SWEAT:

GAY JOCK EROTICA

Visit us at www.boldstrokesbooks.com

Edited by Todd Gregory for Bold Strokes Books

Rough Trade

Blood Sacraments

Wings: Subversive Gay Angel Erotica

Sweat: Gay Jock Erotica

SWEAT:

GAY JOCK EROTICA

edited by

Todd Gregory

2012

SWEAT: GAY JOCK EROTICA

© 2012 BY BOLD STROKES BOOKS. ALL RIGHTS RESERVED.

ISBN 13: 978-1-60282-669-4

THIS TRADE PAPERBACK ORIGINAL IS PUBLISHED BY
BOLD STROKES BOOKS, INC.
P.O. BOX 249
VALLEY FALLS, NY 12185

FIRST EDITION: JUNE 2012

THIS IS A WORK OF FICTION. NAMES, CHARACTERS, PLACES, AND INCIDENTS ARE THE PRODUCT OF THE AUTHOR'S IMAGINATION OR ARE USED FICTITIOUSLY. ANY RESEMBLANCE TO ACTUAL PERSONS, LIVING OR DEAD, BUSINESS ESTABLISHMENTS, EVENTS, OR LOCALES IS ENTIRELY COINCIDENTAL.

THIS BOOK, OR PARTS THEREOF, MAY NOT BE REPRODUCED IN ANY FORM WITHOUT PERMISSION.

CREDITS
EDITORS: TODD GREGORY AND STACIA SEAMAN
PRODUCTION DESIGN: STACIA SEAMAN
COVER DESIGN BY SHERI (GRAPHICARTIST2020@HOTMAIL.COM)

This is for every athlete I've ever fantasized about—going back to high school.

Contents

Introduction: Who Doesn't Want a Jock?

In ancient Greece, athletes were the physical ideal. The models for the statuary of the gods that decorated their cities and temples were athletes. The Olympic Games were established to honor the gods of Olympus with athletic competition between the most godlike of the Greek mortals. The Greek physical ideal of masculine beauty, while rejected by the dogmatic dictatorship over Western culture and thought established by the Roman Catholic Church, managed to survive and was resurrected by Renaissance artists—even if those ideals weren't so easily replicated in real life.

This isn't intended to be a history of male body images—that particular subject has been exhaustively researched and written about in other books—but rather as a lead-in to discussing the modern-day image of the athletic male body and its erotic appeal.

For many gay men, our first crushes were on the jocks in high school. The jocks generally had the most fit, muscular, and appealing bodies—the kinds that launched all kinds of masturbatory fantasies. When I went out for football as a freshman in high school, the locker room before and after practice was a candy store of gorgeous masculine images. Wrestling meets provided another smorgasbord of beautiful male forms, this time in skin-hugging Lycra singlets that left absolutely nothing to the imagination. Basketball players were long and lean, soccer and hockey players had powerful legs and the most amazing butts, and the guys who ran track were also lean with strong legs.

I've often wondered if those high school crushes and obsessions are what translate into the gay male obsession with working out.

I have had many fantasies about professional athletes—my current main crush is on tennis star Rafael Nadal—and over the years, I've written numerous erotica stories about athletes. In fact, the story I'm including in this anthology, "Phenom," was originally published in an erotic baseball anthology called *Fast Balls*. (When I received the call for submissions for that anthology, my mind immediately went back to the late 1970s and a crush I had on Kansas City Royals rookie Clint Hurdle, who appeared on the cover of *Sports Illustrated* with the headline PHENOM.) I've always wanted to do an anthology of sports-related erotica, and so here you have it: *Jocks*.

Interestingly enough, the sport that appeared most in the submissions was hockey; must be those amazing asses and all that fighting and testosterone.

So waste no more time here! Turn the page, and start reading!

—Todd Gregory
New Orleans, January 2012

SWEAT
CAGE THUNDER

I am flat on my back on the mat.
Beaten. Spent. Broken.

He stands over me like a colossus, one foot on either side of my chest.

Looking up, he looks like a giant.

He stares down at me.

Sweat drips off his chin onto my face.

His legs and chest are covered with blond hairs, black now with sweat and plastered down to the skin. His entire body is bathed in sweat. Mine is too, but I'm not sure if it's my sweat or his. The mats are wet, pools of our sweat scattered over the blue surface. His bluish-gray eyes just stare down into mine. Unblinking. Serious. Expressionless.

I start to move, to sit up. He puts his foot in the center of my chest and pushes me back down. His cock is hard, erect, standing to attention. A bead of sweat hangs from the head.

"Did I say you could get up, boy?" His voice is soft, stern, mildly threatening.

"No, sir," I whisper as another drop of sweat hits my face.

His foot remains on my chest.

I am so turned on my erection almost hurts.

Was I so foolish to think that I could beat him, I wondered again; he is an underground wrestling champion, he never loses. Never. He has beaten people that have beaten me, that I had no chance in hell of beating. What was I thinking, taking on the mighty Bill Horton? There were guys out there afraid of him, who wouldn't wrestle him, thought I was crazy for scheduling a match with him. I'd heard the stories.

He likes to hurt people...he's very rough...he broke this one guy's arm...he cracked this other guy's rib...he is so fucking intense...he is crazy, man...

But I hadn't been afraid. I'd contacted him with an e-mail, got a rather brusque e-mail response along with a picture. I'd downloaded the picture and gaped at it. Smooth torso, big pecs, big round hard nipples, flat stomach rippling with muscles like waves on the ocean. Those beautiful, oh-so-intense blue-gray eyes just staring defiantly at the camera. *I'm gonna kick your ass*, those eyes said. I'd gotten hard looking at his picture. I'd slipped out of my clothes and beat off, imaging what it would be like to wrestle him, to get my hands on that body, to see those blue-gray eyes up close, staring into mine. Imagining the feel of his powerfully muscled legs around my head, squeezing as his hard ass flexed.

I'd ordered some of his videotapes, watched him demolish his opponents, who'd never had a chance against Bill Horton. That much was obvious from the moment the match began. He seemed to be able to reverse any hold they put on him, in control the entire time. He might lose a fall here or there, caught off guard suddenly, but his opponent always paid for it. Always. My cock would get hard and I would beat off watching him taking some hapless guy apart. My cock would be hard before I even put the tape into the VCR and hit Play, just thinking about him in his bikini, with those big strong legs, round hard ass, sweating and taking apart some guy who had the nerve to get on the mat with him. Sometimes he would take it slow and make the guy suffer, sometimes it would be fast. But he was always in control, those steely blue-gray eyes blazing with intensity.

Yes, I'd been crazy to think I could beat him.

He did submit to me twice. I was proud of that. A guy I had wrestled who'd beaten me pretty easily had told me he'd never gotten Bill to submit to him even once in three matches. I'd managed to get my legs around his head and hadn't let go, trapping one of his arms so he couldn't get away. I squeezed with all the strength I had in my legs, and he had tapped out. I couldn't believe it. I felt a surge of confidence.

And then, when I'd let him go, he just looked at me and said, "You'll pay for that, boy."

And I had. He knew so many holds, was so strong, too quick for me. He toyed with me at times, getting me into a hold and only applying enough pressure to make it uncomfortable, but not enough to make me scream or beg for mercy. He would taunt me as he held me immobile, whispering into my ear, "Not so tough now, are you, boy? Is this all you've got? Come on, boy, at least make a match of it." Then he'd laugh. "You like being controlled, don't you, boy? You like being submissive."

And my cock, which had gotten hard the minute he'd stripped down to his black Speedo, would ache for release from my red bikini, begging to be stroked, my balls swelling with the need to just let go and squirt out my passion.

At some point in the match he had stripped it off me. The match went on for so long, he'd wrung so many submissions from me, that I'd lost track of time, holds, everything. My bikini had been soaked with sweat, and he tossed it into a corner. It hit with a little wet sound. I was lying on the mat, catching my breath, my back aching from the camel clutch he had just forced me to submit to. He stood over me and slid his bikini down, and for the first time I saw his pinkish thick cock, the heavy full balls hanging just below it. He sat down on my chest and started slapping my face with his cock.

"Suck it," he said and forced my mouth open, and it went in. He started fucking my face, and I licked it, I nibbled it, I gagged and choked on it as he forced it into my throat. It tasted salty from his sweat, but it was good. He pulled it back and I lay there, staring at it. He smiled down at me. "Good boy."

That was when I flipped him off me and got the second submission out of him. I had him down on his back, my legs holding his arms down. I grabbed his wet Speedo and forced it into his face. "You like that, big guy? Huh? How does that taste?" Then I slid my legs down and around his while I held his arms immobile, forcing his legs apart with mine. His armpits glistened with water. I leaned down and started sliding my tongue around in his right armpit, tasting his skin, his water, his smell. He moaned at first, writhing underneath me as I licked, closing my lips then and kissing the wet skin. My mouth was wet with him. I applied more pressure to his legs, pulling them further apart. He screamed out his submission. I let him go and stared down into his reddened face.

"Nice." He smiled up at me. "I like a boy who fights back."

And then he rolled me over. I hit the mat. He positioned his feet behind my knees and grabbed my arms, pulling my chest up and off the mat, my back arching. I felt the pressure start in my shoulders and in my lower back. There was no way out of this hold. There was nothing I could do. It was starting to hurt.

"Give it up, boy."

"No way!"

He just laughed and put on some more pressure. My breath was coming in faster gulps; I focused on the pain, willing it to go away, and when I thought I could handle it he pulled me back a little bit further.

"Okay okay okay! I give I give I give!"

He let go and I fell forward to the mat, rolling onto my back. That was when he stood above me, straddling me, like a colossus, like the muscular stud that he was.

It was as though I was lying at the altar of a god.

He flexes both arms, the biceps muscles peaking, his lats popping out, his pecs moving, veins popping out underneath the pale marble like skin. He kisses one bicep peak and then turns his head and kisses the other. He looks down at me and he smiles. Sweat rolls off his nose and drips onto me. He brings his hands together and applies pressure, one against the other. His shoulder muscles pop out, his triceps bulge, and his pecs tighten, the hard erect nipples coming forward.

My God, he is hot.

"Roll over, boy."

I do.

"Arch that back."

I do, raising my ass up into the air.

He smacks it. "Such a beautiful ass, boy."

I feel his fingers massaging lube into the crack of my ass, my hole twitching as his finger finds it. He slowly starts to stroke my hole. My body starts to tremble.

He is going to fuck me, claim his prize.

I'm his boy, his toy to do with as he pleases.

His finger goes inside me, working my hole, making circles inside me to loosen it up.

Ohmygodohmygodohmygodohmygod

There is pressure from the head of his cock as it presses up against me. A little pain, a gasp, as it enters.

Ohmygodohmygodohmygod

He moans as the whole thing slips in. "Yeah, boy," he whispers.

"Take that big cock up that tight ass." He smacks it again. "Boy has a pretty ass."

My head comes up as I gasp for air.

feelssogoodfeelssogoodohmygodthatfeelsogood

He slides it back and that feeling is so intense, I can't even think anything except about the waves coming through my body as my legs start to shake and then it comes back in hard and I scream a little, just a little because I can't get enough air in to make any real noise because it is such an amazing feeling as he fills me up and then pulls back again, slowly, oh so slowly, and then he is moving back and forth and all I can do is gasp for air, beg for breath, trying to stay focused on the simple mechanism of breathing because I am being overwhelmed with pleasure its all I can think of everything else is being forced out of my head I cant think of anything but the amazing feeling of being fucked by this man, this muscle stud who had used me like a rag to mop up the mats, putting me in hold after hold, forcing me to submit, establishing his complete and total dominance over me, making me his BOY and there is nothing I want more than to please him for him to take his pleasure from me because I am his, I belong to him and him alone, anything you want sir take anything you want from me, I am yours I am your BOY I am yours

And my entire body convulses as I shoot a load, my entire body shaking, convulsing, this pleasure is so intense that I could die from it, it has never been like this before, it is exploding out of me and it feels so intense, so good, so amazingly fucking awesomely good I never want the feeling to stop *mygodmygodmygodmygod*

And when the last bit has come out, he reaches underneath me and rubs the head of my cock.

Now I truly scream, it feels so good I can hardly stand it, and I start to move, trying to escape his hand because I cannot stand the pleasure any more it is too much my entire body is trembling and I can't control it I cannot stop trembling oh my god

And then he pulls his cock out of me and I feel the hot wet drops on my back as he moans and shudders and gasps as his load sprays me, marks me, marks me as his territory.

I belong to him.

He collapses on the mat next to me and pulls me close, and our lips meet in a kiss. We are both covered in sweat, so much sweat that

ANThunDER

my fingers are starting to wrinkle up like I've taken a long bath or gone
for a swim, and he strokes my chest and pinches my nipples.

And finally we pull apart.

He smiles at me.

"Good boy," he says, getting up. "Come on, let's get showered."

And like his good boy should, I follow him into the bathroom.

• 8 •

AFTER THE HOCKEY GAME
JEFF MANN

(for MCB)

The goalie, Matt. That's the man Buddy's watching so intently. Right now Matt's face and body are concealed by the hockey helmet, mask, and padded uniform, but Buddy knows how handsome and well built the man is. He's got butch looks that Buddy loves: a close-trimmed red-brown beard, deep laugh lines, a high-and-tight military haircut, a butt and thighs dense with muscle, and a manly swagger that bespeaks confidence. Last year, they even shared a few blow jobs, back when Matt was still single.

Right now, a Friday night in October, Buddy's high in the bleachers of the Charlotte sports arena, denim jacket resting on his lap so that he can grope his cock through his jeans while he watches the late-night game. The noises of the rink ricochet around him: shouts of the players, scrape of skates across ice, the click of the sticks, the shush of the puck toward the net, disappointed groans or elated yells as the puck's trajectory is deftly deflected by Matt's stick. Buddy's wishing he could follow his favorite athlete into the shower later, burrow his face into the guy's sweat-moist armpits, then drop to his knees and take Matt's thick cock down his throat. Buddy knows how rich those honey-brown pubes would smell bushing around his nose. Too bad Matt e-mailed him to say he has other plans tonight. Probably with Edward, Buddy thinks, fighting back self-pity, Matt's latest sweetheart Edward, the well-to-do IT professional. Hot as Matt is, he always has a steady boyfriend.

Not Buddy. He's a loner; he's never had much luck with men. He's a big guy, no athlete but a perpetual spectator. He's taller and more muscular than Matt but not half as coordinated. Both men are forty; their age and their muscles are two of few things they have in common. Matt's well educated, a lawyer, a city boy from Detroit. He's a cocky Top, agile and self-assured, with flashing blue eyes and a quick grin. He zips around the ice like some kind of arctic angel. Buddy, he's only got a GED. He's a road worker for the Virginia Department of Transportation, a country boy from West Virginia, a bashful bottom. He's very strong—he used to be a power-lifter—with prominent pecs, bulging biceps, and one of those curving, solid bellies so many Southern men develop by their thirties, but he's awkward inside his body. He lumbers when he moves; he feels thick, clumsy, and unsure of himself three-fourths of the time.

Buddy was a nerd in high school back in West Virginia, and very quietly queer, adoring the local stars of team sports but too shy and ill coordinated to be involved in such macho activities himself. For years, while engaging in his own solitary attempts to keep fit—weight-training, jogging, pounding the punching bag—he's been attending public athletic contests of all kinds and developing crushes, on football stars, rugby studs, and hockey heroes. He's been infatuated with Matt for a year now. He wishes Matt were single; he wishes he could see Matt more often.

Buddy grew up a Baptist. His religion made him miserable for years, back when he was convinced that God hated homosexuals. Eventually, he found a Metropolitan Community Church in Roanoke, where he met other gay Christians. Talking with them helped a lot. He's worked it all out in his mind; he knows God loves him and wants him to be happy. Sometimes—during church, or on the side of the road, in his orange road-worker's vest, in the smell of asphalt and traffic exhaust along I-81, he fondles the silver cross around his neck and has little chats with his Creator, praying, "Please, Lord, send me Matt, or a man like Matt. Please send me someone to care for me."

God may be with Buddy always, but no one corporeal sits near Buddy tonight: his broad shoulders and burly frame are surrounded by a circular sea of empty seats. He's used to being alone. He looks intimidating, like he just stumbled out of some mountain holler, and his shyness makes him seem aloof, so strangers tend to give him a wide berth. Guys who like rough/scruff find him hot and handsome, but if they told him that, he'd just laugh. Compliments make him squirm; he assumes anyone with anything flattering to say about him is a liar or a con man. In his own eyes, he's still the insecure acne sufferer from high school, the lard-ass, the butt of jokes.

Buddy's lonely, Buddy's glum. He turns forty-one tomorrow, but he doesn't expect to be in much of a mood for celebration. Just yesterday, Rob, the guy he'd been seeing halfheartedly for a few weeks, dumped him without explanation, so his green eyes are sadder than usual. He watches Matt deflect another puck, rubs his shaved-shiny head, scratches the bushy black beard he grew for Civil War re-enactments a few years back and never got around to trimming, and tries not to cry. Tonight, he's dressed in threadbare jeans and a blue flannel shirt atop an A-shirt, sleeves rolled up to display furry forearms. Since it's supposed to sleet tonight, he's wearing heavy Carhartt boots with thick tread. *You cain't be too careful*, thinks Buddy, resting one boot on a knee while he imagines Matt's balls brushing his lips.

Game's done. As usual, Matt's been ruthless and efficient; his fast reflexes have helped win the game. The rink echoes with shouts, tongue-in-cheek insults, the kind of easy male banter Buddy's always felt left out of, ever since he was a thoroughly incompetent kickball player in grade school. Buddy sits back, resisting the urge to follow Matt into the locker room, watching the small crowd of spectators disperse. On the way out, he finds a shadowy corner where he can steal a nip of bourbon from his hip flask. He's been surreptitiously slurping on it all evening. It helps him feel less bereft.

It's very late, one a.m., and the arena's about emptied out. Through the glass of the exit door, Buddy can make out silvery rain. "Shit," he mutters. Face flushed, he pulls on his Levi jacket, cocks his SOUTHERN HERITAGE baseball cap over his brow, throws open the door, and lopes out to his truck. It's a rusted forest-green Toyota, one of very few vehicles left in the lot. There's not a soul to be seen.

Buddy's got his hand in his pocket, fishing for his key, when he hears a footfall behind him. Suddenly he's shoved up against the side of the truck cab and something's jabbed into his side. A voice, half-familiar, growls in his ear. "I got a gun, tiger. Just keep still and keep quiet."

"What the hell?" When Buddy tries to turn, the hard protrusion in his side pokes deeper and the man slams him even harder into the truck's side. "Shut up! Just be a good boy and put your hands behind your back. Otherwise you'll regret it."

Heart in his throat, Buddy obeys. Cold metal circles his wrists; rachets click. He tugs, but his struggle's of no use. *Fuck! Cuffs!*

"Oh, shit," Buddy mutters. "Oh, hell." The curse words come out sounding like "Sheee-it" and "Hehh-ull." Anger, amorousness, and anxiety always thicken Buddy's country accent.

Rain's stringing winking beads along the brim of his baseball cap and pattering softly on the truck's hood. A strong hand grips Buddy's elbow; the gun traces Buddy's backbone. "Yep. You're caught, tiger. You're caught. You're mine."

Tiger? Matt calls him that. Isn't that Matt's voice? The vowels are Midwestern, like Matt's. Matt's doing this. Matt knows all about Buddy's as-yet-unfulfilled abduction fantasies. He's arranged some kind of kidnap scene. "Who are you?" Buddy hisses. "Matt? Is that you?"

"Matt? Who the hell is Matt?" The stranger shakes him, then slaps the back of his head. "I told you to shut up!"

Ohhhh, fuck, it's not Matt. "Don't hurt me, man! What, what you want with me, man?" Buddy says, mouth dry, deep voice hoarse with alarm. *Lord, oh, please God, help me!* Buddy's knees are trembling now. He's always thought of himself as brave, having howled out many a modern approximation of the Rebel Yell as he's charged across battlefields with his fellow Confederate re-enactors, but feeling a gun bumping his spine is another matter entirely. As brawny as he is, his fear is more powerful. Right now, it's making him as weak as a child. Muscles aren't of much use when you're at gunpoint.

"You gonna keep quiet?" the man behind him rasps.

"Yeah. Yeah. Shit, I'll do whatever you say, long's you don't shoot me. My wallet's in my back pocket. I—"

"That isn't being quiet. I told you to shut up."

"Okay, man, just take what you want and—"

Buddy's frightened words abruptly cease as the stranger shoves a cloth against Buddy's lips. He shakes his head, a brief resistance before the gun prods him again, the stranger snarls, "Open up, or else," and Buddy obeys with a strained whimper. The gag slides between his bearded lips. It's a balled-up jock—Buddy can tell by the ribbed quality of the fabric—and it hasn't been washed for a long time. It's quite a mouthful; when it's all in, Buddy's cheeks bulge. After the stranger's done cramming the jock in, there's a tearing sound, and Buddy feels something tight and sticky applied to his taut lips. The stranger's sealing the jock in place with a long strip of tape plastered over Buddy's mouth and wrapped around Buddy's head. "You're coming with me," he says.

"Oh, fuck, no. Please, no," Buddy tries to say, but the tape diminishes his words to husky moans. He fights to stay calm, taking deep breaths of air through his nose. *Lord, no, please don't let this happen.* Now his captor spins Buddy around to face him and once again slams him back against the truck cab. The guy's got a black face mask on; only his eyes and mouth are visible. That mouth smiles. The two men stare at one another, the one panting against the cloth packing his mouth, the other grinning. Then there's another ripping of tape and Buddy's vision goes dark.

"Time to go," says the stranger after sealing Buddy's eyes. He zips a baggy garment around his bulky prisoner, covers his taped-up face with what feels like a hood, then grips the big man's elbow and hustles him across the lot. Sightless, Buddy stumbles and staggers. Within a minute, he hears the sound of a car door opening, and then he's shoved violently inside.

"Quiet now," warns the stranger, arranging his captive on his side before deftly taping Buddy's booted feet together. "Don't make me drug you."

"Mmm-hmm," Buddy mumbles, trying to keep from the ultimate humiliation of pissing or shitting himself. A blanket's tossed over him. Then his kidnapper's starting up the car. Buddy lurches and sways—his captor takes turns fast—then they're on what's got to be the interstate, where the ride evens out and speeds up.

Buddy bites down on the cloth packing his mouth. He prays harder than he's ever prayed, *Lord, oh Jesus, please help me, oh Lord, oh Jesus,* trying to slow his breathing and tamp down panic. If this were some scene Matt had arranged, it would be an erotic dream come true; Buddy's dick would be rock-hard, what with the bondage and the rank, salty taste of the jock. As it is, his cock's tiny with terror. The backseat air he breathes is musty with old sweat. It's the smell of dirty laundry, gym lockers, sports gear.

"Can you breathe all right?" The disembodied voice sounds almost solicitous.

"Um-mm," Buddy grunts.

"That a yes?"

"Um-mm."

"Good boy." Buddy can almost hear the grin of satisfaction in his captor's voice. "We'll be home in a couple of hours. You ought to take a nap. Once we get there, you won't be getting much sleep."

That sounds like a threat. Beneath the tape, Buddy clenches his jaw, trying not to snivel, fear webbing up his belly and heart. Beneath the blindfold, Buddy rolls his eyes. *Oh, shee-it. A nap? Yeah, right.* He lies in absolute blackness. Inside the cuffs' tight steel, his wrists burn. He rolls onto his belly, trying to get more comfortable and failing. Against the moistening ball of jock-cloth, he murmurs prayers.

❖

Bumps and sharp turns in the road wake Buddy up. Unbelievably, he'd drifted off. It feels like they're ascending a hill.

The car comes to a halt. The driver's door opens and slams shut; the back door clicks open. "Up and at 'em, stud," says the deep voice inside the darkness. Buddy's captor cuts his feet free, then drags him from the backseat. Buddy stands, trying to get his bearings.

Uh-oh. Uh-oh. Oh, no! His abductor can't be Matt. Matt lives in an apartment complex near a busy highway. This is the country. There are no sounds of traffic. There's the tapping of rain, the click of crickets, the lap of what might be water against a shore, leaves crinkling underfoot as Buddy's unseen captor forces him across level ground, and what might be wind soughing through evergreens. That's it. Wherever they are, they're a damned long way from other human beings, from anyone who might help Buddy get out of this.

"No one out here but us," the man mutters as if reading his mind, half dragging, half shoving Buddy along. Up some steps; click of a lock. Warm air wafts over Buddy's tape-sheathed face. He's taken only a few unsure steps inside when his captor removes the hooded garment swathing him and gives him a hard shove forward. Buddy stiffens, expecting to slam into a floor's hard surface, but instead he falls into yielding softness. He's lying on a bed, face buried in blankets. He rolls onto his side and emits an interrogative grunt, "Umm?" which pretty much means, "Where the hell are we?"

A hand falls on his forehead. Fingers run through his thick black beard. "You're one fine big bear of a man. Yes, you sure are. One tasty hillbilly." His captor chuckles, audibly licking his lips. "So fucking fine all trussed up like this. You're wondering what's going on, huh?"

Buddy emits another stifled grunt and nods, frightened heart thumping beneath his breastbone.

"You thought I was some dude named Matt, right? You can call me Matt. On second thought, I guess you won't be calling me anything with all that tape over your mouth." Another low laugh. "We're up in the mountains, in a cozy little cabin. I'll help myself to your money and credit cards later," his kidnapper says, unbuttoning Buddy's shirt. "Right now I'm going to torture and rape you. Word is you like kinky queer shit like that."

Oh, Jesus. Buddy goes rigid, then starts to shake. He relishes a little pain when it's consensual, not to mention a dick up his butt, and the bigger the dick the better, but being abused and screwed by a complete stranger, some sort of crazy criminal, a carrier of God knows what diseases, that's another matter. And who knows what'll happen once the man's done with him? A bullet through the head? Frantic, Buddy snorts in air and starts to shout. His cry for help's cut off, transformed into a short, shrill yelp and a gasp as Matt's weight falls upon him and a firm hand's clamped over his mouth.

"Uh-*uh-uh*. Better not. I got that gun, remember? And this knife too." Metal strokes Buddy's jaw. Beneath the blade's caress, he goes limp. He swallows hard. Hopelessness makes it hard to swallow.

"Keep still now, guy. Time to get you naked. Okay?"

Buddy nods. He lies there, snuffling air, fighting back sobs, as the knife slides beneath his undershirt and slices. In a few minutes, Buddy's naked except for his boots. As soon as Matt's done cutting off Buddy's clothes, the big redneck curls into a scared ball, quivering. One sharp sob escapes him; the rest he chokes back.

There's the snick of a match, then the sound and smell of paper burning, then the thump of wood across andirons, the scent of kindling catching fire. A slurp and a sigh. "Good bourbon you got here," says Matt. "Knob Creek?"

Buddy nods. He hears the rustling of clothes as his kidnapper strips, then feels the bed dip as Matt climbs onto it. Matt unlaces and removes Buddy's clunky Carhartt boots and socks. He crosses Buddy's ankles, ropes them together, and adds several layers of tape. Then Matt pulls Buddy's head onto his shoulder, lies back, and heaves another sigh. Buddy breathes in his abductor's scent. It's strong, musky, the smell of a mature man after hours of exertion. If Buddy weren't so scared, he'd find the aroma downright delicious.

"This is the life. Isn't it?" When Buddy doesn't reply, Matt slaps the side of Buddy's head. Buddy winces. "Isn't it?" Matt repeats. Buddy nods.

"That's quite the chest you've got there, big man. How many pounds do you bench-press?"

Buddy rumbles and shrugs, trying to remember the last time a man gave him a compliment.

"Huh? Huh? What's that? Can't hear you," Matt mocks, squeezing Buddy's thick pecs and playing with the mat of black hair coating them. He lifts the silver cross on the chain around Buddy's neck, tugs it, and drops it.

"Devout sort, huh?"

"Mm-huh."

"Think God'll help you out of this?"

"Mm-huh."

"We'll see. Praying hard?"

"Mm-huh."

"Looks like you're as devoted to the flesh as the spirit." Chuckling, he rubs the solid, hair-covered swell of Buddy's belly. "Biscuits and gravy? Or it is Krispy Kreme? Or Sonic hot dogs? Or just six-packs of Bud Light?"

Matt takes another slurp of bourbon before tweaking Buddy's right nipple, then the left, then the right, then the left. He works them till both are hard. He slides down the bed, rolls on top of Buddy, and sucks them, softly at first, then more firmly, then gently chews them. Buddy moans; for a few seconds, the pleasure herds off the fear, and Buddy presses his torso eagerly against the hungry mouth.

Matt gives each tit a parting nip. He slides back up the bed and wraps his arms around his captive; Buddy's face falls against Matt's torso. "You liked that, didn't you?" Matt whispers, patting Buddy's cheek. "You like those beefy white-trash tits chewed on."

Buddy nods. Despite the extremity he's trapped inside, his cock's half-hard. Tit-work always has that effect.

Matt falls silent. Buddy can feel his captor's chest hair against his cheek, the rise and fall of his breathing. The fire crackles; there's a brittle tapping, rain turning into predicted sleet. Matt pulls the covers over them and starts to snore, arms still wrapped loosely around his prisoner.

While Matt sleeps, Buddy fights the cuffs. They don't give an inch, and now Buddy's wrists are burning again and his shoulders are aching as well. He wonders what will happen to him, if this man will hurt him, even murder him, or take pity on him and let him go. *This is crazy,* Buddy thinks. *I'm so goddamn lonely that it feels good to be held by a man, even in such a scary situation. Whoever this guy is, he may be brutal, but he's warm and tender too.* Buddy thinks about Matt, his Matt, and wonders if he's making love to his boyfriend Edward right now. He thinks about Rob, the hot and hardhearted prick who dumped him yesterday. He thinks about his own death, wondering if the When is tomorrow, if the Where is this cabin. He cries a little, very quietly, and prays again while his captor sleeps and numbness seeps into his cuffed wrists.

❖

Buddy wakes with a start. Matt's hauling his hefty captive up. "Damn, you're heavy." He seats him on the edge of the bed. "Hold still," Matt orders, "or I'll cut you."

Another ripping of tape. To the bands sealing Buddy's eyes and mouth, Matt now adds a long strip he anchors beneath Buddy's chin, plasters up his left cheek and up over the crown of his head, then down along the right cheek, under the chin and over the head again, then yet again, like some patient, repetitive arachnid. The yards of tape are very tight; now Buddy can barely move his jaw. Only his nose is left uncovered.

"Uh-uh! Uh-uh!" Buddy begs, suddenly terrified. All his captor would have to do right now is pinch his nose shut and he'd suffocate.

"Relax, tiger. I know what you're thinking. This isn't about asphyxiation. This is about keeping you quiet for what's to come," Matt says, pulling Buddy off the bed and onto the floor.

"Don't fight me," Matt growls. "Unless you want a bullet through the head. I got the gun right here." He removes the cuffs, then roughly pulls Buddy's thick arms in front of him. Buddy yelps; pain flares through his stiff joints. Matt rubs his prisoner's shoulders and wrists, soothing him as he would a child. "Easy, easy, mountain man," he mutters. "No one's going to hurt you. At least not in any serious way. As long as you're a good boy."

Buddy gulps. They sit there side by side, leaning back against the bed, the smaller man massaging the bigger man's chafed wrists while sleet patters the cabin's roof and wind whistles about the eaves.

"Okay. Here we go." Matt eases Buddy down onto his belly and tugs his arms in front of him. Before Buddy can figure out what's happening, Matt's pulled Buddy's forearms around something hard and has locked his wrists together on the far side.

"It's a support post, tiger; you aren't going anywhere."

Buddy strains; nothing gives.

"Get up on your knees. Lift your butt in the air," Matt orders.

Buddy can guess what's coming now. Even as he struggles to obey, he's begging for mercy. The now-sodden jock and tape-muzzle reduce his pitiful attempts at verbalization to nothing more than an animal's incoherent grumbling.

"Good boy," Matt says when Buddy's in position. He kneads Buddy's butt—it's broad, chunky, and smooth, with thick black hair in the cleft—then taps it with something stiff. Buddy clenches his hands into fists and whines.

"This paddle is solid oak," Matt says, "with metal rivets all through it. They should make for some interesting patterns across your ass, don't you think?"

Matt gives Buddy's butt only three tentative blows before laying it on hard. He beats Buddy for a long time. Buddy gnaws the jock-gag, tugging hard on his bonds. *Jesus God, it hurts.* He starts off bravely, gulping back screams, but soon the pain's mounted to a ceaseless searing, *oh God, no, stop, please stop,* he's howling, thrashing like tree boughs caught in a hurricane, and his desperate and entirely pointless struggles have chafed his wrists raw. By the time Matt's done, Buddy's ass cheeks are covered with tiny diamond indentations the rivets made; the usually pale skin there is bright red and slowly clouding up with a great smudgy bruise, like a thunderhead covering sun. When his torturer caresses his burning buttocks, the sudden tenderness breaks Buddy down. For a good five minutes afterward, while Matt strokes and kisses him, Buddy sobs.

"The kind of butt I most like to fuck is one bruised black and still hot from a beating," Matt mutters as soon as Buddy's weeping has tapered off. "I hear you jack off to rape fantasies, big man. So here you go: What you've always dreamed of."

There's the quick rip of a condom packet. *A condom?* Buddy's relieved and confused at the same time. *Since when do rapists use condoms? And how does he know about my fantasies? Lord Jesus, let it be Matt!*

Buddy moans, a mixture of dread and desire, as gobs of cold lube are spread over his asshole and pushed up into him. Matt takes his time at first, prying Buddy open with gently probing fingers. His prick's entrance is anything but gentle, however. Kneeling behind Buddy, he shoves his cockhead inside with a quick, brutal thrust that makes Buddy flinch and gasp. Ignoring his prisoner's violent head-shaking and unintelligible pleas to stop, Matt keeps pushing till his shaft's swallowed by Buddy's tight pink hole, his pubes are brushing Buddy's crack-hair, and he's impaled his cuffed captive to the hilt. Matt gives Buddy's paddle-reddened ass a couple of vicious slaps before gripping his hips and pounding him mercilessly.

At first Buddy's all suffering. *No, oh God, he's so big, it's agony! Please make him stop!* Getting fucked has never hurt so badly before. The pain of his hole being forcibly taken so soon after that brutal paddling has Buddy crying again, his taped-up face sheened with a wash of tears. But soon enough—yes, this stranger knows what he's doing—something warm and rapturous is building beneath and behind that pain, Matt's cockhead is bumping just the right spots inside him, and, miraculously, Buddy's cock is hard. Now his head's lowered, he's growling with delight, he's shoving himself back onto the very large cock that's driving into him. "Oh, God. Damn. Oh, God. Oh, damn. What...a...tight...sweet...redneck...ass!" Matt gasps. It's not long before Matt's bent over Buddy, sweat-slick chest against sweat-slick back, wrapping his arms around him, biting his shoulders, his hip-pumping rhythm grading into an in-and-out-in-and-out-in-and-out blur. Matt comes, spurting the condom full. He clutches Buddy convulsively and goes limp.

A couple of minutes pass before Matt pulls out, tugs off the condom, rolls his battered and well-plowed prisoner onto his side, embraces him, and slips into a post-come drowse. Eventually, he rises.

"Goddamn, that was great." He gives Buddy's ass a final slap, this blow one of fondness more than punishment, and rises. "Time to get you situated for the night," Matt says. "Now where'd I put that handcuff key?"

❖

This bastard was clearly born to be a kidnapper, Buddy thinks bitterly as his abductor tightens rope about his wrists. *He's fucking amazing at knots. If I was sure this guy was my Matt, if I wudn't so goddamn scared, this'd be hot as holy hell.*

Buddy's lying on a rug at the foot of the bed, in the glow of the fire. Matt works methodically, humming to himself as he hog-ties Buddy—ankles and wrists bound together behind his back—with layers of rope Matt makes additionally secure with tape. As an afterthought, he cinches together Buddy's elbows and then his knees for good measure. He leaves Buddy blindfolded but removes the jock-and-tape-muzzle combo; the tape pains Buddy considerably as Matt peels it off his bushy beard. Before Buddy can start pleading for release, Matt's knotted a bandana between the hapless man's teeth, followed by a second one. "This way, you won't get into any kind of breathing trouble while I sleep," Matt explains blithely.

Now Matt kneads and fondles Buddy's buttocks; they're still burning from the paddle's pitiless blows. Now he adds more lube to Buddy's freshly fucked and aching asshole. Something hard and cold nudges Buddy there. "Open up, big guy," says Matt. "I'm going to plug you for the night." Groaning, Buddy tries to relax. The plug's big. It takes Matt a few patient minutes and costs his captive more than a few twinges and flinches before Buddy's hole is sufficiently stretched for the plug to slide in place inside.

"There you go, mountain man," Matt says, rolling Buddy onto his side, covering him with a blanket, and slipping a pillow beneath his head. "Tomorrow morning, I'm going to rape that redneck ass of yours again. 'I got to git me summora that,' as you ridge-runners say ''round hyer.' Till then, you just keep quiet and try to get some sleep." The bed creaks as Matt stretches out. "You're a big, strong butch guy," Matt murmurs. "I'll bet you can take this for a long time. When you're really, really hurting, give me a shout and maybe I'll set you up some other way." Matt snickers. "Or maybe I won't."

It sounds like a challenge to Buddy's manhood, and so, prideful Southerner that he is, he endures it for as long as he can, longer than he ever imagined he could. The minutes pass, the fire crackles, roof sleet clacks, Matt snores, and Buddy quietly, frantically tries to get loose. *The Lord helps those who help theirselves, Daddy always said.* He wriggles his wrists and ankles around in their tight bonds—*hell, none of it's giving, I ain't going nowhere*—till the skin's blistered and burning. When the arm beneath him goes numb, Buddy tries to shift onto his belly, but, bound so extensively, he can barely move. With great effort and after several tries, he succeeds.

God damn *it.* He lies there panting and huffing, jerking on the short rope tethering his wrists to his ankles. *Big as I am, all this muscle...all it takes is one crazy motherfucking asshole with a gun, a few knots, and some tape, and I ain't worth a damn. All my bulk ain't worth a damn. No fucking way I'm getting out of here. I shoulda fought hard when he first grabbed me. If I'd just turned fast and swung. Damn fool. I've always been a damn fool. And a coward. I shoulda* fought*! Shit, fuck, oh Lord, don't let me die here.* Once more his eyes fill with tears, but this time he fights them back.

Time crawls. Again and again, Buddy twists and strains against his restraints. Against the floor he tries to dislodge the bandanas gagging him, to no avail; Matt's knots are too tight. Inside him, the butt plug throbs. He tightens his sphincter around it, emits a tiny moan, and gets hard. *Shit, this ain't no time to get horny, it's time to get outta here!* Despite himself, he humps the rug, squirms, and sighs. Arousal and fear take turns, stiffening his cock, then deflating it. Worn out with struggle, he drowses, only to wake and struggle further.

The fire's warmth fades. Buddy's trussed discomfort shifts into pang, then sharp pain. His bladder's so full he's afraid he'll piss the floor. He's lost all feeling in his hands. He's shivering. Chilled and hurting, stubborn pride eroded, defiance dwindled into desperation, Buddy starts whimpering and mumbling for release. "Man? Hey, man? Please. Please, man? Please let me loose. I cain't take it no more. I gotta piss. Please, man, I'm hurting bad."

After a good five minutes of such muffled pleas, Buddy's kidnapper wakes. He yawns. The bed creaks. Feet pad toward Buddy, stopping near the hog-tied man's head.

"Four hours. I'm impressed. Had enough, huh?" Matt stands over Buddy, nudging his bearded chin with a toe.

All Buddy can do is nod and whimper. "Please. Please," he implores.

Sleepily, Matt frees Buddy's ankles and knees. He heaves him up, leads him to the bathroom, and helps him piss. "Cold in here," says Matt, shaking drops of urine off Buddy's limp dick. "Ready to sleep with me?"

Spend the rest of the night on the cold, hard floor, or snuggle up with a hairy, warm psychopath? Guess I'll take Door #2, Buddy thinks, nodding briskly. "Uh-huh! Uh-huh!"

"Okay, big guy. Just behave, or else."

Matt unties Buddy's elbows and wrists. Buddy thinks about putting up a fight, but he doesn't know where the knife or gun is, and then the moment's passed, and Matt's locked his hands before him. "You should be a lot more comfortable this way," the deep voice says, forcing Buddy's cuffed wrists above his head and tying them to the bed frame. Matt nestles against Buddy, pulls warm blankets over them, and falls asleep plucking at his prisoner's furry pecs. Buddy sighs, thankful for the other man's heat, and clenches his asshole around the plug, savoring the soreness there, the sense of being filled full. Within a minute, the men's snores commingle.

❖

Buddy wakes to a strange tickling in his groin. Something soft is brushing his cockhead. When he tries to rise, the sharp tug on his wrists reminds him that he's still bound to the bed.

Opaque as the tape is covering Buddy's eyes, still he can tell that the room's no longer dark. There's the soughing of wind, but sleet no longer taps the roof. *Sun's come up. Today's my birthday. Shit. Am I gonna die on my birthday?*

"Good morning, you hot hillbilly. That's my beard on your cock," Matt says, from that world of light and freedom beyond Buddy's blindfold. The titillating brush of whiskers against glans starts up again. "And this is the stubble on my cheek." The brushing is replaced by a maddening abrasion, uncomfortable and pleasurable at the same time. Buddy bites down on the sodden bandanas and groans. When Matt takes Buddy's cockhead between his lips, Buddy thrusts eagerly into him. For a few minutes, there are no sounds but the wind around the cabin, Matt's hard sucking, and Buddy's gagged moans. *Fuuuuck, you're good*, Buddy muses despite himself, bucking his hips against the expert wetness. *You're good enough to hire.*

"Don't want my captive to get too comfortable," Matt says, leaving off the blow job just at the point where Buddy's excited squirming and grunting indicate that he's close to the point of no return. *Hell, man, don't stop now!* Buddy silently begs. There's a rustling and clinking, then Buddy yelps as metal bites into his right nipple. *Tit clamps, shit.* Another stifled yelp as his left nipple's given the same treatment. *Whoa, it hurts, damn, it burns*, but now Matt's tongue is flicking the sensitive nubs, the right one, then the left, then the right, then the left, *oh, hell, yes*, making Buddy's spit-wet dick even harder. Matt tugs the chain between the clamps, pulling and stretching the flesh of Buddy's nipples. Buddy's back arches off the bed; his teeth gnash the tightly knotted cloth. When Matt twists the stretched nips, Buddy gives a sharp sob, nods, and humps the air. This is the sort of pain that, for Buddy, due to some mysterious hardwiring between tits and dick, grades into pleasure almost immediately. It's agony; it's sheer bliss.

Matt gives the chain a sharp tug before dropping it onto Buddy's chest. His beard brushes Buddy's lips, then his clamped nipples. "Your cock needing more attention?" He strokes the quivering shaft.

"Uh-huh!"

"Here you go." Fingers slip something thin and light about Buddy's cock and balls, something that tightens fast. It's a cord. Matt wraps it again and again about Buddy's genitals, then about the base of his balls, finishing around the taut and bobbing shaft of his cock. "Feel good?" Matt gives the bound-up hard-on a soft slap.

"Uh-huh!" *Goddamn*, Buddy thinks, *this is the kinda treatment I've always hankered for. Too bad he's a criminal, 'cause otherwise he'd be the best lover I've ever had.*

"Time to ride you again, tiger." Matt lifts Buddy's thick, dark-pelted legs, resting his captive's calves on his shoulders. He works the plug around in Buddy's ass for a few sweet minutes, which only arouses Buddy more. "Damn, your butt's black and blue. That paddle really tore you up. You do want me to fuck you again, don't you? You sure took to it before."

God, it sounds like Matt. "Tiger," no one's ever called me that but Matt. It's gotta be Matt. Please, God, let it be Matt. Buddy groans, writhes against the probing plug, and nods.

"Say it, or I won't do it." Matt jacks Buddy's prick. "Beg me, you goddamn redneck, you fucking wild-bearded Rebel. Big, hairy, butch dude…big piggy bottom. Beg me to plow you like a whore."

Dirty talk, yum, Jesus, keep it up. "Please," Buddy mumbles around the taut cloth. "Please fuck me. Please. Fuck me like a whore. *Please!*"

Chuckling, Matt eases the plug out; Buddy's ass-ring releases it reluctantly, with a lube-messy pop. The emptiness the plug leaves behind nudges Buddy toward despair. He's never ached so badly to be filled up again. His hole's never felt so ravenous.

"Already nice and open," Matt murmurs. "You want it bad, don't you? You need it bad." His blunt cockhead presses against Buddy's puckered opening. Buddy whimpers, crosses his ankles between Matt's shoulder blades, and tenses his thighs, urging Matt into him. Both men sigh as, with one thrust, Matt's thick cock slides inside. Pretty soon, it's bumping Buddy's prostate just right, so superlatively that Buddy goes wild. Now the bed's rocking with Matt's hard thrusts and Buddy's ecstatic writhing. *Yeah God, ah, yeah God, yeah, fill me up, man, pound me cross-eyed!* And that's when Buddy's captor pulls his prisoner's tape-blindfold off.

Buddy blinks in the abrupt and unexpected flood of morning light. Then he freezes.

*Matt, it **is** my Matt! What the fuck?!*

The swamping sense of relief is replaced almost instantly by rage. Buddy roars. He rears and kicks, dislodging the cock stuffed up his ass. With the considerable strength of his thighs, he heaves his captor off the bed and onto the floor.

Matt crawls to his feet, laughing. "Ouch! Damn. Calm down."

This time Buddy doesn't obey. He keeps thrashing and roaring, white teeth clenched. The words he's screaming—"Goddamn you!

Goddamn you! You scared me shitless! Why'd you do this? Goddamn you, Matt! I'm gonna *kill* you, you bastard! I'll gonna kick your *ass*!"— Matt can only occasionally make out, but the message is clear enough: If Buddy ever gets loose, it'll be Matt's turn to suffer.

"Buddy, calm down. Stop screaming like a banshee and let's talk."

"*Taah*? Anawanna*taah*! Ahwannabrehya*fehsh*!" Buddy shouts, a frenzied garble that Matt correctly understands to mean, "*Talk*? I don't wanna *talk*! I want to break your *face*!"

"Okay, you asked for it. If you won't calm down, I'll have to make you." With all the savage kicking, it takes Matt several risky minutes and a few blows to the ribs before he's caught Buddy's right ankle in a slipknot and anchored the big man's leg to a bedpost. Another couple of minutes, and he's managed to tie down the left leg as well. Even then, Buddy keeps cussing and tossing from side to side. Matt stands over him, arms crossed, waiting for Buddy to wear himself out. After ten solid minutes of enraged struggle, finally he falls still. He lies on his back, stretched out taut in an upside-down Y, panting, chest heaving, throat emitting low growls.

Matt sits on the bed's edge. He strokes Buddy's sweat-wet brow. They stare at one another in the shaft of sunlight streaming over the bed. Buddy's black eyebrows arch. Matt bends, kissing Buddy's hairy breast. "Okay, tiger, I can go take a walk and give you time to settle down. Or I can take those bandanas out of your mouth and we can talk. Choose."

Buddy closes his eyes. His great arms flex, giving his bonds another violent wrench before going limp. "Leh taah."

"Let's talk?"

"Yah." Buddy opens his eyes, blinks up at Matt, and clears his throat. God, Matt's good-looking. Big shoulders, clipped auburn beard, wiry arms, those burning blue eyes. Inside Buddy, the anger's died down to embers, and the old infatuation's asserting itself. "Yah."

"Good choice." Matt tweaks Buddy's chin before working the knots behind his head loose and pulling the spit-soaked bandanas out.

Buddy licks his lips. "Can I have some water?"

"Sure." Matt's clearly worried; he moves very fast to fulfill Buddy's request. Buddy gulps the whole glass.

"Thanks. Y'gonna let me loose?"

"Not till I'm sure you won't bloody my nose." Matt grips Buddy's ball-sac and tugs.

"I *ought* to bloody your nose, man. I thought I was gonna die. I thought you were some crazy criminal, some escaped jailbird liable to kill me."

"You didn't enjoy any of it? You sure seemed to relish getting it up the ass. You always told me you loved a hard butt-pounding more than anything," Matt says, fingering Buddy's taint.

"Hell. Um…Yeah, felt good. Feels good. I—I don't…It ain't so simple."

"Don't lie to me. I saw how hard you got. Several times you were about three strokes short of shooting."

"I woulda been harder if I'da known it was you. If I hadn'ta been so scared I was gonna die."

"Didn't you know it was me?" Matt's hand slips lower; a fingertip strokes Buddy's sticky asshole. "I felt sure you'd recognize my voice. Remember all that online chat we had about your fantasies? How you wanted to be tied up, taken, and used by a stranger? Hell, Buddy, it's your birthday."

"I *know* it's my birthday, you crazy fucker! You arranged all this for my *birth*day?"

"Well, yeah. I did."

"Well, you can be damn sure this is a birthday I'll remember. So where the hell are we? This ain't your apartment."

"Actually, I just bought this house. I recently made partner, so now I can afford it. There's a hot tub, a dock, a motorboat, a big kitchen, guest rooms, just about everything I've ever wanted in a place. We're way out in the country, by Smith Mountain Lake. If you don't end up killing me, maybe we can take a hike in the woods later."

"Hike? I'd have to hike nekkid. Hell, you cut off my clothes! That was my favorite denim jacket!"

"Sorry about that. I thought that would add to the tension. There are jeans, a couple of flannel shirts, a T-shirt, and a Levi jacket, all your size, in the closet. Think of them as birthday presents. Oh, and a black jock strap I thought you'd look hot in."

Matt clears his throat and bows his head. "Look, tiger, we had so little time together last year, just some quick cocksucking. We never got to the hard stuff you said you ached for, the ropes and the paddles, the fucking and the—"

"Oh, God, Matt. I was so scared last night. If I'da only known…"

"It wouldn't have been as exciting then, though. Right? You said you wanted the abduction to feel real. You said—"

"It felt real, all right!" Buddy rolls his eyes. "I just about shit my britches."

Matt grins. "Well, next time you'll know it's me." Matt's forefinger tickles Buddy's hole, then slips inside to the first knuckle.

"Uhhh! Oh, yeah." Buddy wiggles; Matt's finger slides deeper.

Buddy shakes his head. "What did you say? Next time? You gonna kidnap me again? Sweet as that sounds, what about that slick hubbie of yours? The magnificent Edward? So sophisticated! I thought y'all were monogamous. Does he know anything about this? Me lying here all trussed up with your finger up my ass? Feels damn fine, gotta admit." Buddy shakes his head again as if to clear it. "Have you forgotten that fucking paragon Edward?"

Matt bends, giving Buddy's left pec-mound a quick bite.

"Ouch! Dickweed!" Buddy blurts.

Matt's finger slides home. He rubs Buddy's prostate for a few seconds before pulling out, wrapping his middle finger over his index finger, and pushing into Buddy again.

His captive shudders and sighs. "Yeah, yeah. Keep that up."

"'That fucking paragon Edward?' You sound jealous." With his free hand, Matt tugs on Buddy's tit clamps.

God, that feels great. Man, I love my nips hurt. "Jealous? Yeah, I guess I am. I thought you and me hit it off last year…*Harder*, man. Tug 'em harder. Hurt 'em! Yeah! Ohhh, yeah! I thought maybe you and me mighta…but then…uhhhhhh!…you met Alan, and just as soon as that was over, you settled in with Edward. 'Cept for your e-mail notes, I figured you was done with me."

"Clearly I'm not."

For a moment, the two men fall silent, Matt gazing deep into Buddy's eyes. Buddy rocks against Matt's fingers; his asshole opens a mite more. He arches his chest, shifting from side to side to tauten the clamp chain and heighten the torment. "Yeah, man. Oh, yeah… That's…that's…"

"I'm not with Edward anymore," Matt says, flicking his tongue over the fat head of Buddy's cock. "All he thinks about is the next paycheck, the next shiny possession. He's fussy and he's controlling. We're always fighting. He's in love with bullshit. All he talks about is trivia. In fact, he never seems to shut up. Blah blah blah, blah blah blah. I left him last week, actually."

"Yeah?" Buddy gasps. His ass-ring clamps down on Matt's fingers. "So what now?"

"I'm thinking next time around I'd like to try a simpler man, a strong, silent type, a country boy." Matt pulls the tweezer clamps harder; Buddy winces. "A big, hairy-bellied, furry-chested, plump-assed, hopelessly kinky butch bottom. Think I'll kidnap him, beat him, and hold him hostage till he agrees to date me."

"*You* wanting to date *me*? *Me*? A stupid, clumsy, uneducated redneck?"

"You aren't any of those things, my friend. Well, a redneck, yes, but that just makes you sexier, as far as I'm concerned. You're smart in all sorts of ways."

"Why d'ya want me now? Why not before? Why not last year? I fell for you pretty damn hard, if y'want to know."

"I know, Buddy. I'm sorry if I hurt you then. I just wasn't ready. I didn't know what I wanted. I think I do now."

"I know what *I* want," Buddy says, using his ass muscles to push Matt's fingers out.

"Yeah?" Anxiety shadows Matt's eyes.

Buddy's legs tug at their bonds. "I'm wanting you to stuff that dirty jock back in my mouth, unrope my feet, hoist my legs over your shoulders, and finish that fine ass-fucking you started. You've done kidnapped me; you might as well use me hard while you can."

Matt grins. Hurriedly he slides off the bed, fetching the jock. He shoves it against Buddy's lips. Buddy fights him, a show of resistance that excites them even more. When at last Buddy surrenders, Matt stuffs his mouth full.

"Keep that gag in, or you'll be beaten again," Matt growls as he unbinds Buddy's feet. "You disobey me, and next time I'll use my hockey stick on your ass. Okay? I'll beat you till you fucking bleed."

The harsh tone in Matt's voice has Buddy even harder, not to mention the image of being whaled on by athletic equipment. He bites down on the jock. *Fuck, that tastes good.* Meekly, he nods. "Yes, sir," he mumbles.

"One other thing," says Matt, pulling on another condom and lubing them both up.

Buddy cocks an inquisitive eyebrow.

Matt lifts Buddy's legs; his sheathed dick brushes Buddy's balls. "I'm not going to free you until you agree to date me. I think we could have something real, Buddy, something solid."

Buddy smiles around the jock.

"You'll date me?"

"Uh-huh."

"Are you going to kick my ass once I free you?"

Buddy's smile widens. He shrugs.

"Guess I'll have to take my chances," Matt says, plunging his cock up Buddy's butt and beginning a steady rhythm.

❖

Buddy's alone again, but this time being alone isn't a long, sad stretch of indeterminate length, it's just a space in which longing can build till Matt returns.

Sunlight fills the room, slanting across Buddy's brawny body. He's still naked, lying on his back on the huge four-poster. He's tied spread-eagle now, arms and legs splayed and roped to the bedposts. His cock and balls are still trussed up, his tits still clamped, the swollen nubs awash with fiery pleasure. Rope secures the jock still stuffed in Buddy's mouth. Another jock, the fabric rank with Matt's crotch odors, rests upside down on Buddy's face, the waistband wrapped around his head, the smelly pouch positioned over his nose. Buddy takes deep breaths, cherishing the scents.

His roped-up cock sways in the sunlight, his roped-up balls throb, his fuck-tender ass clenches the plug. Every so often Buddy grinds his bruised butt cheeks against the bed just to feel the hard rubber shift inside him, to feel that ever so slight interior hurt that's proof of how hard and lovingly Matt plowed him. Every so often, he thrashes around as best he can, both to remind himself of how inescapably he's tied and to shift his tit clamps, rekindling the blessed burning in his nipples. That first fuck, last night after the paddling, Matt used Buddy's hole with deliberate brutality for his own pleasure. This morning's fuck was tender, all about Buddy's delight, Matt's cockhead massaging his hole's rim, Matt's thick cock shaft opening him wider and wider, filling him full, Matt's athletic stamina making the ride both lengthy and vigorous, his deep thrusts making the helpless prisoner's prostate pulsate and glow till Matt came inside him again.

Buddy flexes his muscled limbs with a mixture of impatience and satisfaction. *Fuck, this feels so hot, to be roped up like this.* His captor hasn't allowed him to come yet, so he's still excruciatingly horny, his prick rearing and full of blood, his balls swollen and tight with dammed-up juice. He looks around the rustic room, at the stone fireplace, the wood walls and beams. He struggles idly, twitching his hips, watching his frustrated cock bounce. When he lifts his head, golden light reflected off lake water blinds him, crimson leaves drift along the breeze. He lies back and sighs, tasting and snuffling Matt's heavy jock scents.

Buddy's happier than he's ever been. *Thank you, Lord, oh thank you, thank you.* He's drowsy too, after his hours of sleepless struggle on the floor last night. His kidnapper's due back soon with breakfast. Later, Matt's explained, the two men will hike through the woods around the lake, taking in the autumn colors, the bright yellow of tulip trees, the scarlet of sumacs, the orange of maples, the gold and spilt burgundy of ash. Tonight, to celebrate Buddy's birthday, they'll have dinner at the gourmet pizza place on the far side of the lake. Back home, after some time in the hot tub, they'll split a bottle of red wine. Then, following some lengthy wrestling, Buddy will end up rag-gagged and bound belly down on the bed, all ready for Matt to ass-pummel again, Buddy's butthole a bull's-eye propped on pillows, eager to be penetrated.

Forty-one? Damn, I'm forty-one. My life might be half over. But I ain't gonna die today. It's Matt. My Matt. He'll take care of me. I'm safe. I think he'll treat me right. Buddy lies there, eyes roving over the room, trying to picture the home he and Matt could make here, *helluva lot better than my trailer, goddamn, look at the oak in this place! And, man, a fireplace in the bedroom too!* imagining what everyone afflicted with loneliness dreams of: a new life. It's the kind of rural retreat a country boy like Buddy has always longed for.

By the time Matt returns, Buddy's drifted off. He wakes to Matt's hand unbinding his cock, stroking it awake. Buddy moans with bliss and bucks into Matt's hand. His brown eyes open; he stares up at his captor.

"About time you came, tiger," Matt says, adding a squirt of lube to his hand before commencing. Buddy tosses and writhes. Matt's fist tightens; he rubs Buddy's glans with his thumb and with the other hand works the plug up Buddy's ass. The tension has built for so long—from the moment those cuffs clicked around Buddy's wrists in that Charlotte parking lot—that it takes Buddy less than a minute to shoot a huge, sloppy load across his belly.

"Nice!" Matt says. Cruelly, he keeps jerking Buddy's now-super-sensitive penis. The sensation's a torment, a crazing tickle, an abrading. Matt snickers; Buddy giggles and whimpers, giggles and begs. Finally Matt stops the sadistic jacking. Without warning, he simultaneously removes his captive's tweezer-clamps.

"Yeeeeeow! Fuck!" well-gagged Buddy bawls. "Oh damn oh damn oh damn!"

Chuckling, Matt bends over Buddy's chest, softly sucking his nips, soothing the enflamed flesh till the pain's receded into dull smolder. Then he cups up Buddy's cum, smearing half of it in his beard and half in his captive's.

"Be right back." Standing, Matt leaves the bedroom. Buddy sprawls limply, cursing and panting. Matt returns with a plate of pastries.

"Ready for breakfast?" When Buddy nods, Matt slips the jock off Buddy's face, unknots the rope, and pulls the second jock from Buddy's mouth.

"Did you enjoy these?" Matt says, brushing the jocks over Buddy's face before dropping them on the bed. "I wore them for weeks, during every game and practice, just for you. I pissed and jacked off in them for good measure."

"Hehhh-ull, yes. Loved 'em! I 'preciate it, believe you me. 'I got to git me sommora that,' like you said earlier. What you got there, Mr. Kidnapper?" Buddy snuggles contentedly against the blankets and closes his eyes. "Smells good."

"The bakery down the road has some selections I think you'll approve of. Try this."

When Buddy opens his eyes, he sees a hunting knife. Transfixed on its tip is a sugar-glazed chunk of golden brown.

"Crullers. Your favorite, right?"

"Damn. That's quite a blade."

"Yeah. I bought this at a sports store just for the occasion. You said you savored knife-play, as I recall. Tonight, after I've tied you up again, I'm going to hold this knife to your throat while I screw you. Unless you think that's too kinky or scary. Unless your butt's too sore. How's that sound?"

"Trussed up and ass-fucked by a knife-wielding rapist? Bring it on! Ain't much too kinky for me. And my hole ain't too sore, promise. Ain't nothing I like better'n a big dick up my butt. Hey, did you really have a gun?"

"No. Well, yes. It was plastic. Say 'Ah.'"

Buddy opens his mouth. Carefully Matt extends the blade; carefully Buddy takes the piece of doughnut on his tongue. He chews. "Oh, yeah. Yum."

Matt pops a sugary chunk in his own mouth. "Yum is right." He pierces another piece and offers it.

Buddy smiles lazily. He flexes his great arms; the heavy bed frame shakes. "Hell, Matt, you make even breakfast a hot scene. You gonna feed me like this every morning?"

Matt rubs Buddy's fur-matted belly, then bends to kiss it. "Every now and then. Special occasions. Like today. Happy birthday, Buddy."

"Thanks, man." Buddy accepts the second bite. "Best birthday ever," he mumbles, chewing. "You can kidnap me *any*time."

They've worked through two crullers and a cherry Danish before Buddy groans. "Let me loose, okay? I'm getting stiff."

"You're not going to punch me?" Matt looks dubious. He runs the knife through the black forest between Buddy's pecs, taps the silver cross resting there, then sheathes the blade and slips it into a bedside drawer.

Buddy grins. "Guess you gotta wait and see."

Matt's barely unroped the big man before Buddy, bellowing, leaps atop him. They tussle on the bed, giggling like fools. Buddy wrestles Matt down, just to salvage some male pride, before allowing Matt to flip him. They end up with Matt's legs wrapped around Buddy's and Matt's hands forcing Buddy's wrists above his head.

"Got you, tiger," says Matt.

"Yep," says Buddy. "You sure do."

"You let me win," says Matt.

"I like it better when you're on top," says Buddy, blushing.

"Fine with me." Matt gives Buddy a kiss before slipping off him. They lie there side by side in a square of sunlight, breaths and heartbeats slowing.

"How do your butt cheeks feel?"

"Nice. Still sore. Still kinda burning. Gonna hurt to sit. That was one top-notch spanking."

"Good enough for me to paddle you again sometime?"

"Lord, yes. Often as possible. You done gave me everything I wanted. This is the kinda morning-after I like the most, man! My wrists and ankles all skinned up from rope, my mouth sore from a real tight gag, my tits all tore up from torture, my asshole raw from fucking, and my ass cheeks all tender from a good beating. Dream come true, man. Dream come true."

"Good to hear. As you can tell, I took careful note of those fantasies you e-mailed me. Want me to take that plug out?"

"Hell, no. Feels super. Leave it in all day. Least till you push your big fat prick up my hungry hole again."

"You are one nasty hillbilly. I love your dirty mouth. Think you could live here? If things work out between us?"

Buddy rolls over. He burrows his face into Matt's unwashed armpit, snuffling the heady scent, appreciatively lapping the salty hair.

"You athletes always smell so damn good," he says, nestling his head against Matt's shoulder. "Live here? You'n me? God, yes. It's nigh about the finest place I ever seen…and hell, all I seen yet's the bedroom."

"Good place to start." Matt wraps an arm around him. "You look tired. Want to take a nap?"

"Yep. All that thrashing 'round on the floor last night tuckered me out." Buddy cuddles closer, resting an arm across Matt's belly.

"You warm enough, handsome? Want a blanket?"

Dear Lord, you finally sent me someone. Someone kind. Someone cruel and kind. Best combo ever. "Naw," Buddy murmurs. "Sun's strong. Feels great."

"Later we can take that walk in the woods. Tomorrow, how about a boat cruise around the lake? Would you like that?"

"Sounds fun. Can we hold hands? Today? In the woods?"

"Yeah. We can. No one out here to bother us. Plus, hell, we're big guys. If anyone gives us any trouble, we'll clobber them."

Buddy nods. "Open up a can a' whup-ass."

"Are you coming to my next hockey game? Next Saturday?"

"Long as you rope and muzzle me after, maybe wear your hockey mask while you beat me with your stick. You know I love all that gear a' yours…Bad boy needs a whipping…" His words make both spent dicks twitch.

"You got it. I'll make that beefy butt of yours burn, mountain man."

"Yeah? Yum. Wouldn't miss it, then." Buddy takes Matt's cock in his hand. "Uh, Matt, look, if, uh, things go good between me and you… you wanna be monogamous, right?"

"Right. Does that work for you?"

"Yessireebob! Okay, so, I know we're both negative, but let's get tested just to be sure, and then, uh, maybe we could bareback…'cause, uh, I really want to take your loads up my ass."

"You want to be my redneck cum-dump, huh?"

"Ohhh, yeah! Real bad!"

"We'll see. Maybe. We'll have to talk about it." Matt rubs Buddy's bald head. "Right now, get some sleep."

"Yeah, I'm wore out." Buddy's voice is slumberously low. "But, Matt? Hey, Matt, can I suck on you some? All that time gagged, I didn't get to suck you yet. You know I got a powerful taste for your cock. Up my ass or down my throat," Buddy sheepishly admits, "I cain't get enough of your cock."

"Go for it, big boy."

Buddy slides down the bed and takes Matt's limp dick in his mouth. "Oh, yeah," he mumbles around the beloved flesh. *'Bout time one a' my prayers was answered. You sure took your time, Lord. What's the Good Book say? No one knows the day and hour of his coming…* Buddy sucks gently as he drifts off. Clutching his cross, he falls into stentorian sleep, Matt's half-hard cock on his tongue, Matt's fingers stroking his beard.

In the Doghouse
'Nathan Burgoine

"Woof."

I stood at my open door and tried not to sigh. Rob gave me his usual grin and a shrug.

"What'd you do this time?" I asked, stepping aside and letting him in. He only had his gym bag with him. In fact, he was wearing grubby jeans and a T-shirt, which meant he'd come here straight from the gym. That wasn't a good sign.

"Why do you always assume it's something I've done?" He went to my couch and sat down, tossing his bag to the floor.

"Rob, we have shorthand for you being in the doghouse. *My apartment* is your doghouse. It's always your fault she kicks you out." I frowned. "Wait. Isn't tonight your anniversary?"

He groaned and rolled his head back on the couch, covering his face with both hands. "How do you remember that? *Why* would you remember that?"

"I take it you didn't?" I crossed my arms.

"We're not engaged! It's only been a year! How am I supposed to remember when we started dating?" His honest bafflement made me smile. Rob was many things—impulsive, supportive, patient, in great shape, and one hell of a kickboxing coach, which was how we'd met—but he sure wasn't a romantic.

"I remember because it was the day after my birthday." I shrugged.

"Shit." He lowered his hands. "Really? Happy birthday."

I laughed. "It's fine, Rob. I'm not as twitchy as Amanda is about that stuff."

"Thank God," he said. Then he frowned at me. "You're all dressed up."

I looked down at myself. "All dressed up" was maybe putting it too strongly, but I was wearing my favourite yellow dress shirt and a nice pair of khakis. It was a very preppy look, but I'd long ago given up on trying to look slick. I had "aw-shucks" looks—complete with the bane of my existence: my dimples—and there was nothing I could do about it. If I rolled with it, on a good day I could almost be cute. Though I had decided on the black silk boxers, just to feel a little naughty.

"I'm going to the Eat Out For Life dinner tonight," I said.

"The…?" He shook his head.

"It's a benefit to raise funds for HIV awareness," I said. "I bought the tickets ages ago, before…" I shrugged. "Well. I felt like getting dressed up and going out."

Rob grinned at me. I knew that grin. Trouble. "Will there be beer at this benefit?"

I nodded, trying not to smile back at him. His brown eyes seemed to fill with liquid mischief when he smiled like that. We'd had more than one misadventure that began with that smile. "Yes, though most people will be having wine with their four-course meal."

"Most people are weird. Beer is way more awesome." He rose. "When do we leave?"

"You are not coming with me in that outfit," I said. I tried not to sound relieved. The thought of going to the benefit on my own wasn't something I'd been looking forward to. I was supposed to be going with Serge. Serge had decided that a younger, blonder model was more pleasing, so I'd had my ass dumped a couple of weeks ago—but only after Serge had accidentally texted me instead of his new boy toy.

Rob made a show of opening his gym bag. "Well, let's see. Other than what I'm wearing, I've got a tank top and some shorts." He grinned at me. I could see how my sister was convinced to take him back so many times. Normally she kicked guys to the curb for much less than Rob had gotten away with over the last year. That grin was so damned infectious.

"Oh for the love of…" I sighed. "Come on," I said, and started for my bedroom. "I think I've got something that'll fit you."

❖

A half hour later, we'd walked to the Byward Market and were seated at one of the most expensive restaurants in the city, and Rob had a glass of beer—they'd refused to bring it to him in the bottle he'd asked for—and I had a nice chilled glass of Conundrum. We were back to our usual topic when he was on the outs with Amanda.

"Thing is," he said, taking a sip, "if she wants me to remember this stuff, she should tell me."

I shook my head. He looked good in the shirt and pants I'd bought early for the cheating bastard Serge's birthday. The shirt was a bit snug on Rob—Serge spent less time in the gym trying to build muscle than Rob did—but the dark brown went well with Rob's chocolate eyes and almost black hair. He'd had to leave the top button undone—which exposed just a trace of his chest hair—and he'd rolled back the sleeves roughly thirty seconds after putting it on. Rob's arms were definitely things of beauty. Once again, I was unsurprised that my sister always forgave him.

Eventually.

"Listen, big guy," I said, "you know I think you're awesome. But you really need to just program this stuff into your phone or something."

"She seemed pretty final about it this time." He sighed. "I fucked up, eh?"

I nodded. "You're in the wrong."

"We can still hang out, right?" he asked.

I smiled. "Of course." It'd made me feel good that he liked hanging out with me. We hadn't done it often, since Amanda was a whole lot of neurotic and clingy, but we'd had some fun. Though usually it was only when my sister had kicked him out, or when she and Serge had both been out of town. We'd usually just sat watching MMA fights, which neither Serge nor Amanda could stand. It suddenly occurred to me that if she did truly dump him, I might not see Rob even that much, and that made me sad.

"Maybe she'll come around," I said.

"You'll talk to her?" he asked. He didn't sound optimistic.

"And say what?" I shook my head. "Did you miss the part about being in the wrong?"

He grinned. "Woof."

I opened my mouth to say something else, and then froze, my gaze drifting past Rob to the door. It couldn't be.

Rob frowned. "What's wrong?"

"Serge is here," I said, feeling my stomach churn. "And he brought his twink."

"Twink?" Rob asked.

They'd just walked in together and were handing over their tickets. I sighed. Serge looked good—of course—the man spent hours in the bathroom before every outing. His moronic blond bimboy was holding hands with him and looking around the restaurant like he'd never seen anything so pretty in his very short and highly oversexed life. Serge looked up and caught my eyes. He raised a hand and waved, a shit-eating grin on his face.

"Ugh," I said, twisting my own lips into a smile and waving back. "Asshole," I muttered.

Rob turned, and when he did, I saw Serge do a double take, his oh-so-sincere smile faltering a little.

"Is he the one with all the hair gel, or the blond guy?" Rob asked.

I hadn't realized that Rob had never met Serge. It wasn't surprising, really. Serge had generally run our social calendar. Amanda thought Rob and I lost maturity when we were around each other—Rob lived by his mantra "Fuck it!" and I seemed to get into the same frame of mind when we were together—so she never wanted to double-date. Sometimes I got the impression that Amanda only spoke to me because she felt it was her duty as a sister. Also, Rob held classes at his gym most weekends, whereas Serge worked out at his office and kept the weekends free for looking good at bars with something cute on his arm.

Which used to be me.

"Hair gel," I said. "Aveda."

Rob turned back to me. "No offense, but he looks like a douchebag."

I laughed. "None taken." I glanced up. "Oh fantastic, now they're coming this way, miserable sons of…Serge! Hi!" I nodded politely.

"Hey, Anthony," Serge said, voice dripping with that false

politeness I'd always heard him use with clients on his cell. "I didn't think you'd be coming tonight." He squeezed the boy-toy's hand. "This is Troy's first Eat Out For Life." He beamed at the cute blond. "Troy, you remember Anthony, right?"

"Yeah," Troy said. He bobbed his head. God, he was vapid.

I gritted my teeth. I really wanted them to go away.

"I'm Rob," Rob said, holding out a hand. Serge looked at him—up and down—then took his hand. They shook.

"You work at the bank with Anthony?" Serge asked. I felt my head tip down. God, couldn't he just walk away and leave me to my humiliation? No, he had to make sure I wasn't here on a date and I hadn't moved on. Then he could take his blond boy home and plough him all night from his position of top dog. Probably literally.

Rob was right. Serge was a douchebag. Why had I ever dated him?

"No," Rob said. "We've been dating for a couple of weeks."

I blinked and looked at Rob. He reached across the table and took my hand, giving my fingers a squeeze. Then he looked at the blond boy toy and added, "My first Eat Out For Life was last year. You're gonna love the food. Are you old enough to drink?"

I coughed, trying—and probably failing—to hide the bark of laughter that burst out. I picked up my wineglass with my free hand and took a sip.

"Yeah," the blond said, oblivious to the barbed comment. "I'm twenty-one." He actually sounded proud.

Serge's smile tightened. "Well, we should go sit. We'll see you two lovebirds at the Balcony?"

The Balcony was the gay bar hosting the after-dinner party. I'd no intention of going there and watching Serge slobber all over his twink all night.

"I'm not sure," I hedged.

"Wouldn't miss it," Rob said. "Enjoy the meal."

The two moved away, thankfully to a table far to the other side of the restaurant.

"Total douchebag," Rob said, turning back to me with a scowl. "What the fuck was that? He thinks he gets to smack you down just because you didn't hop into bed with the next asshole to come along? Fuckwad."

I smiled at him, surprised to find my eyes getting a little wet. "Thank you. You didn't have to do that."

Rob shrugged, and his frown slowly lifted.

The first course arrived.

❖

Rob belched. "So where's the Balcony?"

We were outside the restaurant and walking away from the Market. "We don't have to go to the Balcony," I said. "I hadn't planned on it, even if I had come here with Serge. He was just trying to let me know he'd be there so I could avoid him."

"All the more reason." Rob shook his head. "Besides, all they had at the dinner was that shitty microbrew crap, and I want a real beer. Come on, it'll piss off the douchebag."

I looked at him. He looked back at me with that grin on his face.

"Seriously?" I asked. It didn't strike me as a good idea.

"Fuck it!" He grinned, and I felt myself smiling. "Why not? What else am I gonna do? Woof, remember?"

I held up a hand. "Just don't say 'woof' at the bar. Not unless you want a big hairy guy to hit on you."

Rob blinked. "What?"

"Just trust me on that," I said.

"Okay," he said. "You gay guys are weird."

"Yeah, but we remember anniversaries."

He punched my shoulder. It hurt.

❖

Balcony was packed, but it didn't take us long to spot Serge, who was grinding in the centre of the dance floor with Troy, who had of course managed to lose his shirt somewhere. He had a pierced nipple and flawless tanned skin.

"Ugh. Look at them," I said. "First beer's on me."

Rob gave my shoulders a shake and aimed me at the bar. A few minutes later we had a bottle each, and Rob had tipped half his back already. The music was loud, and thumping, and it was obvious most of the guys in the bar hadn't come from the benefit—or they'd gone home and changed into tight shirts before coming. I felt overdressed and very plain. I forced myself not to laugh as guys started to check out Rob with varying degrees of subtlety. They barely glanced at me.

This was why I rarely came to the bars.

"This is actually pretty cool," Rob said loudly, leaning in to my ear. "The music is good." He seemed oblivious to the looks he was getting—and I couldn't help but smirk at his assessment.

"It's pretty busy tonight. It's not normally this crowded," I yelled back.

He nodded, looking around and drinking his beer. Out of nowhere, he suddenly looped his arm around my shoulder and tugged me in close. I looked at him, surprised, and he winked.

"You came!"

Ah. I turned and saw Serge and the half-naked twink.

"We came," I said, and took a sip from my bottle. Serge nodded, though his eyes flicked up to Rob's arm, casually draped around my shoulder. I couldn't help myself, I put my arm around Rob's waist. Fuck it. For once I'd be the guy with the trophy on my arm.

"Gonna hydrate," Serge said, smiling overbrightly, "and then we'll see you on the dance floor!" They moved past us.

"He's jealous," Rob said, leaning down to my ear.

"Of course he is," I said. "You're hot, and he's annoyed I'm not pining over him."

Rob grinned at me. "I'm hot?"

I rolled my eyes, and shoved him, letting go of his waist. He took his arm back.

"You're hot," I said. "And you know it. Which is a bad combination."

He laughed. "So do we go dance now?"

I shook my head. "No way. You dance like a straight guy."

"I am a straight guy."

"Yeah, well, you dance like one."

"But I'm hot." He grinned.

"Yes, you are," a tall guy said, pausing and tossing Rob a wink.

"Sorry," Rob said, giving me another neck-crushing pull from his arm. "Taken."

I laughed, and the tall guy moved on.

"Dance?" Rob asked. "Come on. You can teach me. I taught you how to kick."

That was true. I'd been a disaster when we'd met. A runner, I wasn't in poor shape, I'd just had zero confidence I'd manage to do anything right in the class. He'd been beyond patient with me, coaching me carefully and steadily until I'd become—in his words—"pretty competent." I tipped back the last of my beer and surrendered.

"Fuck it," I said, and Rob grinned. "It's fairly crowded. You won't look that bad. Come on."

He gave my ass a swat on the way to the dance floor and laughed out loud when I yelped.

❖

A couple of hours later, we were walking home. I was pleasantly buzzed, and Rob had one strong arm around my neck while we walked.

"Admit it," Rob said. "I'm the best date you've ever had."

"You are so freaking full of yourself." I laughed. "And unfortunately, you're right. I'm pathetic."

Rob let go of my neck and stood in front of me. At some point during the dancing, someone—I was pretty sure it was the tall guy from when we were standing near the bar—had slid up to him and undone the buttons on his shirt. The look of total panic on his face when the guy had seen the hair on Rob's chest and said "woof" had been pure gold. I'd rescued him, and Rob had draped his arms over my shoulders while we danced until the guy had left. Rob hadn't done the shirt back up, and I wasn't complaining. He was in great shape—and had just enough chest hair, in my opinion.

"Hey," Rob said, spreading his arms. "Who sent your douchebag ex-boyfriend packing with his toonie?"

I burst out laughing. "Twink."

"What?"

"Troy is a twink." I had to stop walking, I was laughing so hard. "Though I guess a toonie would be a fair price."

"Woof, twink…" Rob grabbed either side of my face with his hands and leaned in close. "You gay guys are nuts."

My breath caught. He was really close to me.

"Hey, faggot!"

Rob turned and got his arm up just as the first of the three men brought the board down.

❖

By the time we were done at the hospital and had finished talking with the police, the sun was coming up. We stepped into my apartment, and I closed the door behind me. Rob walked in ahead and sank onto the couch with a deep groan. His wrist was in a cast. They'd given him a green scrub shirt at the hospital to replace the brown one—which the bashers had ruined.

Before Rob and I had kicked the living crap out of them.

I sat on the couch beside him.

Rob leaned back, shifting his weight, and winced as he moved his wrist.

I felt my eyes well up. I'd held it together at the hospital. I'd tried to call my sister—who hadn't answered any calls from my cell. I'd held it together while they put the cast on Rob's wrist. I'd kept myself from reacting when I'd gotten a text from her: *It's three in the morning! I'm not listening to your messages! Stop defending him! Stop calling! I'm through with him!* I'd held it together at the police station, where two detectives couldn't stop smiling as we described how three out-of-shape idiots had decided to take on two gay guys—never mind that one of the guys wasn't gay—who happened to be kickboxers. Or one kickboxer and one more-or-less-competent student.

I'd even held it together when the police had driven us back to my building, telling us about what the next steps would likely be.

But now we were back in my apartment and my hands were shaking. I leaned my head back on the couch and tried to hold back a sob. I only half succeeded.

Rob opened his eyes and turned his head. "Anthony?"

"Sorry," I said. My voice came out strangled. My whole body was shaking.

"What's wrong?" Rob looked more shaken at the sight of me now than he'd been when the three guys had jumped us. I didn't know whether to laugh or yell at him.

Instead, I started crying.

"Whoa," Rob said, and he sat up, staring at me. He raised his left hand—the one without the broken wrist—and sort of held it in the air between us, not sure what to do with it.

"Sorry," I said. "I...I figured this time I'd be okay." I took a few gulping breaths.

Rob frowned, and his hand finally settled on my shoulder, awkwardly. "This time?"

"I got beat up once already." I sighed. "That's why I started taking your classes," I said. I rubbed at my eyes with the back of my sleeve. "Amanda bought them for me." I shook my head at his surprised face. "It wasn't as bad as tonight, but it scared the hell out of me. God. Is 'hit me' painted across my face or something?"

Rob shook my shoulder. "You were great," he said.

"You took two of them and you had a broken wrist. I got the guy who tried to run away," I said.

"You had my back. And you gave me time to get ready after they broke my wrist." He squeezed my shoulder. "You never take a compliment. You're the same in class. Why do you always beat yourself down?"

"I don't know," I said. "It's dumb. Especially when so many other people seem so willing to do it." I smiled weakly.

He laughed.

"People leave," I said. It came out before I could stop it.

Rob frowned. "What?"

"People leave me. My dad sure as hell couldn't get out of my life fast enough. My mom stopped talking to me when I came out. My step-dad, too. I don't think Amanda even likes me, to be honest. Everyone I've ever dated has pretty much convinced me that I should have just stayed in the closet in the first place. Hell, you met Serge." I shrugged. "I don't have...I don't know. Whatever it is that people like. So people leave."

He kissed me.

One second he was looking at me and frowning like I was saying something in another language, and the next he'd leaned over and I was learning that not only was his stubble fun to look at, it was also made entirely of hot friction. My hand went up to his chest, and I opened my mouth and felt his tongue slip between my lips.

The kiss broke. Our foreheads were inches apart. Again.

"Shit," he said.

"It's okay," I said, and pulled my hand away from the warmth of his chest. "I'm a mess and you're probably still drunk—not to mention being on painkillers—and neither of us have slept and we got attacked..." He was looking at me. His brown eyes were a little wide, and his mouth was slightly open. I closed my eyes. "It's okay, Rob. Really." I opened my eyes again and sat forward. "I'll get some blankets and a pillow—I'll take the couch. You can have my bed." I was rambling. "Because of your wrist."

He looked down at his cast, then at me. He slowly slid off the couch and rose. I sat there and forced myself not to say anything as he walked to the door of my apartment and opened it. When it closed behind him. I shut my eyes, and told myself I would absolutely not cry.

"Fuck," I said.

There was a knock.

I sat up, exhausted physically and emotionally. My body still ached from the adrenaline come-down after the fight. Was I crazy and imagining things, or did he just...?

He knocked again.

I got up and went to the door. I opened it.

"Woof," he said.

"I don't get it," I said, not even trying to hide that I was crying.

"I left. And I came back again. Can I stay here tonight?" he asked.

"It's the doghouse," I said. "Of course you can."

❖

I followed him into my bedroom and tried not to stare as he awkwardly pulled off the shirt the hospital had given him and then stepped out of the pants he'd borrowed from me. His boxers were riding a little low, and I turned around to fuss uselessly in my closet for another blanket. When I turned back around, he was lying on the bed, eyes closed, on top of the covers. He had his right arm flat on the edge of the bed, and his left was up behind his head. It did great things for his arm and chest.

God, he was hot. He was handsome in a scruffy way and muscular, sure, but it was more than that. There was a genuineness to him that was so damn attractive. Okay, he didn't have much in the way of forethought, and the man didn't have the slightest idea how to be romantic, but after he'd kicked the crap out of the first two guys and I'd knocked the last of them off his feet, Rob had turned to me—Rob, who had the broken wrist—and he'd said, "You okay?"

I tugged a spare pillow from the closet and turned to go.

"Don't," Rob said.

"Pardon?"

"Don't sleep on the couch." He'd opened his eyes.

"Okay." I held the blanket and pillow against my chest for a second, then put them on the floor. I stripped off my shirt—I had no idea if I'd ever get it clean—and then tugged off my pants. I felt myself blushing, hyperaware that Rob was watching me and that I'd chosen the black silk boxers. I climbed onto the bed and lay on my back, staring at the ceiling. I couldn't bring myself to look into his eyes.

"Do you want to get under the covers?" I asked.

"I'm not drunk."

I rolled onto my side. Rob was staring straight up.

"I know," I said.

"I've never…" He swallowed. "Well." He turned his head to look at me. "You really think I'm hot?"

I raised my eyebrows. "You're kidding, right?"

His lip curled in a slight grin. "You're pretty hot, too."

"Thanks," I said. It was nice of him to say.

"You don't believe me," he said.

I sort of shrugged.

He moved his left hand from behind his head and reached over. His eyes didn't leave mine as he took my wrist and slowly pulled my hand across the gap between us. I shivered when he led my fingers to his stomach, which was dusted with that lovely dark hair, and then he pressed my hand against his crotch.

He was hard.

My eyes flicked down at our hands, then back to his face. If I crossed this line…

"Oh, fuck it," I said. I slid my hand into his boxers and pulled his dick free, giving him a light squeeze.

He laughed.

I shifted down and took him into my mouth. I'd admired Rob's cock in the shower at the gym, but hard it was a thing of beauty—his cockhead had darkened and his shaft had thickened, with obvious veins that mirrored the ones on his forearms. I swallowed him as deep as I could, until I felt his hardness at the back of my mouth, and wrapped my fingers around the last inch or so of his dick.

"Jesus!" Rob gasped. His left hand rested lightly on the back of my shoulder. "Fuck!"

His back arched a little, and I went to work, feeling my own dick grow hard as I sucked him. I ran my right hand up and across his stomach and chest, letting my finger and thumb find his nipple for a quick rub while I started to blow him in earnest, bobbing my head as far up and down as I could manage, and massaging him with my tongue, swirling it around his cockhead as I withdrew, and then pressing against his shaft when I went down.

"Fuck...Fuck!" he repeated. God, I loved this—I loved having a guy at my mercy like this. I loved sucking dick. I pressed my own hard-on into the mattress while I sucked him. Rob's voice was low, and he was breathing in shorter and shorter gasps the longer I worked his dick. His hand gripped my shoulder tighter and shook a little. His chest shifted under my hand as he moved in little jerks on the bed.

He exhaled in loud gasps and made other noises as he inhaled and pushed his dick into my mouth, raising his thighs off the bed. I moved both my hands to the task, cupping his balls and rolling them in one palm while I continued to stroke him with the other. His cock was wet with my saliva, and his legs were growing sweaty. My own dick throbbed.

"Fuck!" he growled. "Jesus...Anthony...I'm gonna...I'm gonna come."

I let his cock out of my mouth and looked up the length of his muscular body. He looked down at me, face and neck red, breathing heavily.

"So come," I said, and swallowed his dick again. He threw his head back and swore again.

"Fuck...Fuck fuck..." I tugged his balls, and he yelled as he came. He gripped my shoulder so tightly I was pretty sure he'd bruise me, but I didn't care. His body rose up against my mouth. He pumped two hot jets into my mouth, and I barely succeeded in swallowing. I licked and sucked until his dick stopped lurching and his body sagged against the bed.

He lay there, panting, and was looking down at me when I let go of his dick and turned to look at him. I rolled over onto my back, my erection obvious in the black silk boxers, and tugged my dick free to jerk myself. I closed my eyes, rolling my head back, and stroked myself.

"Hey," Rob said, his voice low.

I opened my eyes and looked at him. He'd risen onto his left elbow. He leaned in and kissed me, his tongue entering my mouth aggressively. His right hand—awkward in the cast—he rested high on my thigh. The combination was too much, and I felt myself erupt across my stomach. I cried into Rob's rough kisses.

Eventually, he pulled away. He moved his tongue in his mouth.

"Sort of…salty," he said.

I laughed. "Yeah. A little." I curled up awkwardly, reaching for the tissues beside the bed, and managed to wipe most of the mess from my stomach. Then I got up and went to the bathroom, running the hot tap for a while, and brought back two wet towels. Rob lay back while I wiped him down, looking up at me with that grin. When I was finished cleaning us up, I helped him get under the covers.

"You should take a painkiller before you try to sleep," I said.

He nodded, and I went and got a glass of water and the small bottle the doctors had prescribed for him. He swallowed the pill, and then I slid into the bed beside him. The curtains blocked most of the light, but the sun was definitely coming up.

He closed his eyes, and I watched him for a few seconds, then closed my eyes and finally fell asleep.

❖

I woke up in the bed alone. I stretched, and reached out, and then opened my eyes. I wasn't surprised, really. I bit down on the disappointment and checked the clock. It was almost ten. I groaned and got up, tugging on some boxers and a pair of sweatpants and a T-shirt, and then opened my bedroom door.

Rob had his back to me and was talking quietly into his cell phone. He'd changed into his gym shorts, but wasn't wearing anything else. He turned when he heard me and raised one finger. He winked.

"It's a clean break, but it's still broken," he said, speaking a bit louder now. "I won't be able to do the classes at all today or tomorrow. Or next week, for sure. After that, I don't know yet."

Right. It was Saturday. Normally he'd be giving classes in about an hour.

"I will," he said, after a pause. "Okay. Bye." He shut the phone and smiled at me.

"Good morning," he said. "You snore."

I winced. "Did I wake you?"

Rob shook his head. "No, the wrist did. But you snore. Like a pig. Little grunty snores." He mimicked the noise.

And here I'd thought this morning might have been awkward.

"Did you want breakfast before I kick you out?" I asked, crossing my arms.

"Woof," he said, holding his hands together, like he was begging for mercy. I tried not to be distracted by his arms or his chest. I failed, and he caught me looking. I blushed and looked away.

"We should talk," Rob said.

I smiled. "I know this part." I tried to walk past him to the kitchen, but he took my shoulder in his good hand.

"Anthony."

"No," I said. "It's fine." I tried to move, but he didn't let go of my shoulder.

"Shit," he said.

"Rob," I said. "You're amazing, and you've always made me feel good about myself. You suck at being romantic, but if I'm going to be honest, my sister treats you like shit and you can do way better. As sad as this sounds, you're pretty much my best friend, since all the rest of them decided to stay on Team Serge. I didn't want to screw that up. I hope I haven't. I'm sorry. I shouldn't have kissed you. Or, y'know, sucked your dick."

"I was the one who kissed you," Rob said.

"Yeah," I said. "I remember. That was me giving you an out. Trust me, I had a lot of experience with straight guys in university. Mostly they used the 'I was drunk, I don't remember anything' excuse." I smiled at him, hoping it wasn't obvious I was trying not to cry. "Seriously, Rob, it's okay."

"If I kissed you again, would you stop talking shit about yourself?"

"What?" I said, and then he was kissing me again, and this time I was holding his face and kissing him back and pulling him toward me for what had to be the best and longest kiss of my life. When I fell back a bit, he looked into my eyes.

"Here's what I know," he said, holding up his good hand. He raised his thumb. "I wasn't drunk." He raised a finger. "I kissed you first." Another. "That was the best fucking blow job of my life." Another finger rose, while I laughed. "I have always thought you were cool." He raised his pinky. "In the last year, you've always been the person I've gone to when I felt like shit."

"Okay," I said. My throat felt raw.

"Last night felt great," Rob said. "I knew I liked you, Anthony. And yeah, sometimes I thought about it. About you." He shrugged. "I had more fun at the dinner and the bar last night than I've had in a long time. And I think it was because I was with you. I don't know if that sounds gay. But I don't really care. I fuck up this sort of shit all the time, I guess." He frowned. "Am I making sense?"

"I don't know," I said. "Are you saying you want to date me?"

"Yeah." He nodded slowly. "I guess I am. You're fun to be with. You make me laugh. You like me the way I am. And you've got a great ass."

"Thank you," I said. "That last part sounded pretty gay."

"A little bit, huh?" He sighed. "Look, I'm a mess. I know I don't always pay attention to stuff, and I'm lousy at being a boyfriend. I suck at all the little shit. In fact, I'm probably the worst boyfriend ever."

"If I kissed you again, would you stop talking shit about yourself?" I asked.

"Probably not." He grinned. "But maybe if you gave me another blow job?"

I rolled my eyes, then kissed him again. His left arm wrapped around me and gave my ass a squeeze. I could feel him, semi-hard in his gym shorts, against my stomach. My own dick responded.

"Seriously. Great ass," he said.

"Seriously. Gay," I replied.

"Blow job?" he asked, pressing against me.

"Breakfast first," I said. "Then blow jobs. Note the pluralisation of blow jobs. Omelettes?"

"Deal," he said. "I can probably manage to make the toast."

We broke apart, and made breakfast, and ate. We didn't talk much, neither of us willing to admit that we were rushing, but rushing nonetheless. Finally, once I picked up my plate and carried it to the sink, Rob jumped up and awkwardly pulled himself up onto the counter beside the sink. He winked at me, then looked down at his obviously tented shorts.

"You might remember the pluralisation?"

Rob grinned. "But me first?"

"Greedy."

"I don't..." He blushed and cleared his throat. "I've never. Uh."

I smiled. "Sucked a cock?"

He nodded. "Sucked a cock."

"Well," I said. "You taught me to kick. I can teach you to suck."

He put his arms on my shoulders and leaned forward until our foreheads touched. "But me first, right?"

"You're like a dog with a bone," I said, but I smiled and leaned in for a kiss. He kissed me back, even more possessive and confident than the last time. Then I kissed his chin, and his throat, and his hairy chest, working my way down his body toward his cock as slowly as I could bring myself to go, already looking forward to it.

"Woof," Rob said.

THE WOLVERINES
NATHAN SIMS

The night air was cool and crisp with a bite to it that snuck through the breath, deep inside the skin. It was filled with the scent of fall leaves and fresh-cut grass. Dyson found it odd how death and life could fuse in a single scent.

The warrior sat in the bleachers next to his boyfriend. Around them, the stands were filled with students, family, and townsfolk cheering on their respective teams huddled down on the field.

"Now, which one were you again?" Avery asked, looping his arm through his boyfriend's.

Dyson stifled the urge to pull away. Still not used to public displays of their relationship, he had already gone round one with his boyfriend over the subject. That particular argument ended with Avery leaving him at a club, and that hadn't been the worst part of the evening. Before it was over, Dyson took a pummeling from half a dozen drag queens and went home with a cracked rib and a winged elf supporting him step by step. He gripped his boyfriend's arm. A touch of social awkwardness was better than running the risk of a repeat performance.

"Tight end," he replied, pointing out onto the field as the offense positioned themselves at the yard line. "The one on the end over there."

"Mmm," Avery purred. "*Tight end*, it even sounds sexy."

"Shouldn't you be focusing on why we're here?" Dyson reminded the reporter quietly. "You know, your story?"

"I can work and enjoy myself at the same time," Avery replied, snuggling closer to ward off the chill October night. "I'm exceedingly versatile. You should know this by now."

Grinning wickedly, Dyson leaned in and felt his boyfriend's wavy, copper-colored hair tickle his cheek and asked, "Okay, Mr. Versatile, what would you say if I told you there's a *wide receiver* out there too?"

Avery pulled his glasses down the length of his long Roman nose and looked over their edge. "I'd say pull out that jersey, mister. Someone's headed straight to the end zone tonight!" Dyson chuckled, a single dimple appearing in his left cheek.

Two men sitting in the row directly in front of them turned to each other and laughed. They were middle-aged and had been yelling the name of one of the players throughout the first half of the game. Dyson guessed they were a father and family friend cheering on one of the high school students. Or maybe they were father and uncle, they looked enough alike. But when the one on the left turned back toward the two of them and winked, Dyson figured he might need to reconsider their relationship.

Avery smiled back at the man and said, "It's like a whole new world."

"Tell me about it," the winker agreed. He was slightly shorter than his partner, yet both bore the same fine features that had Dyson guessing they were brothers. "I never thought I'd sit through a game in my life, but Billy here," he pointed to his partner, "was All State Champion his senior year in high school. He would have gone on too, if he hadn't gotten injured. When we started dating, he made me sit through every single game on TV. Now look at me, twenty years later and here I am cheering on my son!"

Delighted, Avery asked, "Which one is he?"

"Number 28," answered their new acquaintance. "The center left of the quarterback."

Dyson followed the man's description and took in the brawny young man squatting down at the yard line. Like his teammates, his helmet bore the silhouette of a howling wolf. The name on the back of his jersey read *Macher*. Dyson wondered which man's surname had won the coveted position across their son's jersey.

"Is he your biological son or did you adopt?" Avery asked. In the half year they'd been dating, Dyson had learned that being a reporter, it was his boyfriend's natural inclination to ask complete strangers wildly inappropriate questions.

"Surrogate," the man replied. "We thought we'd just mix up our batter, pop it in the oven, and see what came out. We had a bet going on whose little guys would make it to the finish line first." The man glanced to his son, then back to Avery and said, "Guess who won?"

"Hush up, Stu, my son's getting ready to play," his partner Billy teased.

Stu gasped in mock offense. "Hateful!"

Billy's response was to holler, "Come on, Cody!" as the ball snapped and the crowd cheered. The play was over soon enough and Avery and Stu continued their conversation.

"So what are you two doing here?" Stu asked, turning the focus on Dyson and Avery.

They hadn't rehearsed an answer to that one. Neither had considered the possibility that they'd strike up a conversation with someone at the game. As usual, though, Avery was quick on his feet.

"Oh, Wain used to play back in high school." The reporter nodded toward Dyson. "I thought it would be fun to surprise him and take him to a game." It wasn't the first time Dyson wondered if he shouldn't worry how easily lying came to his boyfriend.

"A *high school* football game?" Stu asked, bemused.

"Yeah…well…" Avery stumbled for only a moment before recovering. When he did, it came out as more embarrassment than an excuse. "I tried to get Skins tickets from work, but they were already spoken for." Damn, was he good. "Besides, I thought it would be fun for him to relive his glory days."

"So, are you from around here?" Billy asked Dyson. Hearing there was a fellow football player in his midst, he took his first real interest in the couple seated behind him.

"No, I'm from Illinois," Dyson answered. "Just moved here last year."

"You play college ball?"

"No," Dyson said. "We didn't have a team."

"Wain went to a technical institute," Avery explained. An institute where he learned the technique of killing dwarves, trolls, and vampires. Dyson smiled. It was probably as good a description as any.

"I was on an intramural team," Billy said, scanning the field. "Penny-ante stuff after what we did in high school."

"You sound like you miss it," Avery observed.

"Sure I do," Billy replied. "Being out on that field, it's like nothing…hell, it's one of the best experiences of my life."

Dyson knew what he meant. He smiled thinking of the good times back home, before his senior year when everything went so wrong. He remembered the surge of adrenaline as he suited up in the locker room; the crush of bodies in the huddle; and that final, frozen breath of anticipation before the snap of the ball and the play began. He felt it again, arms reaching out to grab him as he slipped by and raced down the field, his muscles stretching and contracting in a miracle of strength and conditioning. He heard the cheers of elation as he reached the goal line, high fives and back slaps accompanying the touchdown.

At the time he'd imagined he'd spend his life in the game. Where else would he be? What else would he be doing? What else did he even know how to do? Well, he'd learned the answer to that question when he'd killed his first wood sprite and then all the creatures that came after. Soon enough thoughts of the field and the game slipped away as a new reality forced itself upon him. The game became nothing more than a fond memory of a former life, one he'd allow himself to pull out and enjoy only on rare occasions for fear its loss would become unbearable.

"It's nice you get to relive it through your son," Avery was saying. "And in such an incredible year!"

"Seven-and-oh so far this season," Billy bragged.

"Not bad," Avery agreed. "I hear they have a new coach."

"New coach," Stu chimed in, "new attitude."

"New attitude?" asked Avery.

"Look at those kids," Billy said pointing down to the field. "They were three-and-nine last year. They were losers. Now look at them. Walking around with their heads held high, like they own the ball, like they're just letting the other team borrow it for a little while."

Dyson leaned into Avery and said quietly, "From three-and-nine to seven-and-oh in a single year? Guess I don't need to ask which team you think is juicing."

As if on cue, the ball was tossed and a member of Cody's team caught it. Instantly three fellow teammates amassed around the kid carrying the ball. Like an arrowhead, one in front and one on each side, they protected their teammate as they traveled down the field in formation. Dyson's high school coach would have wept to see a play work so effortlessly.

The player on the right, closest to Dyson's side of the stands, came in contact with a member of the defense. He shoved the opposing player aside, propelling the kid backward at least a dozen feet before he landed on the turf in a heap. Dyson watched the play in absolute amazement. Cody's team scored and the stands surrounding Dyson went wild, including Cody's two dads, who were on their feet hollering with the crowd.

Dyson barely heard Avery above the din as the reporter raised an eyebrow and answered, "I'll give you one guess. Which team do you think is juicing?"

❖

"Don't you just love that smell?" Avery whispered. The two hid in a stairwell outside the locker room's open doors. It was halftime and the coach for the Wolverines was inside rallying the boys for the second half. Not that they needed it.

After watching them for the first half, Dyson had decided the wolverine really was the perfect mascot for their team. They ran the field like a pack of ravenous dogs, crazed for the ball, tearing through anyone that got in their way. By the end of the first half, the team was already twenty-one points ahead.

"The scent of testosterone and sweat…" the reporter continued as he reveled in the musk coming from the locker room. "A mingling of angst and hubris."

"I'm pretty sure they've got an ointment for hubris now," Dyson offered.

Avery stared at him in disbelief, an eyebrow cocked high above his right eye.

"What?"

The reporter shook his head and chuckled. "It's a good thing you're so damn cute."

"What?!" Dyson blushed. Should he be flattered? Embarrassed? He couldn't quite say.

If Avery intended to respond, his words were interrupted by the coach bringing his speech to a crescendo as the team cheered and the man punctuated it with a single sentence. "Now, drink up, boys!"

"Drink up?!" Avery puzzled. He pulled his phone from his pants pocket and extended it past the corner of the stairwell. Aiming its camera toward the locker room, he snapped several pictures.

"Now get out there and show them who owns that field!" the coach hollered and the team howled their agreement as a stampede of cleats headed in their direction. Dyson grabbed his boyfriend just in time to pull him back into the shadows of the stairwell as the first members of the team passed by.

As they clung together in the darkness, the moment had a not unpleasant effect on Dyson. Their bodies pressed together in the stairwell, their faces close enough to feel each other's breath, the edge of impending discovery mingled with the adrenaline already racing through his veins. Having spent years fighting preternatural creatures to the death, he found this thrill tame by comparison. Even so, it was oddly titillating—the fusing of danger with the proximity to his boyfriend's sturdy frame.

He felt his body respond, and from the way Avery shifted closer, his boyfriend felt it too. The reporter planted his hands against the wall on either side of Dyson, pressing his lover back against the brick, and with the sound of teenage boys storming the hall, he kissed him. Dyson felt open lips greet him and took advantage of the invitation, his tongue sliding deep inside the other man's mouth. He gripped Avery's hips and pulled him closer. Public displays be damned. Who cared if they were seen, not when the end result was sharing a moment like this with his boyfriend?

As their kiss ended, the reporter sighed and buried his face in the crook of Dyson's neck. "You have no idea how many teenage fantasies you just fulfilled."

Dyson grinned and whispered, "Your teenage fantasies were kind of awesome."

"Oh, you have no idea," Avery very nearly growled.

"Wanna try out another one?" Dyson groped between his boyfriend's legs, glad to find he wasn't the only one turned on.

"Definitely," Avery replied, brushing his nose against his lover's, so close their lips practically touched. "Later, though. Once I've got my story."

"Your story, right." Dyson sighed and released his grip on Avery. "Let's get to it, then." He grabbed Avery's wrist and brought the camera into view.

Several images captured blurry scenes of the team seated on the locker room's benches. One was even of the locker room's open doors. Disgusted, Avery deleted each one until, "Bingo! We have a winner!" Two pictures clearly showed members of the team upending small plastic cups full of red liquid.

"Don't drink the Kool-Aid," Dyson intoned as they studied the images.

"Aren't steroids usually injected?" asked Avery. "Not ingested?"

"Usually, but I'm not so sure what you're dealing with here is steroids," Dyson replied.

"What do you mean?"

"When the kid caught that ball in the second quarter, did you see the way the team formed around him?"

Avery nodded. "That cool arrow they made to protect him?"

"The arrow, yeah."

"What about it?"

Dyson shook his head, struggling to find the words. "That formation—it's not the kind of thing that happens naturally, especially for a high school team."

"What are you saying?" Avery asked. Dyson knew this was all new territory for him.

"Something like that takes practice, lots and lots of practice. And practice means time, the kind most high school teams don't have. They're usually just worried about throwing and catching the ball— especially if they only won three games last season. Their coach should be drilling basics, not something like that."

"Well, then how did they manage it?"

"I don't know." Dyson shrugged. "But the way they moved, the way they gelled together, it's like they were controlled by one mind. One brain was guiding them."

Avery shook his head, uncertain what to make of Dyson's comment. "What could cause that?"

"I don't know," Dyson confessed, "but it sure as hell wasn't steroids."

Avery slipped his phone back in his pocket and announced, "We gotta get our hands on one of those cups."

"How'd I know you were gonna say that?" Dyson replied. "Wait here." He edged silently toward the corner of the stairwell. Once he was sure the coast was clear, he signaled for Avery to follow and led the way into the Wolverine's locker room.

The place was a mess. Soiled towels were strewn across the floor. Lockers lined the walls with doors propped open and shirts and jeans dangling from their corners. Sneakers lay cast off beneath benches. Duffel bags were scattered here and there. Water bottles, juice bottles, power drink bottles—dozens of them sat on any surface available. The sting of body odor and medicated ointments filled his nostrils.

Dyson thought of countless Friday nights spent in locker rooms much like this one, readying for games out on fields like the one waiting just outside. The nostalgia hit him hard: the simple rules of the game; opponents whose only goal was to score more points than him; the rush when a play worked the way it was planned. How had he gotten so far away from that point in his life? How had he gotten to the place where every choice he made could have deadly consequences? Where the opponents weren't out to best you; they were out to kill you?

"You miss it, don't you," Avery said.

Dyson attempted a smile but it was halfhearted at best. "It shows?"

"Only a lot," Avery said tenderly. "You know, you could still play. There are leagues out there you could join."

Dyson shook his head. How was he supposed to put it into words so Avery could understand? It wasn't the game or the loss of the game that was eating away at him. It was what his life had become. That was the tough part. It was knowing that he would spend the rest of his life fighting the ghouls and the fey. That he would probably die fighting them. Knowing that, how was he supposed to relive his past or settle for some cheap imitation of it?

With his thumb Avery pushed his wire rim glasses up the length of his nose and said, "You know what I thought when we first started dating?"

"What?"

"So here's this guy, a big-jock-of-a-guy (totally hot)," Avery winked and Dyson couldn't help but smile, "who was a football player back in high school but now he has no interest in the game. Doesn't watch it. Doesn't go to games. Doesn't bore me to tears with stories about his big wins. And even though I couldn't figure out why, for once in my life I didn't ask, because all I could think was: Lucky me! No Sunday afternoons in front of the TV trying to look interested. No thirty seconds of play and then ten minutes of sitting there not knowing what was going on before another thirty seconds of play. None of it. And instead of jinxing it, I decided to keep my mouth shut. But now, being here with you like this, I see why you never talk about it, why you never want to watch a game. It hurts too much."

A Wolverine's helmet sat on a bench near Dyson. He traced a finger along the red stripe running down its center. "It's like a different life, the person I was back then. I felt like I had everything figured out. I knew exactly what was going on. What I would become. It was so simple. But now..."

"Now you're a hero." Avery crossed the room and took his boyfriend's hands in his own. "Now you carry a sword and race into alleys and abandoned buildings to save people without a thought for your own safety. Now you tilt at whatever monster rears its ugly head on a given night." He ran his fingers through the short mat of Dyson's brown hair. "You're Sir Gawain."

Dyson's beady eyes grew to slits.

Avery rolled his own eyes. "Yeah, get over it. It's the name your mother gave you. Who knew how fortuitous her love of Camelot would be? I mean, you have slain dragons before."

"Just the one," Dyson corrected, his eyes shifting to the littered floor of the locker room.

"Just *one* dragon is one more than anyone else has ever seen in their lifetime." The reporter lifted Dyson's face and kissed him. "Anyone can throw a ball," he said when their lips parted. "This, Gawain Dyson, is what you were made to do."

"Yeah, but—"

Before Dyson could finish the thought, voices echoed down the hallway toward the locker room. "Come on, Billy! I don't want to miss the second half."

Dyson and Avery looked at one another, alarmed. Getting caught in the boys' locker room was not exactly part of their plan.

"We need to get rid of their cups," a second voice replied. "Plus, it's a perfect time to clean up and take it back to the car."

Dyson scanned the locker room. The coach's office was on the far wall, its door standing wide open. Dyson and Avery raced inside. Beside the door was a large window that looked out on the locker room. The two men crouched down below it, each stealing furtive glances through its open blind.

"Do we really have to go down there?" the first voice asked. "Can't we just wait till after the game? It'll be crazy and we can slip it out then." The voices were getting closer. It was nerve-racking, wanting to see, yet not wanting to be seen.

"And what if someone catches us? No, better to do it now," the second voice explained as a figure walked into the locker room. It was Cody's dad Billy. A moment later, his partner entered the room on his heels. Avery looked at Dyson in disbelief.

"That thing gives me the willies," Stu said.

"I know it's not pleasant, babe," replied Billy. He pulled the clear plastic liner from a trash bin by the door and knotted its end. It was filled with the plastic cups the team had drunk from before heading back out onto the field. "But if we want the team to make it all the way to state," he continued, "then we've got to make sure that nothing happens to that thing down there, okay?"

Stu sighed heavily then acquiesced. "Okay."

Dyson wasn't liking the sound of this, not one bit. When he chanced a look, he saw the two men heading deeper into the locker room past a sign reading *Showers*. By the time he shuffled to the office's open doorway and snuck a peak around it, Billy and Stu were vanishing behind a door at the end of the corridor past the showers.

"They're gone," he told Avery as he rose from the floor. The reporter joined him, but before he could say a word, Dyson dove in. "Look, I know we came here for your story, but trust me: This has got nothing to do with steroids. There's something else going on here. And I think I should check it out on my own first, so will you please—for once—stay here till I see what's going on, okay?"

Avery studied Dyson a moment, his face expressionless. He leaned in and pecked his boyfriend on the lips and said, "You're cute."

He headed toward the door the two men had passed through. When he reached it, he turned back to Dyson and asked, "You coming?"

Dyson glared at his boyfriend, his beady eyes practically vanishing this time. Avery beckoned him forward, and begrudgingly, Dyson followed him through the door.

If what they'd seen of the school so far had been brightly lit corridors and boldly painted locker rooms, the hallway waiting on the other side of the door was the exact opposite. Insulated pipes ran inches above their heads and down the walls, forcing them to scrape past dingy cinder block that looked like it hadn't seen a fresh coat of paint since before Dyson was born. Caged lights hummed overhead among the pipes, casting light in random rings on the concrete floor every fifteen feet or so. A row of breaker boxes hung on the wall to their right covered in a layer of grime. Beneath the boxes the cables vanished through holes in the cinder block with crumpled old newsprint shoved in to fill the gaps around the cables.

"Well, this is pleasant," Avery observed.

"At least lemme go first," Dyson suggested.

Avery gestured toward the thick shadows that lay ahead. "Lead the way."

"So *now* he listens to me."

"I heard that."

"See what I mean?!"

The two men passed from shadow into light and back again as they traveled down the dimly lit corridor. They came to a brief flight of steps and took them down before continuing down the hallway.

"Where do you think they went to?" Avery asked. As they turned a corner, he had his answer.

Ahead, through an open door labeled *Boiler Room*, they heard Billy say impatiently, "Would you just grab it."

"It's dead," Stu whined. "I don't want to touch it."

Dyson and Avery looked at one another uneasily.

"Either put it in the bag or take the mop and start cleaning up the blood," Billy ordered. "I'm not doing both."

"That's not fair! You know blood makes me queasy."

"Yes, I do."

"Fine, then! Give me the bag."

Avery cast a worried look toward the door and back to Dyson.

"Right about now I'm really wishing you had your sword with you," he whispered.

"That makes two of us," Dyson agreed. He leaned through the doorway.

Billy and Stu stood to the right of a huge steel drum, mounted on its side in a large concrete basin. Pipes crept from the ancient boiler's surface up into the shadows of the ceiling above. On the floor near the two men's feet was a puddle of blood in the center of a red circle. Around the circle's edge were painted several strange symbols. Dyson wasn't sure what the symbols signified, but he knew enough to recognize a magical incantation when he saw one.

The two men were hard at work. Billy stood with a mop, making a first attempt at cleaning up the blood. Stu was lifting the carcass of a mongrel by its tail and lowering it into a black plastic bag. The liner filled with the cups the Wolverines had drunk from sat nearby. Dyson spotted something else too.

Near Billy's feet, just out of range of the blood, was a duffel bag. The zipper was open and a small statue, roughly a foot tall, stood in its center rising up between the zipper's open teeth. Whatever was going on here, Dyson guessed the statue must be at the heart of it.

"Would you hurry up," Billy urged. Stu was doing his best to place the dead dog's body in the bag without letting it touch him. A leg flopped out and he squealed. He attempted to grip it with just two fingers and return it to the bag.

"I'm trying!" he snapped.

Dyson turned to Avery, pointing to the opposite side of the boiler. "Once I'm out of sight, get their attention. I need to get a look at what's in that duffel bag." Avery nodded. Dyson waited until the two men were busy bickering, then crept to the far side of the boiler, out of view. Once he knew he'd made it undetected, he signaled Avery to get their attention. The door squealed harshly as Avery opened it fully and the two men jumped.

"Hey guys, whatcha doing?" the reporter asked.

"Avery!" Stu peeped. He dropped the dog's tail and the carcass plopped to the floor, half-in and half-out of the bag.

Standing in the doorway, the reporter got his first good look at the scene. Dyson watched a look of revulsion register on his boyfriend's face. "A dog? Seriously?! What is wrong with you people?"

"What are you doing here?" Billy asked. From Dyson's vantage creeping down the length of the boiler's steel drum, he couldn't see either of the men.

"I asked you first," Avery replied, the sound of disgust still evident in his voice.

"We-we-we were—" Stu stammered.

"Oh, can it, Stu." Billy snapped. His partner's lips clapped shut and he whimpered peevishly. "Avery, why don't you just go back outside with your boyfriend and enjoy the halftime show? I hear the Stallions added some male cheerleaders this year. You should enjoy that." As an afterthought the man asked, "Where is your boyfriend, by the way?"

Dyson froze. He'd made it to the far end of the boiler, opposite the doorway where Avery stood. The duffel bag with the statue was just a few feet away. If he leaned forward, he could see Billy's shoes beyond the bag.

"He went to the john," Avery answered nimbly. "I saw you guys come in the school and wondered where you were going."

"You always so curious?" Billy asked. Dyson heard a note of disdain in his voice.

"Yeah, it's my job. I'm a reporter."

"A reporter?!" Stu squeaked.

"Shut up, Stu," his partner snapped. "A reporter, huh?"

"Yeah," Avery replied. "The *Washington Post*."

"Oh my God," Stu gasped.

"I'm doing a story on teenage steroid use and heard the Wolverines might be a good place to start."

"The boys aren't using steroids," Billy said derisively.

Dyson stepped around the end of the boiler. Billy and Stu stood with their backs to him. Avery had their full attention.

"Sorry you wasted your time," Billy said with finality.

"Oh, I didn't waste my time." Avery smiled grimly. "Not at all. So what's going on here? Devil worship? You sacrificing animals to the gods of Sunday night football?" He lifted a single finger in the air. "Question: Wouldn't a pig be more appropriate than a dog? Or is that just too cliché?"

Devil worship? Avery was close. But now that he had a clear view of the item in the bag, Dyson put the pieces together. The statue wasn't an idol or an effigy. It was a pitcher—of sorts. A wooden decanter carved in the shape of a wolf resting on its haunches. A broad belly curved up between its legs toward a wide neck that ended at the wolf's open mouth. A tongue dangled from its lips, serving as the pitcher's spout. From the tongue, down the neck, to the belly, the wolf's body was stained red with what Dyson guessed must be the dog's still-drying blood. This was no devil worship. No, the Wolverines were doing something much more dangerous.

"You have no idea what's going on here," Billy said to Avery.

Dyson picked up the carving and said, "Well, I think you're the reason your son's team went from three-and-nine to seven-and-oh in a single season." Startled, Billy and Stu spun toward him. "I think you're doing some sort of dark magic with this totem here. I'm guessing some sort of blood rite that bound the entire team to the totem." He studied the men standing only a few feet away. "How am I doing so far?"

"How did you kn—"

"Shut up, Stu!" Billy ordered, glaring at his partner. He turned back to Dyson, a malevolent smile on his face.

Before the man could speak, though, Avery put the last of the pieces together. "So they got the kids to drink the blood of that dog?!" He looked as if he might vomit.

"I'm betting yes," Dyson said. "The team is bound to the totem somehow. Each of the boys probably had to give some of their own blood to bond with it. Then before the game and again at halftime they drank a bit of the dog's blood. Some of its strength, its agility passed into them."

"They weren't being controlled by one mind," Avery said, referring to their earlier conversation. "Their minds were unified by the blood in their systems."

"Who are you people?" Billy asked, anxiously eyeing the totem in Dyson's hands.

"I told you I'm just a reporter," Avery volunteered. "He's the one you really gotta worry about."

"This is pretty nifty," Dyson said, studying the totem more closely. The carver's attention to detail was staggering. The wide-eyed expression, ravenous for the blood it waited to gobble down and vomit back up again. The upturn of its lips, as if the wolf smiled expectantly, waiting to drink deep from whatever animal might be sacrificed to it. The tail curved up and away from the body before connecting where the tip touched the back of the neck, forming the perfect handle. The fur was carved with precision across its body, turning into arcane symbols at its base. A look at the floor told Dyson they'd used the same symbols for the incantation around their circle. "I've only seen a couple of totems before, but I gotta say…this one's probably the best." He tossed the wood carving from hand to hand like a basketball.

"Be careful with that!" Billy demanded.

"Yes!" Stu agreed, "It was very expensive."

Billy glowered at his partner.

"Well, it was," Stu rebutted then added for the benefit of their two guests, "We found it antiquing in Europe last summer."

"Eastern Europe, I'm guessing." Dyson studied the partners. Billy shot Stu a look before he could say anything further. "I'm impressed you figured out what it actually was. Or did someone over there show you how to use it?"

"So you figured us out," Billy said. He shrugged casually, but Dyson didn't miss the way his grip had tightened on the mop's handle. "So yeah, we found something that gave our team an edge."

"By killing harmless animals," Avery interjected.

"Strays that probably wouldn't make it through the winter anyway," Billy rationalized. "We're putting them out of their misery."

"And what happens when one of those strays is rabid?" Dyson asked. "You know, before it starts showing any symptoms. What happens when the team drinks rabid blood and goes out on the field and tears up their opponents? I mean actually, literally tears them up." The room went silent. "They injure the other team because of the blood they've ingested. Blood you and I'm guessing that new coach of theirs gave them."

"Oh my God," Stu said quietly. It was clear the two hadn't thought through that particular scenario.

Billy shook it off immediately though. "Don't be ridiculous. There's no way."

"Totems don't just give the strength and the physical characteristics of the sacrifice," Dyson said. "The best ones take a bit of the soul and pass it along too. You're messing with something dangerous here. There's always repercussions with magic, especially blood magic like this."

"Billy, what if he's right," Stu ventured. "What if Cody and the others—"

"He's not right," interrupted Billy. "He doesn't know what he's talking about."

"Are you willing to risk your son's well-being to find out?" Avery asked.

"My son is just fine," Billy snapped. "He's a *winner*."

"That's what this is all about?" Avery asked incredulously. "Your son having a winning season?"

"You really don't get it, do you?" Billy disdainfully replied. He turned to face Dyson. "You understand, though, don't you?"

And Dyson did. He understood exactly what Billy was trying to say.

"It's not about the win," the man went on. "It's about the game. It's about being on that field, about *living* on that field. Eating it. Breathing it. Sleeping it! The rush, the adrenaline. Tearing that field up like a titan, like a god. It's about being in the one place you know you were made to be and then not being there anymore, all because of some stupid twist of fate. It's about having it all ripped away from you and never getting it back again, being trapped and knowing you'll never escape. It's about living a second-rate life."

And there it was. Dyson's thoughts, his fears voiced by a complete stranger. Itinerant monster slayer was not what he'd dreamed of being when he grew up, but there it was. There was his life in a nutshell and to hell with his dreams. And when he looked ahead, all he saw were more dark nights, more dangers hiding in the shadows, more bandaged wounds and cracked ribs and a never-ending sea of blood and death. He'd never be able to veer off the course he was on. And if he dwelled on that fact for too long, the finality of it might just drive him over the edge.

Dyson's attention was drawn back to the two men as Stu said to his partner, "Your life is not second rate." There were tears in his eyes. With all the hope and compassion he could muster, he said, "I love you."

Billy smiled, but Dyson knew it wasn't enough. It would never be enough. Even so, the man answered, "I love you, too."

As much as he would've liked to let their moment last, to let them have their happily-as-best-they-could, the fact was these two whack jobs were still feeding animal blood to a bunch of teenage boys. If he was going to stop them before they did real damage, he needed to tuck away whatever bullshit this night had dredged up for him and get the totem as far away as possible.

Taking their moment as his opportunity, he tucked the wooden totem under his arm and sprinted toward the boiler room door. He shoved Billy into Stu as he passed by, and the pair slipped on the puddle of mop water and blood. They tumbled to the ground atop the dog's bagged carcass.

Squeals of disgust and shouts of anger followed him as he grabbed Avery's hand and raced back down the narrow corridor toward the boys' locker room. He took the small flight of steps in a single leap and went crashing through the door into the empty locker room.

"What do we do now?" Avery asked, glancing around frantically.

"We get the hell out of here," Dyson said, dragging his boyfriend out of the room and down the hallway.

They hadn't made it ten feet outside the locker room when they saw the first of the Wolverines step into the open doorway at the far end of the hall. Blinding lights from the field cast the figure in silhouette, his helmet still on his head. A second player joined the first, then another, and another until what looked like the entire team blocked their escape.

In the silence that followed, Dyson heard a growl come from one of the teammates. Soon a choir of voices joined in and the sound rumbled down the hallway toward them. They weren't dealing with boys anymore. The blood in their systems, the blood from the totem was calling to them. Its magic controlled them now.

"Wain, what do we do?" Avery whispered, terrified.

"Up the stairs, go up the stairs—*slowly*!" Dyson added as Avery turned to make a break for it. The reporter obeyed and backed away carefully. He found the first step and then the next and ascended the stairs. Dyson followed behind.

When the first howl ripped down the hallway toward them, they'd made it to the landing between the basement and the ground level. It was followed immediately by thirty other howls as the rest of the Wolverines took up the call.

"Run! Run now!" Dyson shouted, barely audible above the ricochet of baying voices chasing after them.

Avery and Dyson scaled the steps to the ground floor. The building's main entrance was ahead. They slammed into the doors, too late to realize they were chained and padlocked. They raced down the hall to another exit past another staircase, only to find those doors locked as well.

A clamor of yips and growls followed after them as the crazed teenagers reached the school's main floor. The Wolverines spotted the two men at the far end of the hall and broke into a run. Dyson grabbed Avery and took the nearby staircase to the school's second story. They came to a stop in a darkened hallway lined with lockers and closed classroom doors. Ahead, the hall dead-ended at a set of large windows. Lights shining through the glass revealed the windows looked out on the football field below. An idea formed in Dyson's mind.

"What do we do now?!" Avery pleaded as the sound of cleats echoed down the hallway from the level beneath them. Howls and barks merged with the clatter of feet as the team chased after them. "We're gonna be trapped up here!"

"No, we're not," Dyson said. "Just stand aside."

"What?"

"Stand aside."

"Wain, they're out of their minds. They'll tear us apart!" Avery said desperately. The footsteps were getting closer. The first of the team had reached the second stairwell and was climbing the steps to the second story.

"They want this." Dyson nodded to the carving in his hands. "They'll come after me, not you. You'll be fine. Just stand in the doorway over there."

"I can't let you—"

Dyson pecked him on the lips. "You're cute. Now trust me."

"What are you gonna do?" Avery asked, stepping back into the shadowy doorway.

Dyson looked at the windows down the far end of the hallway. "I'm gonna play some football."

"What?"

There was no time for an explanation. The players reached the second floor. They spilled out of the stairwell, flooding the hallway in front of Dyson, snarling and snapping.

"Hey, fellas," Dyson said. He raised the totem to eye level and waggled it in the air. "Looking for this?" he asked.

The hallway erupted in a thunder of howls and cries that threatened to deafen him. Amidst the din, a figure scrambled up the steps, its clothes soaked in water and stained in blood. A disheveled Billy pointed at Dyson and shouted, "Get him!"

The Wolverines broke into a run. The warrior turned and raced for the windows at the far end of the hall. It was a crazy plan, but if he played it right, Avery would be safe and the team would be exposed—if he didn't break his fool neck trying, that is.

As he connected with the glass, Dyson ducked his head and led with his shoulder. The window shattered on contact and he flew forward into open air. Curling into a ball, he leaned into the fall. His shoulder collided with the ground and he rolled, the totem safely gripped against his chest. He leapt up and took off across the lawn toward the football field, the carving clutched tightly under his arm. He glanced back to see the first of the Wolverines reach the shattered window and follow him down. Dyson didn't chance another look to see how many made a safe landing. Instead, he kept his eyes on the approaching end of the field. Passing under the field goal's yellow bars, he raced onto the turf surrounded by the opposing team's bewildered players. From the expressions on their faces, Dyson guessed the Wolverines had left the field mid-play when the totem's magic had summoned them.

He passed the twenty yard line and an unexpected cheer went up from the stands. He shot a look in their direction but found the fans' attention wasn't focused on him. As the Wolverines returned, leaping through the shattered window on the second floor, their fellow students went wild: hooting and cheering, stomping their feet on the metal bleachers. Cheerleaders shook pompoms and broke out in high kicks as the first of the players hit the field. The Wolverines were oblivious to it all, though, their focus solely on Dyson and the totem gripped under his arm.

Out of the corner of his eye, Dyson noticed the first of the Wolverines closing in. He veered away, across the field, passing a dumbfounded player from the opposing team. On the side of his helmet a stallion reared up on its hind legs. "Are you gonna block him or what?" Dyson shouted at the teenager.

His words broke the spell and the player followed after the warrior and the Wolverine chasing him. Dyson sensed a hand reach for him, ready to grip his shoulder. But the hand vanished just as it came in contact. The Wolverine was taken down by the opposing player. Not sure what to make of the chaos surrounding them, his fellow Stallions did the only thing they knew to do. They fanned out to block the Wolverines as they returned en masse. Even those on the sidelines merged on the field.

Dyson raced on toward the fifty yard line as a Wolverine dove for his legs, attempting to take them out from beneath him. The warrior leapt over the player and raced on.

Cheers rose in volume as sixty football players chased after Dyson. The stomping in the stands matched the blood pulsing in his ears, his heart quickening as he ran on, past the forty yard line toward the thirty. A volcano of adrenaline erupted in his veins. His legs pumped beneath him in a symphony of strength and agility. His feet passed across the field in perfect rhythm, legs stretching, lungs filling to capacity as he crossed the thirty yard line and sprinted toward the twenty. Who cared about the totem? Who cared about the end zone ahead? The two were fused perfectly—his present and his past. And damn, if that didn't make the moment worth living.

A Wolverine appeared on his left, ready to tackle him. One of the Stallions players brought the Wolverine to ground. Dyson skirted the pair and ran on toward the end zone. He passed the twenty yard line and connected with the ten. The fans were on their feet. Their frenzied roars spurred him on. He crossed the goal line into the end zone. He laughed ecstatically and turned back to the field as a wave of cheers reached him. But he could only enjoy it for a moment before another wave crashed over him. The Wolverines and Stallions reached him and he drowned in a tsunami of shoulder pads and jerseys.

As the first and then the second and then the third player landed on top of him, the hollow wooden carving in his arms gave way and cracked under the weight. Dyson felt a force ripple out from the broken totem, through the clash of players covering him, and across the field to the Wolverines who had yet to reach him. He watched the eyes of the player atop him grow unfocused for a moment before clearing and the teenager returned to his senses.

"What's going on?" the player asked, unsure how he'd ended up at the bottom of a heap.

Dyson looked up at the teenager. He grinned and said, "Dude, I just totally kicked *all* your asses."

Bemused, the player studied him a moment more as the weight of teenage boys atop them lessened, and the pile began to *unpile* itself.

"Where is it?" Dyson heard Billy shout somewhere above him. "Where is it?!" The man came into view as he yanked players off the heap. "Where the hell is it?!"

When the last of the players was lifted off him, Dyson looked down at the totem in his arms, or what was left of it. The wooden pitcher lay shattered into several pieces, the dog's blood smeared across his jacket and shirt.

"No," Billy said in disbelief, sinking to his knees. "No, no, no." He picked up two of the pieces and tried to fit them together. "It's ruined. Everything's ruined," he muttered.

"Win or lose, your boy and his friends are gonna play fair from now on," Dyson said. "Seems to me somewhere along the way you forgot that's what it's about: playing the game fair and square and taking whatever knocks life gives you in return."

Enraged, the man ripped his eyes from the broken pieces. "You son of a bitch!" he hollered, reaching for Dyson's throat.

It took Stu, a ref, and couple of other parents to pull Billy away. As Dyson watched the man struggle against the hands restraining him, he said to no one in particular, "It might do for both of us to remember that's what it's about."

"You made quite a mess here," Avery said, standing next to him.

Dyson raised his head from the ground and looked at the pandemonium surrounding him. Parents and friends converged on the field checking on the players. Freed from the totem, several of the Wolverines lay moaning as the first effects of the broken limbs they'd received when they leapt from the second floor began to register. At the far end, a group of what Dyson guessed must be school administrators looked up at the broken windows above their heads and back to the players out on the field.

"I guess it is a tad messy," Dyson said, pleased. He folded his hands behind his head.

"Did you have fun?"

Dyson grinned and a single dimple appeared in his left cheek.

"You know," Avery went on, "I have to admit, you were really something out there. I mean, I kinda get why you like it so much."

Dyson's eyes widened. "Don't tell me you're a fan now."

Avery winked. "Let's just say watching my boyfriend get tackled by a dozen teenage boys...I've got a few new fantasies in mind."

Dyson reached out a hand. Avery took it to help him to his feet. Instead, the warrior pulled his boyfriend down on top of him and kissed him.

"What's this?" Avery asked when their lips parted. "A public display of affection? My stars! What will the neighbors think?"

"Let 'em watch," Dyson answered. "They might learn a thing or two."

As the two men leaned in for another kiss, the aftermath of Dyson's final play continued to swirl around them.

REMATCH
JONATHAN ASCHE

I was riding home on my bike when I saw Keith Ledbetter shooting baskets in his driveway. I intended to keep riding, but Keith flagged me down.

"You wanna play?" he asked, dribbling the basketball as he spoke.

The invitation came out of nowhere. We'd been ignoring each other for two years, since high school. I searched my mind for an excuse, the steady cadence of the bouncing ball seemingly growing louder the longer I remained silent. I finally said: "Um, I don't know..."

"C'mon," Keith insisted, "we're not playing in the Final Four or anything. Just shooting some hoops, is all."

"And we all know how good I am at *that*."

Keith had me at a disadvantage. In high school he was good enough to win a scholarship to play college ball—for one of the lower-ranked teams, some school in Tennessee, but it was a scholarship nonetheless. I also played basketball in high school, getting on the team by virtue of being six foot four. (Dad would've preferred I went out for football, but conceded I wasn't built for it.) I developed skill but no love for the game, and by my senior year my indifference became hatred.

Keith and I had been friends, once. Maybe we could be friends again. I leaned my bike against the side of the garage and joined Keith at the center of his driveway.

We had changed since graduating from high school, when we were gangly boys with long hair. Now sinewy muscles thickened our lanky bodies. A tribal tattoo circled one of Keith's bulbous biceps; a thin silver ring pierced my left eyebrow. Keith's dark hair was now cropped close to his scalp and a scruffy beard shaded his face; my curly brown hair was even more unruly, but I was clean-shaven.

Keith passed the ball to me. "You first," he said, smiling. I remembered another time he smiled at me.

High school, senior year: *We had been playing a more serious one-on-one game in my backyard one early fall weekend when one of Keith's attempts to take the ball led to a giggly wrestling match on the lawn. He was on top of me in an instant, holding my wrists to the ground and straddling my hips, his butt resting on my crotch. His weight on me—on my cock—triggered a reaction so spontaneous I didn't realize it until it was too late. I remembered holding my breath, the growing panic as I saw the shock cross Keith's face, and then the relief when his lips curled into a smile.*

His smile became mischievous. "Whatta you want to do now?" he teased, bearing down on my hard-on. I wanted to suck his cock, maybe even let him fuck me, but I couldn't say the words aloud. To say them wouldn't be an answer; it would be an admission.

I looked away, dribbling the ball down the driveway, trying to fight off the other memories that bounced up with it, but I lost the fight and was suddenly transported back to the high school gym in the final seconds of the game against the Baxter Indians, the Indians ahead by one point, 48–47. At the time protesters were calling for the Baxter High School to change its team name and mascot, but the Indians weren't worried about political correctness, just getting the ball away from Tony Winslow. My teammates moved in close to Tony, ready to take the ball—and take the Aronville Lions to the state championship. But I was closer to the basket. Tony met my eyes and in that microsecond I knew the ball was coming my way. *Don't fuck this up, Drake!*

I shook the memory from my head, took a deep breath and jumped, sending the ball into the air. It hit the backboard above the garage door, ricocheted off the rim and dropped to the ground as if repelled by the basket.

"Shit!"

In my mind I heard the Coach Totter shouting, my teammates cussing and rubbing their hands over their anguished faces, like their families had been slaughtered before their very eyes. There were less than three hundred people in the stands, but their jeers could've filled a stadium.

Keith's voice brought me back to the present. "You're just rusty," he said, taking the ball, dribbling it closer to the basket, and making an effortless slam-dunk.

Fucker, I thought, even though I appreciated the flash of bare belly exposed when Keith's shirt rose with his arms as he dunked the ball.

He missed the second time, surrendering the ball to me. This time the ball went in, though first it had to taunt me, hesitating on the rim before dropping through the basket. My anxiety eased—until my follow-up shot bounced off the backboard and into the Ledbetters' front yard. Keith said something as he jogged to retrieve the ball, but I didn't catch it, too busy cursing my incompetence and admiring how Keith's shiny black shorts accentuated the curves of his ass.

Keith became more competitive—and more physical. He tried to take the ball away from me, tried to block my shots. "I thought we were just shooting hoops," I said, attempting—and failing—to keep the ball away from his darting hands.

"What, you think we were playing HORSE?" He laughed, making another one of his graceful dunks.

Then his T-shirt came off. It had been an unusually cool June, but it was still warm, and we had both worked up a sweat. Keith passed the ball to me and then peeled off his shirt, using it to wipe his brow. His torso was more defined than I remembered, his muscles hard beneath lightly tanned skin. Ridges of muscle curved around either side of his abs and around his pelvis, the lines meeting in a V-shape under his shorts. Damp hair clustered between his pecs and defined the line between his abs, making a dark trail from his belly button down to the same spot that V came to a point.

I returned to that moment in high school, when Keith held me to the ground, rolling his hips, the thin fabric of my shorts doing little to dull the sensation of his ass grinding against my cock…

I closed my eyes and pushed my pelvis up between his legs. I wanted to suggest we finish things inside, wanted to show him what I wanted to do, but what he was doing felt too good to interrupt. The spell could be broken with one word, so I lay there silent as he undulated on top of me, rubbing my cock through my shorts. The world around us dropped away as the pleasure rose, until all I heard was my blood rushing through my veins. When I came he slapped a hand over my mouth.

I quickly looked away, forcing myself into the present. Soon I was moving all around the driveway, furiously trying to avoid Keith's attempts to steal the ball. He hovered over me, his sweat dripping onto my back, the heat of his body ten times hotter than the sun, his arm reaching around me, our bodies grinding together roughly as he moved to take the ball. I felt his body press against my ass, felt his dick…

We looked at each other, amazed that things had gone as far as they had. I was still trembling when Keith climbed off me. My shorts had a dark wet spot where my load soaked through, while the front of his protruded lewdly. I took a deep breath, willing myself to offer to return the favor, eager to just to see his cock hard, but before I could speak he said he needed to go inside to use the bathroom, practically running to the back door.

I jumped, taking the ball with me. I grunted loudly as I hurled the ball at the basket as if it were a live grenade. We were at the end of the driveway, almost to the street—from this distance the best I could hope for was the ball might come within three feet of the basket. Instead it sailed through the torn net with a soft swoosh.

"Ho-ly shit!" Keith shouted.

"Couldn't do that again if I tried," I said, smiling broadly.

"Maybe you're a better player than you think."

"Naw. I just got lucky, that's all."

"Maybe," Keith said, smiling like he was in on a private joke. In that smile flashed another moment from our past, one that never stayed buried: my body being thrown against the gym lockers.

"Get away from me, faggot!"

❖

Keith had avoided me for weeks after our "wrestling match," as if our simply walking down the hall together would tip people off about what happened between us. Then he called one Saturday, like nothing had changed.

"How's it goin'?" he asked when I picked up the phone. *"You doin' anything tonight? My sister's sleepin' over at a friend's and my parents are goin' to a party. Got the house to myself."*

We had the house to ourselves now, too, though we locked ourselves in Keith's room anyway. Keith's invitation to join him for a "post game smoke" brought up familiar feelings: exhilaration and terror, the feelings swirling together and making me nauseous. The pot helped.

"Don't they drug test if you're on the team?" I asked from my spot on the floor, leaning forward to hand the pipe back to Keith, slumped on his bed.

He took the pipe from me. "Don't matter, I'm on academic probation. Spent most of last season on the bench, thanks to an asshole English professor."

Keith leaned back against the pillows. He was still shirtless, his T-shirt wadded up beside him on the bed. I was bare-chested, too, reluctantly taking my shirt off as our one-on-one game progressed. (I thought I was still too skinny, but Keith asked if I'd been working out.) Keith brought one of his legs up on the mattress, a gap opening between the leg of his shorts and his muscled leg. My eyes followed long, hairy thigh into the dark cave of his shorts, getting a glimpse of red boxers but no more.

"You play any sports at State?" he asked, putting the lighter to the pipe.

"No, not really." I shrugged. "Haven't played since high school, and I only went out for basketball then 'cause Dad thought I had to be on a team, to prove I'm a man or some bullshit."

"If only he…"

"If only he *what*?"

"Nothin', forget it." Then, his lips twisting into a sly smile, he said: "Just thinking of other things we did in high school."

You and me both, I thought.

His lips curled into a sly smile; his blue eyes glimmered. "Are you still…*into guys*?"

"Why, are *you*?" I asked, turning bitchy when a simple yes would've covered it.

Keith shook his head, grinning like it was a preposterous suggestion. "*Shee*-it, man. I…" He looked away, attempted another hit off the pipe before declaring the bowl cashed. "I've messed around with a couple guys at school," he added, almost offhandedly, dropping the pipe it into his stash box on the nightstand.

I likewise played it cool, nodding like it was no big thing even though my pulse quickened hearing his confession. "Me, too," I said. "Actually had a boyfriend for a while."

Keith's eyebrows jumped, and I immediately wished I kept my mouth shut. "Dude, that's…it was nothing like that with me. Just let this guy I met at the gym blow me."

"Sounds familiar," I said over the drumming of my heart.

His hand sliding into his crotch took my eyes away from his mischievous smile.

My mind jumped back to that Saturday two years ago, when Keith invited me up to his room to check out some porn websites. He started with the straight sites, then called up a gay site under the pretense of making fun of the content. ("Dude, check this shit out.") He asked if I'd ever gotten a blow job, then managed to work the conversation around to proposing we suck each other's cocks, with the assurance no one would ever know. I pretended to resist the idea for about a minute, acting put out when I "lost" the coin toss to determine who went first. It was an act I couldn't sustain once Keith pulled out his cock, already stiffening in anticipation of my mouth. I took a deep breath and wrapped my mouth around Keith's hard-on, trying to mimic what I'd seen porn stars do. It was a clumsy blow job, but that didn't stop Keith from coming in just five minutes.

I dropped my eyes to my feet. Several seconds went by before I spoke. "Guess you're wondering if I still wanna play?"

His hand was still between his legs, squeezing the bulge there and telling me all I needed to know.

"Figured you'd like this better than basketball," Keith said.

At that moment it was that Saturday night, two years ago, and I felt the same excitement and anxiety. I knew why I needed to resist—

I bounced off the lockers and stumbled over the narrow wooden bench. "Fuckin' queer!"

—but my cock was overruling my better judgment, swelling at the thought of messing around with Keith Ledbetter again.

He grinned and moved to the edge of the bed. "You want to?"

Returning his smile, I walked toward him on my knees, easily closing the distance between us. Keith had trouble looking at me as my fingers crawled up his thighs and under his shorts. We both kind of laughed, embarrassed and excited.

Keith leaned back on his elbows and raised his butt off the bed as I pulled off his shorts and underwear. The sight of his cock throbbing against his belly turned my semi into a full-on boner in seconds. Keith's balls hung heavily between his thighs, one nut lower than the other in a pink, hairless sac. I reached for his dick, closing my hand around the thick shaft. It was hot in my hands. He let out a breathless chuckle, watching my hand pulling his cock, not meeting my eyes. A bead of pre-cum bubbled from the piss slit, encouraging me.

My tongue touched down at the base of his dick and slowly traveled to the tip. Keith trembled, gasping as I pushed the tip of my tongue into his oozing slit. His reaction was almost as satisfying as tasting his juices. He moaned softly when I took his cock into my mouth, rising in volume as his dick disappeared down my gullet. "Aw, *dude*."

I swallowed him whole, until my nose was in his bushy pubes, inhaling the salty smell of his sweat. I held his cock in my throat, just long enough to make him squirm, then released it. His hard-on popped loudly out of my mouth, strings of my spit swinging off the glistening head. "Fuck," Keith whispered throatily. Flashing him a conspiratorial smile, I once again took his cock into my mouth, my tongue pressing against its fleshy head and tracing the veins standing up along the shaft. It was a far more accomplished blow job than I gave him that night two years ago—not that he complained then, either.

"Damn, you swallowed *my load?" Keith shook his head, incredulous. I didn't tell him that I thought I was supposed to, or that even though I didn't like the taste, it turned me on. I just smiled sheepishly, wiping my mouth with the back of my hand. "That was awesome." Keith chuckled, shaking the last drops of splooge from his still-hard cock, not caring that it was landing on his bedroom carpet.*

He now thrust into my mouth, groaning as I swallowed his rod. He put his hands on top of my head, stroking my hair. "Aw, man," he sighed dreamily, barely heard over my loud, enthusiastic slurping. I wrenched my mouth away from his cock and moved lower.

"You didn't strike me as the type to shave his balls," I said.

Keith started to ask what type was that but he was moaning before he could finish the question. I licked and nibbled his ball-sac, which had a stronger, sweet-sour smell. I sucked one of Keith's fat nuts into my mouth and tugged, making Keith shudder.

I returned to Keith's cock, sucking it until he was practically writhing on the bed. Then I stood up to take off my shorts. Keith allowed himself a self-conscious smile before averting his gaze, like he didn't want to appear too interested in seeing my cock. I caught him peeking, though, and wondered if he liked what he saw. My dick was slightly longer than his, with a bullet-shaped head, but I thought Keith's cock, thicker and capped with a full helmet, was better looking.

I joined Keith on the bed, startling him as I straddled his hips, just like he did mine when we "wrestled" years ago. His cock pressed neatly into my splayed ass cheeks. A hot pleasure burned up through my asshole and buzzed through my prick. It felt even better when I rocked my hips, rubbing my ass-lips against his stiff dong.

"Kinda' like the first time," I said, gently stroking my cock as I pressed my ass down on his. "Only better."

I leaned in, then, nuzzling his fuzzy face. Our eyes met, and I moved in for a kiss. "No," Keith whispered, turning his cheek to me. "Don't."

"C'mon," I coaxed, kissing his cheek. He faced me again and I seized his lips. His body went rigid, but then slowly relaxed. I kissed him again, swiping my tongue along his lower lip. He turned away, chuckling nervously.

"Man, I don't know 'bout this."

I kissed the side of his neck and nibbled his ear, all while grinding my body against his. His cock throbbed hotly beneath me.

He turned, and again I seized his mouth with mine. This time Keith's lips parted, accepting my tongue inside. He even kissed me back. It was an awkward kiss, but my cock didn't care, pumping out a syrupy stream of pre-cum onto Keith's abs. Keith further surprised me when he brought his hands down on my ass, roughly massaging my firm butt cheeks. I writhed on top of him, kissing him more urgently, my butt rising and falling as I rubbed against his hard-on. I was breathing hard as my mind filled with a blur of fantasies and possibilities.

"Wait, ease up," Keith murmured, nudging me off him. When I rolled onto the bed beside him, Keith sat up and reached for my cock. "I want to try…"

He finished his sentence with action rather than words, leaning down to suck my dick. I gasped, as much from the shock of Keith voluntarily going down on me as from the sensation of his hot mouth on my cock. The last time I was up in his bedroom, Keith had only reluctantly attempted to blow me, and then only because I reminded him he'd promised. I was so horny then my cock actually hurt, as if it had swollen beyond its limits. I doubted I'd last three minutes, and when Keith put his mouth on my cock I was sure I'd come in two. But Keith barely put his lips to my dick before saying he couldn't do it. Instead I went to the bathroom and angrily jerked off.

He had since gotten over his aversion to giving head. It wasn't a skillful blow job, but he wasn't a first timer, either. His "messing around" in college obviously included more than just letting guys suck him off. Regardless, it felt good. Damn good. I put my hand on top of his head and thrust into his mouth. He gagged but recovered quickly. A warm, tingly pleasure flowed through me, growing more intense as Keith worked on my cock. I imagined shooting into Keith's mouth, and just picturing it—Keith's mouth open wide with my spunk splashing down on his tongue—made me shiver.

Keith had another idea. "Guess you been fucked up the ass before?" he asked, looking up from my crotch, hand still curled around my cock.

I nodded.

"You want—can I—?"

"Yes."

For lube, Keith pulled out a bottle of suntan lotion from his bedside table. "Believe it or not, this works pretty good," he assured me.

I watched as he greased up his cock, admiring the size and shape of it but wondering if I'd been hasty in agreeing to let Keith fuck me.

Keith put a greasy hand on my knee. His other hand gripped his glistening boner. "So, how you want it? From behind or…?"

"Hand me the lotion," I said. "You're not the only one who needs it."

"Oh, yeah," he chuckled, tossing me the suntan lotion. "Guess not."

It was his turn to watch, in slack-jawed fascination, as I spread my thighs and rubbed lotion over my asshole. An embarrassed smile tugged at his lips when I slipped two fingers into my chute.

"Now stick your fingers up there," I said.

Keith shook his head. "No, man, I can't do that."

"C'mon. Think of it like fingering a pussy, only tighter."

He grudgingly complied, putting a hand between my legs and

pressing the tip of his index finger against my puckered ass-lips. "That's it," I gasped when that finger pushed into my hole. "Now do it with two fingers."

This time Keith didn't protest. He stretched my asshole with his index and middle fingers. A look of amazement crossed his face as he watched his fingers slide in and out of my hole, as if he couldn't believe he was doing it. I couldn't either. I closed my eyes and moaned softly, my body and cock trembling as Keith's fingers plunged into me.

I told him I wanted to sit on his cock. He lay on his back and I swung a leg over his torso, letting out a pleasing grunt as I sandwiched his cock between my ass cheeks. His eyes were half-closed, his mouth open as I rocked on his boner. Sweat beaded across his forehead. I leaned him down until our bodies were pressed together. I kissed him, and he did not resist.

I lifted my butt off Keith and reached for his cock, pulling it back until the head was at my ass-lips. I sat up, slowly, feeling the tension of his cockhead pushing against my sphincter as I eased my ass down on it. I eased down little more, the tension getting tighter, like a frayed rope about to snap, as Keith's cock nudged my ass-ring open and then...

"Oh, fuck, *yeah*!"

Keith's exclamation rang through the room like a gunshot, but I barely heard it, too busy grunting and groaning through gnashed teeth from the shock of being impaled on his cock. I'd bottomed before, but it had been a while. My hard-on wilted, becoming a semi in seconds flat. Keith asked if I was okay.

"Just need a moment," I assured him, squeezing my ass against his stiff cock.

A moment was all it took for searing pain to settle into a slow burning pleasure. I could feel his cock throbbing against the walls of my ass, his shaft pulsing against the vise grip of my sphincter. I rolled my hips, and Keith let out a sleepy groan as his dick moved inside me. My cock recovered, cautiously raising its sticky head.

I rocked atop Keith, moving in a slow grind, massaging his cock with my ass muscles. He put his hands on my waist—his touch made me shiver—and thrust into me. The room was soon filled with the wet slapping sound of sweaty skin hitting sweaty skin, his thighs hitting my ass as he rammed me. My hard-on was back, bouncing and slinging drops of pre-cum each time Keith sank his dick into my chute.

Keith's face was set in a determined expression: lips pulled back, teeth clenched, eyes focused but unseeing. It was the same expression he had during a game, when he was approaching the basket, about to shoot.

But he didn't shoot now. Instead, he called a time-out. "I wanna fuck you from behind," he slurred.

I obediently climbed off him. Keith got off the bed, and then got back on when my face was in his pillows and my ass was in the air. There was no easing into my chute this time: Keith entered me with one hard shove, making me groan into the pillows as he buried his cock to the hilt. His dick slid into my ass more easily this time, though it was still a tight fit.

It was a hard, ass-pounding fuck. Keith's heavy breathing and my deep groans nearly drowned out the slap-slap-slap of his balls against my ass. He leaned over me, trapping a humid heat between my back and his chest, grunting like a wild animal each time he sank his cock into my chute. I reached between my legs and grabbed my drooling dick, my body quivering upon first stroke. Soon both of us were sounding like wild animals—like enraged bears locked in battle, grunting, growling, and snarling through gnashed teeth.

Keith hooked an arm around my neck and I could feel his hot breath in my ear as he panted, "Oh yeah, oh yeah, oh fuck yeah." The pleasure increased as we fell into rhythm, Keith thrusting, me jerking, our pace quickening the closer we got. Suddenly Keith's arm tightened against my throat and he was gasping frantically in my ear: "I'm coming, I'm coming, I'm—"

We both came. A moan seemed trapped in Keith's lungs as he fired his load into my quaking chute. I announced my orgasm with a ragged gasp, sounding as if I'd just been punched in the gut. I shot my load onto the sheets, my body shaking with each forceful spurt.

We collapsed on the bed, me landing on my own gooey puddle, Keith falling on top of me, his dick still buried in my ass. We were breathing like we'd just played a game with six overtimes, and sweating like it, too. Keith lazily stroked my arm and I closed my eyes, content to go to sleep this way, dreaming that Keith and I were not only friends again, but—finally—boyfriends.

But instead of dreams I got memories, my mind returning to high school during my senior year. After the team lost the game to Baxter words like "fag," "queerbait," and "homo" began to echo down the halls when I walked to class. Keith once again kept his distance, but I wasn't going to let him get away that easily. In the locker room after practice I approached him, asking if he wanted to come over to my house that weekend. He ignored me, so I asked again.

"Get away from me, faggot!"

He pushed me against the lockers. The knob of a combination lock jabbed me in the spine. I stumbled forward, tripping over the bench between the rows of lockers.

"Fuckin' queer*!" Keith shouted before punching the wind out of* me.

I opened my eyes. "I better get home."

Keith and I didn't speak as I gathered up my clothes. I went to the bathroom across the hall to wash up and get dressed. When I returned to Keith's room he was in his shorts and pulling the sheets off his bed.

"Guess I'm out of here, then," I said.

"'Kay," Keith said, not looking at me as he inspected the bare mattress. "Shit, it soaked through."

"So, maybe we can get together again? I can give you my cell number."

He waved me away. "'S'all right, I know where you live."

I was dismissed.

Later, I thought of the many things I could've said. I could've told him that I knew he was the one responsible for making me a social pariah my senior year, telling everyone that I was queer and that was the reason he stopped hanging around me (knowing that I wouldn't be doing myself any favors if I told of the times we messed around). I could've told him that he was queer, that we were on the same team, whether he wanted to admit it or not. I could've punched his handsome, bearded face. I could've kissed him.

But I said, "See ya," knowing I never wanted to see him again.

THE BULL RIDER
JAY DICKINGSON

"And after we had been driven forth before the wind for the space of many days, behold, my brethren and the sons of Ishmael and also their wives began to make themselves merry, insomuch that they began to dance, and to sing, and to speak with much rudeness, yea, even that they did forget by what power they had been brought thither; yea, they were lifted up unto exceeding rudeness.

"And I, Nephi, began to fear exceedingly lest the Lord should be angry with us, and smite us because of our iniquity, that we should be swallowed up in the depths of the sea; wherefore, I, Nephi, began to speak to them with much soberness; but behold they were angry with me, saying: We will not that our younger brother shall be a ruler over us.

"And it came to pass that Laman and Lemuel did take me and bind me with cords, and they did treat me with much harshness; nevertheless, the Lord did suffer it that he might show forth his power, unto the fulfilling of his word which he had spoken concerning the wicked."

Orwell Card looked up with a look of suffering and patient endurance much as the son of the Prophet Lehi must have in the original writing of the history he was reading. "And it came to pass," he continued, "that we were about to be swallowed up in the depths of the sea. And after we had been driven back upon the waters for the space of four days, my brethren began to see that the judgments of God were upon them, and that they must perish save that they should repent of their iniquities; wherefore, they came unto me, and loosed the bands which were upon my wrist, and behold they had swollen exceedingly; and also mine ankles were much swollen, and great was the soreness thereof.

"Nevertheless, I did look unto my God, and I did praise him all the day long; and I did not murmur against the Lord because of mine afflictions.

"So wrote Nephi, in the first book of Nephi, chapter 18, verses 9 to 11, 15 and 16."

The lectern had been placed so that the morning sun shining in through the window would shine directly upon the speaker, and as Orwell looked out upon the congregation one last time, the sun shone upon him, creating what appeared to be a halo of golden light about his head. More than one member of the audience saw, and more than one thought it fitting. Standing there in his crisp white shirt, black suit, and narrow tie and looking out with a beneficence and confidence beyond his twenty-six years, Orwell Card was the stereotypical image of a missionary boy walking up the walkway with Bible in hand, the epitome of all that was good about being a member of the Church of Jesus Christ of Latter-Day Saints. To them, with his closely shorn, straw-coloured hair, eyes blue as the prairie skies, and fair complexion, Orwell Card was the picture of good old country wholesomeness and fundamental religious purity.

As services ended and the congregation began to file out, Orwell extended his arm to Penelope Weiss and the elderly spinster took it and leaned on him for support.

"Orwell Card, just hearing you read from the Good Book makes one feel that she is listening to the Lord Himself," she observed, smiling up at the young man in admiration. "Your sincerity rings out as clearly as a church bell, it does."

"Well, Miss Penny, when I'm standing up there behind the lectern and see you sitting in the front row week after week, your devotion to the Lord and the church is an inspiration such that one cannot help but speak from the heart," he responded.

The senior's steps suddenly became lighter and she became less stooped as she beamed like a teenage girl being complemented by her beau, and Orwell smiled with an inner pleasure as he and Miss Penny continued up the aisle. He had been neither insincere nor obsequious. He really did get inspiration from the senior members of the community, from those men and women who possessed an unshakable faith in their beliefs and who practised what they believed in, and he strove to be like them. When he was home, he volunteered his time at the senior's drop-in centre and at the senior's lodge, Goodwin Manor, assisting the staff on their outings with the residents, helping out in the exercise room, or just volunteering his time to sit and listen to their stories. He did it because it brought him pleasure and comfort.

It was for the same reason that he volunteered at the Rosedale 4-H Beef Club and helped out with the Rosedale Ward Mutual program for LDS youth. He enjoyed being around youth as much as he enjoyed being around seniors, their enthusiasm for life, their energy, and their wholesomeness being as much of an inspiration. He also believed he could be an inspiration to them. He was not the only one. The leaders in the community felt the same. Orwell Card had been an honour student throughout school and was an upright citizen, a faithful member of his church and descended from a prominent and highly respected family, and he was well known in his own right. Athletic, bright, handsome, and personable—there was not a father in the community who would not want his son to chum around with someone as wholesome and successful as Orwell Card, or who would not welcome him as a son-in-law, and there was not a female of marrying age whose heart did not throb a little faster with the mere thought of him.

When he wasn't helping out others whenever he was home, he was helping out at the family farm. Replacing his suit for a torn pair of jeans and an old shirt and well-worn pair of gloves after services, he headed out with his older brother and two hired hands, Jimmy Borden, who had worked for his father as far back as he could remember, and a new hand, Cory Heinmann, a nineteen-year-old up from Salt Lake City, to help replace the fence along the north pasture. It was late July and hot, not a cloud in the sky and not a breath of wind. It was hard work pulling out the rotting posts and putting in the new and stringing the wire back up, but it was good exercise and Orwell welcomed the opportunity to keep in shape.

Midafternoon they paused and sought what little shade the pickup offered them. The four men had stripped off their shirts, and sweat had streaked their dust-covered arms and muscular chests. Jimmy had a thick, black mat with a touch of grey now that tapered into a treasure trail that disappeared under his belt. Orwell recalled the many days he'd worked side by side with the man and had fantasized unbuckling that belt and unzipping the man's fly to discover where that trail led, and doing forbidden things with the hidden treasure. Of course those had been teenage fantasies and he had never acted on them, mostly because Jimmy was married and had seven children and would pound the hell out of him if he ever discovered he had such interests. His brother's hair was only slightly darker than his own, and though they both had a dense mat of hair, neither looked as thick as Jimmy's. Nate was married too and had his own farm next to their dad's. Nate had always been muscular and at one time had even considered professional football. Working his own property and helping his father had kept him in top shape. Orwell did not know why, but even as a hormone-driven, confused teenager he had never had fantasies about his brother, not even on those solitary nights when his hand was his only source of satisfaction.

Unlike the other three men, Cory Heinmann's chest was smooth, not even a few fine wisps about his nipples. Though thinner and more sinewy, hard labour was clearly nothing new to the teenager and he pulled his load along with the other men. He was darkly tanned, obviously spending much of his time bare-chested and outdoors, and darkly handsome with jet-black hair and with eyes the colour of burnt almond, heavily lidded, giving one the impression he was constantly harbouring erotic thoughts. Despite himself, Orwell could not help fantasizing about the young farmhand. Having been encouraged by Nate to tell them about his latest competition at the Calgary Exhibition and Stampede, Orwell had done so willingly, to pass the time, and because he was proud of being a professional bull rider, his livelihood and his passion, As he talked, he saw the gleam in Cory's eyes and he knew he had a fan. When they returned to work, he caught the boy looking at him occasionally, and he knew that look instantly. The boy was having fantasies himself, and they were not about bull riding.

At their next break, Orwell stepped away from the others and, pulling down his fly as he turned his back to them, he hefted out his cock and took a piss. He could have waited, but he was curious. Turning slowly and looking down as he shook off his hose, he carefully glanced over at the others. Jimmy and his brother were in conversation and paying no attention. Cory quickly averted his eyes, but not fast enough. The boy was definitely interested. Unfortunately for Cory, or perhaps fortunately, he did not see the immediate swelling of Orwell's already impressive cock. The teenager purposefully kept his eyes off Orwell, and particularly Orwell's crotch, for the rest of the afternoon.

As they headed back home, Orwell considered following up on

the boy's interest, but reluctantly decided against it. For one, it was too close to home to take any chances. More important, the boy was interested but not likely interested in the version Orwell had in mind. As tempting as it was to follow though on his desires and let things fall where they may, he couldn't do that to the boy. He went to bed and jacked off that night imagining what could have been. Four days later he was up before the sun and on his way to Paisley.

The Paisley rodeo was not a major rodeo when it came to prizes, but it was conveniently scheduled for those who hit the leading rodeos and was popular among the top contestants. It also featured some of the top rodeo stock, the same stock that competed in leading rodeos like Cheyenne's Frontier Days and the Calgary Exhibition and Stampede. So it was that Thursday evening found Orwell leaning against the back pens eyeing his bovine opponent for the next day, a large black bull by the name of Cyclone. Stock providers follow the rodeo circuit just as do the cowboys, and a good bull rider knows his opponent. Every bull is different. Some buck with their hind legs, some leap with all four, some spin and others twist. Cyclone was an apt name for the animal. He was a twister, and riding him was like riding a cyclone. Orwell had seen him in action many times before and had met the drawing of his name with both apprehension and delight; apprehension because he knew the reputation of the bull for inconsistency, making it difficult to read how to ride him and the likelihood he wouldn't last the required eight seconds on his back, and delight because the bull earned half the points the judges awarded and Cyclone never disappointed when it came to giving a cowboy a good ride. In that sense the bull was as much a partner as he was an opponent, and a good bull rider worked with his partner, making the animal an extension of his body. Bulls had a rep just as did their riders, and he knew the judges would have high expectations for the two of them.

"Until tomorrow, big boy," he said softly. Cyclone raised his head and looked straight at him. The look on his face seemed to say, "You'd better come prepared."

As he turned, a figure separated from the shadows and walked toward him. Another rider from his gait. Orwell tensed and clenched his fists, ready. As the stranger approached, the moon emerged from the clouds, illuminating his face. Orwell relaxed.

"Cole."

"Orwell."

"Come to check out the stock?"

The man nodded. "Hear you're riding Cyclone tomorrow."

"You heard right."

"Should be an interesting ride."

"Should."

"Well, good luck to you."

"You too."

The two men parted. Cole Bannick. A good man. Not as good as Orwell, but a good man. After you've ridden the circuit for a while you get to know each other. His relationship with Cole had been distant, professional. That was better than most. Most didn't like him, many feared him, but all admired his bull riding skill and respected him as a cowboy.

Orwell walked the fairgrounds. The carneys followed a circuit also, the bigger outfits hitting the leading rodeos, the smaller ones hitting the small towns. Over the years Orwell had gotten to know them, some better than others. He had a rep among carneys too. There was always some buck ready to challenge him, having heard of him, wanting to prove something. Others didn't like what he was and were on a mission to change him, or punish him. He didn't mind. He liked the challenge. It gave him a rush, and the more challengers he met and defeated, the more his rep grew. He strutted, letting them know he was there.

He paused at the Kinsmen tent for a beer. Alcohol was forbidden by his faith, as were coffee, tea, and tobacco. He figured one out of four wasn't bad. Besides, he didn't believe in all of the tenets of his faith. There were athletes who frowned on alcohol also, but Orwell didn't put much stock in them either. There was no problem in moderation. It had not affected his performance. As he drank, he thought of Laredo. He was a big carney, one of the labourers who worked behind the scenes, setting up the heavy equipment and taking it down. They had met there at the Kinsmen's in Paisley a few years back. The man had heard of his rep and had challenged him to a wrestling match. They'd agreed on the stakes ahead of time. He had won, as he always did, and he'd fucked the man relentlessly and ruthlessly that night, in the dark behind the big generators, using a gob of motor oil for lube and squeezing the man's big balls to make him buck. He had been a good ride. Orwell smiled fondly at the memory.

He seemed to attract trouble. Slim, muscular, and handsome, he attracted women too. He wore a tapered black shirt and tight-fitting black jeans that accented his muscular thighs, his narrow waist, his package, and his compact ass. Women were drawn to him like moths to a candle flame. Their dates, boyfriends or husbands, were jealous, envious of his looks and sex appeal, but he didn't care. In fact he egged them on, getting them hot and bothered, woman and man both, and then left them steaming there on the fairgrounds like the pair of turds they were. He was not interested in a liaison with the opposite sex, but he did enjoy tempting them. He was a desired prize that the woman wanted but would never have, an irritation that the man could not scratch. It reaffirmed that he was in control.

He attracted the same sex also, those who liked their men macho and their sex torrid. Orwell loved to play them also, tempting them, getting them hot, and once they made their move, leaving them panting and wanting, letting them know they were not up to the standards Orwell Card had set. A good bull rider wanted a top-performing bull. He could see the disappointment in their eyes, sometimes the hurt, more often the anger at his arrogance. He didn't care. All men were not created equal, and it was best that they know it. It was a special type of man that lived up to his expectations. He didn't find one that night.

Late the next afternoon, Orwell settled down onto Cyclone's back and the bull snorted his anger and defiance. Laying the tail of the bull rope over the handle and tightly wrapping it around his gloved fingers once, a practice he'd learned from a former junior world champion when he'd just been starting out, and gripping the sweating body of the animal with his legs and knees, Orwell inserted his mouth guard, inhaled deeply, and nodded to the gate man. Most riders took too long to make sure they were comfortable and everything was just right. That just gave Cyclone more time to build up steam, and the longer one took, the sooner he was thrown. He knew. He'd studied Cyclone's behaviour and knew his every quirk and trick, like a good bull rider should. The gate opened and Cyclone shot out straight up into the air with all four feet off the ground and landed with a bone-jarring thud on his hind legs. Orwell had expected that and had raised himself off the bull's back, taking the shock with his legs. Keeping his left hand high in the air, he dug his blunted bull spurs into the bull's ribs. Cyclone responded by kicking back with his hind legs and raising his rump, trying to throw Orwell over his head. Another spur jab and he spun around to the right, wrenching Orwell's body around with him, and then just as quickly flipped to the left. Orwell allowed himself to be flipped, matching his movements with the bull's, keeping a constant rhythm, always in control.

Cyclone was one and three-quarter tons of rippling muscle, not the largest bull in the pro circuit but the most animated and the most powerful. Bull snot and spit whipped through the air as he twisted his head, trying to gore the 165-pound irritation on his back, but Orwell kept his body far from those threatening horns. The horn blew and as Cyclone spun to the left, Orwell released his grip and let the momentum throw him into the air in the direction of his riding hand. Landing on all fours, he scrambled to his feet and raced for the fence, Cyclone's hooves pounding the dirt behind him and his stinking breath blowing hot against his back. It wasn't exactly dignified, but when you're dismounting from an angry bull the last thing you're concerned about is your dignity. The crowd was cheering wildly, and when the announcer announced his score, eighty-three, they went even wilder. With many riders disqualified and even more not making the time, he would easily qualify for the short go Saturday.

Pulling off his gloves, he rubbed his right wrist gingerly. Cyclone had tested its flexibility to the fullest, but he had strong wrists and extra-long-fingered gloves, making them less likely to get caught up in the rope or get pulled off. He acknowledged the congratulations of his fellow competitors and the men working the chutes with a nod and a grin. That was what bull riding was all about, the admiration and respect of one's peers, who were aware of the skill and strength it took to last those eight seconds on a bull's back, the thrill of hearing the crowd cheering, the rush of facing real life-threatening danger, the challenge of pitting a man's strength against that of a bull, and most of all, the exhilaration of doing so successfully and better than one's fellow competitors. In the five years he'd competed in amateur rodeo and the seven he competed in the pros, he'd fractured his left arm, pulled his right out of its socket twice, sprained his right wrist three times, and fractured three ribs. It was worth it. That was what bull riding was all about too. He'd often been asked why he rode bulls. Anybody who wasn't a cowboy, or at least from the country, wouldn't understand. Why does a football player play football or a race car driver race cars? It was for the thrill of the sport, for the sense of achievement and the pride that comes from knowing you are one of the best.

He waited around for the last three riders. Two qualified for the ride tomorrow, one did not. His score was the highest. He would win this event. He could feel it. With a smile on his lips, he turned and headed for the fairgrounds. You could see his pride and confidence in his eyes, and in his walk, and a lot of people saw. When Orwell Card made an appearance, people noticed. As he sauntered down the midway, he was very much aware of the stares. He was slight, five foot six, but make no question about it, that slim frame was compact and all muscle. His tooled black leather boots, silver-trimmed black shirt and Stetson, and tight black jeans complemented his fair complexion, fallow-coloured hair, and slightly darker eyebrows, and added to his sex appeal. Yes, Orwell Card dressed and acted the part right down to his silver 2009 championship buckle and he took just as much delight in the appreciative appraisal by the fair sex and the blatant envy of his lessers as he did in the cheers of the crowd when performing in the arena.

He walked slowly and paused often, checking out those around him, giving those around him time to check him out. He spread his legs openly, invitingly, his package prominently displayed in his tight jeans. He spent extra time hanging around one of the ball toss games, even playing it a few times, the young carney there being particularly attractive and looking like he could give him a good time. The carney flirted back, definitely interested, and Orwell felt his blood rise with the anticipation. The stalking, the unknown, the secret signals and suggestive looks, they were all part of the game and made it all the more arousing. At last he made his opening play, commenting about it being a boring evening, and a long one. The carney did not take him up on it. The teasing had all been part of his game too, to get him to waste his money. Orwell glared at him and considered having his way with him later that night regardless. It would not be the first time he'd forced a man, and rape often was just as good, even better, than consensual. Nobody fucked around with Orwell Card. The young carney stepped away. He was young, but not inexperienced, and he sensed the anger, and he had a good idea why. It was not the first time he'd used his charms to separate a sucker from his money. He was handsome and had come-ons before and he knew how to make use of them. He had never before seen such fierce anger as this, though.

Orwell turned and slowly sauntered down the midway without looking back. Leaving the games of chance, he headed over to the rides. Looking up at the Twister, he glanced out of the corner of his eye. He had, as he had suspected, been followed. While he'd been flirting with the carney, he'd noticed he was being watched, and when one man watches another like that it is because he is a thief or interested in something other than what is in a man's pocket. He was too pretty, too effeminate, for his taste, but he was angry now, and needed to release his anger. He slowly walked over to the Kinsmen tent. The man followed. He found a spot along the bar where it was less crowded. The man stepped up beside him. They exchanged smiles, began a conversation, about the rodeo, the midway, the weather. The man's name was Jason. He was twenty-five, a physical education teacher at the Paisley high school. He lived alone and had a spare bed if Orwell needed a place to sleep.

Leaving the bar tent, Orwell began to head toward the porta potties nearby but they never made it. Slipping into the bushes along the edge of the grounds, he turned and kissed the teacher hotly. As their lips parted, he placed his hands on the man's shoulders and began to force him down.

"What are you doing?"

"I need a blow job."

"I don't live that far away."

"I need it now."

"We'd be a lot more comfortable. And it would be a lot more private."

"You want my cock."

"Yes, but…"

"Unzip my fly and take it out."

"Really, I—"

Orwell had the man on his knees by then, his muscular arms easily forcing the man down. "On second thought, push down your jeans and underwear."

"You're hurting me."

"I'm only beginning." Orwell increased the pressure on the

man's neck where his shoulder blades joined his clavicle, stopping his squirming. It did not take much pressure to send shards of pain through his body. Orwell knew all the pressure points, all one hundred and eight of them. Jason knew if he put up enough of a protest he'd attract someone's attention and Orwell would have to stop. He also knew enough human anatomy to know it would only take the man a second to break his neck, and from the menace in his voice, he was likely to do it. Worse, he might render him unconscious, and then who knew what the man might do or what state he might be found in when he came to. That he could not risk. He unbuckled his pants and pulled down his fly and pushed his jeans and boxers down to his knees.

"Beat yourself off."

Slipping his fingers about his flaccid penis, Jason began to stroke himself, feeling no desire whatsoever. With his other hand he pulled down the other man's fly and took out his semierect pecker. Slipping his lips over it, he began to suck. It was nothing like he had been fantasizing.

Orwell smiled down at the man as his cock hardened between the man's lips. He wondered if he was one of those phys ed teachers who spied on his boys in the showers. He didn't seem the type. He seemed to be much more into men, macho men, men like himself. He considered taking his picture kneeling there beating his meat and sucking his dick and leaving it in the boys' change room where his students could find it. High school students are a horny lot and would welcome knowing someone who would suck them off. He suggested the idea to the teacher. The man looked up at him desperately, his eyes begging him not to do it.

"If you do a good job, I won't."

The man sucked in earnest and worked his tongue over Orwell's knob as he pumped his fist with a renewed vigour and purpose. Orwell smiled down at him sadistically. It had been an erotic idea, but not one he would have followed through on. He seemed like a decent man, if a poor judge of whom to pick up at a bar. He did enjoy the fear in the man's eyes, though, and the reaction he had elicited. With a little training he could see where the teacher could come to enjoy being dominated. He had sensed that in their conversation. That, and the man's desperation. It had to be difficult finding a sex partner being a teacher and in a small town. He was doing the man a favour allowing him to pick him up. The least the man could do was allow him a little rough stuff. As he felt the lust welling up in his loins, he grasped the man's hair and ordered him to deep-throat him. As the man went down further, Orwell threw back his head in ecstasy. When he came, he would pull out and spray the man's face, his final indignity. The teacher would like that. So would Orwell.

The next day the draw matched him up with an ornery bull by the name of Back Bender. He was surprised. Back Bender was considered a rank bull, a difficult ride, and was normally reserved for the leading rodeos where the riders were at the top of their field. That he had been included in the draw was a sign of the calibre of the competition in the short go. He headed over to the back pens to have a look at his new partner. Looking up at him, the bull snorted and pawed the ground.

"Well, you might be one mean son of a bitch, but then so am I," Orwell said appreciatively. It was going to be an interesting afternoon.

"You're Orwell Card." It was more of a statement than a question.

"I am," Orwell said, turning to look at the speaker. He recognized him as a fellow rider, a big man, broad-shouldered and barrel-chested with the biceps of a weightlifter. He looked more like the type of man who wrestled steers rather than rode them. They had never met but their paths had crossed several times. Bull riders were a select group, and sooner or later everyone got to know everyone else. The man had a rep for drinking, and for being trouble.

"Hear you're good."

"I am."

"Hear you're a faggot too. That true?"

"Why do you want to know? Want to sleep with me?" The man flushed a beet red as he glared at him. "Can't think of any other reason that my preference might be of interest to you."

"Your rep for being a smart-ass is true too, I see."

"Can't say I've heard of you, but I suspect you have a rep too. Of being a dumbass."

"I'd take you down right here and now, punk, but I'm going to wait until this afternoon and take you down in the arena. I'll show you who's a man, and who is the best bull rider in town."

"You're a bull rider?" Orwell asked in mock surprise.

"Damn right I am."

"Hmm, from your size and smell I thought you were substituting for one of the bulls."

The man would have charged had his friends not held him back. "This afternoon. You'll find out this afternoon."

"Want to make it interesting? A little wager on the side?"

"Loser matches top prize."

"I'd be happy to take your money, but I was thinking of something more personal."

"Like what?"

Orwell motioned for him to lean close and whispered in his ear.

"Fucking pervert! It's your type that gives sports a bad name. All sports."

"I'll sweeten the pot even more. Besides matching top prize, if you win, I quit riding."

His challenger looked at him in disbelief. "You serious?"

"Always."

"You're on."

"I will be," Orwell responded with a wicked grin.

As the man stormed off with his friends, Orwell continued to smile. The day had just gotten even more interesting. He had seen the man ride several times. He was a mediocre rider. What he had going for him was his size and strength. It was difficult for a bull to dislodge someone of that weight on his back. Technique, on the other hand, was zero. Orwell checked the scoreboard. To his surprise the man, Ty Bronson, was standing second at eighty-two. He had drawn Code Red, a reddish-brown beast known for sunfishing. He was a good bull and could rack up some good points for Ty.

Of the first five riders, two never made the eight seconds, one was disqualified, and the other two had scores below eighty-three. Ty was next. As Orwell had predicted, Code Red gave him a good ride, and Ty was prepared for his trademark belly roll, leaning away from his hand and maintaining his balance. He received a score of eighty-eight. To beat him, Orwell was going to have to match him. As he headed for the chutes, Ty intercepted him.

"Hope you enjoy your last ride, fag," he said with a sneer and a sparkle in his pig-like eyes.

Inhaling deeply, Orwell settled down on Back Bender, and as the flank man tightened the flank strap, Orwell wrapped the bull strap about the handle and his fingers and gave it an extra tug for tightness. Gripping the bull with his knees, he nodded to the gatekeeper and Back Bender leaped out of the chute, straight up. Landing on his front feet, he threw his rear in the air in an attempt to toss his rider over his head, but Orwell was prepared for the move and moved with him. As he kicked his front feet in the air, Orwell moved with him again, constantly in control. Snorting in fury with the failed attempt, the bull began to spin into his hand. Two tons of angry bull spun relentlessly and Orwell felt himself being pulled down the side of the bull, his slim body being sucked into the vortex. Fear suddenly gripped his heart. Being sucked down in the well was one of a bull rider's greatest fears, and one of his most dangerous situations.

Desperately he jabbed his spur into the bull's left side. The rowels on a bull spur aren't sharp enough to cut into the bull or cause any damage, but it was irritating, and distracting enough to bring Back Bender out of his spin. The horn blew. He had made it. Reaching down to loosen his bull rope, fear struck a second time. Luckily the extra tug had tightened the rope enough that he'd been able to keep his grip during the spin, but the spin had tightened it further and he couldn't loosen it. Back Bender was not happy either and he began his trademark jackknifing, throwing his hind legs in the air and then his front, trying to rock his rider off. One of the rodeo clowns got close enough to give the rope an extra yank and Orwell felt it loosen. With the next front leg kick he threw himself off, fortunately stumbling to the left and narrowly missing the back legs as they came up. It was an unplanned but dramatic dismount and the crowd thundered its appreciation with applause and stamping feet. That he had lasted the eight seconds was a rush, and the response of the crowd even greater, but neither compared to the rush he felt as the announcer announced his score of ninety-one.

Picking up his trophy and five thousand dollar cheque, he headed to the back of the grounds for his other prize. That Ty Bronson was actually waiting in the cattle carrier for him was not a surprise. Despite the man's faults, he was not one to back out of an agreement, no matter how distasteful.

"Surprised I'm here?"

"No."

"Then come and take me, if you're man enough."

That Ty wasn't going to pay up willingly did not come as a surprise either. Orwell Card knew how to read men as well as he knew how to read bulls. Stepping into the cattle liner, he slipped the lariat off his shoulder. He had come prepared. Orwell's skills were not limited to riding bulls. Minutes later with the 230-pound bully on his stomach and his wrists and ankles securely tied, Orwell was grateful for the hours of roping practice he'd had on the farm. Actually, tying down the big oaf had been easier than roping and tying down a calf during branding. Unbuckling the belt of the squirming, protesting man and pulling down his fly, Orwell pulled his jeans and boxers down to his bound ankles. Sitting on the man's back, he reached under him, and grasping his cock, he began to stroke it.

"Fucking bastard! Get your hands off there! Messing with my stuff was not part of the bet."

"Come now, Ty. You didn't think I was going to ride you without a little foreplay, did you?"

From his response, the man evidently had. Wrapping his fist about the man's knob, Orwell twisted it and the man jerked with the pain. He ran his fingernail along the rim and the man drew his hips back, pulling his cock away. Slipping his hands under the man's shirt, he tweaked his nipples. Despite his revulsion and anger, Ty Bronson slowly began to get aroused. Continuing until the man was hard, Orwell slipped a nylon cord about the base of his cock and drew it tight, and looped a second, a flank strap to enhance his bucking, he joked, about his balls. Getting up and removing his boots, jeans, and underwear, he lay back on top of the man.

Feeling what was obviously his attacker's cock pressing against his hole and the sudden slackening of weight on his legs, the man did what any man would do under the circumstances—he raised his body and pushed back in a desperate attempt to buck the man on his back off. What that did was drive Orwell's slender, rock-hard cock up the man's virgin asshole. As Ty realized what had happened, he sank back down and Orwell followed, driving his cock the rest of the way up the man's rectum and ramming his body against the metal floor of the cattle liner. This was not Orwell's first man ride. He knew every quirk and trick of his quarry like a good man rider should.

Yanking the man's shirt up, he reached under his body and tweaked his nipples, causing the man to twist and jerk. Being pinned down by Orwell's viselike thighs, which were accustomed to squeezing the thrashing body of a one-and-a-half ton bull, Ty didn't have a chance as he tried desperately to dislodge the slender rider. Orwell continued to pinch and twist the man's irritated nipples as he eased his cock back until the knob was about to slip out of the man's hole and he again lifted his weight off the man's body.

Figuring his struggles had loosened his attacker's hold on him, the man thrust upward, succeeding only in impaling himself on Orwell's stiff, throbbing cock again. Feeling it penetrate deep up his rectum, the man sank back down, driving his exposed erection into the metal floor but unable to sink low enough to pull himself off the prick intruding up his asshole.

"That's it, give me a good ride," Orwell whispered in his ear as he bent over him. "Let's see what a good fuck you are."

The man flushed red with anger and struggled all the harder and Orwell whooped as he raised himself and threw his left arm in the air as if riding a bull. The man twisted and bucked furiously, snorting and grunting just like Cyclone had. Ty inhaled deeply and the rank, fetid stench of wet hay and cattle piss and manure from the nearby pens filled his lungs. Orwell bent over him again, his mouth at his ear.

"Feels good, don't it? My cock up your ass. Bet after this you'll be hanging around the gay bars looking for a partner."

Ty opened his mouth to retort but Orwell reached under him and snapped his index finger against the man's swollen balls, causing him to yelp with pain instead. Hours of chin-ups on the barn rafters at home and in the stables on the rodeo circuit had given Orwell the strength he needed in his arms to hold onto a bull rope. Now he put it to use holding the bully down as he plowed his ass. Ty twisted beneath him angrily and Orwell pressed his body against his, pinning him down. It was hot in the back of the cattle liner and the two men began to sweat.

"That's it, buck your ass. Show me how much you're enjoying your fuck," Orwell panted. Of course Ty stopped, which he slowly realized implied that he had been enjoying it. The humiliation cut deeper than the pain searing his stretched asshole.

Snorting and spitting with anger, he renewed his efforts. Reaching down under him, Orwell squeezed his swollen dick and whispered how it was still hard, proof he must like getting screwed. As he stroked the man's cock he whispered how his tight ass felt like a woman's cunt, and how hot he must feel having a man's cock up his ass. Ty felt filthy and disgusted, but his body could not ignore the stroking of his prick and Orwell's hot, stiff cock throbbing up his rectum and massaging his prostate. He tried to ignore the swelling lust in his loins, but the more he fought it, the greater the desire grew.

He could feel Orwell's naked, muscular thighs grasping his. He could smell the bull rider's sour sweat, and could feel his own running down his ribs. Hearing his attacker's laboured panting, he knew he was about to come. He wanted to come too, but the cord about his balls made it impossible. As if knowing his thoughts, Orwell reached down and snapped his finger against his swollen balls again, combing his pleasure with pain. Orwell slowed down, delighting in the desire throbbing through his veins and through his swollen cock, and delighting even more in the pain and humiliation the man beneath him was feeling. Ty Bronson was the perfect partner, the type of man he most enjoyed fucking.

Reaching under the man's shirt, he repeatedly pinched his swollen, irritated nipples as he thrust his swollen cock in and out of the man's rectum, totally focused on his every action and Ty's every response. Ty bucked and twisted with the pain searing his nipples and his swollen balls as they contracted and he tried futilely to empty them. Delighting in the man's pain, Orwell grunted and arched his back as he filled the man's rectum and he relished the last eight seconds of ultimate pleasure as he emptied his own swollen, sweaty balls.

Finally getting off him and retrieving his underwear, jeans, and shoes, Orwell loosened the man's bonds and exited the liner. Two fantastic rides in one day. What a fucking rush! Orwell raised his eyes and looked unto his God and did praise Him for His blessings, and headed for the midway and a corn dog.

PHENOM
TODD GREGORY

The arms around me hit a grand slam tonight.
        It didn't matter; we lost the game anyway. But I didn't care.
I've never really cared much about baseball. In fact, I'd never been to a
game until our local team signed Billy Chastain. As soon as I saw him
being interviewed on the local news, I knew I was going to start going
to games. It's not that I don't like baseball, I just never cared enough to
go. But all it took was one look at Billy Chastain, and I was sold.

The interview had been one of those special pieces. He'd been a
high school star, played in college a couple of years, and then one year
in the minors, where he'd been a force to be reckoned with; with an
amazing batting average and some outstanding play at third base, he'd
been called up to the majors for this new season, and everyone was
talking about him. I just stared at the television screen.

Sure, he was young, but he was also composed, well spoken, and
seemed mature for his age. He was also drop-dead gorgeous. He had
thick bluish-black hair, olive skin, and the most amazing green eyes.
They showed clips of him fielding and batting—and then came the
part that I wished I'd recorded: They showed him lifting weights. In
the earlier shots, it was apparent he had a nice build; he seemed tall
and lanky, almost a little raw-boned, but once they cut to the shots of
him in the weight room, I was sold. His body was ripped as he moved
from machine to machine in his white muscle shirt and long shorts, his
dark hair damp with sweat. As his workout progressed and his muscles
became more and more pumped, more and more defined, I could feel
my cock starting to stir in my pants. And then they closed the segment
with a shot of him pulling the tank top over his head and wiping his
damp face with it. I gasped. His hairless torso slick with sweat, his abs

perfect, his pecs round and beautiful, and the most amazing half-dollar sized nipples, which I wanted to get my lips around.

I bought tickets and started going to every home game.

Our team sucked, to be frank, and it was soon apparent that there was no World Series or even division pennant in our future that year. But Billy was a great player and everyone was talking about him. He was leading the division in hits and had one of the highest batting averages in all of baseball. He made the cover of *Sports Illustrated* with the headline PHENOM, his beautiful face smiling out at people on newsstands all over the country. There were several shots of him inside without a shirt on, shots I had scanned into my computer, enlarged, and printed out for framing. I made sure my seats were always behind third base so I could get as great a view of him as humanly possible in his tight white pants that showed every curve and muscle of his legs—and the amazing round hard ass I thought about when I closed my eyes and masturbated. Every so often he would look up into the stands and smile, saluting us with a wave.

As much as I wanted to believe the smile and the wave were for me, I knew better.

Tonight's game was the last game of the regular season; our record ensured it was our last game of 2006. The Red Sox were on their way to the play-offs, and we had only taken two games off them all season. We were beaten 10–4. All four runs came from Billy's bat—a grand slam on his first pitch with the bases loaded. The stadium was half-empty; most of our fans had given up on the team at the midway point of the season. But not me—as long as there was a chance to see Billy swing his bat, I was there. And when he circled the bases, he paused briefly at third, looked up to the crowd, and waved at us.

I thought about waiting for the team after the game, seeing if I could get Billy to sign my program, but decided against it. I knew I was more than a little obsessed with him; my friends liked to call me his stalker. They were just giving me shit, but there was a fine line there I was afraid to cross, so instead I went to my car and drove to a small little gay bar close to the stadium. It was one of those places you went to meet friends for a beer or a drink, not one of the places where you went to do recreational drugs, dance to music played at ear-splitting levels with your shirt off and look for Mr. Right Now. The bar was pretty empty when I got there; it was usually only crowded during happy hour. The drinks were cheap but strong; a lot of guys met their friends there to get a nice cheap buzz going before they moved on to other bars in their eternal quest for tonight's orgasm. The bartender was a nice looking man in his mid-forties who popped the top off a bottle of Bud Light when he saw me come in and placed it on a napkin at the bar. I grinned my thanks and took a long pull. The television hung from the ceiling behind the bar was playing a rerun of *Will & Grace* on Lifetime. There were only two other people in the bar, shooting pool in the back area.

I was on my second beer, watching as Grace decided for the thousandth time that her gay best friend was more important to her than any straight man could be—which always struck me as kind of tragic, sad and twisted rather than uplifting—when the door opened. I didn't turn and look to see who was coming in—I didn't care, and I wasn't looking to get laid. I was on my second and final beer before heading home, and I preferred to be lost in my thoughts about Billy and how he looked in those tight white pants rather than doing the *shall-we-go-to-my-place-and-fuck* tango with a stranger. It'd been a long day, and I was looking forward to sleeping in the next morning.

I took another swig and almost fell off my bar stool when the person who'd walked in stepped up to the bar a couple of stools down from me.

I'd recognize Billy Chastain anywhere.

He was wearing a sleeveless navy blue T-shirt with the words *Crew Cut Wrestling* written in yellow across the front, along with the image of two men in singlets wrestling. His jeans rode low on his hips, and as he leaned forward on the bar while showing his ID to the bartender, his shirt crept up in the back and the jeans rode down a little further, showing off the red waistband of his tight gray Calvin Klein underwear. The way he was standing showed off that oh-so-perfectly round ass to anyone who wanted to look at it. My mouth went dry and I took another swig of my beer as the bartender handed him a bottle of Bud Light. He stood back up and took a drink. He saw me out of the corner of his eye and turned to look at me, giving me a friendly nod as he put the bottle back down.

I turned my eyes back to the television screen as fast as I could.

Another episode of *Will & Grace* was starting. My heart started pounding as he moved down the bar toward me. "I know it's bad form to say this," he said in the husky voice I'd heard on television a million times but always made the hair on my arms stand up, "but I really *hate* that show. In the real world, a gay man would have told Grace years earlier 'you're single because you're a neurotic self-absorbed cunt who's completely unlovable with no redeeming qualities whatsoever. Why would any man want you?'"

I laughed. I'd thought the same thing any number of times. I turned and looked at him, managing to remain calm on the outside while on the inside I felt like I was going to turn into a pool of jelly at any second. "Will's no better than she is."

He nodded. "He's a lawyer in New York with a nice body, a gorgeous apartment, and he's kind of handsome—and he'd rather hang out with that crazy bitch instead of getting laid, yet he can't figure out why he's single? How the hell did he get through law school if he's that stupid?"

I tapped my beer bottle against his. "Exactly."

He tilted his head to one side and squinted his eyes a little bit. "You know, you look familiar."

"Do I?" I struggled to keep my voice from squeaking. "Well, I know who you are. Billy Chastain, the phenom."

He laughed. "Yeah, that's me." He took another drink from the beer. "Man, this beer is good. I don't drink while I'm in training, but the season is now officially over, and man, does this taste great." He looked at me again. "I know who you are. You've been to almost all of our home games—you sit up behind third base, right?"

"Guilty as charged."

"Big baseball fan." He grinned, and I could feel my cock stir in my own jeans.

"Not really." I grinned back at him. "More of a big Billy Chastain fan."

"Really?" He stepped closer to me and put his hand on the inside of my leg. I felt an electric shock that went straight to my balls, and my cock was now achingly hard. He licked his lips. "How big?" He moved his hand into my crotch and lifted his eyebrows, his eyes getting wider. "Nice."

This can't be happening, I thought. *This has to be one of the best wet dreams ever.*

"You got any beer back at your place?" He lightly brushed his shoulder against mine.

"Um, yeah."

He gave my cock a squeeze and I thought I might come right there in my pants. "Mind if we go back there?" He winked at me. "You got a car? I take cabs."

"Yeah."

"You up for it?"

I finished my beer in one gulp. "Sure."

All the way to my apartment, he played with my cock. It was hard for me to focus on driving. We made small talk, me barely able to get out more than two words at a time. I parked and we walked up the flight of stairs to my front door. My hands shook as I unlocked the front door. Once we were inside and the door closed behind us, he grabbed me and pulled me to him, our bodies pressed tightly together as he tilted his head down, pressing his mouth onto mine. I sucked on his tongue and his hands came down behind me and squeezed my ass. My cock was aching, and I put my hands on his chest. I pinched one of his nipples and he moaned. He tilted his head back as I kept pinching, not letting go of his erect nipple. "Man," he breathed, "that drives me crazy."

I slid my hands down and pulled his shirt up. He raised his arms, his lats spreading like wings as the shirt came up and over his head. He dropped his shirt to the floor, and I kissed him at the base of his throat, moving my mouth down to his left nipple. As I sucked on it, I pinched the other. He moaned and started thrusting his crotch forward. A little wet spot appeared on the front of his pants. I didn't let up, sucking and licking and sometimes playing with his nipple with my tongue. He leaned back against the door, his head back, his eyes half-closed. I traced my tongue to the center of his chest, and then slowly slid it down to his navel. I undid his pants and they dropped to his ankles, and I put my mouth on his hard cock through the underwear. I played with the head of his cock with my mouth until he put both hands under my arms and pulled me back up to my feet.

He smiled at me and then pulled my shirt up over my head,

tweaking both of my nipples before putting his mouth on my right one. He toyed with it, played with it, and I couldn't believe how good it felt, and then he too was sliding his tongue down my torso, undoing my pants and pulling my underwear down. My cock sprang free. He looked up at me and smiled. "That's a beauty, man," he said before putting his mouth on it.

I moaned as he tongued the underside of my cock and licked my balls. I still couldn't believe it was happening. Billy Chastain was sucking my cock—no one was going to believe this.

He stood up and smiled, putting his arms around me and pulling me close to him. He kissed my ear and knelt down, picking me up. I wrapped my legs around his waist and kissed his neck. He stepped out of his pants and carried me through the living room and into the bedroom, the whole time sucking on my earlobe while I ground my cock against his rock-hard stomach. He gently set me down on the bed and took off my shoes, then pulled my pants and underwear off, dropping them to the floor. I sat up on my elbows, watching as he took off his shoes and socks, then the underwear came off. His cock was long, thick, and hard, and bent a little to the left. He had trimmed his pubic hair down, and his balls were shaved. He smiled at me, then climbed onto the bed next to me. I turned and we kissed again, his tongue coming into my mouth while I reached down and put my hand on his cock. He pulled me on top of him, our cocks grinding together as we kissed. His body felt amazing against mine, his skin soft yet hard at the same time, the power of his muscles radiating through his skin.

"I want you to fuck me," he breathed into my ear.

Oh, God.

I reached into my bedside table and pulled out a condom, opening the package with my teeth. I sat back on my knees while I slipped the condom on, then squirted some lube onto it. I then put some lube on my fingers, sliding them into the crack of his ass until I found what I was looking for, and started spreading the lube around. His eyes closed. "Just do it, man." He breathed, spreading his legs further and tilting his pelvis up.

I started slow, placing the tip of my cock against his hole, gently applying a little pressure until the head went in. He tensed for a second, then relaxed. I went in a bit more, slowly, working my way in as he relaxed and got used to me being inside him. When I finally pushed all the way in, he gasped, tensed and relaxed; his eyes opened wide, he grinned at me. "Wow, that feels amazing."

I started moving, slowly, sliding in and back out, then back in. With each deep thrust, his beautiful body shivered and quivered, moans escaping from his lips as I worked his ass, reaching up every once in a while to tweak his nipples, which obviously drove him insane. As I felt my own orgasm rising within me, I pounded faster and deeper and harder, and finally as my come started to build, he shouted out "Fuck! *Fuck! Fuck!*" and his entire body shook as he started shooting his own load. The sight of him drenching his chest with his own come got me pushing harder and I screamed out as my entire body convulsed, my own load shooting into the condom.

I collapsed on top of him, my cock still inside him.

He kissed the top of my head. "That was amazing."

"Uh-huh."

We lay like that for a few minutes, my ear pressed against his rib cage, listening to his racing heartbeat and his breathing.

Finally I sat up and pulled off the condom, dropping into the trash. "Let me get you a towel. Or do you want to shower?"

"Can I shower in the morning?"

I smiled. "Oh, that can be arranged." I tossed him a towel and he wiped his chest down. He tossed it back to me and I wiped my crotch down before getting back into the bed. He put his arms around me.

"Thank you," he said, kissing me on the neck again and nuzzling against my throat. "That was amazing."

"Yes, you were," I replied.

He smiled and yawned. "Do you mind if we sleep a little? I'm kind of worn out—the game and all." He winked at me. "And all."

"Sure."

He turned onto his side and I curled into him, kissing him good night on the mouth. He placed his head down on the pillow as I turned off the lights. Within a few seconds he was breathing regularly.

I snuggled up against him and put my own head down on top of his arm. We fit together perfectly.

My friends weren't going to believe this—but then, I wasn't sure I did either.

I could lie like this forever.

It might just be a one-nighter, and that was fine with me. I wasn't going to get ahead of myself and make plans for our future together or anything.

But he wasn't leaving my place in the morning until I'd seen that big dick shoot another load all over that ripped torso.

And on that note, I finally fell asleep.

HOCKEY STARS ON TOP
JAY STARRE

It was the play-offs, a nerve-wracking period for every player on the team. At twenty-two, Kevin was older than his two line mates, Paul and Sven, who were both just nineteen. He was the natural leader in the trio due to that two-year age gap and the relative maturity it gave him.

It was Sven who initiated the stress-relieving tactic that worked for them, but it was Kevin who encouraged it, then cranked it up to the next level at every opportunity. It turned out to be the perfect way for them to remedy their pent-up emotions, and soon they engaged in the practice after every game.

None of them drank, and drugs were out of the question. That left driving fast cars or gambling or extreme sports—or sex. They chose sex.

Sven, the Swedish American from Minnesota, was the biggest of the line mates at a towering 6'6". He was in the shower with both Kevin and their third, Paul, when he sprang one huge boner.

"Hey, dudes, sorry about this. Can't help it. I'm so fucking horny! No time to go out and get me some with all this practice and the fucking game schedule, and Coach after us all the time to get our rest and crap like that. Maybe I should just pump one out right now? No one else is around but us. Do you mind?"

Sven was already pumping his soaped up hard-on while he chattered on. He was the talkative one of the three, the most easy-going, and the least able to keep his thoughts to himself. He was a little bit naïve, but very likeable.

Paul didn't say a word, but his big blue eyes got bigger as he stared right at that massive soaped-up dick in the shower beside him.

He was the shortest of the trio and built like a bull. Now his bull-cock was growing too; it was fat and thick and had an uncut monster knob at the end. He didn't say much because truthfully his English was not the best. He was Quebecois from Montreal and had managed to get along in his native province without speaking English for most of his life, until he came to the States to play for his current team alongside Kevin and Sven.

Kevin's cock wasn't immune to the hot sight of his teammates sporting huge boners, and within spitting distance too! He made a quick inner calculation, weighing the fact they were alone in the locker room while the rest of the team showered and changed in an adjacent room, that neither Sven nor Paul was likely to tell anyone what went on between them, and that Sven was right. They needed to relieve their sexual frustration somehow.

Besides, they played on the same line in every game. He was the center while these two were his forwards. The closer they were and the more they were in tune with each other, the better they would play. That was an undeniable fact.

"Great idea, Sven. Let's whack one off. See who can shoot first," he replied cheerfully.

He knew what he had to do. He moved in closer to Paul, who was in the middle shower, and draped a long arm over his shoulder as he began to soap up his own cock. Sven, on the left, let out his bray of a laugh and moved in closer on that side.

It was not unusual for Kevin to put an arm around one of the pair. He was always the one to embrace them after a goal, slap them on the shoulder or chest, or affectionately squeeze the back of their necks with his big hand. So Paul wasn't uncomfortable with that arm across his shoulders and mustered the courage to grab his own cock and begin stroking it.

Three randy young jocks with boners, it didn't take more than a moment for them to get into it. Sven had no inhibition at all, pumping and groaning and thrusting his hips toward the two other cocks nearby. Paul's round mouth opened and his gorgeous eyes got even bigger as he tore his gaze from Sven's towering pole to Kevin's thick pipe. His hand flew up and down his soapy shank, the foreskin peeled entirely back to reveal the purple knob at the end.

Kevin moved around, his arm still draped over Paul's shoulders, and aimed his cock at the other two. With each upward stroke, he thrust it a little closer. He knew what he was doing, already thinking ahead to where this jerk-off session might lead.

"Hell yeah! Fuck! Jerk it, dudes! I'm so fucking horny! Here it comes!"

Naturally Sven couldn't keep his mouth shut no matter what the situation. His gasped-out announcement came just as Kevin managed to thrust his cock-head against the tip of Paul's and within an inch of Sven's. That slippery bump was enough for Paul. He shot at the same time as Sven.

The tall Swede was a squirter. His cum flew upward in an arc of spurts to spatter his line mates. Paul's cum bubbled out in a sticky flood, smearing Kevin's cock-head as the short hockey player thrust against it while moaning deep in his throat.

Kevin felt all that cum hit his chest and stomach and flood over his own cock. The sight of his buddies gasping, moaning, and shaking all over as they unloaded was so incredible, he joined them in a laughing eruption of his own. He shot all over Paul's gooey cock, adding his cum to the mess.

"Fuck, that was hot! Can we do it again after practice tomorrow?"

Sven seemed totally at ease with the aftermath, three oozing cocks and three flushed jocks. He grinned broadly as he asked Kevin for permission to repeat the jerk-off session. Kevin chuckled as he pulled his arm off Paul's shoulder and slapped him playfully on a cheek of his husky butt. "Sure. Something to look forward to. How about it, Paul?"

Paul offered a sheepish grin while nodding enthusiastically. It was no surprise that he didn't say a word.

Both Sven and Paul were more passionate than ever at practice the next day. They passed the puck back and forth like they were two halves of a whole, playing as if they could read each other's minds.

The big blond whooped it up, skating up to Paul and playfully checking him, while Paul offered his shy grin and stared up into the taller blond's pale orbs with a sparkling intensity. It was obvious they shared something, a secret in this instance. Some of the other players even commented on it.

Kevin had sensed their fun and games could lead to something bigger. Now he knew it was true. He formulated a plan right then and there. After practice when he led them into one of the empty locker rooms to change, the other two were raring to go.

Sven tore off his gear, grinning like a kid in a candy store. "Can't wait to jerk off again with you dudes. Let's get naked and get nasty!"

His massive cock was thrusting out in front of him as he raced to the showers. Paul, so much shorter, jogged after him, his fat cock bobbing between his beefy thighs. His big round ass jiggled as he ran and Kevin's cock jerked and leaked as he followed.

Under the shower spray, Sven cavorted and sang, teasing Paul by waving his huge boner at him and playfully slapping it. Both Paul and Kevin had to laugh at his idiotic display, although Kevin knew it was only one side of the giant jock. When they lost a game, he took it badly and had to be cheered up by the more levelheaded guys like him, or his mood would infect the quiet players like Paul.

Now, with the prospect of more fun in the shower, the tall blond was raring to go. Soaking wet, his shoulder-length hair plastered back over his high forehead, he lathered up and moved in on Paul showering beside him.

"Time to stroke, dudes! Let's see who can hold out the longest this time!"

Kevin joined them with his cock as stiff and soaped up as the others. He launched right into his new plan, to the startled cries of his line mates. Instead of stroking his own cock, he reached out and grabbed hold of both of theirs.

"*Oui*...fuck...*merde*...yes," Paul blurted out as his bright blue eyes nearly popped out of his head.

"Hell yeah! That feels so fucking good, Kev," Sven agreed, then immediately reached out to take hold of Kevin's soapy cock.

Of course Sven would follow where Kevin led, being the least inhibited of the three. The plan was working out so far! Even Paul joined in by reaching out to seize his buddies' boners.

The three of them worked furiously at pumping a load out of each other. Sven's earlier challenge had them groaning and squirming to see who could jerk the other off and make them come first.

The trio formed a sexy huddle as they humped each other's fists, the tall blond Sven, the stocky dark-haired Paul, and the lean copper-headed Kevin. Sven and Kevin were very smooth while Paul was furry, and all of them had muscular, sport-honed bodies.

They worked themselves into a frenzy, Sven's enthusiasm infectious as he used his massive hand to yank and rub his line mates' cocks as fast as he could. Paul squirmed between them, his own hands squeezing and jerking just as eagerly.

Kevin knew what they felt because he felt it too. Holding his buddies' hot and throbbing rods in his hands was much better than holding his own. The very idea of how turned on his teammates were turned him on even more.

He'd cranked it up a notch, and successfully, but seeing the looks of intense pleasure on his line mates' faces, he knew the time was ripe for a little more. Instead of jerking off the other two, he reached around them and placed one hand on each of their asses. Big, solid hockey-player butts, one smooth as velvet and the other lightly furred, the round cheeks tensed and jiggled under his palms. He pulled them even closer by his grip on their butts as they continued to jerk each other off.

"Hell yeah! Uhhnnnnn! Squeeze our asses! That feels so fucking hot," Sven grunted out.

Kevin did. He squeezed and massaged each of their big butts while the pair jerked each other and him off. And Paul, although he didn't voice his pleasure, seemed to be enjoying the butt-massage the most. He wriggled into Kevin's hand and whipped his hand up and down Kevin's cock, his pursed lips wet with drool and his blue eyes intent on Kevin's.

The copper-haired center not only squeezed and massaged their hefty asses, he pulled the cheeks open and dared to peek over their shoulders, or around Sven's in the taller jock's case, and get a look at their cracks. He spotted Sven's pink pucker deep down in the pale butt-valley, and Paul's crinkled slot buried between the jock's massive and furry mounds. That view had him on the verge of blowing, but it was Sven who once again precipitated the end of their jerk-off battle.

He reared up on his toes, his pale ass tensing under Kevin's fingers and his gigantic hard-on stiffening into a rigid pink bat, then he squirted. Spurts of jizz arced up to spatter the shorter Paul's face, which had him bug-eyed and pulling back. Still, he was unable to help himself, and followed Sven's lead by shooting a gooey wad of his own.

"Sorry, Paul! Got some cum on your mouth! Lick it off, dude, why don't you?" Sven teased as he continued to shoot more gobs.

Paul shook his head and crinkled his nose, but otherwise ignored Sven's nasty jibe as he too kept on spewing.

Each of the pair had a hand on Kevin's cock and whipped them up and down in an attempt to get him to shoot too. It worked. The feel of their clenching butt-cheeks under his hands and the ripe smell of their cum did it for him. He let out a big groan and blew.

They closed in together in a huddle under the shower spray, their cocks touching, their arms around each other's waists and their mouths almost close enough to kiss, although that wasn't going to happen—at least not yet. Kevin was tempted to lean in and lick Sven's cum off Paul's chin and pert nose, but knew the stocky jock wasn't quite ready for that.

Then disaster.

They lost the next game. Sven actually scored with an assist from Paul, but that's all their team could do against the hot goalie on the other team. They were down to do-or-die, facing elimination in the next game if they didn't win.

Sven plopped down on the bench in the locker room and unlaced his skates so slowly it was as if he was mired in molasses. Paul was undressed and heading to the showers while Sven was still at it.

"Are you coming?" he asked hesitantly, his cock already growing into a fat tube.

"In a minute," he answered, his hang-dog expression almost laughable.

Kevin offered Paul a smile and a wink as they showered together and waited for Sven to join them. The dark-haired Quebecois looked worried, although his hard-on remained stiff and ready.

Sven came shambling in, his dick hanging limp and his pale eyes downcast. As soon as he stepped under the shower between the other two, Kevin made his move. He'd planned on upping the ante anyway, and it seemed now was the time for a gamble.

"I think I know what will cheer you up, buddy."

Before Sven could reach for the soap, Kevin dropped to his knees in front of the tall blond and leaned forward to swallow up his dangling dick.

"Oh fuck! Hell yeah, Kev! Suck it, dude!"

Sven's lengthy cock reared up in Kevin's mouth like a rocket about to blast off. Kevin grinned around the stiffening pole while using his tongue and lips to wash the head with wet spit. The lanky blond could hardly contain himself, groaning and thrusting as he reached down with one hand to grasp the top of Kevin's head and out with the other to seize Paul's beefy arm and pull him in close.

"Try it, you'll love it, dude!" he dared Paul.

His bright grin was a testament to his rapid mood change and Paul was immediately responsive, although he didn't know if Sven meant for him to try sucking his cock, or try getting his cock sucked.

Kevin didn't leave things to chance. He latched onto Paul's rearing boner and pulled him closer by it, then pulled off Sven's cock to dive down over the Quebecois's. Paul babbled something in French and immediately began to ram in and out of his kneeling line mate's wet mouth.

Kevin switched between the two stiff cocks, the long pink one and the fat purple one. His two line mates humped his mouth while emitting either grunts or nasty words of encouragement.

One thing the kneeling center didn't let them in on—this wasn't his first time sucking dick. He'd sucked a few before, discreetly, and done even more than that with other willing dudes. But that was his own little secret. For now, he spat, sucked, and gurgled like it was all new to him.

He grabbed hold of their asses like he'd done the last time and squeezed. They seemed to like that and humped his face with even more enthusiasm. He shouldn't have been surprised, though, when the tall Swede made a startling move.

"Looks like a hell of a lot of fun, Kev. I want some of that," he blurted out, then dropped to his knees in front of Paul beside Kevin and dove over the stocky forward's fat pole.

Kevin almost laughed, it was so ludicrous to see the giant hockey player down on his knees with the shorter jock's thick knob between his slurping lips. He smacked his pink lips and bobbed up and down while looking up with his pale eyes to stare into Paul's surprised bright blue ones.

The center continued squeezing Paul's beefy ass as Sven sucked, then reached out and took hold of Sven's hand to place it on Paul's other butt-cheek. The Swede took the hint. He began to work over that hefty cheek with his palm and fingers as he sucked and licked the forward's fat cock.

The two of them took turns sucking on Paul's cock, sometimes both licking it at the same time while they played with his big butt. Kevin even slipped his fingers into the crack and dared to stroke his puckered hole, but didn't test him by poking into it, although he really wanted to.

Sven grabbed Kevin's cock with his free hand and the center followed suit. Now they jerked each other off while they sucked Paul and played with his round ass.

Slobbering over the beefy forward's thick cock, it was inevitable that sooner or later their mouths would meet. It was Sven who kissed Kevin over Paul's gooey cock-head. Open mouthed and slobbering, he pressed his lips against his line mate's and offered a really sloppy kiss before diving back over Paul's flared knob.

It was that kiss that did it for all three of them. Paul couldn't hold back any longer, his cock wet and jerking, his ass warm from all that massaging, and his hole twitching from the tantalizing fingertips running across it. He emitted an explosive grunt and shot.

His cream came out in a gooey flood. Staring into Sven's eyes, Kevin sucked it up and swallowed it. Sven's pale blue orbs widened and he groaned and bit his lip as he shot too. Kevin's hand on his cock flew up and down, which seemed to increase the arc and distance of his blow. His nut cream flew high up between Paul's spread thighs to spatter his ass-crack in a gooey splat.

The taste of Paul's cum and the feel of his cock pulsing between his lips was so hot Kevin also shot. He flooded Sven's hand with his spunk.

Sven's bad mood had been successfully allayed. The trio enjoyed a laughing shower together amidst promises that they'd win the next one.

That next game was a brutal contest. But when they were up against the wall, the team rose to the challenge. By one goal in overtime, they staved off elimination. The team retired to their locker room to celebrate while Kevin and his line mates slipped away to their own room and their own celebration. Of course no one questioned this practice, as virtually all hockey players had their little quirks during play-offs which they followed religiously to ensure good luck.

This time, Paul was so cheerful about their win, he took Sven's smirking dare and dropped to his knees in the shower room to suck off both Sven and Kevin, and with surprising enthusiasm.

"Hell yeah, Paulie! Wrap those sweet lips around our dicks! Give us some throat!"

Once Sven got started there was no way to hold him back, and poor Paul gurgled and choked as that lengthy pink pole searched out his tonsils. But the kneeling hockey star was not one to shirk from a challenge, especially if it came from his fellow forward. The two did have a friendly rivalry going, and even now in the showers, it showed.

Kevin got down on his knees to help him out and this time it was Paul and Kevin who sucked off the tall Swede and played with his high, round white butt. He continued with his nasty spiel, daring them to suck deeper and urging them to kiss each other over his lunging cock.

Paul's big eyes looked into Kevin, tentative but hopeful, and the center understood. Paul wanted to kiss him but was too shy to do it. Even though he already had a mouthful of cock, kissing seemed just a little bit more intimate.

Kevin placed a hand behind his neck and pulled Paul's face against his own. Their lips touched, wet with spit already. Kevin opened up and slowly teased the jock's lips with the tip of his tongue. Paul groaned and opened up. They kissed passionately while Sven humped their cheeks and laughed above them.

The tall Swede was so turned on by the sight of his two line mates kissing, he shot. His cum flew so high it missed them entirely and splattered the shower wall behind them. The other two continued kissing while they jerked each other off, and it was only moments later they blew a load too.

Out of the showers and starting to dress, Kevin decided it was time to go for it all.

"This is a lot of fun, but it's time for one of us to bottom. Any takers?"

"What do you mean, Kev? One of has to take a dick up the butt? Not me! It should be Paul."

"*Moi?* Hell *non*, it's your big ass that looks like it needs a cock up it," Paul blurted out, his longest sentence of the season.

"Hey, let's not argue. I've got an idea. How about we make it a contest? Whichever of the three of us gets the most points in the next game gets to decide who's on the bottom. Okay?"

Sven agreed right away. "That's fair. Sure, what the hell."

Paul, still a little riled at Sven's automatic assumption that he should bottom, was slower to agree, but when Kevin put his arm around him and cheerfully reminded him that he was the top scorer of the three already, he brightened up and took the challenge with a smirking glare at the Swede, who only laughed it off.

The series was tied and this final game would decide which team moved on to the next round. Neither team was willing to surrender without a fight. But it was Kevin's line that made the difference in the end.

The screaming of the fans, the cursing of their rivals, the grinding, bumping, slamming, and racing across the ice was frenzied and relentless. Thirty seconds before the end of the third period, Kevin scored and they had won. They were on to the next round.

Because he'd scored the winning goal, Kevin had to speak to the media flooding the ice before he could escape to the locker room. He found Sven and Paul waiting for him, excited but tense and not yet changed out of their sweat-soaked gear.

Sven spoke up at once. "So, Mr. Big Shot, you scored the most. So who's it gonna be? On the bottom? Who's getting a dick up the ass?"

Kevin grinned at them, enjoying the moment as the pair looked up at him and practically begged him with their eyes. He knew it wasn't really so much about not wanting to get fucked as not wanting to be the loser. He had already thought of what he would do if he scored the most, and who he'd choose.

"Knock yourselves out, boys! My butt is yours, if you know what to do with it!"

Both their mouths dropped open, but only for a moment as Sven whooped it up and began to tear off his gear. Paul giggled nervously as he followed his line mate's lead. Kevin took his time, reveling in their excited mood and certain he'd made the correct decision.

In fact, the two forwards were so greedy to fuck, they couldn't even wait to get into the showers, and as soon as they removed the last of their gear, their sweat-soaked jocks and cups, they swooped in on the lean center.

Sven wrestled the laughing jock down onto the bench in the center of the change area. Face-down, his own sweaty jock still on, his two line mates went for his rearing white butt. The solid mounds were smooth and pale, outlined by the straps of his olive green jock, and wide open with his muscular thighs straddling the bench.

"Hell yeah! What a sweet butt. Look at that hole, Paulie! Who gets to fuck it first?"

Of course Sven had to make it a contest between the pair. Kevin intervened with a challenge of his own. "Whoever licks it first gets to fuck it first!"

"Fuck yeah! I know you want to get in there and eat some sweaty jock asshole, Paulie, but you probably don't know how to do a good job of it. Let me show you!"

It was proof of how far they'd come. From merely jerking off in front of each other in the shower, they'd grown so keen on their fun and games, nothing seemed too nasty for them. Sven, with a big grin on his face, dove for Kevin's crack.

Paul held the round cheeks wide open with both his hands, his fat cock rearing up between his thighs as he knelt by Kevin's head and watched with wide eyes. Sven did not disappoint, sticking out his huge tongue and swiping it across the sweaty valley while giggling between licks.

Kevin gasped and wriggled his ass up into that raspy tongue. His asshole quivered and pouted as tongue ran over it, and he thought of the upcoming fuck with cautious excitement. The Swede's cock was about a foot long, and Paul's was thick as a beer can. Fortunately he'd brought lube!

Sven got into licking ass with a vengeance. Not only was he enjoying the taste of sweaty butt-crack, he was also putting on a show for his rival. Paul would have to work hard if he was to outdo the blond in nastiness! He licked with his tongue up and down the entire crevice, right down to the strap and cup that held Kevin's cock and balls, then up to the strap that ran across his tight waist. He settled on the snug hole and stabbed at it as Paul held the round cheeks wide apart for him.

Then he fingered it. Kevin reared up and grunted as the first finger-tip prodded his tender ass-lips, then wriggled his round butt wildly as Paul added a finger of his own to the spit-gobbed probe.

Sven licked and spat on that pink hole as both he and Paul vied to see who could shove a finger deeper into it. The initial pain was irrelevant as a heated ache took over and the pair of fingers began to drive in and out and stretch both his sphincter and the tunnel just beyond.

With two fingers probing his gut, and Sven's lips and tongue teasing his crack, Kevin knew the inevitable wasn't too far off. "Get some lube out of my bag and shove your cock up my ass, Sven!"

The Swede still had his face buried in the center's spread crack, his long blond hair splashing across the ivory cheeks as he and Paul dug around in the tight pink butt-slot. At first it seemed like he hadn't heard. He was obviously enjoying the ass feast!

Paul tapped him on the shoulder as he admitted to his own desires with a nervous giggle. "Go on, Sven. My turn to lick ass."

That had the tall blond rearing up out of Kevin's butt and chortling. "You go ahead, Paulie! Lick that butt while I get us some lube so we can fuck it."

Paul moved in as Sven stood up and went for their line mate's hockey bag. While he rummaged in it for the lube, Paul straddled the bench behind Kevin, grabbed his rearing butt-cheeks, and dove for hole.

His enthusiastic slurps matched Kevin's loud moans and compelled their blond line mate to rush back to the pair with his giant hard-on swinging between his long legs. He stepped over the bench right behind Paul and groaned with excitement as he stared down at the hot sight of his buddies at play.

Kevin was face-down with his firm ass spread over the bench, his olive green jock outlining the smooth cheeks. Paul was on his belly too, his short dark hair stark against his line mate's ivory butt-cheeks as he worked his tongue up and down the deep valley between them. His own big ass was spread over the bench as he leaned over and ate jock butt.

Sven squirted clear lube all over his cock, then half squatted so he could plant his giant meat in the crack between Paul's husky butt cheeks. He rubbed the slippery fuck-shank in that crack and grinned as Paul's body jerked and he grunted loudly around the hole he sucked on.

"Fuck, this big sweet ass of yours is so tempting! I should fuck it while you eat out Kev, Paulie. But a deal's a deal. Maybe next time

I'll get my chance if I score the most! Now get out of the way so I can shove my big cock up Kev's butthole!"

Paul rose out of Kevin's ass crack with a smack of his lips, face flushed bright red and big-eyed. He didn't comment on Sven's remark about fucking his ass, but did rub his ass back against the slippery shaft briefly before rising to get out of the blond's way.

"Come around here, Paul. Sit in front of me," Kevin said. He wanted something to take his mind off his trepidation about the inevitable gut-plowing Sven had planned for him, and Paul's fat cock was just the thing.

Paul obeyed, straddling the bench in front of Kevin and bending over to hold the center's ass cheeks open for his line mate. Of course his plump boner reared in Kevin's face, and the center quickly seized the opportunity to bury his face in the Quebecois's lap and slurp it up.

"Hell yeah! Suck that fat cock while I work on your ass, Kev! I better finger it first, though, so it's stretched out before I try to ram this giant thing up there!"

And he was true to his word as Kevin felt a pair of slippery fingers settle on his pink hole and begin to probe. He reared up toward the fingers and wriggled his ass around them, knowing that would help ease them in. His sphincter was tight, and the best way to loosen it enough to take Sven's big poker was to do exactly as the blond planned.

He wriggled and heaved while Sven kept those two lubed fingers right on target, laughing as he pushed and twisted. Their combined efforts worked. Both fingers sank knuckle-deep. Kevin gurgled around Paul's thick shaft as his entire body jerked. Sven laughed louder and couldn't resist ramming deeper with his fingers.

"Fuck! So fucking tight! My cock is gonna get the vise treatment! Feel it, Paulie, it's hot and steamy and pulsing!"

Paul was just as eager as Sven to get into the center's lubed hole. He slid a hand into the smooth crack and aimed his fingers at the pink slot. Sven slipped his out and Paul shoved his in. Kevin grunted deep in his chest, but already could feel how much easier those fingers slid into him than Sven's had a few minutes earlier.

The two took turns fingering Kevin's hole, digging deep and twisting, pulling out with a slurp, then shoving right back in. The prostrate hockey star wriggled around those burrowing fingers while sucking cock and driving his own jock-covered dick into the bench beneath him.

Sven was laughing and muttering nonstop, but gave no indication he was ready to replace fingers with cock until he actually did. Kevin felt a pair of fingers yank out of his hole, then something blunt and thick slide in. The blunt heat kept on coming, deeper than those fingers and thicker too. Steadily and thoroughly, cock sank into him.

"To the balls! Hell yeah! I love it, Kev!"

He felt the full weight of his line mate's big body over him as Sven buried his cock completely. The throbbing pole inside him was almost more than he bargained for. But Sven relented and began to withdraw, easing the gut-churning pressure as he pulled all the way out.

Just as Kevin felt the emptiness of that withdrawal, fingers dug into him, both Sven's and Paul's, and he reared toward them, feeling wide open now and ready for more.

"Fuck yeah! Your hole's real sloppy now, Kev. Here comes more cock!"

With fair warning this time, Kevin pushed upward and outward with his stretched sphincter and managed to swallow the promised cock with relative ease. It drove balls-deep again.

The sweet, throbbing heat was awesome. He found himself loving it. And with a cock in either end, the copper-haired hockey star squirmed back and forth over the bench and took it. Sven dished it out, slamming in and out, grunting and laughing, lube squishing and sweat dripping.

Paul held open Kevin's ass for his line mate, and also slid his fingers into the crack to feel the piston-drill of cock in hole as he squirmed around the center's slobbering mouth in his lap. All three were getting a thrill ride, but Kevin felt like he was getting the best deal. It seemed that his sacrifice was no sacrifice at all!

The Swede pummeled Kevin's ass, his lengthy pink pole driving in and out at a faster and faster pace. He was usually the first to blow, but this time he didn't seem willing to give up that sweet ass any time soon.

It was Kevin who couldn't hold back. His cock, trapped in his cup and being mercilessly mashed against the bench by Sven's savage pounding and his own wild wriggling, swelled up to the bursting point. The rub and thrust of cock up his ass and against his tender ass-lips and aching prostate pushed him beyond his limit.

"Damn! I'm coming...with a cock up the ass," he blurted out around the head of Paul's fat cock.

"Shoot it, Kev! Shoot your wad with my big fucking cock pounding your sweet fucking ass!"

His load filled his cup while his body thrashed all over the bench and he buried his face in Paul's lap, snorting in the ripe sweet stench of his sweaty balls. All that squirming, and the convulsing of his asshole as he blew his nut, had Sven's cock trapped in a prison of palpitating ass-lips. He surrendered to his own orgasm.

"Hell! I'm blowing too!"

He pulled out just in time to squirt. His pink cock, rigid and jerking, erupted a spew that flew all the way to Paul's powerful torso. It spattered his furry chest and dribbled down his rippled abs.

The stocky Quebecois thrust up into Kevin's wet mouth and blew. As cum splattered his chest and dripped down over Kevin's copper hair, he blasted a load deep in the center's throat.

The trio were totally played out after that wild fuck and the brutal game beforehand. They barely managed to limp into the showers and wash up. While they showered together, Kevin laid out their strategy for the rest of the play-offs.

"Whoever has the most points at the end of each game will decide who bottoms afterward. No arguing. Agreed?"

Sven was all smiles as he nodded his assent while Paul offered his sheepish grin and agreed with a single *oui*.

And for the remainder of the play-off run they followed that plan faithfully. Even this went according to Kevin's earlier design. The other two followed his lead, and when they scored the highest, both Paul and Sven gave up their own sweet asses instead of ordering one of their buddies to perform the duty.

Teamwork, sacrifice, and putting their teammates ahead of themselves, wasn't that what sports was all about? Kevin thought so, and it seemed he'd been proven right. They won the championship that year.

JOHNNY LAREDO
AARON TRAVIS

This is the true story of how I met Johnny Laredo.

If his name sounds familiar, that's because Johnny was once a star, sort of. Not anymore. Johnny hasn't been on television for three or four years now, long enough for a lot of his old fans to have forgotten him. Oh, occasionally we'll run into somebody at the supermarket or on the street who recognizes him and asks for an autograph. But not often.

Which doesn't mean that Johnny doesn't get looked at just about every time we step out of the house. People look. People stare. I can't say I blame them. They can look all they want. But Johnny is mine.

And thereby hangs a tale.

This all happened a few years ago, right here in Fort Worth, Texas. It was the middle of the summer and hot as hell. I remember, because that was the summer that something called the Polynesian flu hit town. I was the first to get it, probably from some cracker coming in the clinic to have his bitch spayed.

That Saturday night when I first laid eyes on Johnny, I was at home lying in bed, completely miserable, blowing my nose and flipping channels by remote control. There wasn't a damn thing on worth watching—an old Ronald Reagan movie, sitcom reruns, the local news, a werewolf flick on the Spanish station, and of course that goddam 24-hour Christian network. Typical Saturday night TV in Cowtown.

I kept my finger on the button and watched the channels flip by.

"If you really loved me, Billy, you'd—"

"We're asking Mrs. White about the new, improved—"

"Win one for the gip—"

"Tornadoes are expected along the—"

"Flames of hell, consuming all the hummasexials, adultras, fawnicaytas!"

And then I flipped the channel one more time, and saw something that made my fever-weak eyes snap wide open.

I hadn't seen professional wrestling on TV since I was a kid. Even then, I'd seen it in only glimpses because in our house it wasn't allowed. My mother looked down on it; wrestling shows were for people who didn't know any better. And even as a kid I could see through the staged falls and rigged matches. Heroes and villains, cosmic Good and Evil shrunk down to a hard, lifeless core that the truck drivers and housewives could turn on to. When I was a kid the theme was still World War II, the Big One, being played out every Saturday night. The heavies were Nazi types in black leather with crazy German names, or pumpkin-shaped "Sumo" wrestlers. The heroes were hardcore American working types, big homely guys just a little past their prime with broad shoulders and broader waistlines, heroes the ranchers and fry cooks in the crowd would identify with.

The heroes usually won, and the audience, self-styled martyrs to a world of racial busing, welfare chiselers, militant fags and women's libbers, could taste that sweet unstained victory of Good over Evil. Occasionally it was arranged for the villains to win, so the crowd could feel the rush of righteous indignation. Anyone with sense enough to get out of the rain could see through it. When I was older I got involved in high school wrestling, the real thing, and kept it up through college; my opinion of pro wrestling went from *joke* to *bad joke*.

But that feverish August night I discovered that TV wrestling had grown up, at least a little, and in a wonderful way.

There on the screen, talking and looking me straight in the eye, was one of the most gorgeous young men I had ever seen. Age: twenty-two, maximum. Hair as black as ink, wavy and short. Bright blue eyes, smooth pale skin, red lips, square jaw. He looked like he had never shaved; his forehead and cheeks blushed warm pink.

He was practically naked, dressed in shiny blue trunks, high white socks, and sneakers. He was lightly tanned, hairless, perfectly proportioned—an absolutely flawless physique. There wasn't a hint of coarseness; he didn't have weightlifter's body, and certainly not a typical pro wrestler's. He was sculptured and lean, like a gymnast.

I put down the remote control and willed the TV camera to stay right where it was.

He stood with his hands on his hips, leaning down to a microphone held up by a short, pudgy announcer who was practically a midget. His lines were the standard claptrap ("Yeah, well, we'll just see how much of a man Killer Klaus Kurtz *really* is when I get him alone in the ring next week!"), but he didn't sound at all stupid. His voice was deep and soft.

My heart was melting. And draining molten into my cock, where it rehardened like cooling steel.

The camera panned away from the young wrestler to a close-up of the announcer, who pointed his finger at the screen and barked like a used car salesman. I growled at the TV. Then I heard the announcer: "And we'll be right back to see Johnny Laredo take on Big Donovan, right after these messages!"

I sat up in bed, fisting my erection slowly, while on the screen a skinny housewife in a cheap wig and a sleeveless blouse explained how a certain detergent got her husband's T-shirts really, really white.

Finally I was back in the coliseum, and the kid they called Johnny Laredo was jumping over the ropes into the ring. His opponent was a real monster—Big Donovan was a toothless, snarling, drooling bald giant with enough extra lard on his frame to heat a small city through the winter.

But Johnny—oh, Johnny. That face. That body. Talented, too. He played to the camera with the natural instinct of a star, moved with the fluid grace of a young gymnast, showed off every perfect muscle as he danced around the ring. And when he fell, he fell hard, sprawling against the ropes and grunting while Big Donovan pounded away, making his pretty face into a mask of pain, wrenching in agony, suffering like a martyr for the screeching audience. Suffering for me at home with my greasy fist around my dick.

When he scrambled up, flexed his arms and leaped, he was like moving sculpture. The camera caught him in a hundred shifting poses, each one more breathtaking than the last. Bent double with his ass reared up. Pinned on his back with his long, sleek legs in the air. Down on his knees with his arms twisted behind his back and his massive shoulders straining. Finally, straddling Big Donovan and holding him down, his torso gleaming with sweat, a blush of triumph on his angelic face.

It was over too soon. My final glimpse of him was his victory strut around the ring, his muscular arms held aloft and a beaming smile on his face while the crowd went crazy with excitement.

The housewives and truck drivers weren't the only ones excited. I had been slowly masturbating the whole time, my eyes glued to the screen. There was another commercial and I held off, thinking there might be more of Johnny. But when the show returned he was gone, and the next match was between a couple of female midgets. I switched it off.

My hard-on told me I was more recovered from the flu than I'd thought. I laid back in the darkness and made myself feel good, thinking about the amazing revelation of Johnny Laredo.

❖

From then on, I always had something to watch on TV before I went out on Saturday nights. And the more I watched, the more I started seeing how carefully choreographed Johnny's movements were. It wasn't just me and my dirty mind, I was sure. I wasn't just imagining it.

It was the poses—Johnny on his back with a look of agony on his face and his legs wrapped around his opponent, who huffed and puffed and bounced his gut against Johnny's rock-hard buns. Or Johnny on top, with the thug's head trapped between his iron thighs, while the announcer's gloated over Johnny's physique—"Isn't he an amazing young athlete, ladies and gentlemen? Just look at those muscles!"

What was all this but shifting images of man-to-man sex, sucking and fucking, with some sadistic violence and submission thrown in? How could even the dullest audience miss it? Or maybe they weren't missing it. Maybe they were taking it all at face value on the surface, but secretly, subconsciously feeding off the thrill of seeing Johnny nearly naked and posed for sex.

I had the hots for Johnny Laredo.

One Saturday night they announced a special offer of free eight-by-ten color glossy photos of Johnny to the first fifty people at the coliseum door. No way was I going to go down and fight the crowds. But I had to have one of those pictures.

How to get one? I racked my brain for five minutes, then came up with one of those crazy ideas that you'd never believe could change your life. It almost seemed like a joke at the time. I wrote Johnny a fan letter. I made it special.

I found a ruled pad of paper and a number two pencil, then grabbed the pencil like an icepick and scrawled out a letter:

> *Dear Johnny Laredo,*
>
> *Hi my name is Tom. I am seven years old. I am your BIGGEST fan. Could I have a pitcher of you? I would like a pitcher of you IN ACTION. Thanks you a hole lot. My daddy heped me to rite this letter.*

Yeah, I thought, a picture of you in action. Like down on your hands and knees naked with your cute little ass in the air and your hard cock up against your belly. Or maybe on your knees with your mouth wide open…

But I was willing to settle for a simple shot of Johnny in his tight blue shorts.

I read the letter over and had a good laugh. I mailed it to Johnny Laredo in care of the coliseum and forgot all about it.

❖

The next Saturday afternoon I was busy with a friend in the bedroom when the doorbell rang downstairs.

The friend was Gary. Back then he was one of my steady tricks, a college freshman who still lived with his folks down the block. Blond, blue-eyed, and slender, and hot as a pistol. One of those proud little whoreboys, the type who think about nothing but sex. Gary came out early. I met him when he was just out of high school and barely eighteen. He pecked through the screen door of my back porch one afternoon and asked if I wanted to subscribe to a magazine. I invited him into the kitchen and the next thing I knew he was cupping my crotch and asking if I'd like a blow job. The way he swallowed me in one gulp, I could tell he'd had a lot of experience.

I'd been seeing Gary at least one weekend afternoon a month. It was a trip, watching him fill out and mature into a young man.

Watching his appetites grow. Feeding those appetites. I was the first to fuck his ass, and the first to spank it. After that he was always after me to get rougher and meaner with him; it's something a lot of guys seem to expect from me. Can I help it if I happen to have a ten-inch dick, shoulders as wide as a barn door, and a face so ugly it's cute?

That Saturday afternoon, upstairs in the bedroom, I had Gary stripped naked and kneeling with his back to the wall, right under the window that faces the street. I stood at the window with my hands pressed flat on the sill. The old man across the way was mowing his lawn. Kids on bicycles were doing wheelies in the street. I smelled the grass and felt the streaming sunlight on my naked chest while I gently rocked my hips and listened to the soft thump of Gary's head banging against the wall and the low, gurgling sound of Gary choking on my cock down his throat.

Every now and then Gary made a little whimper while he gagged. Maybe it was from the pleasure he was giving himself with both greasy fists around his short, stubby cock. Maybe it was from the sting of the tit clamps I'd put on his pert little nipples, linked together by a chain I could reach down to tug on whenever I wanted to feel him swallow me extra-deep.

Gary was working hard to get me off, loosening up his throat like a whore's cunt, but I was teasing him, giving him a hard ride, fucking his face with long, relentless thrusts. He kept choking and spewing saliva all over my balls and my thighs. Whenever he seemed to adjust I'd reach down and tug on his clamped nipples, listen to him whimper and fuck his throat a little harder.

Every now and then his long blond lashes would flicker open and he'd gaze up at me with glazed blue eyes. Then he'd shut them tight and suck harder, hollowing his cheeks, sliding his sweet red lips down to the thick root of my cock. His blond hair was dark with sweat, plastered across his forehead. His whole face was slick with spit.

I threw my head back and shut my eyes, savoring the sweet ecstasy of having ten inches of sensitive meat buried down an eager-to-please teenage throat. I was close to coming, ready to pull out, when I heard the sound of a car pulling up and coming to a stop on the street just below. I looked down and saw a long purple limousine parked in front of my house. The windows were shaded, so I couldn't see any faces. I suddenly felt self-conscious, standing there on the verge of shooting a load all over Gary's twitching, cock-hungry face.

Then the limo doors started opening. I automatically stepped back from the window. Gary thought I was teasing him. My cock slipped out of his throat and popped from between his lips. He made a low whimper and fell forward onto his hands and knees to crawl after it. A second later the doorbell rang. I stepped back toward the window to see if I could get a glimpse of whoever was on my doorstep. My cock speared between Gary's wide-open lips and went all the way down his throat. He wasn't expecting it—he sprayed a throatful of mucus all over my crotch and sounded like he was drowning. Then I heard him gurgle contentedly and felt his throat muscles begin to ripple exquisitely up and down my shaft.

I couldn't see the front doorstep very well from the window. But I could see well enough to catch a glimpse of something that made me yank myself out of Gary's throat and start searching the room for something to wear. The doorbell rang again. I stepped into a pair of old, faded jeans and headed for the stairs. My hard-on kept popping the buttons open.

"Tom?" It was Gary behind me, sounding forlorn. "Tom, don't be long, huh?"

I turned around and grinned at him. He was hunkered down beneath the window, pulling his hard cock out from his crotch and letting it go, so it kept slapping his hard belly. His lean, hairless body was slick with sweat, his chin was glossy with spit, his jaw was hanging slack. His face had the glazed look of a cocksucker who's been gorging himself for hours and still hasn't had enough dick.

My dick throbbed and two buttons popped open on my 501s. "You come while I'm gone," I growled, "and I'll spank your ass." Gary moaned and looked like he might faint. He squeezed his aching red cock with one hand and reached up with the other to pull on his clamped nipples.

The doorbell rang again. I bounded down the stairs, through the hall, and across the living room. Just as the bell rang again I pulled the door wide open.

There were five of them in all, a little delegation gathered on my doorstep. Four of them were dressed in polyester double-knit suits and ties. The fifth was Johnny Laredo, wearing snakeskin boots, skintight jeans, a white felt cowboy hat, and a sky-blue T-shirt that hugged his big, meaty pecs like a second skin.

Johnny Laredo, in the flesh. Standing on my doorstep. My heart was pounding in my ears, and not just from rushing down the stairs. My cock was pounding in my jeans, and not just from Gary's interrupted blow job.

One of the men started talking, smiling the whole time. He was in his fifties and wore a bad hairpiece, had two solid gold teeth and a whiny East Texas Bayou twang. "Howdy, suh, good aftahnoon. Is little Tommy heah? We got a big s'prise for the little feller."

"A surprise?" I said. I tried hard to look at the guy, but my eyes kept straying to the hard plates of muscles inside that sky-blue T-shirt. I could see Johnny's nipples through the thin cloth. While I watched, they seemed to crinkle and stiffen before my eyes. I glanced up at his face and could have sworn he blushed before he lowered his eyes. His face was almost too beautiful to look at.

The bossman gave me a big, glittery smile. "Wahl, now, suh, little Tommy-boy sent Johnny heah, the best goddam wrassler in this state, pardon mah French, he sent Johnny a real sweet fan lettah, and we gonna s'prise him with a little sump'n."

"Uh, I'm afraid Tommy's not here right now," I said. "He's gone to his grandma's. Uh, with his mother."

The man frowned. "Ah see. Yes, Ah see. Wahl, where's 'at? Cross town? We wanna give his s'prise to little Tommy in person." I caught him glancing suspiciously at my hands. There was no wedding band there, of course.

"Uh, out of town," I said. "Out of state, actually. Oklahoma. That's where my wife lives now. My ex-wife, that is. She came by and picked up little Tommy and they drove out of town this morning."

"Ah see. Yes, ah do believe I see." The man looked at me shrewdly. For the first time I noticed that one of the men had a camera on a strap around his neck. So that was it—a publicity gimmick, something for the papers: *Wrestling Idol Johnny Laredo Answers Little Boy's Fan Letter in Person!*

"Wahl, Ah'll give you these things innyway, suh. You'll make sure little Tommy gits 'em, won't you?" The man winked and then elbowed one of the others, who handed me a wrapped package. It was eight inches by ten—a framed photo. There was an envelope taped to the wrapping.

"Hold it!" The photographer nosed in to catch the package changing hands.

"Don't be so trigger-happy, Darryl!" the bossman snapped. "Put 'at camera away. We won't be takin' inny pitchers today."

"But, Boss—"

"Hush up!" The man glared at him, then turned back to me with a sickly sweet smile. "Wahl, we'll hafta be goin' now. You say hello to little Tommy for us." He turned and headed for the limo, waving for the others to follow.

"Hey, wait a minute," I said. "Don't I get to shake the hand of little Tommy's idol? I remember helping him to write that fan letter. Why, I'm sort of a fan of Johnny Laredo myself."

They stopped in their tracks. Johnny glanced at the boss, then haltingly stepped toward me and put out his hand. The movement made his biceps swell up and fill the tight sleeve of his T-shirt.

I took his hand in mine. I looked at his face, so close I could have reached up and stroked his smooth cheek. He lowered his eyes, first down to my naked chest and then to the big bulge straining at the buttons of my jeans. He looked up and our eyes met for just an instant. There was something in his eyes that I couldn't quite make out.

"Come on, Johnny!"

He pulled his hand from mine and turned to go.

I watched them pile into the limo, then I closed the door and bounded up the stairway, clutching the package and the envelope. I ran to the bedroom window just in time to see the long purple doors slamming shut. One of the passenger windows rolled down and for just an instant I saw Johnny staring up at the window, looking me straight in the eye. Then the car wheeled around and sped off.

I felt something warm nudge against my crotch. It was Gary, masturbating with both hands and undoing the buttons of my fly one by one with his teeth, poking his tongue between the flaps to lick at my cock and balls. He undid the last button and it tumbled out, slapping him across the cheek. He tried to catch it with his mouth, but I stepped back. I reached down for the chain and pulled him hissing to his feet, then led him by his nipples to the bed. I reached into the dresser drawer for some lube and rubbers. Gary crawled onto the bed, purring and wriggling his ass.

Considerably later, after a long hot shower, Gary got dressed and went limping out the back door, with a grin on his face that wouldn't go away. I was grinning, too, as I unwrapped the photo. The color was garish and the frame was cheap plastic, but it was Johnny. He was posed in a crouch, his shoulders hunched, his face set in a scowl. Even snarling he was beautiful. The inscription read: *To Tom Richardson, my BIGGEST fan, from Johnny Laredo.*

The envelope contained two front-row tickets for next Saturday's match at the coliseum.

❖

Little Tommy couldn't make it, I'm afraid, and neither could his equally-mythical mom, so Big Tom went by himself. I turned in the extra ticket at the box office and found my seat.

The arena was a madhouse. Kids ran up and down the aisles in rolled-up jeans, screaming and howling like animals. Women with cheap permanents and bad makeup sat grim-faced, waiting for the kill. Men with big beer guts hanging over tight jeans burped and told dirty jokes.

I wasn't too out of place, in my freshly shined cowboy boots and my Western belt, hand-tooled with acorns and leaves all around with my name embossed on the back. I hadn't worn it since high school. Thirty-inch waist, and it still fit.

I looked up and down the front row. A gaggle of grade schoolers was off to my left, along with an old woman doing her knitting—she was a regular I recognized from the Saturday night broadcast. On my right there was a group of middle-aged men in overalls, spitting tobacco juice on the floor and acting rowdy.

I looked over my shoulder and saw that the camera crew was stationed just a few rows behind us. Good, I thought—that meant the action would be played to my side of the ring. I squirmed in the hard wooden chair and waited for the lights to dim.

The evening got off to a slow start, for me at least. I couldn't get too excited about Big Donovan taking on Eric Samples, the Hillbilly Hooligan, or pseudo-Sumo wrestler Moso Hirohito rolling his three hundred pounds of excess lard all over gone-to-seed bodybuilder Mickey-Mike Michaels, but the crowd warmed up right away. They were like wild animals, a seething mass of humanity plugged into a weird repressed sex and violence trip. They screamed, they hollered, they rose to their feet and shook their fists like football fans at the Super Bowl. At one point the little old lady got so carried away she tried to crawl over the ropes and attack Moso Hirohito with a knitting needle. Some security guards escorted her kicking and screaming to the exit, with a ball of yarn trailing behind.

Then, finally, came the golden moment. The match we had all been waiting for: Johnny Laredo vs. Killer Klaus Kurtz.

Kurtz entered the arena first, to a raucous chorus of hissing and booing. I suppose at one time he must have had quite a body. His shoulders and arms were certainly massive, but generously marbled with fat; his gut was enormous. He was wearing a leather face mask and a leather harness and wore a German iron cross on a chain around his neck. He strutted around the ring, thumping his chest and bellowing insults in a ridiculously phony German accent.

Then Johnny came springing down the aisle from the dressing rooms. A wave of cheering replaced the catcalls. As he jumped over the ropes, I could almost feel the love that was pouring out from the audience, almost see it, as if it were a palpable thing like wind or light.

Unfortunately, the crowd was doomed to disappointment. Johnny didn't do well that night. I could tell early on that he was scheduled to lose, and he did. He played it magnificently, suffering beautifully and always getting back up to take more punishment from that brute Klaus Kurtz. I couldn't quite bring myself to join in with the screaming hysterics around me, but I can't deny that I felt the rush of sharing Johnny's struggle against evil, and tasted the bitterness of his defeat.

The view from my seat was breathtaking. I was almost close enough to touch Johnny, and at times I could actually smell his sweat as he began to glisten and sparkle under the hot lights. I watched his body as he buckled, flexed, pounced, and shuddered under the impact of Klaus's blows. They met, locked arms, broke apart, circled each other like wary beasts.

The images were like the most intense pornography, seen under glaring lights in 3-D. Johnny on his back, wrists pinned above his head,

his long, lean legs spread open and wrapped around the Killer's waist—
Johnny breaking free to roll forward and flip Kurtz onto his back with
a thud, then scampering on top to trap Kurtz's face between his sweaty
thighs—Klaus struggling free, getting to his feet and flinging Johnny
against the ropes—Johnny, dazed, falling to his knees—Klaus, with a
sneer of triumph, knocking Johnny face-down to the floor—Johnny,
trying to rise, thrusting his ass high into the air, wiggling his butt above
unsteady, wobbly legs, flexing his taut buns inside his skimpy nylon
trunks. Pointing his upraised ass straight back at me.

My palms itched. My mouth watered. My dick went stiff. And
then—

Johnny looked back through his legs, his cheekbone pressed to the
floor, his mouth crooked, like a young man in pain, or skewered on a
cock. His eyes were barely open. His eyes were *on me.*

He saw the lust on my face. He knew what his pose was doing to
me. Our eyes locked. He froze that way, his ass thrust toward me as he
looked back at me, pleading with his eyes.

Suddenly Killer Klaus rammed him from the side and sent him
tumbling. It wasn't planned that way. Johnny looked dazed and Klaus
looked chagrined. They tried to get back into the rhythm of the fight,
but their timing was shot. The match lost momentum, and when Johnny
went down to defeat there was a certain spark missing. The crowd could
tell, even if they couldn't tell why. Their boos at the end were a little
forced and confused.

Johnny left the ring with downturned face and a towel over his
slumping shoulders, looking more defeated than he should have. I
watched him trudge to the dressing rooms. He turned at the door and
scanned the front row until he caught my eye. He bit his lip and then
disappeared.

I thought about leaving then, but it was easier to stay put and savor
the weird high Johnny had given me. The next match started, but the
wrestlers moved before me like ghosts. I barely heard the noise of the
crowd, vague and distant like a roaring ocean.

Suddenly a little boy was standing in front of me.

"For you, mister." He thrust a folded piece of paper under my nose.
As he ran off I caught the glint of a quarter clutch in his little fist.

I unfolded the note.

Meet me afterward? At the north exit.—J.L.

I looked over my shoulder. He was standing at the door to the dressing rooms wearing a blue silk robe, staring at me. I nodded, and he slipped out of sight.

❖

During the last match I went to the parking lot and drove around to the back of the coliseum. Johnny was waiting for me on the steps, sitting with his hands in his pockets. I had expected to see him dressed the way he had been on my doorstep, in boots and jeans, but he was wearing sandals and cut-offs and a red T-shirt. His hair, still damp from his shower, looked jet black.

We exchanged glances as he squeezed into the bucket seat. I drove slowly to the exit, glad to beat the rush.

"Hi," he said.

"Hi."

"Nice car. I like sports cars."

"Thanks. Anywhere in particular you want to go?"

"Well, there's a little bar off the expressway where some of the guys go after the show."

Just what I didn't need, I thought, a bunch of his wrestling pals hovering around us. "You want to go there?"

He thought about it. "No."

"Okay," I said, "I know a place. Bert's. Kind of a funky establishment, in a little hotel downtown. Saturdays they've got a guy who plays acoustic guitar."

"Sounds great."

We didn't talk any more during the short drive to Bert's. I glanced at him every now and again, thinking how beautiful he looked under the glow of the shifting street lamps.

Johnny ordered coffee and piece of coconut pie. I had a Lone Star. "You have a nice house," he finally said.

"Yeah, got a good deal on it."

"It's so big. You must make a lot of money. What do you do?"

"I'm a vet. As in veterinarian."

He smiled, showing off his perfect white teeth. "No kidding?"

"No kidding. I got a couple of assistants who take care of the pet work—dogs, cats, gerbils. I'm more interested in horses. One of these day I'm gonna find a place out of town and raise horses of my own."

"You like horses?"

"Yeah. I like to ride." Whether by accident or not, at that instant the calf of his bare leg made contact with mine under the table. I saw him blush, but he didn't pull it away.

"You really from Laredo?" I said.

He laughed. "Shit, no. Chicago."

"What are you doing in Texas?"

"College student. Pre-med; got a scholarship to SMU. Made the gymnastics team this semester."

"No kidding?"

He grinned, showing off the most perfect teeth ever to bite into a coconut pie. "The wrestling's just something I fell into. Started back in Chicago, my first summer out of high school. Did a stint with Larry McMasters and the WPWC. He's the one who came up with the name Johnny Laredo. Came down here and I stuck with it; the hours fit and the pay's not bad."

"So what's your first name, really?"

"Oh, it's really Johnny. Just not Johnny Laredo. You live in that big house all alone," he said suddenly, "just you and little Tom?"

"Well, as long as we're being honest, all that stuff about my ex-wife and little Tommy was a bunch of crap. I'm the one who wrote the fan letter. Hell, it was kind of a joke, really. But I'm not sorry I did it."

"Neither am I," he said. His leg pressed against mine just a little harder.

Suddenly I didn't want to be in Bert's café any longer. "My house?" I said.

Johnny nodded.

❖

We stepped into the living room. I tossed the keys onto the coffee table and switched on the lamp behind the sofa, coloring the room with a dim amber haze.

I walked to Johnny, looking him straight in the eye. I put my arms around him and felt him press his firm chest against mine. I kissed his neck, his ear, his lips. I eased my hands downward into the silky depression at the small of his back, then onto the hard rounded ledge of his buttocks. His body felt warm and firm inside his clothes.

"Johnny," I said, speaking quietly into his ear, "I want to see you naked."

He stepped back, out of my arms, and undressed until he was the way I was used to seeing him, wearing nothing but his underwear and socks. His jockeys were scooped low in front, made of sheer black nylon. I could see his hard-on inside, like a short, thick club.

"The back," I said, my mouth dry.

He turned around to show me his ass. The heartbeat in my cock was like a hammer as he bent to roll down the skimpy shorts to his ankles and step out of them. He stayed that way, bent over and clutching his ankles. He flexed the stretched muscles of his thighs, making his buttocks pull apart and spread wide open. Johnny was able to do things with his gymnast's body that I'd never seen before.

I wet my middle finger and pressed it against his hole. It quivered against my fingertip, then opened for me. Johnny gasped. I felt him clutching at my finger from inside, milking it with his ass. He opened and closed his taut cheeks, squeezing my hand and releasing it. I thought about what it would feel like to have my cock inside him, with him squeezing like that, and I suddenly felt dizzy, as if all the blood from my head had rushed into my cock.

Johnny pulled himself off my finger and folded gracefully onto the floor. He turned and faced me, kneeling. My middle finger was where he had left it, poking into mid-air. Johnny looked at it for an instant, then closed his eyes and took it into his mouth and began sucking on it. I sawed it in and out, finger-fucking his mouth, watching his eyelids flicker and his cheeks cave in.

I pulled my finger out of his mouth and traced the tip over his moist red lips, using my other hand to unbutton my jeans. My hard-on tumbled out and slapped the side of his face. Johnny blinked, staring at it cross-eyed. He split his mouth wide open.

I stepped back. Johnny followed on his hands and knees, his eyes almost shut, his mouth hanging open. Hungry for cock.

I made him crawl halfway across the room, backing up step by step. When I reached the stairs I stopped. Johnny looked up at me and made a whimper, as if to ask if he could finally have it. I nodded. I threw back my head and felt my cock swallowed up by his warm, moist throat.

He wasn't quite as good a cocksucker as Gary. But I guess I might have been a little disappointed if he had been. Besides, he could always learn. Gary had. All it took was being hungry enough.

I let him suck me to the point of coming, then gently pushed his face back. He hadn't touched himself the whole time. His cock, hard and dry, pressed up red and swollen against his belly.

"Let's go upstairs," I said.

I didn't tell him to crawl. He did it on his own, creeping on all fours up the stairway, his ass clenching and relaxing as he made his way. I followed behind him, with my cock sticking out of my pants like a compass needle aimed at his hole.

He crawled onto the bed and laid himself out spread-eagled, clutching the corners of the mattress with his hands and feet, lifting up his ass and spreading his thighs. I was in no hurry. I moved as if I were in a perfect dream, first lubing up my cock, hard as a steel rod, then slipping a condom over it, then lubing it some more.

I crawled into the space between his thighs, gazing down at the etched muscles of his back, and navigated my cockhead to the lips of his hole. He rose up a little and swallowed the head all by himself, letting out a little gasp of pain. I eased down into him, letting gravity force the whole thing into his bowels. Johnny twisted and squirmed and cried out, but he never stopped clutching the mattress. Once I was all the way in I pushed myself up on one hand and grabbed a handful of his black hair with the other, like a rein, and started riding.

Johnny was amazingly strong, lifting his whole body spread-eagled, rearing back to meet my thrusts, wrenching his hips back and forth on the bed, pulling against my hand in his hair. His back erupted in a river of sweat. He began panting and moaning, then making short, whimpering squeals, and then finally a long, ecstatic groan as I came inside him and felt his insides spasm from his own climax.

❖

"Johnny?"

It was a month later. Johnny and I were floating on the bed, spooned together, his back against my hairy chest, his ass cradled in my lap, my half-hard cock nestled up his butt.

Earlier we had watched the broadcast of his match with Junior Jackson. Johnny was worn out. He'd put on a good show. For me, he said. The wrestling show was long over, and the station had signed off. The screen had turned to blue snow.

My arms were around him, my fingers absently stroking his nipples, all swollen and erect with a little hickey around each one. The blue glow of the television made Johnny's sleek flesh shine like silver.

"Johnny?"

"Yeah, Tom?"

"I want to ask you something, Johnny. It's kinda crazy."

"Yeah?"

I couldn't see his face, but I knew his eyes were open, staring into the darkness through droopy lids.

"Would you like to move in here with me?"

From the crinkle at the corner of his eye I could tell he was smiling. "Yes."

"You mean it? Right away?"

"Why do you think I always call it your big house, where you live all alone?" He cooed the words sleepily and snuggled his ass against my crotch. My dick began to stiffen again.

"It could be a good deal for you, Johnny. You're pre-med—I took a lot of those courses, went through all that grad school shit. I could help you out. And I make plenty of money. You could quit the wrestling if you wanted to—"

"Tom, I'm convinced already." He breathed a long, slow sigh and squeezed his ass around my dick. I slid my hand over his hip and wrapped it around his stiff cock. The boy I lusted after on TV. Johnny Laredo the wrestler. I smiled. The look on his face was so peaceful, I knew in that very instant that it wasn't a passing thing, that something would come of it.

"Wanna fuck me again, Tom?" he whispered.

"All night, Johnny—all night long!"

PUT IT IN ME, COACH
LOGAN ZACHARY

Shane was my best friend since kindergarten, and if he wasn't staying over at my house, I was over at his. We played every sport growing up, and his dad encouraged us, since he coached at the high school. As a child, I asked him, "Put it in me, Coach, instead of "Put me in, Coach." That became a joke between us, but it stopped in my preteen years.

There were the Friday and Saturday nights where we spent cuddled under a blanket, watching movies we weren't supposed to see, like *A Clockwork Orange*, *The Exorcist*, and *The Revenge of the Pom Pom Girls*.

The hide-a-bed folded out in Shane's living room, and his dad, Coach John, would watch movies with us. Coach John owned a camper and many tents, and Shane would often invite me on their father-and-son camping trips. We'd travel anywhere from the Black Hills of South Dakota to the shores of Lake Superior or our own exotic backyard in the Upper Peninsula of Michigan.

Ghost stories told around the campfire made for spooky fun. Coach John was young when he had Shane, while my dad and mom had me late in life. My parents were Shane's grandparents' age, so my Dad didn't like to camp or take many family trips.

Saturday nights were sauna nights at their home. Shane, being of Finnish descent, had a sauna in their basement. The sauna stove had Lake Superior rocks that were heated, and when water was thrown on them, the door would bang open from the sudden expansion of the water into steam.

Cedar branches were used to beat on each other to clean our pores. and when we were done, we'd sit with towels wrapped around our waists outside as we cooled off. In the winter, we could jump into the freshly fallen snow in the backyard to cool off, and then we'd race back into the sauna to warm up.

Shane's dad had an amazing body. Coach John had a furry, sculpted chest, which I hoped mine would look like when I grew up. He had long, strong, hairy legs that ran fast, and he had narrow hips and a large penis that hung between his legs. John was the football and track coach at the high school, which helped him stay in great shape.

In high school, Shane started to drink and party as my schoolwork focused my attention toward the medical field. We still hung out at times, but Shane always seemed to be too busy for me. Shane didn't go out for sports, much to his dad's disappointment, but I ran track and helped out with the sport injuries on the sidelines during the football season.

A month after our high school graduation, Shane was involved in a car accident and died. My parents moved to Arizona my freshman year in college and sold our house. To keep my Michigan citizenship, I moved in with Shane's parents.

John's wife left my sophomore year, unable to live in the house that Shane had grown up in. So when I returned to their home for the summer, the house was different.

As I unpacked my suitcase, John asked, "Mitch, what do you want for supper?"

After driving all day from college, my back was sore and I was exhausted. "Whatever you want."

"Pizza and beer?" he asked.

"Perfect."

❖

After supper, we took our beers out to the backyard and sat in the deck chairs. Coach John clicked my bottle with his. "It's great to have you home for the summer."

"Thanks for letting me stay with you."

"My pleasure. This old house gets mighty quiet these days. It's

Saturday night, I was going to turn on the sauna. Did you want to take one tonight?"

"I wasn't planning…"

John's face fell, and I stopped.

"I guess my back would feel better if I hit the steam."

"I'll go heat it up." John jumped up and headed into the basement to turn the heater on.

❖

An hour later, I wrapped a towel around my waist and walked barefooted down the basement steps. Opening the wooden sauna door, I inhaled deeply. The cedar scent and steam mixed as I breathed in. My skin was instantly covered with sweat and steam. My towel clung to my legs and butt. I could feel it absorb as much moisture as it could and hang heavy around my hips.

The wooden floor and bench greeted me, and I filled the wooden bucket with cold water and added a few drops of eucalyptus to the pail and used the dipper to mix it up. I threw a scoopful onto the rocks. Steam hissed as the water evaporated instantly. The door opened and banged shut. That was a good one.

Memories of the past flooded my mind. Shane and I would see who could get the biggest bang. We'd sit on the top bench, throw the water on the rocks, and feel the hot humid wall of steam after the water vaporized.

I closed my eyes and inhaled deeply; eucalyptus and male sweat. I felt my towel relax its hold around my hips and open on one side.

I settled back and let my mind go blank.

The sauna door opened and a cool breath of fresh air entered. Coach John stood in the doorway with two cold beers, his hairy chest tanned from the sun.

"Do you mind if I join you? I brought beer." The bottles dripped water as he entered.

I pulled the edge of the towel back up and covered my lap. Seeing his body and hairy chest made my cock jump. I could feel it start to slowly swell. Great. This was not the time to get an erection with my friend's dad.

He was forty-five, if my memory was right. Twenty-three years older than me.

John handed me the beer bottle and stepped on the lower bench. "Is there room up there for me too? Or would you rather sauna alone?"

My hard-on grew to twice its size, and I worried that he would see it. I set my beer on the bulge and shifted over. The edge of the towel flipped down, flashing my upper thigh and part of my ass.

John settled down next to me. His hairy knee brushed against mine, and I had instant full-on wood.

If he saw it, he didn't say anything. I looked down at his lap and saw his thin towel clinging to his body. It hugged his cock and showed the ridge at its tip. How much bigger and thicker it was now than I remembered. Most things seemed to be smaller when I came back home, but not his dick.

John reached over and grabbed my knee and squeezed. "I'm glad you're home. Have you had any charley horses? Do you remember how you'd wake up screaming in pain with one?" His hand grabbed my calf and massaged it, looking for a muscle knot.

Sweat beaded across his hairy chest and matted the beautiful pelt. Only a few gray hairs sprung out from between his pecs. His deeply tanned skin darkened with the heat and sweat.

"I've been lucky and haven't had one in a long time." I breathed in; a delicious male scent assaulted my nose, and my cock jumped and throbbed with each heartbeat. Wetness formed around the end of my cock and soaked into the cotton towel. I threw another scoop of water onto the rocks, and the sauna door opened and banged shut.

"You always enjoyed banging the door."

That wasn't the only thing I enjoyed banging, my mind said. A hot wave of humidity rose up, and the sauna temperature soared twenty degrees. Sweat ran down my face and burned my eyes as more poured down my back and funneled into my butt crease. I watched the thermometer needle hit 125 degrees and felt my body hair heat up. I ran my fingers through the damp locks as my scalped burned. "Wow."

"I know, it feels great." Coach John still squeezed my calf. "Shane always liked banging the door too." He closed his eyes and let his head fall back as he remembered his son.

"I need to start out slower and use smaller scoops of water." I pulled the towel tighter around my waist and stood up. Quickly, I scooted to the edge and sat down on the next bench lower. The air was a few degrees cooler, and I could breathe in without it burning my nostrils.

John laughed. "Getting out of the habit? Aren't there any steam rooms or a sauna at college?" He moved over to sit behind me with one hairy leg on each side of my torso. He reached forward and touched my neck. His fingers massaged my tight muscles as his coarse hair tickled my shoulders and sides.

My erection throbbed in my towel, and it felt as if it would rip through the fabric.

John's hands worked over my shoulders and up my neck. He caressed forward and started to descend over my pecs. He found my nipples and circled them.

They rose into tight little peaks under his touch. My head fell back into his lap and brushed up against his groin. I could feel his arousal, but his hands were working magic across my body. My hand slipped under my towel and adjusted my hard-on, flipping it up to lie on my belly. I found my fingers stroking my sensitive flesh and milked out pre-cum, wetting the mushroom tip. I swallowed hard and inhaled deeply. Musky male sweat teased my senses.

John's cock brushed the back of my head.

I wanted to turn around and take him into my mouth. I wanted to suck on that massive cock, lick the salty sweat from his balls. I wanted to have his body next to mine, rubbing, caressing, kissing…"

John's hands worked lower, combing through the hair on my abs. His finger circled around my belly button and slowly slipped inside. Sweat and humidity made the entry easy. He pulled out of my navel and brushed over the towel around my waist. The cotton fabric loosened from my hips, and my erection leapt up.

"Move forward a bit." John slipped down from the upper bench and straddled my backside. His legs brushed against mine, and his hard-on slid down my back and settled against my ass. His hand slid lower across my abs and found the thick bush of pubic hair. His fingertip found the root of my cock and stopped.

I turned to face him, and he kissed me. His lips found mine, and his tongue slipped inside and tasted beer and all man. My tongue sought his and when they touched, we stopped, surprised at our actions.

Sweat broke out over both of our bodies, and we were overheated.

I grabbed the wooden bucket and poured the cool water over us. The brisk rinse awakened me, and my arousal swelled and throbbed.

"Your back is so tight. Relax."

Relax? You just kissed me, you felt me up, and I'm going to burst into flames. How can I relax?

A bottle of baby oil sat next to us, and Coach John dumped some over my back.

I felt the hot oil run over my skin.

John rubbed it in, and he applied a palmful over my lower back.

My towel dropped down and exposed my ass. I felt him massage my butt and worked the oil into my crease.

He poured more oil onto himself. His hairy body slid along the wooden bench as his legs easily rubbed and slipped alongside of mine.

Heat soaked into my body, but I couldn't tell if it was from his body heat or the sauna.

John's towel opened and his aroused state rode up and down my back. His balls slipped between my cheeks, and the hair rasped against my ass. The baby oil and our sweat made our bodies glide easily against each other.

I stood, ready to bolt, when John moved forward, and his cock slid between my cheeks. My legs released, and I sat back down on the bench and landed on top of Coach John's cock. It filled my crease, and he pulled it out from underneath me.

"Oops, sorry," he said. He pulled his towel around his waist and tucked the loose end in. His erection strained against the cloth. "I need another drink. Do you?" He handed me the beer and took his own.

I grabbed my towel and pulled it close around my waist as I accepted my beer. I took a long drink on it, the cold cooling me off and calming my nerves. I sat back and took a deep breath.

Coach John flopped down next to me and drained his beer. "I think the heat and the beer got to me. I'm going to shower and cool off." He walked over to the corner of the sauna where the shower was and turned the knob. Water poured out of the head. John removed his towel and showed his perfect furry ass to me.

I downed the rest of my beer and continued to stare at him.

He stepped under the water and let it cascade over his tanned, oiled body. His butt cheeks flexed as he shifted his weight from one leg to the other. He grabbed the body wash bottle, but it slipped from his fingers. He bent over to reveal a hairy crease and a perfect pink pucker.

I closed my eyes, memorizing every detail. How many times had I jacked off to the image of his naked body as I grew up? I couldn't count.

Coach John washed himself, soaping up with thick lather that smelled like coconut. He rinsed off and turned his back into the spray. His massive cock stood straight out in front of him.

I didn't remember it being that large. I've never seen nine and a half inches before, but I did today.

He finished his shower and turned off the water. He grabbed the towel and started to dry off. He looked at me and smiled. "I'm heading out to the backyard to cool off. Join me when you're done. I'll have another cold beer waiting for you."

"Okay," I said to his tight ass as he passed by and left.

A cool breeze blew into the sauna as the door opened and John left.

I let loose the breath I had been holding and fell back against the bench. What the hell had just happened? Crazy from the heat? The Beer? What?

My hand caressed my erection and stroked the sweat and oil along my shaft. I needed a release so bad, but I was worried Coach John would return. I stepped under the shower and washed quickly, cooling off as the cold water cleaned. I wrapped the damp towel around my waist and exited the sauna. A wave of humid heat and cedar followed me. My bare feet flapped on the cement floor as I headed up the stairs and out into the night.

John sat in a deck chair, his towel draped over his lap. He raised a beer to me as I sat down in the opposite chair. The night breeze cooled my skin, and I could see the steam rise off my body. The beer tasted great, and I inhaled deeply.

We sat in silence looking up at the night sky and admiring the blinking stars. After the beer was gone, I tightened my towel and stood. "Hey, I'm beat. I'm going to turn in."

"Good night, Mitch. I'm glad you're home."

I walked into the house, found a dry towel, and slipped into bed. I tried to sleep, but my body wouldn't relax; my erection throbbed under my sheets.

The back door opened, and I heard Coach John come in. He used the toilet and didn't flush. I'm sure he was afraid of waking me up. His bare feet padded past my room and stopped at my door. He stood there for a long while.

I pretended to sleep.

He entered the room and neared the bed. He pulled the covers over my bare shoulder and gently touched my hair.

"Are you having trouble sleeping?"

"How did you know?"

"I'm having trouble too." He was naked. His cock was hard, and he shivered.

"Are you cold?" I pulled the covers back and invited him to join me.

He sat down and slipped between the sheets.

I moved over and our feet brushed against each other. He was so cold. "Let me warm you up."

He turned his back to me, and I spooned him.

I tried to keep my hips away from his ass, but he pushed back against me. His ass cheeks sandwiched my dick.

"Mitch, my, have you grown."

"Thanks, John, you were always my role model."

"Is that so?" He rolled over to face me. His cock rubbed alongside mine, and he wrapped his arms around me. His cold, hairy body felt so good in my arms. He smelled of cedar and coconut.

I pressed against him harder and looked into his eyes.

"Is this too hard for you?"

I felt his huge cock. "It feels great."

"That's not what I mean. I was worried that I had gone too far…"

I brought my mouth down on his and stopped him. I kissed him deeply and opened my mouth to let my tongue taste him.

He pressed against me harder and opened his mouth to tongue me.

He tasted wonderful. I remembered that one Friday night when we had watched *The Thing* and scared ourselves so bad, Coach John had to sleep with us. How I treasured that night so many years ago. His warm body snuggled against mine, keeping me safe from aliens and other monsters in the night.

I could feel pre-cum ooze out of my cock and smear across his hairy belly.

He reached down and stroked me. He pulled along my shaft and fingered my hairy balls.

I was so close; a few more strokes, and I'd lose my load.

John rolled me onto my back and straddled my body. He slowly moved down my torso, his hands exploring every inch along the way. My neck, my pecs, my nipples. He rolled my erect nipples between his teeth and sucked on one and then the other. He inhaled deeply.

I extended my neck and allowed my body to enjoy his mouth.

He licked between my pecs and teased the patch of hair he found. He continued down my chest, my rib cage, my abs. He traced the muscles with his tongue. As he circled my belly button, a wave of pre-cum flowed out of my cock and filled my navel.

"A surprise treat for me," he said. "Thank you." His dipped his tongue in and savored the sweet fluid. He drank every drop from me and continued lower.

My cock tapped his chin, and I could feel his razor stubble.

He ran his chin down my shaft and worked it side to side on my balls.

I grabbed his head as my fingers combed through his hair.

He moved between my legs and brought them up. He spread them and sucked one ball into his mouth. He rolled it around before taking the other one in. He worked both in and swallowed.

My balls hang low, and he drew them all the way in, up to my shaft. He grabbed my cock and squeezed.

I could feel his saliva and my juices run between my ass cheeks.

He let my testicles slip from his mouth as his tongue licked to my hole. It circled the opening, around and around, seeking entry and tasting me, the deep dark center of my being.

I moaned with pleasure. I grabbed the bars of the headboard and opened my ass wider for him.

He drilled in deeper, pressing past the tight muscle, and worked to relax me.

"Do it," I said. "Stick it in me. I want you, deep inside. Please."

He smiled and wet my hole more and reached between his legs. He stroked his cock a few times and brought it to my crease. He ran it up and down, teasing my pucker.

I pushed down on him. "Put it in me, Coach, hurry."

He stopped. "You used to say that as a kid." He then guided his dick to my wet opening and pressed forward. His thick shaft slowly entered and stopped. The mushroom head was swollen and took a little extra time and pressure to pass the muscle.

I bore down on him and forced him inside.

He slowly continued forward, his dick going in deeper as he jacked my cock.

My ass relaxed and swallowed him to the hilt. He kissed me before starting to retract. My whole body wanted more, faster, harder, deeper. I grabbed onto his butt cheeks and pulled him back into me.

"I've wanted this for so long," he said. His words came out in short gasps as he rode my ass. He quickened his pace and drilled into me.

"Oh yes," I moaned, "me too."

He milked me, and he humped me, faster and faster.

His hand clenched down on me, his pelvis slammed into me, and he collapsed on top of me.

I felt a white heat fill my bottom.

Coach John's whole body spasmed and continued to press in deeper. He pulled out slightly and then rammed back into me one last time. Seconds later, he pulled out of me and lubed up my dick. He pulled my hips to the edge of the bed and hovered over my hard-on. Slowly, he descended on me. His tight ass sat on my dick and pressed down, swallowing me whole. Three times was all it took for my cock to unload its contents.

I humped him as hard as I could; his tight ass sucked all the cream out of my balls and into him.

John rose slowly off my dick and lay on top of me, both of our bodies too sensitive to move.

After our breathing and heart rates returned to normal, Coach John snuggled next to me. Our bodies fit together perfectly. He held me to his hairy chest as his hands pulled me closer.

My butt pressed against his semi-hard dick. I grabbed his hand

and held it close, our fingers intertwined. My eyes drooped as my body finally relaxed, and I started to nod off.

John pulled me closer and kissed my head. "Sleep, Mitch, we have all summer. Welcome home, son."

"Put it in me, Coach."

And he did.

Finish Line
Jeffrey Ricker

Elliott's friends thought he was crazy when he told them he was starting to train for a marathon. They had a point. Elliott hadn't run any further than to catch a closing elevator door in maybe fifteen years. His idea of a workout was a nice brisk sit.

It showed, too. After his thirty-fifth birthday, his metabolism ground to a screeching halt, and his waistline picked up the slack by expanding rapidly. He got winded going up more than two flights of stairs. His doctor started using phrases like "pre-hypertension" and talked in grim tones about prescribing statins for his cholesterol level.

Worst of all, men were starting to look right through him as if he weren't there—which was odd, because there was so much more of him.

"It's not getting fat that I'm worried about," he said to Angela, the department admin who had the best candy jar in the office. He ate a fun-size Snickers as he talked to her and he silently vowed, like he always did, that it would be his last piece of candy.

"What are you worried about, then?" she asked. It occurred to Elliott he had never seen her take a piece of candy from her own jar.

"Closing my eyes and never opening them again."

She shrugged. "Sounds like you're having your midlife crisis. Just go on the Lipitor or whatever and buy a sports car like straight men do."

Elliott looked toward the mirrored elevator doors where his funhouse reflection seemed even more pear-shaped than the reality. "If I'm having my midlife crisis at thirty-five, does that mean I'm only going to live to be seventy?"

Angela put the lid back on her candy jar and didn't answer.

❖

As it turned out, this time Elliott was right: the Snickers *was* his last candy bar. That evening he went to the mall to get a new case for his phone. Instead, he wandered into the sporting goods store. His attention was drawn by the larger-than-life black-and-white poster in the window of a runner, shirtless, hands on his hips as he stared into the distance somewhere over Elliott's head. Elliott's gaze drifted downward to his own reflection in the window.

It was time for a change. He went in.

Thirty minutes later he walked out, his wallet two hundred dollars lighter and the bag in his hand containing a pair of running shoes, thin thermal pants, and a hooded jacket. He stood for a moment outside the store thinking, *Now what?* He waited for things to feel different, but maybe that would happen after his first run.

Which was a disaster.

He walked out of his building the next morning feeling slightly ridiculous in his running gear, like an imposter. He lived in a loft on Washington Avenue. Running west would take him past the restaurants and into the midtown warehouse district, but east was more interesting, with the Arch and river beyond the downtown office buildings. He turned right and began to jog slowly, wondering how fast was too fast. At the end of the block, he felt fine, so he picked up his pace.

He got exactly three blocks further before his lungs burned too much to breathe and his knees wondered what the hell he was doing. He was still blocks away from the river. He turned around and walked home.

❖

"Three blocks?" Angela asked the next day. "That's it?"

"Running's harder than I thought," he said, shifting from one foot to the other, then winced. When he woke up that morning, his shins practically screamed at him. In response to Angela's questioning look, he said, "Shin splints, I think."

She sighed. "If you're going to stick with running, it sounds like you need a trainer."

"A trainer?" The first thing that came to mind was how expensive that would be. "It may be hard for me, but it's still just putting one foot in front of the other."

"Until you fall and break your neck." She reached under the desk for her purse and began rummaging through it.

"What are you looking for?" he asked.

"My personal trainer's card. I don't use her anymore, but I went to her before my trip to Hawaii. Ah." She extracted the card and handed it to him.

He looked at it. "Magda? Her name is really Magda?"

"Her name is really Magda."

"She's good?"

"Actually, she's a hateful, tyrannical bitch. Which makes her a perfect personal trainer. Trust me on this. Anyway, the company covers half the fee, so you might as well."

Elliott slipped the card in his shirt pocket. "I'll think about it."

He reached for the candy jar. Angela snatched it away and put it in her desk.

"No candy for you."

❖

After work, he went to Angela's gym, which was an unassuming-looking place in a strip mall. Magda was no longer there, the woman at the front desk said. Apparently, being a hateful tyrant wasn't a good way to attract repeat business.

"If you want to get in shape for running," she said, "you should talk to Jeremy. He's good with that."

She pointed toward the back, where a man in a blue shirt and track pants stood near the squat machine. Elliott was relieved to see Jeremy wasn't a typical gym bunny. In fact, he was shorter than Elliott, and a little on the scrawny side. His handshake was strong, though, and when he smiled he revealed even, perfect teeth. Elliott tried not to hate him for that.

"So what's your goal?" Jeremy asked.

"I want to run a marathon."

It was out before Elliott even realized what he'd said. A marathon?

He couldn't even make it a mile, and now he was asking to go…how long was a marathon, anyway? He couldn't remember.

Jeremy, for his part, didn't bat an eye when Elliott told him this. "Okay," he said, "what's the farthest you've gone so far?"

"Let's just say I'm starting out pretty much from scratch," Elliott said. He'd probably have to 'fess up about his pathetic first attempt and his shin splints before long.

Jeremy waved a hand. "Not a problem." He crossed his arms and leaned against the squat machine. The way he stared at him made Elliott feel like he was having that dream where he showed up at work in his underwear.

"So," Jeremy finally asked, "how long do you have?"

"Pardon?" *Do I look terminal?* Elliot wondered.

"How long until your marathon, I mean."

"Oh. Well…I haven't decided which one to sign up for yet."

"That's good, actually. If you'd said you'd signed up for something like, next month, I was going to have bad news for you."

"So, how long do you think it'll take to train for it?"

Jeremy crossed his arms and contemplated the floor between them. "Six months should do it."

"Six months?"

"I know it's not a long time," he said, not catching on to Elliott's incredulity. "Most people in your shape, I tell them we need at least nine months. But I think if you're really committed, we can make it work in that amount of time. What do you say?"

A week later, Elliott wondered why he'd said yes. Jeremy didn't explain from the outset just how much of Elliott's life he intended to overhaul. He weighed him. He measured his height ("Six feet," Elliott told him; "Five eleven and a half," Jeremy responded), his waist (Elliott wore 34s, but Jeremy pointed out that he was actually a 35 and should have been, for his age and height, a 33 at worst or, ideally, a 32), his shoulders, his chest, his inseam, his shoe size.

Elliott asked, jokingly, "Are you going to make me a suit or help me get in shape?"

"When we're done, the suit that would fit at these measurements is going to fall right off you," he replied.

He made Elliott keep a food journal for a week and record every bite of everything he ate and drank. When they went over it, Jeremy crossed out half of it.

"I thought pasta was supposed to be good for runners," Elliott protested.

"With alfredo sauce and cheese garlic bread? I don't think so. And lay off the beer."

Elliott groaned. "You're killing me here."

"Actually, I like to think maybe I'm saving your life." He shut the notepad and slid it across the table. "But if you're not interested—"

"No no, I'm interested." Elliott flipped the notepad back open. "It's just that—well, I like beer."

Jeremy laughed. "So I can tell," he said, and reached over and patted Elliott's belly.

Jeremy went on to list all of the things that Elliott could and/or should eat (mostly mundanely healthy and likely tasteless). Elliott caught little of it—fortunately, Jeremy wrote most of it down in the notepad—because he was too preoccupied with the flock of birds taking flight in his stomach where Jeremy had touched him.

"You're skipping happy hour a lot," Derek said.

"I know," Elliott replied. He had known Derek ever since his first newspaper job out of college—Derek liked to say they were the only two gays in the village. Elliott could have corrected that misconception, but Derek was a reporter and never had reason to go down to the press room like Elliott. That's where Elliott met the third gay in the village, who was a bit burly and blue-collar and apparently had helium in his ankles, which suited Elliott just fine but probably would have met with disapproval from Derek. After Elliott went on to become an art director at a magazine and later for a not-for-profit, he and Derek still met regularly for drinks, darts, and show tunes on Tuesday nights at the Loading Zone.

They were playing 301 and Elliott was winning. He just needed twenty-five points to go out. "I've been a little busy lately."

"Oh? Doing what?"

Elliott threw. Twenty, and he had two more throws to get five without going over. Tricky. "Just work stuff," he said and threw again.

Ten. Crap. The electronic board clucked at him disapprovingly. Served him right for lying. He retrieved his darts and returned to the table where their drinks waited—a cosmo for Derek, Diet Coke for Elliott, a choice that had drawn a raised eyebrow from Derek.

Derek ended up winning, and was a little disappointed when Elliott begged off a rematch because he had to meet Jeremy at the gym at six the next morning. Not that he told Derek why. Angela at the office was the only person he'd told about his training plans.

"And why's that?" she asked when he informed her of this.

"I don't know," he said, because he thought he really didn't.

"Are you afraid they won't be supportive?" she asked.

"I can't imagine why they wouldn't."

"Yeah, me neither. So what else is it? You're not ashamed of trying to be better, are you?"

It sounded so ridiculous when she said it, but he felt there was an element of truth to it. As he tried to put his finger on it, he noticed something missing from her desk.

"Where's your candy jar?"

"I decided to retire it for a while." She opened her desk drawer and pulled out a Tupperware container. "Baby carrot?"

❖

It wasn't fear of doing better that made him keep his marathon ambitions to himself, he realized the next day. It was the fear of trying to do better and failing spectacularly, to say nothing of publicly. He decided to talk with Jeremy about this when he went to the gym.

When Elliott walked in, Jeremy was doing curls and wore a sleeveless shirt. He was using a 100-pound barbell (Elliott himself struggled with a 50), and for the first time, Elliott noticed Jeremy's arms weren't small at all. After he'd racked the weights and toweled off his face, he led Elliott over to the treadmill for a warm-up.

"Failure? Not gonna happen," he said. "You're running that marathon."

"But what if I don't make it that far?" Elliott asked. "Then everyone knows I'm a failure."

Jeremy reached across the treadmill and hit the Pause button. "I'm not going to let you fail. If I did that, I wouldn't be doing my job right.

I know it seems like we're going slow now, but it'd be worse to start too fast and then get injured. Believe me, we'll pick up the pace soon." Jeremy smiled and gave Elliott's arm a single pat. "You're gonna be amazed how far you can go by the time I'm done with you."

Elliott felt his face flush and smiled before he could restrain himself. Jeremy hit the Resume button and the treadmill started back up. At the same time, he glanced toward the front door and his smile vanished. "I'll be right back. Keep at this pace for another minute and then go up to 4.5."

Elliott watched Jeremy walk up to a blond woman in a severe black suit, her hair pulled back in a ponytail. He couldn't hear anything the two of them said, but her body language was tense and hawkish, Jeremy's equally brittle in response. He went away for a moment. The woman turned toward the gym interior and, noticing Elliott's stare, gave him a "What?" look. He glanced away. Jeremy returned a moment later and handed her an envelope. She handed him a key ring. Even from a distance, Elliott could read his lips. *There. Go.*

"No trouble, I hope," Elliott said when Jeremy returned.

"Nothing you need to worry about, sparky," he replied. "Hey, you're supposed to be going 4.5." He reached over again and punched the Speed button.

❖

For their first run, Jeremy had Elliott meet him at Forest Park. It was a Thursday morning in mid-April, the weather already veering from mild into warm. Still, the morning was cool enough that Elliott wore a long-sleeve shirt and track pants. Jeremy wore shorts and a tank top. Elliott tried not to stare.

"You sure you're not going to be too hot in that?" Jeremy asked.

"I don't know." Elliott looked down at his outfit. "Am I?"

Jeremy made a gesture that was not quite a shrug. "Just let me know if it starts to feel like too much."

The trail around the park was already filling up with runners and bikers despite the early hour. They started out walking, then the Garmin on Jeremy's wrist beeped, and they picked up the pace to a slow jog.

"Don't hold yourself so stiffly," Jeremy said. He let himself drop behind so he could watch Elliott's stride. "You can move your shoulders, but don't lean forward too much. And try to keep from bouncing up and down. You want your momentum to go forward, not up and down."

"Sorry."

"And stop apologizing so much. You're doing fine."

"Sorr—I mean, okay."

"You worry a lot about doing things wrong, don't you?"

"I don't know. Doesn't everybody?"

Jeremy shook his head. "You have to be willing to make mistakes, otherwise you won't allow yourself to take any risks big enough to matter." His Garmin beeped again. "And...walk."

Elliott slowed down and noticed he wasn't even out of breath yet. "Already?"

Jeremy laughed. "One foot at a time, sparky."

❖

Derek was the first to comment on the change in Elliott's appearance.

"You need some serious wardrobe help," he said when Elliott walked into the Loading Zone. "You look like you're wearing dad jeans."

Elliott set down his Diet Coke and opened his dart case. "I've had these jeans for, I don't know, three years at least."

"Well, at some point between then and now, they turned into dad jeans. You need to go get some that fit."

"That's because you've been losing weight," Angela pointed out the next day. She stopped by Elliott's desk to drop off mail and he asked her if they looked like dad jeans to her. She made him get up and turn around, then declared that yes, sadly, they did. "Haven't you noticed?"

"I guess not," Elliott said. "Jeremy told me not to worry about weighing myself at this point."

"Well, bless his heart, but maybe you should bend his rules just this once."

That night he weighed himself. He'd lost ten pounds already, and they weren't even up to a 10K run yet. In fact, they hadn't done much running at all, as far as Elliott could tell. On most of their runs, they spent more than half the time walking. The rest of their workouts, Jeremy had him in the gym lifting weights or taking the twice-weekly yoga class.

"You're starting from zero, basically," Jeremy said when Elliott asked him about this. "Pretty soon you'll be flying. You just have to trust me." He tilted his head down and smiled. "You trust me, right?"

Elliott didn't see that he really had much choice. He'd already signed up for the Chicago Marathon that October. He wasn't about to quit now.

Although he told Jeremy he could be patient, Elliott's subconscious started sending him different signals. That evening he had a dream about Jeremy. They were in the park, getting ready for a run (though it was one of those dreams where the place didn't look anything like the place actually did in reality). The funny thing was, besides there being no one else around, Jeremy was wearing a suit and tie.

"Are you ready to run?" he asked Elliott, who wore shorts and a tank top. The sun was high and intense; it was the kind of day where the brightness bleached out the details.

When Elliott said he was ready, Jeremy started to take off his suit. A bubble of alarm swelled in Elliott's chest as he realized Jeremy didn't have anything on underneath it. He began picking up clothing as Jeremy discarded it and tried to make him put it back on. Soon, though, Jeremy was completely naked except for running shoes and socks. He turned away and said, "Keep up if you can."

Instead of pursuing him, Elliott just watched Jeremy's backside as he receded into the distance. He knew then that this was just a dream, and that realization was enough to jar him awake—but not before wondering whether Jeremy's ass looked that perfect in real life.

❖

"I think I'm getting a crush on my trainer," he confessed to Angela over lunch. They were sitting at the lunch counter at Whole Foods, which faced the windows and the parking lot. It was easier to admit his awkward infatuation when he didn't have to face her.

"Isn't he straight?" Angela asked. She dabbed some wasabi into her soy sauce and stirred it with her chopsticks.

"I think so," he said, "but he gives off these mixed signals."

"Like what? Inappropriate touching?"

"Not really." Since Jeremy was his trainer, Elliott basically paid him to touch him in what otherwise would be highly inappropriate ways.

"Does he make inappropriate statements?"

"Like what?"

Even though he wasn't looking at her, Elliott could practically hear Angela rolling her eyes. "I don't know. Maybe something like 'Gee, you look really hot' or 'Let me suck your dick'?"

"Ha. Ha. Very funny." Jeremy had, of course, told Elliott on numerous occasions that he looked hot—because Elliott still hadn't figured out how to dress appropriately for the weather, and Jeremy typically made him slow down and drink water in those cases.

"Oh please," Derek said at darts that week. "Do *not* get another crush on a breeder."

They were playing cricket, and Derek had just closed out the bull's-eye. Elliott was losing badly.

"What do you mean, 'again'?"

"Two years ago," Derek said. "The guy in the mailroom who delivered packages to your department. If I remember right, you checked out *his* package on many occasions."

Elliott threw—and completely missed the board. "Why do I get the feeling all my so-called friends are making fun of me?" he grumbled.

"Because we are, and because you make it way too easy." Once Elliott retrieved his darts, Derek lined up and took aim.

Elliott grabbed his Diet Coke and wished it had a whole hell of a lot of rum in it. "You know, just once I would like to get a little fucking support from people who claim to be my friends."

Derek lowered his dart without firing and turned to Elliott. "Oh, honey." He put his hand on Elliott's shoulder. "I kid because I love. And because I want you to stop wasting time on boys who will never like you back."

Elliott wanted to say something in response, something touching, but Derek turned back to the board and raised his dart. "Now, stop distracting me while I'm kicking your ass."

❖

After that, Elliott put thoughts of Jeremy to the back of his mind, where they mostly stayed. He focused instead on all of the changes Jeremy was working in his life: He upended his routine and turned into a morning person. Instead of staying up late drinking with friends or watching movies on Netflix, he set his alarm for five so he could drag his ass to the gym by six. The altered topography of his refrigerator's contents was reflected in slow changes to his body, alterations that he never noticed but that other people commented on. Still, Jeremy told him to hold off on buying new clothes. "We're not done changing you yet," he said.

Whenever Jeremy talked about remaking Elliott's body (which he did a lot), Elliott couldn't resist a tiny surge of excitement. It was even worse when Jeremy helped him stretch after a workout or a run. When he had Elliott lie on a table and raise a leg while Jeremy slowly pushed on it ("This really gets your hamstrings," he explained), Elliott resorted to mentally running through the multiplication tables to keep from dwelling on what it really looked like Jeremy was doing.

Then he went home and jacked off furiously in the shower.

Despite all that, he managed to maintain what he thought was a reasonable (if not healthy) perspective on his relationship with Jeremy, which—first and foremost, he reminded himself—was a business relationship.

All of which wound up left by the side of the trail when they went on Elliott's first ten-mile run.

He met Jeremy in the park at six, a little earlier than the usual time for their Saturday long runs. Jeremy had mapped out a course that would take them from the edge of the park east through downtown and back. It was mid-June, and the morning was already warm and on its way higher. Three miles into the run, Jeremy peeled off his tank top and tucked it in his waistband.

On the way back to the park, Jeremy lifted his water bottle to his lips, and all that came out was a hollow gurgle.

"Shit. I'm out," he said.

"My place is just up the block," Elliott heard himself saying. He hoped that Jeremy would say he could get by with what he had, but instead he said, "Cool." Why hadn't he kept his mouth shut?

They stopped at the front door of his building and Elliott pulled out his keys. Jeremy put his tank top back on while they waited for the elevator.

"Nice building," Jeremy said.

"Thanks," Elliott replied, which seemed like the dumbest thing to say. "I mean, I like it, too."

The elevator ride to the fifth floor passed in silence, and soon they were walking toward Elliott's corner unit. He unlocked the door and led Jeremy down a long hallway along the outside wall—Jeremy ran his hand over the exposed brickwork and made an approving sound.

The hall opened into the living area, with the kitchen off to the side separated by an island. Jeremy headed for the water dispenser in the refrigerator while Elliott said he had to go to the bathroom.

He let the water run in the sink for a minute after he'd finished washing his hands. His reflection looked flushed, his face still shiny with sweat, a bit of his light brown hair plastered to his forehead. He pushed it out of the way and turned off the faucet. His shirt was soaked. His shorts were flimsy, skimpy, and too short. His mind was a blank, and for the moment, he was grateful for that.

When he came out of the bathroom, Jeremy was standing right there, taking a drink from his water bottle. Elliott yelped and jumped back a little, stumbling (*Really smooth, Elliott*, he chastised himself), but Jeremy put out a hand to steady him and laughed a little.

"Whoa, sorry," he said. "Didn't mean to startle you there."

A short silence drew out, and Jeremy got that thoughtful look on his face that Elliott had gotten used to seeing when he was deciding how far Elliott was ready to go. He reached around Elliott to set his water bottle on the vanity inside the bathroom.

"Actually, I *totally* meant to startle you," he said, pulled Elliott close, and kissed him.

And not just any kiss. This was a shove-you-against-the-wall-and-clamp-on-like-you're-the-only-source-of-oxygen-in-the-room kiss. Somehow, Jeremy managed to yank Elliott's shirt off without Elliott ever noticing the kiss had stopped. Jeremy took off his tank top again. Elliott put a hand against Jeremy's chest so he'd have a moment to catch his breath.

He couldn't believe he'd actually thought Jeremy was scrawny when he first saw him. He wasn't bulky, but every ounce on his frame seemed solid. Dark hair, slick with sweat now, outlined the curve of his chest and continued in growing profusion down his belly until it vanished into the waistband of his shorts, which were tented out like an exclamation insisting on being heard.

Elliott couldn't resist. His hand fell from Jeremy's chest and grasped that exclamation. Jeremy's head fell forward and rested against Elliott's collarbone. His breath was shallow and quick.

"Where's your bedroom?" he asked. It was barely above a whisper.

"Are you sure this is a good idea?" Elliott asked once he'd led Jeremy through the doorway beyond the kitchen. They stood at the edge of his bed, which he hadn't bothered to make that morning.

"Actually, I'm pretty sure this is a terrible idea," Jeremy said. He knelt at Elliott's feet and began tugging at his shoelaces. At the same time, he leaned his face into Elliott's shorts, cupping his mouth over the bulge there.

Elliott gasped and placed his hands on Jeremy's head, holding him there even though Jeremy made no move to break away. With one hand Jeremy kept tugging at Elliott's shoe while he slipped his other hand up the leg of Elliott's shorts. At that point, Elliott decided he really, really liked the skimpy running shorts.

Even so, he stopped Jeremy again. "I thought you were straight."

Jeremy gave him a merciless squeeze. "You're kidding, right?"

"But the blond woman at the gym a couple weeks ago—"

Jeremy looked thoroughly confused but still kept stroking Elliott. Then realization seemed to dawn. "Oh, Heather. My ex-roommate. She moved out and stiffed me a month's rent and hadn't even given me her keys back." Finally he gave up on Elliott's shoelace. "Jesus, get these things off."

Elliott kicked off his shoes, and Jeremy pushed him backward onto the bed while tugging Elliott's shorts up and off his upturned legs. Naked, suddenly exposed, Elliott laughed half out of giddiness and half out of nervousness now that Jeremy could finally see how he looked underneath his clothes.

Jeremy pulled off his own shorts before catching Elliott's legs mid-fall. Grinning in almost drunk-looking joy, he lowered one to his hip and held the other against his chest. He tilted forward slowly, extending Elliott's leg much the same way he did at the gym after a workout. Still warm from the first half of their run, Elliott was even more flexible. They were nearly face-to-face.

Jeremy scooted Elliott forward until there was enough room for him to crawl onto the bed. Without needing to be told (or ask, Elliott noted with a little amusement), Jeremy leaned over and practically yanked the drawer out of the nightstand, then began rummaging through it blindly.

"Hey, slow down." Elliott sat up. Gently, he took Jeremy's hand and found the condom and lube himself. "What's the rush?"

This time, Jeremy was the one grinning in embarrassment. "I seem to remember telling you the same thing a few times, sparky."

Elliott carefully tore open the wrapper. "I like it when you call me that," he said as he rolled the condom over Jeremy's dick. Rising up to his knees, he pushed Jeremy back onto the bed and straddled him. "See? Sometimes you just have to take your time."

Jeremy grinned, rose to his elbows and kissed Elliott. "Yeah, maybe you should show me more."

For the next half hour, Elliott did exactly that.

Elliott felt like he'd had an out-of-body experience after they'd both come. Jeremy lay on top of him, his head once again resting in the curve between Elliott's neck and his collarbone.

"God, we reek so bad," Jeremy said.

"I want to do that again," Elliott said.

"Shit."

Elliott glanced up. Jeremy was looking at the bedside clock. He rolled off Elliott and out of bed. "We've got to get cleaned up and run."

Elliott just wanted to lie there for a while and enjoy the dizzy, light-headed feeling that had come over him after Jeremy had, well, come over him. Instead, Jeremy took his hand and pulled him to his feet.

"Hey," Elliott protested, stopping before Jeremy could lead him into the bathroom. "Again I ask, what's the rush?"

"It's going to take us an hour to run back to the gym, and I have a client at one-thirty."

"Oh. Should I be jealous?"

Jeremy grinned. "Of seventy-year-old Mrs. Matheson? I don't think so."

❖

With that, the tempo of their long runs changed: run, fuck, run. As the distances became progressively longer, the logistics became more of a challenge: On the sixteen-mile run, they went out to the Katy Trail, running out four miles from the trailhead at Defiance toward Augusta, then back to Elliott's car, where he wound up laid out on the backseat. Jeremy fucked him while keeping lookout for any other trail walkers. (Though they were usually out and running long before anyone else showed up, Elliott was still glad he had tinted windows.) Afterward, they ran another four miles toward Weldon Spring and St. Charles, then back. Elliott typically spent the rest of his Saturdays on the sofa or in bed, exhausted.

❖

"You have got to be kidding me."

Derek's incredulity at Elliott's revelation that he was dating his trainer was only slightly less than Angela's had been. ("I'll be surprised if you're still fucking him by the time you get to the starting line," she'd said. "Happy for you, but surprised.") Derek, on hearing the news, set his darts on the table and picked up his beer.

"So," Derek said after a long drink, "he's gay but you can't tell anyone because dating a client would be a conflict of interest and potentially unethical?"

Elliott nodded. "And he might get fired."

Derek shook his head. "At this rate, you might as well be dating a straight guy."

"I don't think a straight guy would give head as well as Jeremy does," Elliott muttered, loud enough that Derek would be sure to hear it.

Derek tossed a sour look in his direction. "Now you're just being mean." He and his boyfriend had broken up a couple weeks earlier, and he was the sort of person who could dish out much more than he could take.

"I promise I'll bring him in and introduce you once the marathon is over," Elliott said.

"Assuming it lasts that long."

"Oh, thanks. Now who's being mean?"

As it happened, Elliott thought later, maybe Derek and Angela had a better grasp of the situation than he'd given them credit for. Still, he was caught off guard in September, less than four weeks before the race, when Jeremy said they should probably cool things off.

"Just for a little bit," he added quickly. They were at the gym, and Elliott was in the middle of a bench press. "My boss is getting nosy. I let slip about our training runs outside of work, and she wanted to know why I wasn't billing for them."

"Seriously?" Elliott racked the weights and sat up. He felt an overwhelming urge to go out to the parking lot, figure out which car was hers, and key it.

"You're almost done anyway," Jeremy said. "You've got one more long run coming up, and then you taper off until the real deal. Piece of cake."

Jeremy made it sound so easy, but when Elliott tried to recall how many of his long runs he'd done alone, he came up with zero. He visualized flaming out in the middle of his twenty-miler and limping back to his car in defeat. For added effect, in his imagination, it was raining.

And there was one other thing he hadn't thought about before: Jeremy wouldn't be with him on race day either. He'd be running on his own.

"No, you won't," Jeremy said when Elliott voiced this anxiety. "You'll be with thousands of other people, and you'll have six months of training under your belt. You'll be ready."

It sounded to Elliott like Jeremy was trying to convince himself of that fact as much as Elliott. "But...I just...it's..."

"Hey, deep breaths." Jeremy placed his hand on Elliott's chest, and gradually Elliott tamped down the rising panic. "I told you to have faith, remember?"

"Yeah." Elliott wiped away the sweat of panic. "And now you're not going to be there."

Jeremy looked hurt. "Don't you get it? I didn't mean faith in me. I meant faith in yourself."

❖

Elliott left that training session fifteen minutes early, in a huff. He went out that weekend and, true to his prediction, his twenty-miler was his worst performance yet. He ran out of gas after mile fifteen and mostly walked the last five.

It even rained.

His three-week tapering schedule went smoothly, but he was just counting off miles without much caring how he felt about them.

"Oh, hell no," Derek said when Elliott mentioned offhand that he might not go up to Chicago for the marathon. "You're going to run that damn race if I have to tie you up, throw you in the trunk, and drive you up there myself."

"Please, you've been playing doubting Thomas the whole time." Elliott threw the last dart of his turn—missed the 20 again—then took a sip of his drink. He stared at the glass suspiciously. "I wanted a rum and Coke."

Derek stepped up to the throw line. "Yeah, well, you'll drink Diet Coke and you'll like it. At least until after Sunday."

"Jeez, what's with you?"

Derek set down his darts, grasped Elliott by the shoulders, and turned him to face the mirror above the bar. "That's what's gotten into me. Look at you. I don't remember the last time you looked this good. I bet your cholesterol's below two hundred now, isn't it?"

"One seventy-eight," Elliott muttered. Looking at himself in the mirror, standing next to Derek, he tried to glimpse some of what his friend apparently saw. The changes had been so gradual, though; had they really happened?

"I'm going to kick your ass if you don't go up there and run that fucking race," Derek said. "Do you understand?"

"Yes, Mother."

Derek raised an eyebrow but said nothing. He turned back to the board, picked up his dart, and threw it. It landed dead center in the bull's-eye.

"Good. Now go buy the winner another beer."

❖

The morning of the race was cool, but not as chilly as Elliott had expected. He had on a long-sleeved throwaway shirt that he'd take off once he'd warmed up. He'd been prepared for that. What he hadn't been prepared for was just how big a crowd of 45,000 runners looked. Nevertheless, he'd managed to make his way to a spot in the open corral where he could see the five-hour pace team's lollipop-shaped sign, which was the pace he'd trained for.

"You sure you're not going to be too hot in that, sparky?"

Elliott didn't have to turn around to know who it was, but he did anyway. Jeremy's grin was so wide it was almost painful how happy he looked.

"You're here," Elliott said.

"Wow, nothing gets past your eagle eye," Jeremy said, then stepped closer and kissed him. Elliott was already too surprised by Jeremy's presence to be that much more surprised by the kiss, but that didn't keep him from enjoying it. Nearby, someone whistled, then a voice yelled, "Guys! Get a room!" At that point they stopped kissing and cracked up.

"How the hell did you find me?" Elliott asked once they stopped laughing.

"Fortunately, you're tall. Also, I figured if you followed any of my directions, you'd be near the five-hour pace setter."

Elliott didn't have to look at him skeptically for very long before Jeremy finally said, "Fine, I've been looking for the last half hour. Pretty soon I was just gonna start yelling 'Sparky!' until I found you."

"I still can't believe you're here." He looked down at Jeremy's shorts and shirt—and his race bib—and it finally dawned on him. "You're running?"

"I figured I'd done all this training with you, and I didn't have anything else to do this weekend…"

Elliott wasn't about to fall for that. "Registration closed months ago. You were planning to run this all along, weren't you?"

Jeremy smiled and shrugged. "Guess you caught me again. I signed up as soon as you told me you had."

Elliott did a quick mental backtrack. "That was at least a month and a half before we—um…"

"Went the distance?"

"That's one way to put it, yeah. So what did your boss have to say about this?"

"Considering you fired me weeks ago, there wasn't any conflict of interest anymore. I just told her my boyfriend was running this race and I wanted to be there."

"Your boyfriend." Elliott smiled. "I'm an idiot, aren't I?"

"Good thing that's endearing. But I told you I'd make sure you got across the finish line. I figured it would be bad form if I wasn't even at the starting line in the first place."

They had three minutes to go before the start. Jeremy took Elliott's hand. They faced the sea of people in front of them and, somewhere beyond that, the starting line.

"You know," Elliott said, "you can probably run this a lot faster than I can."

Jeremy just smiled and shook his head. "Not gonna, though."

"I guess this time we can't stop on the middle and have sex either."

"Kind of ruins your chip time. We'll just have to save that for after."

"I'm okay with that."

Up ahead, the starting horn sounded. As far back as they were, the crowd didn't start moving right away. It would take a while for the momentum to reach them, but Elliott heard the thunder of feet against the pavement. Jeremy gripped his hand harder.

"You ready?" he asked.

Elliott nodded. "I'm ready."

THE RAVISHING OF SOL STEIN
TROY SORIANO

Never have I seen him dry. Not even once. It's almost beyond any explanation as to why and how he is always sweating, but his perpetual dampness knows no season and makes any fabric he wears insignificant. Even when it's snowing sideways, he somehow walks in glinting with perspiration. He comes into the gym sweaty. He gets sweaty here. A minute after getting dressed after his workout, he would stand before you, already sweating again. Is there any time of day or night that he is not somehow glistening? It was as if he was a god, and the agreement upon leaving Olympus, was that he would be allowed to venture anywhere in the world, provided the thinnest sheen of his clear, clean sweat stay upon him at all times, a membrane that would permit him to exist in our world and move among us in this mortal environment, a skin on top of his skin, not just keeping the world from him, but also keeping him ever so slightly apart from the world. I had the feeling that if you wiped it too much away, kept it off him for too long, you might harm something quintessentially him.

His physical efforts stamp their imprint on his sleeveless T-shirt daily, a kind of sweat Rorschach I can't hide from as he goes by me in the gym, more effectively revealing the dark truths of my inner state than a dozen inkblots on as many white cards. No fluffy clouds, some days I think I see his face in the design, a face below his face, this one more *in* on my intentions toward him. Other days, I think I see my own face staring back at me with intensity. Monday I swear I see a skull leering at me in the shapes his sweat makes there. Tuesday, friends having tea.

After checking him in, handing him a towel, and *have a good workout*, I openly stare at him from the front desk at the gym where I work, and the inscrutable patterns his toil soon renders on his clothes never fail to tease me from my sanity. To the treadmill, to the Smith machine, back to the treadmill. Over the course of about two hours, the patterns steadily make their way down from his shaggy armpits and clean neck, down further to his dangling, jangling, sweat-heavy, too-small for him silver nylon shorts.

Squats on the Smith machine admit to all who will dare to look that yes, sweat now clearly soaks through the top of his white jock strap, dimming the color from bright white to a fine gray in that exact spot where what was merely the back any chump on the beach could admire any day of the summer suddenly became the ass that reads like a personal gift for the lucky few. Watching him make sweat appear from nothing, to then have it explode all over himself, where it slowly, sensually, outlines the shape of his body, is to me as if I am watching fireworks in slow motion while "Bittersweet Symphony" plays in the background. Except instead of up into the sky, they rained down to the earth, kaleidoscope spin-art against the sky of his body, where his face outshone the sun.

Follow him down the hall to the locker room any day, where it would be easy to note a dozen good qualities. There is charity there—someone took the towel he had set out for himself on the bench, no worries, he can grab another from me at the front desk. There is fraternity there, a friend catches his ear by the sinks and wants to talk about his loss of job, and there he is with only a towel around his waist, patiently listening while making eye contact and comforting the man, his steadying hand on his shoulder. Magnanimous, a friend wants to take a picture with him, in the locker room of all places, even though they are both shirtless, *come on, let me try out my new camera* he says, it's a little funny-awkward but ah what the hell, and there he is with a smile, his arm draped around the guy. An hour later, unbeknownst to him, this image is already propagating like a beast all over the Internet, doubling its number of appearances there every few minutes, saved onto ever more hard drives, USB drives, soon made the background on phones, personal computers, backed up onto the memories of whirring towers tucked into closets, handled by servers in windy towns he would never deign to visit. Oh well, he would say, life is just a laugh.

Modesty? Ah, here is the conspicuously deleted entry in the thick catalog of his virtues.

❖

Nowadays everyone has their locker room etiquette sorted out. There are gay gyms and straight gyms, some mixed gyms, and people generally know how to dial down, or ramp up, their open admiration of another man's physique in these too-small rooms, always depending on well-marked, and long ago blazed, trails. You can look for 2.5 seconds at most any part of a naked man, that's free. More than that, and you're inviting something. Trouble or a party. An enemy, or perhaps a new friend. But be discreet. If you can't handle it, just keep your eyes to yourself the whole time. That's what most guys do.

If a guy really has a problem with nudity, he wouldn't be in the locker room, right? He'd just come into the gym wearing his workout clothes, leave wearing them too—and only go to the bathroom for a piss. And if you got it, you can walk around with thick and swinging meat—why not? Swinging slowly, back and forth, heavy dick and balls, to the shower, back, to the urinal. Because, hey nobody really cares, or should. If it bothers anyone too much, that says something too, only those struggling with themselves have a problem with the naked body, in a locker room, at a gym!

No one wants to seem like they are struggling with their sexuality in *that* place. The guys who changed out of their jeans with a towel wrapped tightly around their waist, they were either completely gay and having a breakdown about it, or neurotically religious. And anyway, the confident, sorted-out-with-himself man with a big dick shouldn't have to be modest just because one guy feels offended by the sight of a monster trouser snake, he shouldn't be impaired simply because seeing it slowly takes the shy guy's composure completely, making him want to jump over a locker room bench to worship it, all while he supposedly in his mind has a problem with it. That guy is tortured, but no one else is. And no one is going to say anything to the proud man in a locker room, especially if he is as fit as Sol.

It was generally agreed that if anything, we should be encouraging guys like Sol to be naked in more and more places during his day.

Here's where it got complicated. And I never really figured out why. But given all this, him getting naked still did set a subtle panic loose in the men's locker room. And it was as if he was aware of it, and didn't like it. But what he didn't like wasn't the flattering attentions of others, not at all, he didn't like that they were so embarrassed and awkward over their obvious attraction to him. He felt bad it had to be that way, and looked for a way to change it.

So as soon as he started dressing or undressing, he became much more gentle and kind in his movements and words. If he noticed someone staring at him, and they were like a deer in the headlights when he caught them, instead of murmuring *fag* under his breath like a guy like him might do in some sad 'burb of America, he would just say brighten a little and say *oh hey how are you? Good? Okay*...with a reassuring, confident nod as waves of visible relief crashed over the stunned man's face that his face wasn't going to be smashed in. It was a brilliant tactic. Now they still admired him, but they probably also left him a little bit more alone.

They had an expectation of being reprimanded for their ten seconds of gulping down his image with their eyes. In the end they were not chastised at all, but in fact the opposite—rewarded with his subtle smile. You might be a fan, but he would make of you a friend. Even so, with all the allowances he permitted, to be himself, comfortable, it was always the same—when he first walked in and put his clothes into a locker, a dozen guys immediately chose lockers close to his, and started and finished their workouts in time with his in the hopes of a front-row seat for the best show of their week. As pathetic as it was, I couldn't really blame them, and I counted myself among his lowly fans; I was maybe even the most pathetic one.

A funny thing desire is, even if a guy got lucky, it always seemed to go by too quickly. A guy like Sol can change clothes fast, and before you knew it, you couldn't exactly remember the details of his physique and wanted badly to see it again. It was like trying to remember the taste of your first ice cream. The sweetness is in the tasting. You could remember it, or you could just try to go get one. And so people, other men and even women, were always pent up in their hunger to see him, even if they just had. He just had the decency to be nice about it.

His niceness is exactly what was so intimidating about him, because it made him human. You really didn't want to be like a thousand other people who would paw him with their eyes, but then again, how could you seriously not be? He really didn't seem to mind, and come to think of it, he might have even liked it.

Here he is at his locker, bold as brass. But brass can't help but be bold, can it? After all, it's both gold and *shining*. A lot of good it would do for brass to be timid. He stands there in his pinstripe suit, then suddenly he is there with his pants around his ankles and implausibly, sock garters, elastic strained around his prominent calves. He has forgotten to take his jacket off first, and so in an unbuttoned all the way lavender oxford, undone tie loosely draped around his neck, messed-up dark blond hair, gray eyes, with his pants coming down, he is nearly toppling over. If the computer in your mind is taking mental pictures of this for later, it will lock up at this point.

He sits down bare ass on the bench, which moves significantly under his weight, and starts to undo his shoes. His black socks and dress shoes look so powerful, refined and civilized, you could believe that mankind has come a very long way indeed from the primordial ooze and dank caves that were once his berth; that is, until he opens his legs a little and stretches back, and you see his balls. The computer in your mind will now fatally error.

Looking at them, they almost do not make sense. These are not a gentleman's balls. These are two Caveman-needs-to-populate-the Earth motherfuckers. Each ball alone looks like two or three of any other man's balls. Surrounding them but not on them is a cloud of natural (not trimmed) mid-length golden brown hair, which is matted down and slick with sweat, against his upper and inner legs.

This hair is not heavy as it goes up his stomach toward his abdominals, but it *is* thicker as it tucks into his upper-inner thighs, and in particular down and around, and into his ass crack, surrounding most densely the spot where his asshole must be, like he tucked a handful of auburn cotton balls right over his asshole, becoming then less dense, finer, and more sporadic in each and every direction outward from that exact center, making the overall pattern of the soft golden hair on his sumptuous ass look almost exactly, if you stood back to admire it, like a bull's-eye. When I pass through the locker room as he is changing and see what I just described to you, I almost have to cough out of disbelief, lust, or excitement. I really can't say which it is. I definitely feel altered.

Standing there, shifting his weight from one leg to another, taking his time undressing out of his work clothes and preparing for his workout, texting on his phone, folding his clothes carefully, saying quiet hellos to whoever, subtly shining, gleaming with sweat before he has even started working out, he puts on his light gray compression shorts. Seconds after he has pulled them up, visible on the outside of his compression shorts, his left ass cheek has already delineated itself from his right ass cheek with a razor-thin line of demarcating sweat. The perfection of this line, its appearance out of nowhere, and the speed with which it had materialized, was as if I had just seen a miracle.

Pretending to check the football scores on the TV hanging down from the ceiling in the middle of the room, I watch as this line of sweat spreads outward from the center of his ass cheeks, growing thicker and denser in just the time I stood there. It spreads outward from the center of his ass in both directions so that the first few inches to the left and right of his butt crack are now visible. In the roughly two minutes it takes for him to pull on his fingerless gloves, the sweat has outlined every shape his ample balls and ass made, on the outside of his shorts, sketching it out for you, what the situation was inside them. If it wasn't for the nylon shorts he eventually pulls over them, in his compression shorts, he stands basically naked. But before he does, he takes his time, he walks around and has a sip of water at the drinking fountain, he stretches in the dry sauna that's in the corner of the men's locker room, and I memorize what I love about his look. Those massive balls, the uncut meat, average length but much thicker than most guys. Dazzling. But I always did like my bread buttered on all four sides.

This wasn't the mischievous attitude of a guy half flaunting a bulge in underwear that he knew fit him well, what we jokingly refer to as plum-smugglers: big, full testicles very much in-your-face, but decently tucked away, still displaying a large and admirable bulge. There's a ton of those guys who do exactly that amount of flaunting in the world. No, this was bulge-upon-bulge, too big to ignore. This was Sol Fucking Stein, and if he was smuggling the plums, he sure as hell wanted you to know where they were at all times, that they were both jaw-achingly beautiful and promptly leaving your vicinity, and if you fucking liked plums you might think about getting up off your arse and following him and letting him know somehow, because any second now someone else would, and then you would be the sorry piece of shit licking plum juice off *their* chin. Well, there were a lot of things in life I didn't know, but I knew that I wasn't gonna be that guy, no matter what.

He stands there, almost steaming. If you stared long enough, you could almost smell him, but frustratingly, could not. My thoughts blur—is he coming or going? Wait, did he just work out or is he starting? Does he notice when I go by him two, now three times? How long have I been away from my post?

And too soon, just like that, every day he would be gone. And I would be jogging back to the front desk, smiling and joking, giving a chubby gal a tour of the yoga room, signing her up for a two-year membership, making my commission, shouting out workout tips as I go by the members, the whole time thinking:

Give me a black eye when I make a pass at you, Sol Stein, or please show me what you want, because I need to stand out from your legions of fans, and I really do not know how to, believe me I don't, but you gotta know that it is always on my mind. And I am gonna figure out how to if it's the last thing I do.

After I had worked at the gym for about nine months, eventually it was time for me to close up by myself. I was kind of surprised that any one person was given this responsibility, honestly; a gym seemed to me like a little fortress of valuable equipment, luxurious amenities, and pricey retail products in the form of supplements as expensive as four-star meals. It just seemed a lot to give any one person the keys to. But I guess there were upscale retail shops with as much or more to lose than any gym, and they must all eventually trust their staff. There was nothing at Gucci or Hermès I wanted. But to run butt-naked through the women's locker room, free weight area, and reception desk with your friends would be priceless.

A lot of young kids fantasize about being let loose in a mall unsupervised all night long, it's basically the teenage dream, but I am twenty-seven, and somewhere in the back of my mind, when it finally happened, I realized that much more than that, I had always wanted to lord over a whole gym by myself, all night.

I fantasized that I would call up the directors of gay porns and tell them to shoot their next feature here, fantasized about throwing parties and inviting all my friends, having sex all over the place, jacking off in the mirrors that people checked their *Surya Namaskara* out in, about playing whatever music I wanted, and most of all going through everyone's lockers, ransacking the lockers of those who were mean to me every day and peeking into those guys' lockers who were nice to me.

So when the day came that I was staying late giving a young couple a tour and trying halfheartedly to get them to sign up by pushing the free towel service, and I saw the whirling keys headed through the air toward my head from my boss, I caught them with true excitement. He waved me over to his desk and I excused myself. I was told not to be nervous, that everyone that worked there had a night that they had to close up shop, that most people hated it, but that it was easy and even if everything went wrong, as long as I did not close early, and set the alarm when I left, nobody would have a problem with me.

"Feel free to work out when you're done with your shift, that goes without saying."

"Great. I wanted to get a workout in today."

This massive-to-me perk was normal. Encouragement of personal fitness is one of many things I liked about working in a gym. Maybe some of my friends looked down on me for my job, as they worked at banks and the mall, but who else could go to work not wearing underwear all day? Still, you could say I was very shocked when he added:

"Oh, and I know it's a grody thing to ask of you, but if anyone leaves their stuff locked up in a locker overnight, you gotta use the bolt cutters and cut the locks off. Open them up and empty them out before you leave. It's not usually very many people—maybe six or seven lockers, out of five hundred that are locked. The members know they are not allowed to claim a locker and keep stuff here overnight, but a few always try to. Just cut the locks off. Wear some rubber gloves if you...you know...gotta touch anybody's stuff. You don't have to wear the gloves, but you can."

He seemed genuinely grossed out and somewhat apologetic for having to ask me to do something so dirty.

"Okay," I laughed gently, "but what do I do with the stuff that's in the lockers?"

"That's the weird thing! Most of these people that try to claim a locker, there's nothing in there when you finally open it. I dunno, throw whatever's in there in a trash bag, we'll keep it with the lost and found stuff."

"There's a lost and found? I never seen—"

He looked at me admiringly and added, "Good night! Remember to turn off all the TVs. There's…twenty-three of them," he said with a wink. "Just count down as you go. Or you can do all of them with one remote…it's around here somewhere…"

The first night was pretty slow, and I was a bit timid to really own the space after hours. I felt like everyone I knew during the day was still there, watching me. I put on the music I wanted to hear, wore some slightly more revealing workout clothes than I might have normally chosen, kept flashing myself my dick as I lifted weights, stupid stuff. I really didn't do much differently than I would have if it had been noon in a packed gym. But it was raining and beautiful out, peaceful.

Even though there were so many windows at the gym and it wasn't that late, I found it interesting that no one really looked in. If a gym isn't open and the members can't enter, it was almost as if the building didn't exist. Myself, I am always looking in windows of closed buildings.

Word soon got out that I didn't mind locking up at night, and pretty quickly, I was doing it every night, and timidity turned into temerity regarding what I did after the last patron left at midnight. I was calling a dozen of my friends over to work out, I'd turn the music up, play inappropriately raunchy tunes, guys were walking around shirtless in compression shorts and barefoot. We'd sit in the dry sauna and talk and drink and horseplay. Sure it was late, but curiously I never had the slightest difficulty getting a single friend to come over to the gym at that time. I guess I was not the only one whose fantasy it was to have total freedom in a gym, a different kind of gym, one that was a little more rowdy and fun. It was like a whole other gym, a bar-gym, a nighttime gym, a better gym. It wasn't dirty and downscale like a sex club, it was still luxurious, but no one was in charge, and we could choose who we wanted to be there.

I never went into the women's locker room. Every locker could be locked in that room, for all I knew. But no one complained or mentioned it. After my friends left every night, I would go into the men's locker room before I left, cut all the locks off the lockers, and vacate any stuff that was in there.

I found amazing things. A Walkman from the 1980s with a Wham! cassette still in it. Square-cut bathing trunks from the first time they were fashionable. A man's locker is the closest we men get to the privacy of a woman and her purse; these were little soul-cabinets. I found an intense little journal of one man's progress to bodybuilder size, noted the crushing intensity and judgment with which he regarded himself, the pencil writing small and strained. I found gay porn in the same locker as a Bible with many passages underlined in red. A love letter to a woman, never sent. Old photos, half-drunk protein shakes, wrestling shorts, jock straps, and enough compression shorts to open my own athletic shop.

I never eroticized the clothes I found, and they weren't too erotic, honestly. Even though I suspected I was a piggy kind of guy, and figured I would find it sexy to feel up all these guys' clothes, something was missing. I mean I would open the lockers, and if there was a soaked-through sweaty jock strap in there that looked appealing, yeah, it would definitely make me very quickly raging hard, but even as I touched it, I would feel respect that this was someone's intimate item of clothing. As fun as it would be to feel it up, wrap it around my hard cock, and jack my load into it, it wouldn't be like spending a sexy night with Sol. There had to be something special about sex, I thought, in order for me to be supremely turned on, amused but not a little disappointed in myself.

My lording over the gym at night had pretty much run its course and I was bored with all variations of wild boys I could think of in about three weeks. Sure, sometimes my friends would still come by and work out, or we'd watch a movie in the men's lounge, or a hot couple I knew would want to have sex in some backstairs corner of the place after hours, and I would just smile and tell them sure, just clean up after. Mostly I was back to just working out at night, alone, lifting weights while classical music played in the background, as my only fringe benefit of having the keys to the kingdom. I had been doing that for a week or so when Sol Stein walked in front of the front desk to leave, to then slowly turn back toward me with a question.

"Is the gym...open late now?"

Completely panicked. I literally found it hard to speak.

"Wh...what?"

"Is the gym? Open late now?"

I chuckled guiltily.

"Well...well...why, as a matter of fact it, it—"

"—because it would be really convenient for me to work out then sometimes."

I decided I must get it together and not miss my chance.

"*Sure*. Of course. I mean, not for everyone? But yeah," I said completely earnest. "Come by tomorrow. We will be open."

"No matter how late?"

"No matter how late."

He smiled, pleased. "Fine."

He slapped the desk once, settling the matter for good.

I would invite none of my friends that night. Movie night would not be happening. If anyone but Sol Stein showed up, I would turn off every light and sit in the dark until he got there, and then every light would come on, for him.

The next night at midnight, sure enough Sol Stein did show up. But so did more potential new members than we ever had show up at closing time. My boss was so impressed by our potential for a record sales month that even he stayed an hour later. Sol came in, did his biceps, and that was something nice, but everything was somehow wrong. The gym was too loud, the phones were still ringing—other than it being a Saturday night, it couldn't have been less like a date! I did think I saw Sol looking at me at the front desk while I was talking to some new members. I caught myself looking at him nearly every day. But I never thought I noticed him looking at me before.

When I approached my boss later that night with an idea, it sure didn't go the way I planned.

"Sir, I was thinking. You know I have been staying late, and a lot of people seem to come after midnight. I was thinking that maybe we should increase our hours on the nighttime side to accommodate—"

"Scratch. Uh-uh. I appreciate the idea, but as a matter of fact, I have been getting some comments that the gym is too loud after closing time from some of our neighbors in offices nearby. Apparently they pull some late nights in some offices in this building and they think you're having a party in here. Just get the gym closed and go home. Don't even work out here then."

"Oh, okay."

"And I will close up tonight and tomorrow. Thanks. Go home."

I could say I was disappointed, but the little fuckups in my life were too common for me to be too surprised at them. I knew somehow that I would have a moment, sometime, to tell Sol what I thought of him. I mean, I didn't even know him really. But I thought I would like to at least have the chance to. I thought, deep down, that I still would. I just didn't know how, but no mistake—I surely kept the flame alive.

When Monday night came and midnight too, I was turning off the twenty-third television in a blacked-out gym, standing in front of the little computer by the door with flashing green and red lights, setting the alarm when, in the dark, I noticed heat at my back and a figure suddenly behind me.

I jumped around. It was Sol.

"I thought you were staying open later."

I decided if Sol and I were going to progress, I could start by being more direct with him.

"We never really were staying open later. I wanted to lobby for longer hours, and I was just hanging around here alone at night, sometimes letting my friends in. But we aren't really open. In fact, they pretty much shot down my idea for changing the hours. I am sorry, Sol."

"Oh. Well, it's no big deal. I liked your idea, though. A lot of us keep late nights."

I smiled so deep within me. Him liking an idea of mine was a good start. I had other good ideas, too.

He looked different in the low light of the city then. Softer and more vulnerable. It sounds crazy, but I felt like we were boyfriends right from that moment, I could feel myself about to give into him, in exactly the way I would many times when we would someday be boyfriends, so that after he was walking away for a minute I ran after him and said:

"*Sol!* I know you came all this way, and I did tell you that you could. I'm sure it's just, you know, good customer service if I go ahead and let you work out, at least for tonight."

He turned around and walked right up to me, and I saw his gray eyes and his stubble and smiled. He simply said *okay* in the softest way and walked past me back to the building. He had spoken in a voice I never heard in all the months of overhearing his small talk with everyone at the gym, in a tone I didn't know could ever come out of him.

I put some music on, only turned on the lights overhead where he was working and kept the rest off, and decided I would work out in the same area.

He laid back at the chest press bench. I did military press at the Smith machine nearby.

"It's nice like this. The minimal lighting. I wonder why gyms are always so glaring. This music's perfect. Really relaxing."

I decided I just needed to drop the intrigue of the obsessive fan if we were really going to know each other. I didn't say anything for a couple minutes and just let his remarks warm the air. I decided to let myself feel his equal.

"Maybe you should open your own gym," he added.

I smiled huge.

"Half gym, half library. Half espresso bar. What else could I pack in?"

"Internet café? Laundromat!"

We laughed.

"What do they have you do exactly, to close up?"

"Oh, all kinds of things. I gotta turn off the TVs. Shut the Jacuzzis off. Let's see, uh, cut the music. Just a bunch of tedious items. Tally up the cash. Though I usually can work out before I leave, so that's nice. Oh, and I have to cut the locks off the lockers and toss the stuff inside into a trash bag. Does it sound gross?"

"Gross? No. It sounds *interesting*, though. You must have found your share of odd items. Or is it just…?"

I rolled my eyes conspiratorially.

"It's everything. Sports jerseys, sweatpants in size XXXL. A ton of caps. Cuff links, used jocks, sock, uh, garters."

Sol guffawed out of nowhere. "Ha, I bet. You must have found something of mine sometime in there. Sorry if you did. You shouldn't have to clean up after people, really."

"Never."

"Never?"

"Never have I found anything of yours."

He smiled earnestly, with intensity. "You don't think so? I'm sure I leave things all the time."

"Nope. You have never forgotten anything in the gym after you have left."

He laughed in wonder at my confident conclusion.

"Yeah, but how can you know—"

"Because I pay attention to you," I whispered, low under my breath.

"I'm sorry?"

"Because I…have, and do, pay a hell of a lot of attention to you."

Sol laughed nervously.

"You always choose the same locker. 333. Then, a few months ago, you switched to 111. For months, you chose 333, every time, and then you suddenly switched. You will do 222 once in a while but never 444. You like numbers, repetition of numbers. Anyway, you are back to 111, and I don't know what it means to you, it's just something that I *know* about you. If you look stressed, you will sweat first from your neck, a torrent, a kind of Niagara Falls. If you are feeling great, you sweat from around your waist first. You never wear a jock strap. Only compression shorts. You talk to people who stare at you. One time you dropped your MP3 player and before you picked it back up, I caught the text on the screen, something called 'The Most Beautiful Song In The World' was playing and I didn't hear even a bit of it, but I always wondered what it was, almost every day I do, in fact."

We both realized we had stopped working out. I was about to cry, just from stress or pent-up desire for him, simple exhaustion. But I fought back, and finished what I had to say. I walked up to him and touched his face, near his dripping temples.

"And above all, you are always sweating. I see, I make out, shapes in the sweat on your sleeveless T-shirts. I call it my Rorschach. I make out forms in the sweat-dark shapes you make, against a maroon T-shirt. And one gray shirt, but not often. One with purple letters. TCU Football. I don't know what that is either. You haven't worn that for a long time. But the last time you wore it, it was sopping wet here, here…here."

I touched where his left underarm was, his neck, and his right underarm. Then I laid my flat palm against the very center of his solar plexus. "But it was most sweaty right here."

Just then there was a clanging at the front door.

"Excuse me."

I thought it was someone trying to come in, and ran over. But it was the cleaning crew. They explained that they were going to be coming earlier than they used to, and that I had to leave so they could work. They knew the layout well, so the dozen-member team just started roaming all over, Windexing, vacuuming, emptying trashes. Flicking a few more lights on.

"You gotta leave," the manager of the team said flatly to me.

"Okay. I just gotta, you know, turn off the TVs, then I'll leave."

As I was ticking off every duty I had to take care of before I left, jogging up to where the rows of TVs were, Sol was walking with his gym bag back toward me, toward the exit. My stomach sank. I was sure he was never gonna be my friend or boyfriend now. I suppose there was some consolation that I probably wouldn't get a black eye.

"Sol—"

"Well, good night. Thanks for staying open for me. See ya tomorrow. Don't forget to cut the locks off."

He laughed. He was making fun of me. This was gonna be the beginning of us having tension when we saw each other, and this time he wouldn't do anything to mitigate it for his, or especially my, comfort.

In despair, I went into the men's locker room. I had been so regular cutting them off lately, maybe members were getting the point, because there were none to cut off that night.

Or so I thought. At 333, hanging there in the low light the skeleton crew worked in, was a single, thick, gleaming lock. I was confused, annoyed. I dreaded seeing what was inside. A little humiliation, no doubt.

It took several tries and I couldn't get it. I called the foreman of the cleaning crew over, and together we got the lock off, with one of us on each side of the bolt cutters. When it swung open, the director of the cleaning crew saw what was inside first. I had fallen on my ass with the bolt cutters on top of me.

"Oh great. Congratulations for what's inside, buddy! Now I gotta go work."

He laughed at me, I said thanks to him and opened the locker door. Inside was a jock strap, hanging from a hook in the top of the locker. It was gleaming with sweat, size XL. And there was a note.

You were right about all that, by the way. Except I do wear jock straps. I was wearing a jock strap tonight. It's my only one.

I grabbed it with both hands, and for the first time really let myself bury my face in a man's jock strap. Right there in the men's locker room, I immediately rubbed it on my chest, against my cock, where the leg straps crossed over, right where his asshole would be especially, I ground that area into my dick. I put it all of it in my mouth at once and closed my eyes, laughing as it popped out.

Placing its pouch right over my nose, I swabbed my face with it, anointed. I was having a blast. This was like when a kid has a crush on you in the third grade and they send a note saying *I like you*. But about a million times better than that. *What a nice guy*, I thought as I put his jock strap under my shirt and held it to the center of my chest and, without meaning to, fell asleep, with a straining erection.

I awoke to the sound of some gaudy radio hit by the pop princess of the week loud in my ears, and one of my coworkers kicking the bottoms of my shoes hard. Members were changing all around me, and my boss wanted to talk to me.

People walking by his office would see him yelling at me for a good forty-five minutes for many reasons. News of my late-night parties finally reached him, my using the gym as my own personal clubhouse, nightclub, and singles bar. I felt bad, but not terrible. For some reason I still held Sol's jock strap in my right hand as I took the abuse from my boss. Something about there only being fifty lockers in play in the women's side of the locker room, because I never went in there. And what was I holding in my hand? Was that a member's property?

And at this I walked out. Still holding Sol's jock of course, always, for the next few unemployed days, holding his jock. In fact I was still holding it when the phone rang and I heard his voice on my home phone.

"Hello?"

"Hello." I could tell, even though I could not see him, that he was smiling, and that made me laugh a little, though I didn't think he could hear it.

"How did you get my number?"

"I pressed them tonight about what happened. Your boss seemed pretty mad at you. He was more than happy to give me your number when I explained that you I was sure you were in possession of some of my personal property."

I laughed a little hard. "Yeah. That I am," I said, twirling it in my fingers, suddenly hoping that he didn't want it back. "I'd hate to part with it, but maybe you could loan it again—"

"Do you want to come over and have some quiche?"

"Some, uh, quiche?"

"Are you seriously busy? I mean, what am I saying, you've joined, I'm sure enthusiastically, the ranks of the unemployed, how can you be busy?"

"I could be busy. But I'm not too busy for quiche. Never too busy for quiche," I said, at first having a hard time imagining him cooking that, but quickly making sense of it. *Hearty food, a little bit country, a little refined...*

"Great. I'll come get you. Your boss gave me your address, too. He sure as hell hopes I kick your ass."

He came to pick me up about thirty minutes later. On the way to his house, he explained a lot of things. That he was flattered by everything I noticed about him. But more than that, he appreciated that I would always make eye contact with him, instead of only looking at his body, dick, and ass. Above all, he liked that I was up front with him about my desire.

"As many people as seemingly admire my looks. I'm alone most of the time. No one seems to have the guts to let me know what they really think. But I have needs, too, you know?"

Sol lived downtown, a thirty-minute drive from where I lived.

His place was nice. Spare, but had warmth, little furniture but what was there was sumptuously comfortable. Nothing on the wall in the living room, still there was a low leather sofa, wide, with soft blankets all over it. A large painting leaning against the wall made for some bright color and a medium-sized sculpture by that. No TV, but many books.

It was very warm in his place, and even though it was soon to be fall, I was surprised he'd have the heat on already. As if answering my mental query he spoke up. "There's a bakery downstairs. This room is always warm. Sometimes I open all the windows just to be comfortable."

"Don't you get cold?"

"Do I look like I get cold to you?"

He looked at me with finally some vulnerability in his eyes and walked over close to me.

"As if your constantly damp state is not the best thing about you, Sol."

"It isn't." And right here his voice softened—"Not the best thing, anyway."

"I wouldn't count it as a disability."

I excused myself to use the bathroom and maybe splash some water on my face. After I came out of the toilet, I realized I stood facing his walk-in closet. Maybe I had spent too many days breaking into people's personal things, but I walked forward and flicked the switch on.

It was a wide room, with new, dark wood flooring, and recessed lighting, and a small, perfectly square skylight. On the right were many nice suits on gleaming hangers. Some polo shirts, some tees. On the left, it was like someone took the Under Armour section from City Sports, gave it to Sol to wear, and he did, and then scattered it all over a dozen cedar-lined shelves. In other words, to me, it was the smallest, best curated museum in town. I flicked the light back off and committed myself to really be inside it, sat on the floor of his walk-in closet with his suits in front of me and his workout clothes flung on shelves behind me. There was still some space to lie down and spread out in between.

I looked ridiculous. Unemployed, sitting in a dark closet of someone I didn't know that well, his dirty underwear sticking out of my pocket. Maybe I should be completely miserable. But I wasn't. Sol's jock strap is like the perfect *amuse bouche* to me, and I fucking hated that job. This jock isn't just any man's. It is Sol's. His sweat, to me, is just like sunlight to a freshman on spring break. I can never get enough of it.

I prop myself up on my elbows a few minutes later when Sol comes in without turning the light on. He takes all his clothes off and stands there in the dark. And then he starts talking.

"Your name is Argus Heberling. In Greek mythology Argus was

a giant with a hundred eyes, which I always thought fit you because I don't know a lot about you, but I could always sense that you are observant, and that is kind of like knowing a lot, in itself. It means eventually you will know a lot more. Your hair is always a little spiky in the middle of your head but lies down soft around the edges. You wear sunglasses at work if you are having a down day, which has been more lately. People let you do this, not because it's allowed at your job, it's not, but because you look handsome in them and they are enjoying you in them, and so, say nothing. You have a heart tattoo on your upper inner left arm, in an unusual place, where it is not easily seen. For a long time it was just a heart. But then a couple months ago, you added wings to the heart. Which I only know because you wore a tank top exactly two days out of the past six months. And you love classical music. Absolutely love it. When you are working during the day, you tend to play classical music, even though your boss and coworkers tell you it is inappropriate for a gym, and members complain."

He kneeled down naked beside me as he said this last part. "You see, the reason I know this, is when you would work out those last weeks when you closed by yourself, I would come in, curious, and sit on the couch in the lobby and sometimes listen to the music you played when you were lifting weights, alone. I would sit there and read just for the hell of it, and I would watch you. And while I did this, I always heard *Reverie* by Claude Debussy, Mozart, string quartet, the adagio. Arthur Grumiaux on the violin. Myaskovsky. Haydn. Piano trio. Number 27. But your absolute favorite song. The song you played more than any other while you worked out, was Gymnopédie #1, by Erik Satie. Or, as I like to think of it, The Most Beautiful Song In The World."

We sat in silence for a few stunned minutes.

"You were stalking me. As I was stalking you. Is there a name for that?" I said, with a bit of a tear in my eye.

"No," he said, and licked the tear from my eye as soon as it had appeared. "Don't try to think of one."

I made him stand up, and I took my shirt off. With his jock strap still half sticking out of the right pocket of my jeans, I took my shirt off, shoes and socks. I unbuttoned all the buttons on my jeans so they started to fall off me a little.

"You're so sweaty, Sol."

"All the time." He added, "Would you like me to take a bath?"

"No. But I'd like to give you one."

I started licking his forehead. He was a little taller than me, though much broader, and he bent his knees a little to receive my unusual expression of affection.

I am going to give you a tongue bath, I whispered, into his hair.

"A tongue bath. Sounds like a bath that gets you dirty."

I never gave anyone a tongue bath before, but the thought always deeply intrigued me. And I couldn't have a more willing partner. I started, slowly, from his face, worshiping with my tongue every inch of his sweaty body.

I had wanted to do this for so long that I took my time, savored the wild, sensual taste, feel, and smell of him. I licked his nose on both sides, I sucked on his lips, I licked his closed eyes and gnawed on his stubbled chin, which made him laugh.

I took care, taking seriously my job to clean him, cleaning the sweat off his neck for ten minutes, and under his arms, taking bales of his underarm hair into my mouth, sucking the sweat from his long underarm hair, letting the primordial feeling overwhelm me. Licking over and over until I didn't taste any of his salt.

There was nothing gross here, there was nothing of him I didn't want. Nothing I could discover in my care of him that would have put me off my worshiping.

His pectoral muscles I grabbed with both hands to lick, and suck on; his muscles were full of moisture, a too-full sponge. You could wring or knead with your hands any muscle group on his body and your hands would slide slick across them, easy.

I laid him down on the floor, in the dark. And laid him face-down beside me. I let my drool drop down from my mouth into the crack of his ass, and let gravity press my face into it, swirling my tongue and kneading his ass cheeks apart as I did so.

Like throwing a football, like swinging a bat, like doing squats, a good rim job is actually done from your legs, you can't just use your lips or your mouth. I used my strong legs and all the force of my body to push my whole face deep into his ass, ramming my face in, over and over, making him moan loudly in pleasure. Proving my fitness to please him. Sol slammed his fist on the floor repeatedly while he squirmed.

I sucked on his leg hair, like a dog, the back of his kneecap, I lay on the floor, luxuriating there, as he put the heel of his sweaty foot in my mouth and then the flat of his feet. I licked clean and sucked on the toes of both of his feet—you would have thought that he was doing something very kind for me, seeing how happy I was there, and you'd be right. And as fast as I cleaned him, he stood there pouring sweat on me still, as I sweated underneath him, working so.

After I had licked both of his sweaty feet clean, Sol sat down on my face and lowered his balls into my mouth. I was flattered that he thought I could get both of them in my mouth at the same time, but I sure had fun trying to. I slathered them with tongue love, dutifully. Until he couldn't take it anymore and sat forward and spread his ass cheeks on my face so that I was able to see that his ass cheeks were deeper and sweatier than I had previously thought when I tongued him there before. But now, like this, it was only too easy to reach the very red center of the bull's-eye.

It was convenient that he was on top of me, so that when he lost control, it was simple for him to go to from this position to really planting both knees on either side of my face, to point his hard cock down my throat. Thrusting deep into my mouth, he fucked my open throat wildly while letting the weight of his upper body throw him forward on me, grinding on me like this, needing it. And there we were. In the dark, wet, sliding on each other, falling in love with it.

But I wasn't prepared for him to stand up after a few minutes of this, grab his compression shorts from out of his gym bag, and wring them out over my face. I felt the drops of the sweat that was like his secret sweat, the sweat closest to him hit my face. This quickly drove me over the edge, and I smiled, loving it as I grabbed my meat and jacked myself off. The look of me there and the sensuality of it all soon made Sol lose it and add his sperm to the sweat he'd just baptized my face with; his load mixed with his sweat and ran all over my face. He knelt down to kiss me. I lost my load then, and it went all the way up to my face from my dick in a jagged lightning pattern.

We emerged from our impromptu man-cave, grabbing bits of his clothes to wear as we sauntered out. Our choice reflected our playful mood, him wearing a pinstripe jacket and no shirt, pajama bottoms and slippers, and me wearing my jeans, no underwear, with one of his ties draped around my neck.

We chowed down on his excellent quiche like civilized gentlemen. And gulped down bowls of coffee.

Sol asked, "So where are you gonna work now?"

"I really don't know." I looked at him in his pinstripes. It was as good a look to be around all day as gym shorts were. "Maybe I'll work at a bank."

"I know a bunch of people who work at a bank. I could talk to someone."

I took a bit of the quiche. It was good. Something about the piquant flavor and our recent explorations led me to say something I never thought I'd say.

"A writer is what I really want to be."

Sol broke into a slow smile like the one a friend gets when you tell them a really good idea.

"A writer." Something about the way he said it made it sound deliciously subversive, and then I was sure that it was what I was going to do.

He took a big bite of his own quiche, and putting it square in his mouth said with anticipation and absorbed thought—

"I like that. I don't know *any* writers."

THE RICE MAN COMETH
MARK WILDYR

Roger Rice Rierdon received the snap, dropped back into his own end zone, and watched in dismay as his receiver, Donny De Santis, was brought down by illegal interference. Rice did a 360 to evade a lineman and kept on going. He stiffed a tackler, headed for a hole, and went into his swivel-hipped, broken-field dash. A defensive guard loomed up but was off balance, so Rice ran right over him. He wiggled through grasping hands and arms like a wet eel.

At midfield, he eluded the last obstacle and turned it loose, breaking into a flat-out piston run that left everyone behind. The excited crowd roared, and the public address system thundered a familiar refrain. "And the Rice Man cometh, ladies and gentlemen! The Rice Man cometh!"

The red flag on the play was declined, and his one-hundred-five-yard run led the Wilson High Chargers to their first state championship in five years.

Hours later, those swivel hips swayed to music at the after-game celebration back home. On what should have been the greatest day of his life, Rice felt off-kilter, unsettled. He looked over Cindy Malvern's shoulder and caught a glimpse of Donny dancing with his girl. Everyone else in the room would have taken the look in Donny's eyes as dreamy, but Rice recognized boredom when he saw it.

Pleading exhaustion, they left the dance early. After dropping off the girls, they discussed the game on the way to Donny's house.

"They had no defense, man."

Rice snorted. "Then how come my ass was shagged every play until the fourth quarter?"

His friend glanced over and gave a dazzling smile. "Guess your ass was too slow till then."

They laughed. He admired Donny's big brown eyes. He'd heard the cheerleaders say those eyes could get into any bed in town.

As tired as he was, Rice was reluctant for the evening to end when he pulled the Mustang to a halt at the curb before the De Santis house. Donny must not have felt the same way because he punched him on the shoulder, thanked him for the ride, and went inside.

❖

Their status as heroes lasted only until basketball season, and then life returned to the mundane. The weekend scrimmages at the park or on the field helped, but something indefinable had happened to Rice. His grades and relationships suffered. The schoolwork he could do something about, but something else was going on…inside. When Cindy claimed he wasn't really interested in her and broke it off, he was stunned to realize he didn't care.

The coach, who was also his counselor, picked up on Rice's malaise and shared years of high school experience, telling him of jocks who grew depressed when their careers ended. It was a natural letdown, but he'd get over it. Besides, he had college ball to look forward to.

Rice knew it was more than simply a letdown, but he couldn't put his finger on it. He got more out of a conversation with Donny than the one with coach.

"Hell, Rice Man, you oughta be counting your blessings, not singing the blues." They were sitting in the 'tang and sucking on some illicit beer. "Man, you got everything."

"Everything?" He snorted. "Like what?"

"This great set of wheels, for one. Your folks got money, so you don't have to work. You got a scholarship, good grades, a good-looking girl. Well, you had one till you blew her off. Shit, you're the best-looking cocksman in the state with a big dick and a pair of balls. What else do you want?"

He grinned. "Been checking me out? Shit, Donny, you got those things, too."

"Yeah, right. That's why I work down at the warehouse loading and unloading crates. And that's why I drive the Rattletrap." Donny referred to his twenty-year-old Ford.

Rice's belly muscles tightened. "As far as a cock is concerned, I hear it's nip and tuck who's got the biggest one. Maybe we oughta measure and settle it once and for all."

"Well, you'd win that one hands down, because I couldn't get it up for you."

That stung a little. Why? He didn't know, but the mental image of the two of them standing face-to-face in a cock contest got stuck in his mind.

Later that night as he lay in his dark bedroom with semen drying on his chest and belly he realized he'd held the image of Donny De Santis in his head as he masturbated. Ah, man, what was going on? Well, the guy was as pretty as a girl. He chuckled. Hearing that always got a rise out of Donny, who took it as a slur on his manhood.

But it was true. The guy had clear, dark skin that never saw a pimple. He took so much teasing about his long, curling lashes and big, brown moon-eyes that he threatened to start wearing glasses whether he needed them or not. Years of Youth Athletic Football League and high school ball hadn't bent his straight nose or scarred his broad mouth. The rest of him followed form…good shoulders, deep chest, flat belly, manly hips. It was the same right on down to his soles. Rice might be Wilson High's Nordic Thor, but Donny De Santis was its Mediterranean Adonis.

The two of them had formed a bond when they joined YAFL. They were both six-year-olds at the time, and they'd been inseparable ever since, sharing illnesses and joys, victories and defeats. As he thought of their years together, Rice edged closer to what was really bothering him: They wouldn't play ball together next year. He was going one way, Donny another. How could he make it without the big lug? Shit, how would Donny survive without him?

But that wasn't all. They'd shared about everything over the years as they grew from awkward, gawky kids into teenaged jocks. But they hadn't shared one another.

Rice sat straight up in the bed. Where the hell had that thought come from? He tossed and turned another hour, but it wouldn't go away until he jacked off again.

❖

Over the next few days, he came close to saying something to Donny a dozen times, but at the last second, he'd clamp his mouth shut. They were going to scrimmage this weekend over at East End Park. He'd find a way to say what was on his mind then.

But there was a special order down at the warehouse, which meant Donny had to work late that Saturday. Rice wandered over to the park by himself and joined in a football game. In a perverse frame of mind, he was pleased it was tackle, not touch. Perfect for releasing pent-up frustration.

In some way he didn't quite understand, Rice liked these informal contests better than the games on the gridiron. The absence of hundreds of spectators shouting encouragement and calling his name bummed him some, but sandlot games gave him something else. The players weren't wrapped up in padding and protective gear, which made it more personal. His fingers met raw muscles and dug into living flesh. And when the other guys tackled him, it was almost like they were groping him. It was a turn-on…kinda.

And then there was the sweat. Even this late in the year, when the really hot months were behind them, a little running around on the field kicked off the hypothalamus and produced rivulets of wet, musky sweat loaded with pheromones. The briny stew didn't get soaked up by thick uniforms and contained by plastic helmets; it covered everyone and everything. Got in their faces. Stung the eyes. Put salt on the lips.

As the afternoon wore on, he couldn't tell whether the film covering him was his own secretion or that of half a dozen other guys. This was man-to-man. The way the game ought to be played. They were like fucking gladiators. Shit, sweat turned him on.

❖

Rice had agreed to pick up Donny at the warehouse that evening because the Rattletrap was acting up. He got there early and parked at the far end of the building. Zipping his windbreaker against the chill night air, he strolled toward the loading dock where Donny's crew was still working on a big trailer.

He plopped his butt down on a stack of pallets at the corner of the building where he was sheltered from the breeze and out of the reach of the harsh warehouse spotlights. Invisible to the workers on the dock, he stretched his legs in front of him and watched the crew work. He was fascinated by the play of muscles down Donny's back. By the way his biceps bunched and flexed. By the strong thighs.

Rice didn't even feel it coming, he just suddenly had an erection. He pressed his hand over the boner. It felt good. His eyes still on Donny, he yanked opened his fly and freed his cock. It was big; he knew that from years in a locker room. He skinned the foreskin back. Ahh. He stroked his rod, starting slowly and then getting into a rhythm. Faster. Harder. His breath grew ragged as he edged toward the precipice. His eyes never left Donny.

He missed a stroke when his friend paused for a moment to stare in his direction. Instead of alarm, Rice experienced a rush. He came unexpectedly, shooting cum all over his jacket. He ignored it, pumping through a great orgasm while staring at the trim, athletic figure of Donny De Santis. As he shuddered through his ejaculation, he felt something. What? He swallowed hard. He didn't know. Just… something. Something different from when he and Cindy did it.

As his breathing calmed, the cool night air chilled his wilting penis. With what seemed a tremendous effort, he pulled out his handkerchief and swiped at his jism. Shit, there was too much of it. He'd shot a bucketful. With his dribbling cock hanging out of his britches, he waddled awkwardly back to the Mustang and cracked the lid on a bottle of Crystal Springs to wash himself off.

By the time he got back to the stack of pallets, the work gang had assembled on the dock to pull on coats and retrieve lunch pails. Rice waited until Donny had almost reached the stacked pallets before stepping forward.

His friend gave a tired smile. "Been waiting long?"

"Naw. Just got here," Rice lied. "You look beat."

"Kinda. Think I'll go on home."

"Got a six-pack in the car. Coupla beers first?"

"Sure. Might relax me. Sorry to crap out on you."

"'S'okay. Ready to pack it in myself."

Rice drove to a remote park he knew would be deserted this time of evening. Twilight was fading and darkness was settling in. Neither of them spoke during the short ride. He suspected Donny dozed off a couple of times. They remained quiet during the first couple of beers even though Rice had things to say. He just didn't know how to say them.

He had realized something when he whacked off watching his friend work. He wanted Donny. Well, at least he was curious about wanting him. And it was more than just wanting to know who had the bigger cock. Way more. The revelation scared the hell out of him. But it was exciting, too.

"You over your blues or whatever?" Donny broke the silence as they worked on their last bottle.

"Guess so. Figured out what it was, anyway." Now! Now was the time to get it out in the open. To let Donny know how he felt. He weaseled. "You?"

"Me? Didn't know I was moping around."

"Do you realize how long we've known one another? You've been my main man since I was six years old. Played ball with you for twelve years." Rice lost his nerve. "Now we've played our last game together."

"Yeah. I thought about that, too. But we're still friends. We've still got one another."

He swallowed hard. "Yeah. Best buds."

"Gotta pee, man." Donny broke the silence that followed. "Let's go to the pisser."

Rice kicked over the motor and drove to the other side of the park. They got out of the car and went in together. The urinals had little modesty panels, which was all that saved him from embarrassment. His cock reared its head as soon as he pulled it out. From the corner of his eye, he watched Donny stare resolutely down at himself while he emptied his bladder. Rice stuffed his unruly cock back into his pants before the monster grew too much.

"What the hell do you have all over you?" Donny asked as they washed their hands at the sinks.

Rice glanced in the mirror. Dried, flaky spots stained his jacket.

"Be damned," Donny said, grinning at him in the mirror. "The Rice Man jerked off all over himself." He laughed.

Rice felt like his cheeks were on fire. "Like you never do it."

"Not so sloppy," Donny admitted with a smile. "It's worse when you get it on your pants."

Rice relaxed. "Yeah. When you wash them off, everybody thinks you peed your pants."

"What's more socially acceptable? Pissing your pants or coming in them?"

"Coming is definitely more adult." He went weak with relief as his friend let him off the hook. But Donny kept snickering while Rice swiped his jacket with a wet paper towel.

When he glanced down at the other boy's groin, Donny went quiet. He looked up and knew he'd been caught. Confusion twisted Donny's features. Abruptly, he turned and headed out the door. "Night, Rice Man," he called over his shoulder. "See ya Monday."

"Hey, wait. You're riding with me, remember?"

By the time he dried himself off and went outside, Donny was halfway across the park, running like he'd caught a pass and the other team was hot on his heels. Even though he was a good mile and a half from his house, Rice knew better than to go after him. With a frustrated sigh, he drove straight home.

❖

Donny seemed to have forgotten the whole awkward episode by Monday. He acted like his usual laid-back self. Rice had fretted over the encounter all day Sunday, and that pissed him off. The Rice Man wasn't a pussy. He didn't go around worrying about what other people thought. Of course, Donny wasn't exactly "other people." No sweat; everything turned out okay.

The week passed slowly, but Saturday eventually arrived. This time, Donny got off work at noon and showed up on the soccer field at the park where they scrimmaged. The other guys always insisted the two of them play on opposite teams. Otherwise, it was an unequal contest. Today was no exception.

Rice gave Donny a grin as the two sides lined up. The center hiked the ball, and the contest was under way. Donny dropped back, faked a pass, and headed for the weaker side of the line…the left side. Rice anticipated his move, but wasn't quick enough to prevent a gain on the play. He felt the strength and vitality of Donny's thighs as he wrapped himself around them. Both of them bounced off the turf once or twice. He got up and offered a hand. Donny accepted, but scooted the ball a few inches forward with a big wink.

Aw, shit. Let him get away with it. They huddled and went to the line again. It was a pass this time, but Rice got a finger on the ball and tipped it away. The third down was a run. Donny took the hike and charged right over his own center. Rice was out of position, but he put his swivel hips to good use and charged into his friend from the side. He was a little high, and his arms grasped Donny's thighs. As they tumbled, his left palm pressed against his opponent's package. Even in the excitement of the action, he could feel that Donny wasn't wearing a cup. He was half-hard. Rice couldn't help himself. He squeezed.

Donny got up and gave him a funny look. Neither of them said anything as the lines reformed. Rice inhaled. Sweat. Funky, sexy sweat. And some of it was Donny's. He sniffed his hand before remembering he was in public. He swiped his nose to make it look natural.

The next three plays were passes. After that the ball went to Rice's team. He took the hike and went wide to the right. Donny followed him. He faked a pass and then charged. Donny wasn't fooled and nailed him at his own scrimmage line, but he but tackled him around the torso. Dumb. Rice gained another couple of yards before going down. That wasn't like Donny.

The teams were pretty evenly matched, so the game seesawed back and forth. The Rice Men—that was the name of every team he played on—were up by six when Donny charged through his line and headed right for him with the pigskin tucked under his right arm. He feinted left...and then headed right in an all-out run. He almost got past, but Rice got one hand on his left leg, managing to slow the runner. Then he brought his other hand around and had him...right in the crotch. Rice held on as they hit the ground in a tumble. He ended up on Donny's back with a hand trapped beneath his basket. Despite himself, he squeezed Donny again. The cock in his palm responded.

Suddenly, Donny rolled over, throwing him off his back. He scrambled to his feet and glared, his hand hovering protectively over his fly. Without saying a word, he whirled and stalked off the field.

Fending off questions about what had happened, Rice shrugged and said he guessed Donny sprained a wrist or something. Sprang a boner was more like it, but he couldn't say that.

Despite repeated calls, Donny wouldn't answer his cell phone and ignored his tweets. Rice tried again Monday afternoon after his friend didn't show up for class. This time, he dialed the home phone. When Mrs. De Santis said her son didn't feel like taking the call, he offered to come over. A chill rolled down his back when she said that wouldn't be a good idea.

❖

Tuesday, they saw one another in the hall before homeroom. Their eyes met briefly. Then Donny dropped his gaze and walked on by. Rice swallowed hard and followed him into the room. Their assigned seats were side by side, but the bell rang before he could say anything. At next bell, Donny dashed out the door and headed for Trig. Rice had a social studies class. Donny managed to elude him the rest of the week, even going so far as to miss two homeroom classes to avoid sitting beside him.

By the time Saturday rolled around, Rice's head was so fucked up he considered skipping the scrimmage. But when he arrived, his heart played a tattoo in his chest. Donny was there, and he sure as hell couldn't avoid him on the field.

But Donny did his best to do just that, passing or handing the ball off more than running it himself. An hour into the game, when the sweat was pouring and the bodies were getting steamy, Rice ran over the center and headed right for Donny. He almost eluded his grasp, but Donny managed to get an arm around him and hold on. They went down and rolled. He ended up on bottom with Donny's nose no more than four inches from his. Those brown eyes stared right down into his soul. He saw something there, but it was fleeting. Then Donny's face tightened in anger…fear. Rage? But just before he scrambled up, Rice felt it. A boner. An erection. Hard and hot against his groin.

"Fuck you, Rierdon. Fuck you to hell." His best friend for twelve years, turned and walked back to his own side of the field.

After that, the game turned nasty. Rice's hurt turned to anger, and he dealt with it the only way he knew how…throwing everything he had into the game. They drove their teams hard, too hard. Some of the guys began to complain, to ask what was going on. Rice simply played as rough as he could, and Donny matched him blow for blow.

The game broke up early. Rice was glad. His anger had burned itself out. The sweat was no longer doing it for him. Now it just smelled like sweat, body emissions. He was turned off by it, defeated by it. Shit, he'd just lost his main man.

❖

If Rice thought he'd been in the doldrums before, now he was in the pits. He hated to get up in the morning. He grew surly with people when it was uncalled for. He and Donny might as well have lived in different towns…states, even. Donny went out of his way to avoid seeing him. Rice walked around disoriented half the time. He started looking for fights, but nobody would take him on. Donny probably would have, but that was one step he wasn't willing to take.

It came to a head with one ring of Rice's cell phone the Friday afternoon school broke for the holiday season.

"We need to meet," Donny's voice growled in his ear. "We gotta get this thing cleared up."

"You name the time and place."

"I've got a six-pack. Coors."

"Light?"

"Yeah."

"Okay, how about East End Park. An hour."

As Rice showered, he wondered if he was cleaning up for a fistfight. If Donny came at him, would he put up a battle, or just take it? He deserved anything he got, probably. But he wasn't just going to stand and take a beating. He finished rinsing off and nodded. He'd defend himself, but he wouldn't try to put his friend down. While he was drying off, he got a woody that wouldn't quit. He seriously considered jerking off but decided against it. He dressed with difficulty—his hard-on kept getting in the way of the zipper.

When he pulled in behind the Rattletrap at the park, Donny got out and walked back to the car. He seemed uncertain, but Rice couldn't read his face. Donny wore something between a scowl and a frown.

He opened the passenger's door and slipped into the seat. The six-pack went on the floorboard at his feet.

"Drive," Donny said.

"Where?"

"Anywhere. Down to the river. Up on the mesa. Anywhere."

Rice kicked over the motor and pulled out of the park. Neither of them said a word as he drove to the mesa and parked where they could look down on the town spread out below. The sun was down and a few lights were beginning to pop on.

He leaned back in his seat and glanced at Donny out of the corner of his eye. They both spoke at the same time.

"I'm sorry—"

"Shit, man, I'm—"

Rice rode right over him. He wanted to get it out of the way. "I'm sorry I was such a shit. But I didn't know how to handle it."

Donny met his eye. "*You're* sorry? Man, I was the one being an ass." He paused. "Yeah, I know what you mean. I didn't know how to handle it, either."

"I shouldn't have…you know, groped you."

Donny blinked. "Groped me? Hell, I shouldn't have got a hard-on."

They turned in the seat and looked at one another. Rice spoke first. "You mean you got all pissed at me because *you* got a hard-on?"

Even in the twilight, Donny's flush was apparent. "Yeah, I got embarrassed and didn't know how to handle it. I thought you'd be hacked off at me."

"So you cold-shouldered me for a month because you got a boner for me?"

Donny turned away and looked out the window. "Well, yeah."

"Man, I thought you were pissed at me because I grabbed your pecker."

Donny's head swiveled. "You mean you did that on purpose?"

Rice gave a nervous laugh. "Well…*yeah*. I squeezed it, didn't I?"

"Let me get this straight. You were feeling me up?"

He swallowed hard. "Yeah. Couldn't help myself."

"How come?"

"Because I…I…"

Donny clapped his hands to his head and laughed aloud. "I don't believe it. The Rice Man's at a loss for words. That's rich."

"You don't have to make fun—"

Donny put a hand on his arm. "I'm not laughing at you. I'm laughing at what a couple of dolts we've been. I've been fighting to keep from doing the same thing to you."

"Why didn't you?"

"Afraid to. It's not like getting in a car with a girl. She knows exactly what you want. A guy wouldn't be expecting you to put the moves on him."

"How long have you been thinking about it?"

"Tenth grade," Donny replied promptly. "You?"

"I'm slow. Just the last few weeks." He pulled two more beers from the pack and tossed one to Donny. "Have you ever…you know?"

"Just with girls. Never thought about it with a guy—until now."

"Me neither." Rice turned in his seat as two cars rolled up onto the mesa and rumbled toward them. "Shit!" he muttered with feeling.

Donny eyed the approaching vehicles. "Maybe we oughta slow things down a little. Think about this some more."

"I…" He tried to work some saliva into his mouth. "Yeah, sure."

Four of their teammates and two girls wanting to party piled out of the vehicles. Donny threw himself into the mode, and Rice figure he was embarrassed at being caught up on the mesa with just the two of them drinking. Donny probably figured the whole world would know what they'd been talking just by looking at them. Guilt does that to a guy. Maybe after the beer was gone they could go off by themselves. Naw. The moment had passed.

The weather was a little raw the next day, but a few guys showed up for the scrimmage. Rice couldn't really get into the game until Donny drove up in the Rattletrap after his shift was over at the warehouse. As soon as Rice saw him, his armpits sprang a leak. This was nervous sweat, the kind that carries body odor, but he'd smeared on the deodorant that morning, so maybe he'd be okay.

Donny threw himself into the game, and it soon became a personal contest. But it wasn't the vicious battle of the last Saturday. This was good, old-fashioned masculine rivalry. And then it happened.

Donny brought him down from behind and ended up atop his back with his hand trapped at Rice's groin. And he squeezed. Not once, but twice. The second time, there was more to squeeze. Rice was damned near hard.

He called a run, and again it was Donny who chased him down. When they got untangled, he had to walk hunched over to keep his erection from being so pronounced. Donny flashed a broad grin. Rice was so fucking happy, he scampered forty yards for a touchdown on the next play.

Now it was Donny's turn. Every time he ran the ball, Rice brought him down, making sure he had a hand between those long, strong legs. He squeezed and rubbed every chance he had. The last time they got up, there was no way Donny could hide his erection, so he called a time-out and plopped down on the cold ground to wait it out.

While everyone was gathered around talking and resting, the wind came up, and they decided to call it a game. One by one, they wandered away until only Rice and Donny were left. They stared at one another without speaking for a long moment.

"I've thought about it. A lot," Rice said.

"And?"

"I say go for it." Donny's big eyes fascinated him.

"You think that's a good idea?"

"Yeah. You?"

Donny dropped his gaze. "I'm scared of you, Rice. I'd just be one more notch on your belt. And I'd…" His voice died away. "I'd be hurt. It would mean more to me than just another conquest."

"Hell, Donny. Don't you understand what I'm trying to say? I've got feelings for you. Been trying to deny it, hide it…make it go away. But it won't! I'm fumbling around trying to deal with it."

"What kind of feelings?"

"I'd say it, but it would sound goofy."

"So sound goofy."

Arms on his knees, the cold from the ground chilling his butt, he stared at the brown grass between his legs and forced the words out of his mouth. "I love you, man."

Donny avoided his look when he glanced up. "I love you, too, Rice. Have for two years. About went nuts every time you got serious over some girl. But I learned to handle that. Figured as long as you kept to girls, I'd be all right. But if you'd ever started looking at another guy, I'd have knocked his head off. I'd have fought for you, Rice Man."

"Let's go somewhere now. Right now!" His cock stirred at the thought.

"And do what?" Donny shot back at him. "You gonna suck my cock? Let me fuck you? You expect me to suck yours, let you fuck my ass?"

"I…I don't know." He was stunned by the mental images. "We could start off slow and see where it goes? Maybe we can figure something out."

"Maybe. But in every relationship, somebody's dominant and somebody's submissive. Can you see the Rice Man being submissive?" Rice paused before shaking his head. "So that means you expect me to be," Donny went on.

"Shit, I don't know! All I know is I want to be with you. I want to see you, Donny. Hold you in my hand. Have you hold me. I want you!" He enunciated the last three words slowly.

"I guess I do, too, but I don't want to do it in the backseat of a car. I want it to be better than that."

"Man, I don't think I can wait. I'm about to pop a vein down there."

Donny grinned and stared at his groin. "I know. I can see. Got my own problems over here."

"Let's at least go to the head or somewhere and do a little groping."

"Don't know if I could stop."

"Shit!" Rice thought for a moment. "Look, my folks are leaving tomorrow to go Christmas shopping up in Albuquerque. They're planning to stay over a couple of nights to visit some friends. I'll beg off the trip so you can come over and spend a couple of nights. But keep your hands off yourself in the meantime. I want you primed and ready, not wilted and worn out from jacking off."

"Okay. But you gotta promise me the same thing. I work tomorrow, you know. So if I show up, I'll be hot and sweaty."

"Sweat's a turn-on, you know."

Donny's eyebrows climbed. "It is? Not for me."

"So I'll shower, and you won't. See you tomorrow night."

"Damn, Rice, tell me this is going to be okay."

"All I can tell you is that I want you and need you." He took a deep breath before saying those words again. "Don't you understand? I love you."

Donny flushed. His Adam's apple bobbed as he swallowed. "How many times have you used that line?"

"It doesn't matter how many times I've said it before. This is the only time it's counted."

❖

Rice looked at the clock for the umpteenth time. He'd fought all day to keep from jacking off while thinking about tonight, but now he wondered if it hadn't been for nothing. Donny hadn't actually committed himself to show up, but he hadn't said no, either. What was it he'd said? *If I show up, I'll be hot and sweaty.* He'd agreed to forgo shooting his wad. Wasn't that a commitment?

But it was eight thirty and no Donny. No phone call. No contact. The guy wasn't even answering his cell. When he hadn't heard anything by nine, he gave up. Stripped to his shorts, Rice lay on his bed and fought his disappointment.

Maybe it was better this way. No! No, it wasn't better. He closed his eyes and conjured an image of the sexiest human being in the world...his world, anyway. He hardened immediately. Pretending it was Donny's hand, he began to stroke himself.

The doorbell made him start. He got up and glanced out the window. The Rattletrap sat at the curb. Without bothering with a robe, he rushed to the front door and threw it open.

Donny's eyes swept his near-naked form. "Did you start without me?"

Rice flushed. "Gave up on you is more like it. I was going to bed."

"At nine o'clock? Hey, man, sorry I'm late. But I had to work another half shift. The Christmas season's a heavy time at the warehouse.

Thought about stopping for a beer or two. Nervous, you know." He stepped inside and closed the door. "Then I decided it wasn't a beer I needed."

"I tried calling you."

"We leave our cells in the locker room."

When Donny wanted to shower, Rice decided he was going to quarterback this outfit and took charge. "No way."

"You're really serious about this sweat thing?"

"Like you wouldn't believe." He reached out and rubbed Donny's neck and sniffed his finger. "Am-fucking-brosia."

"What?" Donny laughed aloud.

"You can laugh, but I know what I want. I want to lick the sweat off you."

"Gross. But if it's what you want." He followed Rice into the bedroom.

There was an awkward moment as Donny undressed, but it passed as soon as they stared frankly at one another. Rice smiled. It looked like Donny could get it up for him after all.

"First, I want to settle the big cock contest." He stepped forward and grasped Donny's hard prick, laying his throbbing tool on top of it.

"Looks like a draw to me," Donny said.

"And another legend bites the dust."

"Yeah, but nobody will know except the two of us."

Rice led his friend to the bed and pushed him over onto the mattress. None of his experience with girls came to his aid. He didn't know what to do. Oh, he knew, he just didn't know what Donny would permit. He placed his hands on his friend's shoulders. Donny's came to rest on his torso, searing his flesh.

"You're so fucking handsome," Donny whispered. "I've got the biggest man in this town naked on a bed, and I don't know what to do with him."

Rice reached out a hand and clasped his arm. "What do you want to do?"

"Kiss you."

"Don't sweat it, man. Just do it." Rice didn't quite know what to expect. What he got was a wet buzz that ranked up with the best he'd ever had. "Wow!" he exclaimed when they parted.

"Yeah. Wow! That was good, Rice."

"Again." It was longer, more intense, more emotional this time. When he caught the faint musk of Donny's sweat, he moved down to his neck, licking the perfect olive skin before returning for another kiss. Donny's hand wandered down his torso and took a firm hold on his erection. "Uhhh," he moaned into Donny's open mouth.

Donny pulled away and rolled over on top of Rice. Their cocks throbbed side by side. Donny kissed him again, gently thrusting with his hips. Rice shuddered. His nipples felt like they were firecrackers ready to go off.

When they broke apart, Donny put his head face-down on the pillow beside him. "You know, most guys have to grow *out* of fucking around with their buddies. We had to grow into it."

"Yeah. Know what I figure?" Rice was excited by the gentle motion of Donny's hips. "You said there had to be a dominant one. I don't buy that. We'll be a partnership."

Donny raised his head and studied Rice's eyes. "Partnership? What do you mean?"

"We'll make a pact. Whatever I do for you, you'll do for me. Whatever you do for me, I'll do for you."

"Do we rule anything out? Make any rules?" Donny's hips still moved slowly back and forth.

"Just that one. You don't ask anything *of* me you won't do *for* me. And the other way around."

"Are you saying that if I take you in my mouth, you'll do the same for me?"

"That's what I'm saying. That way neither one of us is dominant."

Donny's lids slid halfway down over his eyes. "Rice, you ever heard of premature ejaculation? That's…what…I'm…having. Right now!" Donny groaned and lunged hard against him. "Ohhh!"

A warm liquid flooded his belly as Donny continued to squirm. Rice held his friend's head between his palms, forcing him to meet his gaze. "How was it?"

"Bad, man! It was sooo fucking bad!" Donny laughed maniacally.

Rice hooked his heels around Donny's legs, thrusting and grinding with his own hips. Lubricated by Donny's cum, it didn't take long. "Oh, man! Oh, Donny! I'm getting it." His jism spurted between their muscled bellies and mixed with his lover's. He groaned and hunched for a long time. Chill bumps played down his back as the ecstasy died away.

Finally, they were still. Donny lay atop him, his heart thudding. "How do you feel? You know, about what we did?"

"It was A-one! Super! Ranks right up there. How about for you?"

"You aren't ashamed or disgusted or anything?"

"No. Why? Are you?"

"Rice, I don't think I could be disgusted by anything I did with you."

"Then you're all right with it?"

"It was great." Donny laid his forehead against Rice's. Their lips teased one another. "I was afraid."

"Afraid of what?"

"That you'd get turned off afterward and tell me to leave."

"No way, man. Not ever! You think we can make do with just belly fucking from now on?"

There was silence for a moment, and then they both spoke at once. "No."

"Look," Rice said, "let's shower and rest for a while."

The shower was a mistake. They never got their rest. First, Rice licked Donny all over—before the water washed away all the sweat, he claimed. Then Donny lathered his back…and his front. Rice's cock got excited again. Donny's dick responded to the sight.

Donny got to his knees and looked up at him. "Partners?" When Rice nodded, Donny took the end of Rice's big cock into his mouth. He gagged and almost retched, but he backed off and tried again. He did better this time, closing his lips over the glans and gently bobbing up and down on the shaft.

Rice leaned back against the shower wall and spread his legs. Donny's hands stroked his thighs, cupped his balls, moved to his ass. A finger slid up and down his crack. Speechless, Rice stood on trembling legs until he knew he was going to lose it. Fantastic! A girl had blown him once, but it was nothing like this. This was *Donny* doing this wonderful thing for him.

"Don…Donny!" he warned. "I'm coming."

Donny pulled away at the first spurt of cum, but after a second, he took Rice in his mouth again and sucked up the remainder. Rice would have slid down the side of the shower if Donny hadn't propped him up. After working his way through the longest, most intense orgasm of his life, he looked down at his friend.

"Man…oh, man! Oh, man!" He grasped Donny beneath the arms and hauled him to his feet, kissing his lover while in the grip of a passion that exceeded anything he'd ever experienced before. He pulled away, met Donny's level gaze, and sank to his knees.

"No." Donny pulled him back up. "Let's go back to the bed."

This time, Rice lay atop the other boy. He began his lovemaking with a long, slow kiss and moved down Donny's brown torso, kissing and licking all the way. He made his lover squirm by biting his nipples. He made him wiggle by sucking on his navel. He made him gasp by tonguing his testicles. And he was damned well going to make him come by sucking his huge cock. Amazed to find that taking a man's penis in his mouth wasn't unpleasant, Rice set about his task with characteristic enthusiasm. He didn't try to go too fast, but swallowed as much of that big column as was comfortable. He knew before Donny warned him that his friend was coming because his balls drew up in his hand. Even the sperm flooding his mouth wasn't unpleasant—because it was Donny's.

❖

Donny was the same witty, funny guy the next morning that he had always been. They dressed and breakfasted and talked as casually as usual—except they touched one another more. Before Donny went off to work, Rice pulled him into an embrace. He felt Donny harden as they kissed.

"Are you really okay with it?"

"I'm better than that, Rice Man. I want some more." Then he was gone.

Rice tried to read a book he had to write a report on when school resumed. Then he walked around picking up things in the house, but he didn't do either very well. Midafternoon, the phone rang. Donny wanted to hear his voice. At seven, it rang a second time. Donny again. He was going to be late. A semi just came in.

Donny brought a pizza when he came, which was fortunate. Eating was something Rice had forgotten about since they had breakfast together. After they ate, Rice stripped Donny, made him lie down on the bed, and licked away salty sweat before massaging Donny's tired back muscles. As he felt the sinews loosen, Rice began to harden. For the last few minutes of the back rub, his cock rode the crack between Donny's naked buns. Donny spread his legs; Rice rode deeper.

Donny reached around and fingered the pre-cum lubricating the tip of Rice's turgid cock. Suddenly, he arched his back and guided Rice to his sphincter.

"Donny!" Rice gasped. "I don't know if I can…"

"Don't worry. I won't ask you to reciprocate. But I want to see if I can do it."

Rice shoved his hips slightly, penetrating Donny's flesh a fraction of an inch. "But we made a rule."

"Fuck the rule. Better yet, fuck me. I want you inside me." Donny lifted his butt, and the rosebud opened. Rice moved forward; his glans disappeared. "Ahhh!" Donny muffled his cry in a pillow. "No. Don't stop. But go slow. Just go slow."

"But I'm hurting you."

"Like blue blazes!" Donny exclaimed. "But I want it. Please." Rice gently fed him more of his cock, ceasing when his lover's cries became too loud. After a moment's rest, Donny gasped. "Now! More."

It took a long time for Rice to enter him completely. When he was in, he leaned his weight against Donny's back and licked away the sweat from his brow. Then he began lazily thrusting in and out. As Donny relaxed beneath him, Rice became more animated.

"R…Rice, it feels better when you pull almost all the way out and then give it to me. Long strokes, man! Oh, yeah! That hits the sweet spot, bro. I don't know how to describe it, Rice Man. I feel you sliding all the way inside me. And it's stroking something that feels just great. Man, fuck me!"

Rice kept at it steadily, easing off each time he approached the edge. Donny lay spread beneath him murmuring encouragement, expressing pleasure.

"Okay, give it to me," Donny said. "Give it to me hard. Bring me over the edge. You're gonna make me come. Fuck me, Rice. Fuck me hard. Harder! Give it to me!" Donny lifted them both off the bed with his powerful thighs.

Rice did his best. He used those hips that made him so good on the gridiron. He used them like a broken field runner. He used them like he was in the clear and was pumping and churning away, eating up the distance. He used them like a man used them on a woman. Then he groaned out loud and froze against Donny's butt. "Oh, shit!"

"The Rice Man cometh!" Donny shouted. "In me!"

And so he did.

Goran's Run

Joseph Baneth Allen

My first clear memory of Paul Goran is of him stepping out of the shower stall twenty years ago in the home team locker room at McKethan Stadium.

Tiny beads of remnant water from the shower nicely accentuated the firm lines of Goran's nearly smooth body. Damp ringlets of tawdry blond hair were strewn across his forehead.

Back in 1989, lithe bodybuilder-type physiques had not been considered desirable for college ballplayers aiming to break into the majors by coming up through the minors. Lightning reflexes and speed were, and still are, considered more important for a ballplayer to possess than mere sculptured muscle. Goran had all three qualities wrapped up in a neat package standing six foot three, along with an honest, affable smile when he caught sight of my dad and me approaching.

"So you're the enterprising young man who caught my homer," Goran cheerfully said. He nonchalantly grabbed a white terry cloth towel from the nearest locker side bench and wrapped it around his waist for modesty's sake.

Meeting Goran under these circumstances had been a wild stroke of Gator fanboy good luck. Dad was, and still is, a devout, a Florida Gator fan. Just having turned twelve a few weeks back, I still really wasn't a Gator or any type of sports fan at that particular moment in my life.

Dad had taken me that Saturday morning to the game in hopes of that actually seeing a game would jump-start an interest in at least watching all things athletic on the television. It had been a long two-and-a-half-hour drive from Jacksonville to Gainesville. Dad assured me with each passing mile that I would love baseball as much as I loved to read science fiction novels by Andre Norton. Jacking up the volume on my Walkman had done little to blunt his enthusiasm.

The parking lot at McKethan Stadium was packed to capacity by the time we had arrived. Dad managed to squeeze his Plymouth Reliant into one of the few spots remaining in the overflow parking lot. The game was the first time the University of Florida had hosted an NCAA Regional baseball game at any of its stadiums across the state. So this second-to-the-last ball game of the season had been heavily promoted as a grudge match between the Gators and the Louisiana State University Tigers.

Dad had considered it an act of divine providence that he was able to get two tickets to the game we were about to see. A few months back the NCAA had announced its selection of McKethan Stadium to host one of its regional baseball games at the exact moment he used his American Express card to purchase two tickets at the Ticketmaster kiosk in the Avenues Mall.

I had still been wishing that the game had been sold out and Dad was watching it televised back in the comfort of our home until sheer dumb luck had enabled me to catch Goran's second inning homer.

Looking back, Dad had managed to score good seats in the grandstands.

Goran, a senior, was a second baseman. He was fourth up to bat during the second inning. A man on first base was all the three Gator teammates before him had managed to accomplish. His first attempt at hitting the ball was rewarded with a strike. LSU senior Brandon Reynolds was on the pitcher's mound for the Tigers.

Dad nudged me and pointed out to the field.

"Both Goran and Reynolds were chosen as All Americans by the Southern Conference back last year," he told me. I sighed inwardly, bored to near tears by the thought of having to endure watching strike after strike. Yet I gave Dad a slight smile. He and everyone else around me were definitely excited by the game play so far. No matter how much I wanted to be anywhere else other than at McKethan Stadium, I didn't want to be a total snot-nosed kid and completely ruin the day for him. I loved him too much to do that, even though I absolutely hated him for bringing me to this game.

Ball back in hand, Reynolds took a few moments to size Goran up again before making another pitch—a fastball. Bat and ball connected with a resounding whack that was lost in the din of the roar of the Gator fans as they stood up and cheered.

Goran's homer soared over right field in the general direction of where Dad and I were sitting. People around us were cheering, standing up, and watching the skies to see where it would land. Some already had catcher's mitts stretched out to catching the incoming ball against the blinding midafternoon sun.

From my vantage point, I could see that the ball would just fall short of the railing and would land in the aisles below our seats. Lacking a catcher's mitt, I quickly improvised, dumping the remainder of my soda into the concrete floor of the bleachers.

Holding the plastic cup in both hands, I leaned out over the narrow railing as far as I dared. The ball came in fast and furious. The cup rang like a bell when it slammed inside.

It also stung like hell. I had almost dropped my hard-won prize into the seats below me. It was then that I felt a hand tightly holding onto the back of my belt. Startled, I turned around to discover that it was Dad who had such a death grip on me. A funny mixture of sheer relief and joyous pride danced on his face and brown eyes.

"Dad! Dad! Did you see? Did you see? I caught the ball!" At that moment, I really didn't understand the excitement I was feeling. I'm sure the smile on my face had been wild and extremely goofy looking.

Not wanting to lose the prize within it, I clasped the cup tightly against my chest. I really wanted to cry. The stinging pain in my hands hurt so badly. Yet I was afraid that if the tears flowed or I started complaining about the pain, this magical moment I was sharing with Dad would end with him embarrassed and ashamed of me with all these other people around.

"Great catch, Spence!" Dad replied with a grin equal to my own. "If your luck holds out, someone from the team will invite you to meet Paul Goran after the game. He'll sign the ball for you then. Of course, make sure that your old man is invited to come along with you too."

I simply nodded vigorously in agreement as we headed back to our seats. Dad had been correct. Within minutes, a Gator team representative with a bushy salt-and-pepper mustache found us and invited both myself and Dad back to the locker room after the game. It was only then that I had realized that in all the excitement, I had missed Goran rounding the bases.

Goran's homer was the first of the game and the only one from either team to go into the stands. The Gators had won by a margin of one run—the final score being 4–3.

Dad and I waited until the crowds thinned a bit before making our way to the Gators' locker room. "Do you think Paul Goran will sign this for me?" I asked Dad. My hands still had their death grip on the ball.

"Probably not that one, Spence," Dad replied carefully. He was being careful not to diminish my newfound enthusiasm for baseball in any way. "When you offer it to Goran; he'll probably thank you and autograph another ball for you in return. Ballplayers like to keep their homers to carry the good luck over into the next game."

We were met at the locker room entrance by Ryan Goetell. Mr. Goetell was the Gator team representative—a wry middle-aged volunteer alumni booster, Dad had told me earlier—who had tracked us down in the stands and issued us the backstage invitation. He greeted us by name and a smile before ushering us past the security guards and inside.

"Hey kid, great catch!" several of Goran's team mates called out as we sought out where Goran was amongst his teammates—who were in various stages of undress. Some actually applauded as we walked by; a couple players reached out and patted me on the back.

My cheeks were flushed with embarrassment. I was growing more nervous from all the unexpected attention and praise being heaped upon me with each passing second. Nobody at Mandarin Middle School would have cheered and given nerdy me thumbs-up for catching a homer. Despite always making sure to wear white socks and dress in the regulation gym shorts and T-shirt with the school logo, I was just average in phys ed—not chosen first but at least not chosen last. None of the star athletes at my middle school would have appreciated being shown up by me on the field.

"Paul, this is Spencer Hamill and his father Ed," Mr. Goetell said. He stepped to the side to let us interact with each other, but not before I had caught him discreetly eyeing various undressed ballplayers.

Goran appeared genuinely happy that I had caught his homer with my improvised catcher's mitt. He held out his hand. "It's always great meeting a future star catcher."

As we shook hands, a jolt ran through me. My heart wanted to burst out of my chest as I looked into his blue eyes that twinkled at some inner amusement. I just couldn't get any words out. Dad came to my rescue as he shook hands with Goran.

"Spence is a bit shy around strangers," he said. "It's his first time watching a game in a stadium instead of the boob-tube."

Natural shyness over Dad's improvised white lie was not the reason why I was tongue-tied. Actually seeing Goran nude for a few brief moments and now talking with him was more exciting than catching his homer for reasons Dad had absolutely no clue about. Instinct had warned me long ago to remain silent about being attracted to guys, not girls. Even now I was careful not to let my eyes linger on any particular undressed player for too long, unlike Mr. Goetell.

"No way! Really?" Goran asked. "Then I'm doubly impressed by your actions, Spence. Not everyone would have been quick enough to figure out how to catch an incoming ball with a drink cup.

"Soda, not beer, right?" He gave me a sly wink.

Everyone laughed, including me.

Summoning up enough courage while praying my voice wouldn't crack, I held out the homer. "Would you like to keep this homer?"

"Oh, no way, Spence," Goran replied. He did, however, pluck it out of my hand. "You keep this ball. It's special. I will put my Johnny Hancock on it for you, though."

Goetell had been waiting for that cue. He held out a black magic marker pen to Goran.

"Will you be here for next week's game?" Goran asked as he went about autographing the ball. He handed it back to me once he was finished.

He had signed it: *Great Catch, Spence! Your Friend, Paul Goran.*

"Thank you!" I said a bit breathlessly after reading what he had written. With a goofy smile I held it up to show to Dad and everyone around us.

"Can't make it up here next week," Dad said with heartfelt regret. "On Monday, I have to fly up to Denver to teach a weeklong Six-Sigma Green Belt training seminar for a group of midlevel CSX managers.

I won't be back in time for the season's last game. Spence here still hasn't gotten his driver's license."

Both laughed while I groaned inwardly at Dad's utterly lame joke.

"Well then, hopefully you and Spence will be able to come out to watch me play if I get drafted by the Jacksonville Expos," Goran easily replied.

"Dad will take me to all the Expos home games?" I looked up and gave Dad my best "oh please, please" look. Usually I only gave it to him when my allowance had run out and I wanted another new book to read.

"Sure Spence, we'll go to all the Expos home games, provided you keep your grades up," Dad cheerfully said. My parents always made sure that "the catch" was always linked to how high my grades were.

"No worries, Spence; you only have to get straight As for a year." Goran laughed. "With a great deal of hard work, and a little bit of luck, I should be picked up by the Florida Marlins by the end of the next season."

Not trusting my voice out of fear it would crack again, I just nodded in agreement. Goran shook my hand again to seal our deal. Dad would tell me later during the drive back home that the Jacksonville Suns were affiliated with the Montreal Expos—a Canadian team. Much to my chagrin, he also went into great detail on how the team was a member of the Southern League and a class Double-A affiliate.

Only Goran's confident prediction about his rosy future never came true.

The Gators carried over their win against the Tigers, winning the last game of the conference season. Once again the Southern Conference had named Goran to the All Stars. The Gators named him MVP. He was summa cum laude with an undergrad degree in civil engineering. The baseball draft was just less than two weeks away. The Expos changed their name to the Suns and realigned themselves with the Florida Marlins. Only it didn't matter.

By then, Goran had vanished.

On the day prior to graduating he was still packing up all his stuff and clothes in assorted boxes and two suitcases in his dorm room. The next day he was gone.

I had only learned of his disappearance by a passing comment from some sport commentator on television. He stated that Goran would have been drafted in the second round by the Jacksonville Suns if he just hadn't up and walked away from what would have undoubtedly been a stellar baseball career. Later in my bedroom, I must have stared for hours at the homer he had signed for me, wondering why he left it all behind.

Only the flame of my newly awakened passion for sports hadn't entirely diminished with Goran's disappearance.

Every year since then, Dad and I managed to attend a few of the Suns home games. By then Dad had splurged a bit, and I had a brand-new catcher's mitt. I never caught any other ball, though, that had been hit by a player. Goran's run had been a once-in-my-lifetime experience and it would continue to have an impact on me in ways a twelve-year-old boy couldn't have even begun to imagine back then.

After graduating from the University of North Florida in 2000 on the five-year plan with a degree in broadcast journalism, I managed to turn a low-paying jack-of-all-trades position at WPXC-TV in Orange Park, Florida, into an assignment editor position up at ESPN's studios in Bristol, Connecticut.

Most of my daily routine was sitting in editorial meetings and handing out assignments to erstwhile reporters to cover the usual broad-spectrum sporting news stories, and making sure that they filed their stories on time and on or under budget. I used most of my precious free time to research and write a book about past and present sports mysteries.

Despite being my muse, Goran's disappearance did not make it into the pages of that first book. Sure, it remained as a niggling little thought in the back of my mind. Yet the story of one college ballplayer dropping out of sight for reasons known only to him did not fit into the scope of the book I was writing at that time.

Solving Sports' Greatest Mysteries by Spencer Hamill was published by Perseus Books back in March of 2003. It peaked at number two on the *New York Times* nonfiction best seller list by September and stayed there until February of 2004. I had been given my pink slip by ESPN for writing a popular sports book under their radar by the first week of May of 2003, when it started to really climb the charts. Only by then, it didn't matter.

Largely due to the book's success, A&E approached me to turn the book into a twelve-episode series in 2005. A series of television and radio interviews I had previously done for the book, including, ironically, one with my former employer, had already proved that I was personable and photogenic enough to host the show. It debuted as one of the highest rated shows on the cable network for the fall season.

Dad enjoyed taking full credit for jump-starting his now "famous" son's interest in sports, and I let him.

A solid season of continuously being in the top tier of highly rated shows on A&E, coupled along with strong sales of the DVD set of the series, heightened an interest and demand for more episodes and books on sporting world mysteries. I happily complied with writing the companion books for the series *Solving Great Sporting Mysteries of the Olympics* and *Solving Sports' Greatest Mysteries of the Ancient World*, which I also hosted.

With three solid bestsellers and series under my belt about sporting mysteries, it seemed only natural that I turn my attention to researching and writing *Solving College Sports' Greatest Mysteries*. Naturally, Goran and his odd disappearance once again came to mind.

Yet including him in this new book wasn't a done deal.

To guarantee continued success of my highly profitable series, Carol Tidwell, my editor at Perseus Books, had final say over which college sports mysteries I could explore in this new book. The bigger the mystery, the bigger the buildup it could be given by the publisher's multimedia arm, and of course, by extension, the new series.

Carol was on the fence about including Goran's story—if there truly was one—as a chapter in the new book. She's a sweetie, but is tough as nails when it comes to her job of doing the grunt work of editing anybody's book acquired by Perseus. Convincing Michael Reeves, my producer at A&E, to include Paul Goran's as a full-length segment had been a cake walk. Yet Carol expressed some reservations over a conference call we had to discuss book chapters.

She felt I should roll Goran's disappearance into just a few paragraphs in a whole chapter devoted to college athletes who dropped out of sight before achieving their professional promise. Without a full chapter about Goran, I wouldn't be able to justify a full-length episode devoted entirely to him. So I agreed to meet with her in person in her office by Friday to convince her of the need to include Goran's mystery disappearance in the latest book.

It was just the excuse I needed to come up for air after having been so deeply immersed in researching material for the latest book's other chapter.

I decided to make the two-day drive up to NYC from my home in St. Augustine, Florida. My motivation for avoiding flying was not wanting to risk one of my prized possessions: the baseball that Goran had signed for me about twenty years ago. It probably would have inadvertently been "lost" by overly zealous TSA airport screeners

With the exception of being able to seduce Francisco Ramirez—a hunky, twenty-something Latino college student who had been manning the front desk at the Fort Lee Regency Hotel where I stayed at in Petersburg, Virginia, on the first night of the long drive up the eastern seaboard on Interstate 95—the trip up to NYC was pretty uneventful.

Perseus Books is headquartered in a typical steel and glass high-rise in Manhattan's Midtown South District. Carol greeted me warmly with a hug and we exchanged a few casual pleasantries before she ushered me into her side office. Even if she had the corner office, the view would have still sucked—another high-rise blocked out the sky.

Once the door was closed, her facial happiness visibly evaporated a bit as we sat down on the well-worn leather couch in her office. I brought the acrylic cube container where Goran's ball resided out from where it was tucked away in my briefcase and offered it to Carol to hold.

Her eyes widened in delight as she held the ancient baseball with the reverence she felt it deserved. Holding out her left index finger a fingerbreadth away from the clear protective surface, she traced out the curve of Goran's writing on the ball. She smiled at me.

"Spence, you've definitely got me hooked on how you came to love sports," she said. "I chucked as your teenaged self rebelled against being dragged to a ball game by your dad. How you caught Goran's homer was way cool. Mike undoubtedly could make an authentic looking 'reenactment' segment out of it that would awe viewers and keep them watching—especially the women and men who'd drool over the shower sequence."

"But you still don't think he's worth a full chapter in the latest book," I said.

Carol gave me a half, almost sad smile.

"Goran got you interested in sports. He's one of your childhood heroes. You noted that in the draft. Are you sure that you can honestly deal with, and write about, what you find out about him?" she asked. "Childhood idols often cast different shadows when viewed through jaded adult eyes."

Carol is not just my editor and publishing world mentor. She's also one of my closest friends. Not every writer can claim being the best of buds with their editor. Inwardly, something about the Goran chapter troubled her. I could see it reflected in her green eyes. Her normally full lips were stretched in thin lines. Otherwise, she would have had this conversation over the phone and not asked for face time to talk about Goran.

I decided to cut to the heart of the matter. "My potential disillusionment over Goran isn't what's throwing up your editorial cautionary signs," I noted. "Did you find out something about him that I missed in my initial research?"

Carol ran her hands through her short ebony hair. From past experience, it was a sure sign something was bothering her.

❖

"Your research, so far, shows that Goran's parents never filed a missing persons report on him with the Gainesville Police," Carol said. "Neither did his coach. Ditto for his agent. His teammates and college buds never raised concerns. His girlfriend, assuming he had one, didn't raise any alarms.

"To me, that's a sure indication that he dropped out of sight for a specific reason. A reason everyone around him obviously knew about and were comfortable keeping silent about—even if they were opposed to it.

"Have you given any thought that Goran might not want anybody poking into his past, much less trying to find out where he is today? Sometimes, someone's past should remain deeply buried for good reasons."

Carol had caught me flatfooted. I knew she was speaking from hard-learned experience in her own personal life. Nearly forty years ago, she had given up an infant son for adoption when she wasn't able to care for him after divorcing her abusive husband. Finally giving into the desire to find out if he was happy with his life, she tracked him down. He was happy all right. Only the bastard wanted absolutely nothing to do with her. It still hit her hard.

She was also right. My basic assumption was that Goran would be somewhat happy to be reunited with the boy—now man—who had caught his homer. It'd make for a great television moment and no doubt boost book sales. Only I hadn't really considered the notion that the reality would be the polar opposite of my fantasy and that sheer anger, and not unadulterated joy, would be his reaction.

"Let's compromise," I offered. "I was going to take two weeks off anyway before making the plunge and do the actual writing for this book. My plan had been to kick back in a cabin rental in Maggie Valley. Instead, I'll do some additional leg work to see if I can learn anything more about Goran. At the end of the week, if you don't think it's worth pursuing, I'll hit the Delete key on him."

Carol chewed her lower lip a bit while she considered my offer. She resembled my mom whenever she did that. I also realized that it was an indication of some hidden fear she had yet to give voice to.

A few uncomfortable seconds passed between us before she finally spoke. "People who often leave behind all traces of their past lives like Goran did usually are afraid of someone or something." Her eyes widened a bit as they locked onto my blue ones. "What if it was a person he was afraid of who is still around?

"If so, have you considered that he or she might not want you snooping around into any shared past with Goran that's been buried now for decades?" she asked.

Truthfully, I hadn't. Carol didn't like how my face honestly reflected that answer.

"I'll check in once a day," I offered. "Just say the word and I'll haul ass pronto out of where ever I'm at the moment. You can send in the cavalry if I don't check in."

Carol snorted back a laugh. "Past experience has taught me only too well how you follow my instructions. Seduce any more hotel clerks on the drive up here?"

I responded by giving her my best look of unabashed innocence. She looked at me sternly before wild giggles escaped from the prison of her lips.

We talked for a while longer about various chapters in the book before we called it a day. After deciding on Chinese for dinner, we ate at Jimmy Sung's on Forty-fouth Street. We then caught a performance of *The 39 Steps* at the Helen Hayes Theatre before calling it a night. I dropped her off where she currently camped out—the Berkley Park apartment building on 340 East Twenty-ninth Street. I reiterated my promise to check in daily and gave her a chaste kiss on the cheek before she got out of my car. Upon seeing that she had safely gotten inside the building, I drove over to the Washington Square Hotel.

I normally stay at the Washington Square Hotel whenever I'm in NYC. After I checked in, I went to my room and fell into an exhausted sleep once I had slid between the sheets—alone.

Next day, I was retracing my long drive along Interstate 95 in the direction of Gainesville. It was tempting to overnight again in Petersburg, Virginia and listen once again to Francisco moan *"más fuerte, por favor...sí...sí..."* as each thrust carried my cock deeper inside his hungry quim. He was a total bottom slut. Happily, I remembered enough of four years of Honors Spanish from high school to happily oblige his begging requests for more of my cock.

Yet I drove past Petersburg without stopping.

Repeat bedroom romps can result in swirling rumors that can swiftly tank a broadcast career. While Mainstream America readily embraces gay actors and talk show hosts, the group collective still heavily frowns upon and rejects any active athlete or sports journalist who visibly strays from the expected norms of the heterosexual sporting world. So, following the example of a few of my colleagues and a few sporting figures I paled around, I remained deep in the cold closet.

Any leads as to what happened to Goran and why he had chosen to walk away from becoming a professional ballplayer were colder than hiding in the closet. Before e-mailing the latest outline on the book to Carol, I had contacted the missing persons department in Gainesville Police Department.

For the promise of personally inscribed copies of my three previous books, and the new one when it came out, Sergeant Chris Halvosa happily played "Dumpster rat" and dived into all the missing persons reports filed in Gainesville and the rest of the state of Florida for 1989.

"Afraid my search turned up nothing," Halvosa said. He had

called me back the next day to report back on his findings. "Funny, you'd think that his parents would have at least filed a missing persons report on him if he just up and walked out on everyone and everything he was working toward."

Part of me was relieved that Goran had obviously left the life he had worked so hard for behind for reasons known only to him. He couldn't have chosen a better time to disappear. The Nancy Grace era of the twenty-four-hour crime news cycle had yet to fully kick in—otherwise he'd have been the topic du jour with intense speculation by talking heads for at least a week. His photo would have been plastered across the television screens every seven minutes or more with "breaking updates."

"I also looked into morgue records for any John Does found during the time he disappeared and five years out," Halvosa said over my thoughtful silence. "Nobody matched his description. You may want to try getting in contact within his parents."

I thanked him and promised to take him and his wife or girlfriend out to dinner the next time I was in Gainesville.

"The books are enough, besides, I'm single," Halvosa said.

"By odd coincidence, so am I." Before the call ended, I had gotten him to accept my dinner invitation along with his address to mail the signed books I had promised him. Carol had said nothing about seducing hunky-sounding police officers.

Under different circumstances I would have followed up on Officer Halvosa's suggestion. However, earlier research into Goran's family life had shown that talking to his parents had been impossible for nearly a decade now.

Edward and Rachel, Goran's parents, had called Pensacola, Florida, home for all their married life. Growing up there, Goran eventually became a state All Star high school baseball player at Escambia High School. His parents were killed in a head-on collision on the Cervantes Street portion of the Old Spanish Trail on U.S. 90 back in the late evening hours of May 23, 2002. The drunken driver of the other car survived with just a few scratches, with a few years' prison time added to the mix.

Resthaven Gardens Cemetery in Pensacola was where they were now spending eternity.

While Goran had been an only child, he did have quite a few cousins. Both sides of his family were scattered across the southern United States.

Stephanie Longfellow was the solitary relative of his who had somewhat guardedly consented to talk to me over the phone after I had tracked her down to an address in Darien, Georgia. All of Goran's other cousins politely told me "no comment" before severing the connection.

Stephanie refused to take me up on my offer to meet with her in person at the restaurant of her choice in Darien.

"There's really nothing I can tell you about Paul," Stephanie told me by way of an explanation. Her voice carried a wistful sadness. "I only met him briefly once at a reunion the family held back in the summer of 1987 over at Ginnie Springs, Florida.

"Paul was nice enough and his girlfriend was very pretty," Stephanie recalled. She hesitated a moment. "I remember her as looking lonely. Poor thing didn't have a good time, half lost among strangers. Wish I could remember her name for you. Paul occupied most of his time at the reunion with...oh, what was his name...um...it was a state name...Dakota—one of his friends from the dorm, I think."

"Would you happen to recall Dakota's last name or anything else about him?" I had hopefully asked.

"Not really." Stephanie hesitated a bit; I sensed she was struggling to recall any details about Goran's mystery friend. "Dakota was just an average-looking guy. Looking back now, it does now seem a bit odd that Paul was so chummy with somebody who, to put it kindly, wasn't athletic. I'm sure you know how an athlete usually is only good buddies with other another athlete."

I did, but wisely refrained from making too caustic a reply out of fear of alienating the sole fairly friendly information source I had in Goran's family.

"Did Paul show up for his parents' funeral?" I asked.

"No, he didn't," Stephanie replied. A twinge of old smoldering anger colored her voice. I had definitely touched upon a family sore point. "My parents called him to break the news. Aunt Rachel was Mom's youngest sister.

"They had found a contact number for him among his parents'

records. Mom told me, he just broke down crying when she broke the news about his parents to him.

"Now here's the odd part, Mr. Hamill. Once Paul regained his composure a bit, he asked Mom to take care of the funeral arrangements and estate. Then he hung up.

"Mom finally had to give up trying to call him when the number was disconnected a month later. Nobody's heard a peep from him since then."

We talked for a few minutes more, but I learned very little. Once his parents' final debts had been settled, Stephanie's mother had put the money, nearly a half million now, in a trust account for Goran.

"A dusting of monthly compound interest is the only action that account ever sees," she told me. "Mom's foolish for not just having him declared dead."

There had been more than just a twinge of envy in her voice when she volunteered up that informational tidbit.

Stephanie then politely excused herself with a promise to give me a call if she thought or found out anything more about Goran and his whereabouts. I wasn't going to hold my breath waiting for a call that would never come. All I knew now was that he was at least still alive when his parents died, but had never touched the money set aside for him.

Still, she had given me a fresh new lead. All I had to do was see if anyone in the Gator Alumni Association remembered who Dakota was and where he was now—assuming he was a sophomore at UF like Goran was back in 1987. It should be easy to learn who he was, since Dakota was an uncommon enough name.

Maybe then I'd be a few steps closer to finding Goran, or at least figuring out what had happened to him. Besides, a potential dinner date with Sgt. Halvosa and playtime afterward with his handcuffs beckoned and helped provide more than enough motivation to bypass home in St. Augustine once I crossed the Florida state line the next day. Gainesville is only about a three-hour drive away from Jacksonville.

Carol was kept in the dark about that part of my Gainesville itinerary when I checked in with her as promised. A cop was a relatively safe lay. Unlike the military, American police departments had yet to fully embrace gay officers in their ranks. So Sgt. Halvosa wouldn't kiss and tell, keeping both our careers safe.

Calling the Gator Alumni Association would have been simpler than just appearing in the flesh at the campus office. Yet past experience had taught me that lips are more readily loosened by using the shock and awe approach of a sudden and unexpected "celebrity" author appearance.

Upon arriving in Gainesville, I lucked into getting a room at the Hilton near the university. From there, it was just a short drive to Emerson Alumni Hall—the on-campus location for the alumni association.

Once inside, my shock and awe effort with Stacey Fischer, a stout blonde and friendly receptionist at the front desk, was rewarded with her quickly arranging an interview with Ryan Goetell, the Gator Reunions & Events Coordinator. His name tickled at the back of my mind as Stacey escorted me down the hall to his office. Once inside Goetell's office, memory flooded back to me. He had been the one who introduced Dad and me to Goran almost twenty years ago.

Now it was my turn to be shocked and a bit awed. Goetell had been the last person I had ever expected to bump into when I first started out to find out what had happened to Goran. He had aged well and was still as wiry as the first day we met all those years ago. Only the neatly trimmed silver hair atop his head and mustache with just the barest trace of black sheen betrayed his age. His vibrant dark brown eyes widened in surprise when he'd recognized the faint traces of a boy he briefly met years ago in the man now standing in front of him. I also recalled that he had rather discreetly liked looking at naked young men.

"I can't believe it," Goetell happily cried out. Laughing, he got up from his chair and embraced me in a full bear hug, which I returned. "Little Spencer Hamill, now all nicely grown up and a famous sports author to boot."

"Still looking to catch any stray homers?" he jovially asked once we were at arm's distance again. "Sit down, sit down."

"Nope," I replied with a light smile. I sat down in the comfortable-looking leather wing chair he gestured me toward. His office décor appropriately reflected "Gator Pride" with photographs and assorted baseball and other sports memorabilia. "Nowadays I'm just trying to find the second baseman who used to hit homers before he dropped out of sight."

Goetell sat in an identical chair next to mine. "Paul Goran? Oh yes, I recall that he did just pick up and leave. From what I recall, he never even picked up his diploma. The undergraduate office just finally got tired of having it on file, so they mailed it out to his parents back in 1997.

"Tragic, how they were killed by some worthless drunken driver. I heard through the alumni grapevine that he really dropped off the face of the earth after that."

I did my best to keep my composure despite the fact that my stomach was twitching a bit nervously. Either Goetell had excellent recall or he had brushed up on Goran because he had advance warning I was combing through the ballplayer's past.

"I'd like to say that my command of all things relating to Paul Goran was due to the blessing of having a photographic memory." Goetell laughed. A little bit of my bewilderment must have slipped past my usual nonplussed journalistic facial façades. "In truth, your editor called our media relations department earlier today and gave us a heads up that you're looking any information about Paul Goran. So I brushed up a little bit an ancient history in anticipation of your arrival."

"I'll have to thank her for paving the way later today when I speak to her," I said. *After I spank her for pulling the rug out from under me*, I silently added. "Was there anything in the alumni records to indicate why Goran left like he did?"

Goetell just shook his head negatively. "Absolutely nothing—not even any disciplinary actions for behavior on the field or off. Goran was just about as straight an arrow as they used to come by. He even maintained a 3.5 grade point average."

"He definitely wasn't exactly a typical ball player for back then," I agreed. "Did the records have any other contact information besides his parents?"

"Just them, I'm afraid."

I decided to toss out the one lead Stephanie had given me and see if I scored any hits. "What about Dakota—a friend of his who probably was a Gator around the same time as Goran?"

"Don't recall anybody by that name off hand." Goetell cupped his chin in his right palm. "I'll have to dig into the records to see if I can find out if there was an alumnus by that unusual names. Shouldn't take too long now that we uploaded all alumni records years ago."

Goetell went back behind his desk. With a few clicks of the mouse and deft keystrokes, he found Goran's friend. "Dakota Coty was in the same graduating class as Goran. Of course, I really should get Dakota's permission to give out his contact information to you."

He winked at me as the printer was powering out to spit out the contact information. "Still, I must admit to being curious about what happened to Paul Goran. He definitely would have gotten into the Majors."

"He was a strong hitter," I replied. "No doubt Suns owner Peter Bragan would have run that train bell a lot for Goran."

No Jacksonville Suns victory at the Baseball Grounds is official until the bell is rung. It had been a gift from a friend of his who worked for CSX, and for the past twenty seasons it has been mounted on a wooden frame that sits next to Bragan in his open box at the Baseball Fields of Jacksonville where every Suns home games was played.

All Suns batters also know better than to ever touch home plate after hitting a home run without hearing a bell clanging in the background.

Goetell gave me the printout on Dakota and another hug before we parted company at the alumni association. "Hey, why not join me for dinner?" he asked. "Wife's off visiting family, and I hate eating alone."

There are times when a man has to give in to the desires of his inner boy. So I accepted his invitation to dinner to the Olive Garden. Afterward we both ended up in bed back at my hotel room.

Goetell definitely was a demanding and satisfying "Daddy." His naked body had only lost a fraction of its once-youthful firmness. His body was almost smooth with the exception of a salt-and-pepper treasure trail that trailed down from an "innie" belly button. A gorgeous seven-inch uncut cock was surrounded by a neatly trimmed black bush only dusted with silver. Kneeling, I eagerly milked Daddy Goetell's cock once he guided my head down to it.

His cum was hot, sticky, and sweet tasting. I swallowed; savoring every drop I could drain out of his still-hard cock. I lifted my eyes upward.

"Good boy," Goetell said, just a little breathless. "Now Daddy's going to make his baby boy feel really good."

Once we were on the bed, he made me come twice—eagerly milking each drop of jism out of my cock—as my ass kept perfect rhythm with the steady sliding of his fingers in and out of my quim. I was moaning incoherently by the time his cock began a gentle entry inside me.

The house phone roused me from a deep slumber around seven the next morning. For some reason I had fallen asleep before Goetell had left. I thought nothing of it as I trudged barefoot to the bathroom. Road trips combined with about two hours of sex with a commanding Daddy are exhausting.

I quickly showered, shaved, and packed. I twice tried calling Coty, but nobody answered. I left a message the second time. He lived in Lakeland, Florida—just a few hours away by Interstate 75 and a few state two-lane highways. A photo of a Coty as a UF student had been included on the printout that Goetell had given me. Stephanie had been spot-on in her assessment of him when he attended that Goran family reunion with Paul all those years ago. With a round face framed by birth control glasses and frizzy black hair, Coty definitely didn't epitomize "athletic" material with his average, somewhat pudgy build.

Breakfast was just a toasted sesame seed bagel with cream cheese and a glass of orange juice hastily downed at the hotel's restaurant. By the time I had checked out, it was just pushing nine o'clock in the morning.

My plan had been to reach Lakeland by at least two o'clock in the afternoon.

My cell phone vibrated just as I hefted my luggage into the trunk—alerting me to an incoming text message. It came from Coty's number.

Who is this? Coty's text asked.

A sports writer looking for Paul Goran, I replied. *Ryan Goetell gave me your number.*

A minute passed before a reply came back. By then I had gotten into the car and had cranked up the air to escape the triple-digit heat of the morning.

Goran died years ago. Have nothing to say. Don't contact me again.

How did he die? I texted back.

Coty didn't reply.

He was lying, of course.

If Goran was dead, then Stephanie wouldn't be admiring that nice chunk of change in his trust fund from afar. Under her stewardship, it would have been drained dry. Of that I had no doubt.

I decided to try texting Coty one more time. I had nothing to lose.

I'm the one who caught Goran's homer back in 1989.

About two minutes passed before the phone rang. Coty had nibbled on the bait I had dangled out in front of him.

"Why do you want to find Pauly?" Coty warily asked. His voice had an almost neutral accent. It was impossible to detect which part of the country he originally came from—a trait I assumed he had picked up from studying acting at UF.

"Because he changed my whole life when I had caught that ball he hit out of the field at McKethan Stadium," I honestly replied. "In that one moment Paul Goran became my role model. I wasn't going to be a sports star like him. There was never a chance of that. I just strive to be the best I can be—just like he did back then."

"What will you do if you find him and he wants nothing to do with you?"

I swallowed hard. "Then I thank him and walk away."

"And write up what you find out about Pauly in your book?" So Coty had been in contact with Goetell. Otherwise, he wouldn't have known about the book.

"No, I'll protect him just like you and Ryan are doing."

Coty snorted. "Don't you mean 'Daddy' and me?"

"Okay, I slept with him," I admitted. It was safe to admit that with nobody else in the parking lot. Still, I kept my vocal volume low. No sense in outing myself to strangers in the hotel parking lot who might know who I was. "Obviously you did at least once; otherwise you wouldn't have known what role Ryan likes to play."

I really wanted to ask if Paul had slept with Goetell too, but decided against it. No point in pissing off the only individual who might be able to tell me where Goran was these days.

"Touché." He laughed for a few seconds before sobering up. "Pauly sometimes still talks about the kid who used a drink cup to catch a homer he hit. Maybe seeing that you turned out all right might get him back on track after all these years."

"Why did Goran walk away from his dream of a major league baseball career?" I asked.

Coty sighed heavily. "Pauly made just one doozy of a mistake. He brought a married man back to his dorm room. One of Daddy Goetell's older alumni friends back then. The guy had a heart attack as he was riding Pauly hard. No criminal charges were filed on the condition that he'd just quietly go away.

"If he didn't the college would ruin him with the publicity of a sex scandal. Back then, it was the only option available, so he took it just to keep his parents in the dark.

"Sad thing was, his parents suspected that there was something between me and him. Sadder still, we were—and still are—just friends without the benefits. Once they even called to tell me that they didn't understand but they loved Pauly anyway. They should have told him that before it was too late for them and him. And before you ask, yes, I told him. He's never really gotten past over that cluster-fuck he created back then."

"Did Goetell know?" I asked. My innards were twisting inside in anticipation of the answer.

"Who do you think helped Gator U cover it all up?" Coty bitterly replied. "Probably even knew about his dead friend's weak heart. Bastard had a notion to keep Pauly out of sight as his own personal boy toy, for a while anyways, until the next new boy came along. Goetell loves keeping his boy harem fully stocked. Only Pauly put a kink in that plan by up and walking away from everything and everyone who mattered to him."

I quietly let out a deep breath that I had been subconsciously holding. In previous imaginings of mine, Goran had walked away from everything for a variety of reasons. Hiding out from a sex scandal hadn't made my top ten reasons why he walked away from pursuing a baseball career.

"Where can I find him?" I asked, knowing full well he had the answer.

"He never left the state," Coty said. "He's in Yulee. Works days as a shift manager at a Gate Gas Station there. He rents a small unit at Cedar Park Apartments, number 268B. The complex is off of North Brisbane Road."

I quickly wrote the information Coty had given me on the hotel invoice. "Are you going to give him a heads up that I'm going to see him?"

"No," Coty replied. "Pauly would just run again if I did that. I think it's time for him to face past mistakes, instead of running from them."

I agreed and thanked Coty. He just grunted and broke the connection.

Yulee would have been the last place I ever would have thought to look for Goran. It's a typical small town just about ninety minutes away from where I lived in St. Augustine. Sure, it's home to a world-class golf designed in part by Arnold Palmer, but Yulee owes the bulk of its economy to the Yulee Tradeplex—a small strip mall including a Winn-Dixie, a stand-alone Lowe's, and a Super Walmart.

There was only one Gate Gas Station in Yulee, but I just drove past it and found Goran's apartment complex around four o'clock in the afternoon. Number 268B was a bottom unit. The parking space with his apartment number was empty, so I just parked in the nearby visitor parking about fifty yards away and waited.

I broke out my laptop from the trunk and began writing up everything I had learned about Goran. I also liberated his homer from my luggage.

A gold Saturn Ion that had definitely seen better days pulled into parking space for unit 268B shortly after six o'clock in the evening. I got out of my car as the door to the Saturn opened.

Despite having a shorter haircut than when I last saw him, Goran was instantly recognizable when he got out of his car. His lithe muscular body nicely filled out the standard uniform of Gate managers—black knit shirt with tan pants—just he had done with his Gators uniform. It just now expressed world weariness instead of the youthful exuberance he had once carried himself with when nothing but a future in baseball was knocking on his door.

I still a few feet away from Goran by the time he got to the front door of his apartment.

"Paul!" I called out. "Catch!"

Startled, he turned around to see who I was. With an overhand pitch with my free hand, I threw my treasured ball at him.

My pitch wasn't perfect. The ball swerved a bit to the right of him. Still, Goran caught it with the old ease of the ball player he had once been.

He turned in over in his hands for a few moments. He mouthed the words of the signature and looked up at me. Shocked surprise was mirrored in his tired blue eyes and face. Coty obviously hadn't called to let Goran know that I would be paying him a vist.

"Spence?" Goran asked. Half lost in a memory of bygone glory days, he just couldn't quite believe it was me—little Spencer Hamilton all grown up, to paraphrase Goetell. Or that we had reconnected after all these years. At least I hoped we had. I wasn't sure, because his memories also contained the pain having everything he had strived for taken away from him.

"The one and only," I replied with a goofy smile. I felt a bit awkward standing there with my laptop in hand. "It's good seeing you after all these years. Hope you feel the same."

My fantasy had been that he would welcome me with open arms. Goran didn't. He turned around and unlocked his front door. Without waiting for an invitation, I followed behind him and closed the door behind me. After all, he was still holding the ball. He sat down on a futon.

Placing my laptop down on the coffee table, I knelt in front of him. His eyes had the haunted look of a condemned prisoner just about to be escorted into the death chamber.

"Dakota told me just about everything," I told him. "How UF covered up the sex scandal you were involved in. Why you felt you had to cut yourself off from your family. He still loves you, you know that, right? Only thing I'm in the dark about is why you walked away from him."

"Spencer, I…I…had no choice," Goran replied. He was a bit hoarse. "Dakota thought I was straight. I knew he hated me. How could he not? Not only did I lie to him, I screwed around, just because I could. Only look what happened. I fucked over everyone I ever cared about real good."

I took a deep breath while I cupped his face between my hands. Goran's tears trailed along the edge of my fingertips.

"Paul, it's time to stop running from the past," I gently told him. "Not everyone who entered into your orbit fell into the sun. I didn't get burned in your downward spiral. I'm where I am today because I kept running toward you."

Goran wanted to believe me. His eyes reflected the inner struggle his conscience was engaged in. I decided to try giving it a push in the direction he needed to go. My lips brushed against his dry ones.

Goran leaned back into the futon, pulling me down with him. Years before I had used to masturbate to the image of him kissing, sucking, and fucking me. Now, in the reality of the moment, I was the one seducing him. As our mutual kissing became more passionate, my hands began exploring the firmness of his body as they slid underneath his shirt and inside his pants.

Most of our clothes were scattered in the living room by the time we had moved to the top of his bed. I paused only long enough to remove his briefs and mine, tossing them onto the floor.

My lips and tongue explored every inch of the body my younger self had spent many a stroke session fantasizing about. Goran moaned as my tongue teased the tip of his cockhead. I eased as much of his nine-inch cock down my throat as I could without gagging. He liked having his cock sucked while I gently tweaked his nipples.

His quim tensed when I first penetrated it with a finger. It was tight. So it had been a while since Goran had a cock inside him. By the time I had loosened it up with three fingers, Goran was begging me to fuck him. I paused only long enough to slide a condom on. Then I placed his legs over my shoulders and gladly obliged him.

Before I finally fell asleep, I remember the feel of Goran in my arms. He was nuzzling against my chest.

Goran was no longer in my arms by the time I had finally woken up. Nor was he in the bed or anywhere in the room.

After recovering my discarded boxers from the bedroom floor, I wandered into the hallway leading to the living room.

"Paul?" I called out. No reply came.

He wasn't in the living room either. Under my laptop on the coffee table near the futon was a white piece of paper neatly folded over. I lifted it out and opened it—a farewell message from Goran.

Hey Spence,
    Don't bother locking the door behind you. Packed up everything I needed while you slept. You were right. Thanks.

It's time to stop running. Only running I'm going to do this time is right to Dakota—if he'll still have me. Just make sure to include everything when you write about you and me.
    Best Regards,
    Paul

P.S. Stephanie's expression ought to be priceless when she learns I've returned back to the land of the living...

I chuckled a bit, conjuring up the image of how Stephanie would react to not getting to dip her hands into his trust fund. Then I considered his request.

Hell, Goran wouldn't be the only one I would be outing.

I'd be outing myself as well. I powered up my laptop.

He was right, though. I owed it to us both to be honest and tell our story in its entirety to the world. It was time I stopped running too. Carol, though, was going to have a conniption. Ditto for my producers and the network once I revealed I was gay and so was Goran.

So I took a deep breath, composed my thoughts once the desktop took me to a fresh page in MS Word, and began writing...

My first clear memory of Paul Goran is of him stepping out of the shower stall twenty years ago in the home team locker room at McKethan Stadium...

SHUTOUT
'NATHAN BURGOINE

Y ou've got Popov," Bart said.
"Will I need penicillin?"

Bart frowned at me. "What?"

I stared back. "What's pop-of-whatever?"

Bart laughed, long and hard. I crossed my arms while he calmed down. Laughing suited Bart—he was built like a walrus and had the moustache to match. He always played Santa at Christmas, too. He was the best boss I'd ever had, so I tried not to picture killing him while he laughed at me.

"Sorry," he eventually said. "Mikhail Popov."

"Popov is a person," I said, getting it. "New client?"

He nodded, looking like he was about to guffaw again. "The hockey player."

"Okay," I said.

"You still don't know who he is, do you?"

I shook my head. "No idea."

He grunted, chuckling again. "Best damn goalie the Sens have had in years. The Thunder did his shoulder in. He's done TENS already, and his coach says he's ready to start building up his strength again."

"The Thunder?" When Bart looked like he was going to laugh again, I waved it off. "Not that I'm opposed to some easy stuff, but…"

"You're a boy," Bart said.

"I'm aware of that." Now I was even more confused.

"He's got a…history." Bart colored. "With the girls." This sort of thing bothered him—the poor man wasn't good with even light banter.

"Last time he was here he let his mouth run off a bit with Becky, and she hauled off and slugged him."

Now I knew who this guy was. I tried and failed to hide a smirk. Becky was my closest friend and confidante at work. She was pretty patient, but when she hit her limit, you didn't want to be nearby. She'd ranted about this guy before, but the name hadn't stuck in my memory—she'd mostly referred to him as "that asshat."

"He earned it," Bart admitted. "But the point being I want none of that this time. And you're less likely to, uh…" His blush went from red to sunstroke. "Y'know, get starstruck, or whatever."

"I get it," I said. I was one of only three men on staff. And I was definitely the only guy on staff who wouldn't give a crap that Pop-whatever was a hockey star. I cracked my knuckles. "When do we start?"

"He's in at three." Bart seemed relieved. "Everything by the book—his coach will be all over our ass to clear him to play as soon as possible, but you know the rules."

I did. And I agreed with them. "Nobody goes faster than they should."

Bart clapped me on the shoulder. "You're a good kid, Geoff."

It was my turn to blush and feel uncomfortable. "Thanks, boss."

❖

"You're my trainer? You're what, nineteen?" The words were a mix of annoyance and disbelief. There was only a trace of Russian left in Mikhail Popov's accent. I fought the urge to ask him to say "nuclear vessels."

"I'm thirty-two," I said, a little stung and flattered both. Life with dimples. "Only I'm a physiotherapist, not a trainer." We were in one of three private rooms we had for clients who wanted or needed some privacy. One of the nice things about being in a government town was no lack of government clients. They were recession-proof.

Popov frowned. "I already did the physio crap. I'm good." He raised his arms up, and I could see him struggle a bit with his right shoulder. He might be good, but his shoulder wasn't.

"Good, huh?" I said.

"I'm great," he said, and scowled.

Shoulder notwithstanding, that was true. Apart from the scowl, he was pretty freaking hot. He had the dark Russian thing going for him— black hair, eyes a deep enough brown it was hard to see the pupils, and a scruffy unshaven look I chose to ignore, so I wouldn't get hives. The man needed a razor. But the man had fantastic legs. It was apparent that hockey was a damned good workout for the thighs.

I lifted my gaze, not wanting to be caught glancing at his calves.

"One," I said, holding up a finger. "It's not crap." I held up another. "Two, you had a full subluxation of your left shoulder and gave your rotator cuff a really bad day." My third finger rose. "Three, you're stuck with me until you get good enough to go back out on the rink or whatever, so let's play nice."

Popov leaned back. "On the rink or whatever?"

"Let's see your range of motion," I said, feeling myself blush. "Stand in front of the wall. I want you to walk your fingers up, like this." I showed him what I wanted him to do. He remained on the seat, glowering at me.

"Do you even watch hockey?" he asked. I couldn't decide if he was amused or angry.

"Not if I can help it," I said. "Come on, step over here. Let's see how restricted your movement is."

He slid off the seat awkwardly, and I saw him wince despite himself. That surprised me. Not that he'd be in pain—he'd definitely be in pain. But he seemed like a macho type, with all the crap that came with, so I figured he wouldn't show it. Not to mention the painkillers he must have been on.

He did his best, but it wasn't much. I bit my lip, wondering if Bart knew how far we had to go here.

"How old are you?" I asked. I'd already looked at his birth date, but I often asked a client this, just to see their reaction.

"I'm thirty-four," he said. "But I'm in good shape." I gave him points for not lying and made a mental note to look into the general age of hockey players. I'd worked with a few athletes before, including an Olympic swimmer, and most had been younger.

I nodded and gently took his arm. Even after being immobilized and unused, it was a fine-looking arm. He was built and had that perfect amount of dark hair on his forearm. I gently turned and drew his arm a little bit, asking him to let me know when and where things felt off, and after about half an hour, I was pretty sure this wasn't going to be a fun process for anyone involved. He was quick to snap at me, and his range of motion was really restricted.

"Fucking hell!" he growled. "Are you a fucking sadist?"

I released his arm and made a note. "No," I said. I waited a couple of breaths. "You've got a really bad situation here."

He nodded, and swallowed. "Just tell me."

By the time we'd finished chatting and discussing some of the options, it was obvious from the sweat soaking through the front of his T-shirt that Mikhail was in real pain.

"We're good for today," I said. "You okay?" He'd winced again when he got up to go.

He smirked, brushing it off. "I'd hoped I'd get that feisty chick again."

"Becky?" I said. "She said something about taking up kickboxing."

He winked. "You gotta love a woman with strong thighs."

"I prefer men." I shrugged. "But strong thighs are always a plus."

He gaped a little at me, and I have to admit I took some pleasure in the panic in his eyes. So much for being Mr. Tough Guy. I smiled nonchalantly and told him I'd see him tomorrow. He nodded and was out of there like a shot, though I could tell his shoulder was giving him hell.

❖

"Pop-Tarts?" I said, incredulous. I'd done a search on Mikhail Popov when I'd gotten home. The results had been half-athletic and half-tabloid—the tabloids showing him with any number of large breasted women, whom the newspapers and the women themselves seemed to take pride in referring to as "Pop-Tarts." None of them lasted very long, and they even had a Facebook group for themselves.

Ick.

On the athletic side of things, I saw that Mikhail Popov held the current record number of shutouts for the Sens—even I knew what that meant—and his current season, prior to his injury, he'd had a 0.941 save percentage. The article clarified the statistic included the "bad year" after his knee surgery. The number itself didn't mean anything to me, but he was the goalie, so I assumed he stopped a heck of a lot of pucks.

I found a video online of the accident itself. It involved a guy much bigger than Popov—a player on the Leafs named Gregory whom everyone called "the Thunder" for some reason. It had apparently been an "accident"—goalies weren't supposed to get smacked around, but it didn't look so accidental to me. I understood the whole "Thunder" thing once Gregory rammed into Popov on the clip. The sound of the impact was like a thunderclap. Gregory got another in what I assumed was an endless string of penalties, and Popov stayed prone on the ice. I rewatched the clip, and I could see the moment when Popov had landed just the wrong way on his shoulder with the other player's weight on top of him. I could all-too-easily imagine the crunching sound. I winced and touched my own shoulder, remembering.

I closed the laptop and rubbed my face. He was in great shape. He'd definitely done as he'd been told by his doctor, but he was impatient.

I was sure he wasn't going to be playing any time soon.

More than that, I wasn't sure if he was going to play again at all.

❖

"Okay, stop."

Mikhail had been slowly raising and lowering his arm for about ten minutes. His arm was shaking, his shirt was nearly soaked through, and he was clenching his jaw so tightly I could see the veins in his neck.

He kept going.

"Mikhail," I said. "I said stop."

He kept going.

I leaned in close and gently stopped his arm from rising. He seemed to come back from somewhere far away and glared at me for the interruption, sweat beaded on his forehead.

"What?" he snapped.

"I said stop."

He let his arm drop—slowly—and exhaled. "Fuck."

"You can't push yourself like that," I said. He wasn't like of most patients I'd worked with. He was absolutely going to do everything he could to get back to where he was before being injured. But he was trying to go too fast.

"I'm going to lose the season," he snapped.

"Yes," I said. "You are."

He glared at me.

I took his shoulders and met his gaze. "Do you feel the difference?" I asked. Even through his T-shirt I could feel the heat radiating off his right shoulder. "You're injured. There's nothing wrong with that. I am not going to sign off on you this season. There's no miracle to be had."

"You fucking f—" He bit off the word. His face flushed, and he looked down. He was a little pungent, and the white workout shirt was stuck to him. I could see the dark hair at his throat and was suddenly aware that I was inches from his face and holding his shoulders. The unsaid word hung in the air.

I let go.

"I told you already, go ahead and swear." I forced myself to grin. "You can call me whatever name you want. I won't be offended."

He sighed. "It doesn't help."

"That I'm not offended?"

Mikhail actually laughed. He looked back up at me. "I'm not good at being injured."

"I can tell." I gave him a pat on his good shoulder, and he leaned away.

"You hitting on me?" He narrowed his eyes.

"I don't think I'm cut out to be a Pop-Tart."

He smirked. "You don't have the tits."

"Yeah, well, you're not my type, either."

Trouble was, I was lying. He was hot, grumpy, foul-mouthed, stubborn, and completely inappropriate.

Which was exactly the sort of guy I seemed to find attractive and also the reason I was perpetually single.

At least he was straight.

"Let's get you into the tub," I said, then tried not to stare as he worked his way out of his shirt. His chest was pumped and covered in those fine dark hairs. He had a thick build—not a gym bunny physique, but someone who knew how to throw around weights to get strong.

Not my type my ass, I thought.

He grunted as he pulled the shirt off, and once again I realized he was in way too much pain. I couldn't understand why he was struggling so much.

I had a sudden realization.

"Are you taking your painkillers?" I asked.

His eyes dodged mine. That was answer enough.

"Look," I said, wondering how far into lecture mode I could descend before I got another curse out of him. We were up to four "fucking sadists" already today. "I get that you're a tough guy. I do. And I happen to agree that pain is a very important piece of feedback your body gives you, but they prescribe painkillers for a reason."

Mikhail shook his head. "No." He looked at me, jaw set. Not for the first time, I wished I was taller than him. It was hard to aim annoyance at someone bigger than you.

"Mikhail," I began, wondering what I could come up with to get the macho jerk to take his medication.

"I'm an addict."

The three words completely stalled me.

"What?" I said.

Mikhail's smile held no mirth. "About four years ago, I had to have knee surgery." I'd seen the scar. That had also been when he'd worked with Becky. "They gave me pills. I liked them." He shrugged his good shoulder. "I got hooked. And I got clean." He looked into my eyes. "That's why I don't take them."

"Oh," I said.

He seemed mad he'd said anything. "Keep that to yourself."

I nodded. "Of course. I can keep a secret."

He looked at me for a long time, then nodded. "Okay. Time for the tub, right?"

❖

"I want to go skating."

"No."

"On the canal," Mikhail clarified.

"What part of 'no' was unclear?"

"Fucking sadist," he groused. "It's for charity. For kids."

I frowned and crossed my arms. He'd actually made a little

progress and had been listening to me. He hadn't sworn at me all day. Now I figured I knew why. He'd been buttering me up.

"What is it, exactly?"

"It's for Winterlude. Some of the players get together with some kids on the canal. We skate with them, pass a puck around, sign shit. Some of the kids are from CHEO, and they really look forward to it." He looked at me, dark eyes wide with false innocence. "It's not about me, Geoff."

CHEO was the Children's Hospital of Eastern Ontario. Winterlude included turning the length of the Rideau Canal into the world's largest skating rink. I should have said no anyway. I narrowed my eyes.

"You're gonna disappoint children?" Mikhail shook his head, tutting. "You're a horrible man. Some of them are pretty sick, you know."

"Asshole," I said.

"I can go?" He smiled. He knew damned well he'd gotten me.

"Yeah, but no passing the puck, and I'd be happier if you didn't skate at all. Seriously, Mikhail," I added, when he pumped his left fist into the air.

"Come along if you don't trust me," Mikhail said.

"Fine," I said, and he looked at me, surprised, but didn't say anything else.

❖

I was beginning to realize why Bart had been so stunned when I'd not known who Mikhail was. The kids lined up on the canal sure seemed to. Most of the kids were out skating with the rest of the team, but there were a few—some with broken bones, some with the bald heads and pale skin that announced bigger worries—that were at the sidelines where I stood with Mikhail. I tried to stay out of the way, watching as Mikhail signed his name on jerseys a helper handed him from a large box. I was wearing one myself, which Mikhail had signed. I felt a little silly, but wasn't going to complain about another layer in the freezing Ottawa winter air. The CHEO kids each got a jersey, too, and most of them had a few questions for him—more than one about his shoulder.

"I'll be back on the ice when he says so," Mikhail said, pointing at me. Suddenly, the eyes of most of the kids—and not a few of the parents—were on me.

"Hi," I said, and waved. Lame.

"He's my physiotherapist," Mikhail said.

Once all of the kids from CHEO had had their turn, most of them had left right after to get back to the hospital. The sun was getting low on the horizon, but the canal was still full of kids, and a second line had formed. I shivered in the cold air, but had to admit that it was fun to watch the hockey players interacting with their fans.

While I watched, I saw there was a young skinny kid waiting in line. He didn't seem to have a parent with him, unlike most of the other boys—and a few girls—in line. I pegged him to be about nine or ten until he glanced up and I realized he was just really short. I smiled ruefully to myself, remembering how little I'd once been.

The kid slowly made his way through the line until he was only three people away from being the next to talk to Mikhail. At which point, a couple of much bigger kids—brothers, from the look of them, shoved him out of the way roughly and cut in front. No one else seemed to notice, including the adult with the two bigger kids, who was talking on his cell and barely paying attention.

"Hey," the little kid said.

"We're in a hurry," one of the bigger kids said and gave him a shove. The little guy fell down.

I was moving before I realized, and when I got there, I raised my voice. "Sorry, sir, these two just earned a penalty. Back to the end of the line."

The man blinked at me, frowning. He held his phone away from his ear for a moment.

"What?" he said.

"These two cut in and then shoved him down," I said, helping the smaller kid back up. He stared at me, turning red. I was probably embarrassing the hell out of him.

"We've been waiting for a while," the father started to explain.

"And as hockey fans, you know the penalty for fighting," I said, hoping I was at least somewhere close to the mark. "Back to the end of the line."

He looked like he was going to argue, but I aimed a "try me" look at him, and he took his kids by the shoulders—both of them wailing about how unfair this was—and marched them to the back of the line.

"You okay?" I asked.

The little guy nodded at me. I stood with him until it was his turn. He looked like he was fighting back tears. I studiously ignored that and chatted with him about nothing.

"What's your name?" Mikhail asked him, once we were at the front.

"Finn." Once in front of Mikhail, the kid's frustration had vanished.

"Well, Finn," he said. "How would you like an autographed puck, too?"

Finn lit up. Mikhail personalized the puck specifically for him, and the kid raced off with it clutched in both hands after tugging on the jersey—which was so long he was nearly tripping over it.

Mikhail went to sign the next jersey and winced visibly. He was pale.

"Okay," I said, speaking up. "You've had enough."

Mikhail blew out a big breath. "Sorry, kids. You know what the doctors are like."

There was a chorus of moans. The father with the two bullies glared at me. I shrugged at him.

"Hey," Mikhail said. "I'd stay, but he says I have to go. But how about I come back again before they close down the canal for the year?"

The moans became cheers. After a few more moments, we turned, and started off down the ice. Mikhail swore under his breath.

"You're feeling pretty bad, aren't you?" I was annoyed at myself for not noticing sooner.

"Yeah," he admitted. That made me feel all the worse. He was admitting he was in pain? Damn.

I looked around. "Come on," I said. "I'm closer."

I knew he was in rough shape when he didn't argue.

We got to my car, and I helped him into the passenger seat. I did his seat belt for him and then went around to the driver's side. It was freezing, and I blasted the heat as soon as it came through the vent.

"I'm not far from here," I said. "You can crash at my place."

"Thanks," he said. He'd closed his eyes.

"You were amazing with those kids," I said. "Polite, even."

He laughed. "They don't make me do things that hurt and then tell me not to skate."

I stopped at a red light. "There's nothing I'd like better than to have you back on the ice and doing what you love," I said. "But I'm not setting you up to fail."

We idled for a while.

"I'm pretty sure you made that one kid's whole year," I said.

"Hmm?"

"The little one. Finn?" I glanced over. Mikhail was looking out the window.

"Ah," he said.

The light changed. We were almost at my place.

"It was really cool," I said. "He reminded me of me at his age."

"You were a small kid?" Mikhail asked.

"The smallest," I said. "Had the crap kicked out of me on a regular basis. This is my building."

I pulled into the underground parking and parked in my spot.

By the time I'd helped him get his boots and his jacket off, Mikhail looked about ready to topple over. I led him to my bedroom and flicked on the lights. He sank onto the bed, exhausted.

"Are you hungry or thirsty?" I asked. It was getting dark.

He shook his head. "No." He struggled out of his jersey and started to tug off the sweatshirt beneath. His chest was as good to look at as always. I glanced away.

"Is there anyone I should call?" I asked. "The latest Pop-Tart, or whoever?"

He laughed, once. "No." Then he looked up at me, and for a second, I could have sworn he was embarrassed. It passed quickly.

"Go ahead and sleep," I said, and closed the door behind me.

❖

I woke to the smell of coffee. Groggy, I frowned at my living room ceiling until I remembered why I'd slept on my couch. I rose, a little stiff, and went to my kitchen, scratching my chest and trying to wake up. I'd slept in my jeans under a blanket on the couch. It hadn't been the best sleep I'd ever had; it had been a bit too cold to be comfortable.

Mikhail had his back to me and was only wearing his boxers. I'd seen him in his trunks at work, of course, but somehow this seemed more intrusive. I swallowed. He had a fantastic ass and large, muscular thighs. His calves were a thing of beauty. His back was wide and strong.

God, he was hot.

I cleared my throat.

Mikhail turned. "I made coffee." I tried and failed to avoid glancing down at his hairy chest and stomach, and then a bit lower, where… His boxers seemed a little full in the crotch. He tucked left, apparently.

I aimed my gaze back up.

Okay, well. Everyone has morning wood, right? I was certainly feeling it.

He was rumpled and his hair was sticking up. It was adorable. And sexy. He was staring at me, though, a little smile tucked into the corner of his mouth. I realized I hadn't said a word to him yet.

"Sorry. Not a morning person. Thanks," I said, and opened the cupboard where the mugs were. I handed him one, then got one for myself.

My kitchen wasn't big. He was close enough to me that I felt awkward, and when he poured the coffee his left arm brushed mine. I stepped back, almost jumping from the touch.

He looked at me. "I thought I wasn't your type."

He was teasing me, the jerk.

I took a long gulp of coffee. He'd made it strong. It was fabulous.

"Fine," I said. "You're exactly my type." I raised my free hand when he grinned. "But that's not a good thing. My dating life is full of one self-centred macho bastard after another that gave me nothing but grief. Not worth it, no matter how hot they were."

"You think I'm hot?" He sipped his coffee.

I rolled my eyes, putting my cup down. "You know you're hot." I reached past him. "I'm afraid I don't have any Pop-Tarts. You want toast or bagels? I might have some—"

He put down his coffee and took my arm in his weak hand. I froze, and he pulled my hand down until he pressed my palm against his hard-on. He felt thick and hot.

His dark eyes didn't leave mine.

"Uh," I said.

His left hand cupped the back of my head and pulled me in. His stubble was rough against my lips, but his tongue was insistent. I felt my own confusion giving way to something more basic. I squeezed his dick.

He broke the kiss, our foreheads still touching, and smiled.

"Breakfast later," he said, and then tugged me toward my bedroom.

❖

I was sure this was a bad idea, but every time I tried to come up with reasons to stop, he'd kiss me again and I'd forget what it was I was upset about. His hard hairy chest was a delicious friction against mine, and I had my hand down the front of his boxers before we'd made it into my bedroom. He had a thick cock, and I could feel the heat of his pulse in my hand.

The moment the back of his legs hit the bed—which I noticed he hadn't made—I broke out of our tangled arms and slowly slid down, kissing his chin, and his throat, and stopping at one of his lovely dark nipples for a while before I made my way across his stomach to the patch of dark hair leading downward. When I pulled on his boxers, his hands took either side of my head and he tilted me to look up at him.

Aroused, he wore a sort of bashful smile, and I heard myself chuckle before I leaned forward and took his dick into my mouth.

"Fuck," Mikhail grunted, and I took it as a compliment. His length was average, which was good, since his girth was giving me a bit of a struggle. I swallowed him, aiming to bury my nose in his dark hair and just succeeding. My hands gripped his strong thighs.

His grip tightened in my hair, and I went to work on him, tasting the salty muskiness of the day before and licking around his shaft and cockhead in alternate strokes. He grunted again, rubbing my head with both hands and breathing in long slow breaths.

After a while, his hands pulled me from his dick, and I looked up at him again. He tugged me up, and I rose back to standing. He crushed me against him—gripping strong with his left arm, and awkwardly pulling at my jeans with his right. I pulled back enough to undo the button and zipper for him, and managed to step out of my jeans and underwear in one move.

Our cocks rubbed together with urgency—his hard thighs were incredible. My hands dropped to grip his ass, and he did the same. His kisses were almost possessive, making me lean back at the strength of them.

Finally, he moved backward a bit and sat on the edge of my bed, pulling me with him. I knelt, my legs to either side of him, and I wrapped my arms around his neck, finally looking down at his face from above. We were both breathing heavily and grinding ourselves against each other.

"Tell me you've got some lube," Mikhail said, one of his fingers teasing me and making me arch against him.

I leaned over to get to my nightstand, and Mikhail gave my ass a friendly slap. I yelped, laughing, and tugged open the drawer.

I knelt beside the bed while I rolled the condom onto him, and he leaned back, resting his weight on his left arm while I worked. His dark eyes were intense, watching me while I worked, and every time I looked up at him, they were locked on me. His chest hair was dark with sweat, and I wondered if we were hurting his shoulder.

"Lie down," I said, nodding to the pillows.

He shifted onto the bed, his hard dick aimed high, and lay on his back. I crawled up onto the bed and was more than generous with the lube. He was a thick guy. He took the bottle from me and squirted some onto his left hand and fingered me again. I leaned over him, trying not to rest any weight on him, but rubbing our dicks together while he teased my ass with his slippery fingers. I kissed him again, deep, and then rose, taking his dick in one hand and lowering myself down onto him.

"Jesus," I gasped as I relaxed his cockhead through. He was so hot after the cool slickness of the lube, and I felt every bit of his thickness. I lowered myself slowly, eyes shut tight, aware I was moaning as his dick filled me.

I opened my eyes when I had his length inside me, and he was staring into my eyes. His jaw was clenched. I rose, lifting myself half off him, feeling his hardness moving inside me, and he rumbled deep in his chest.

"Stay there," he said, his voice gravelly with need. I braced my hands to either side of him, arching my back slightly away from him, and resisted the urge to sink back down onto his hot cock.

He gripped my waist with his left hand, and then pushed up with his pelvis, driving his dick back into me. Those powerful thighs thrust upward at me, slapping against my ass.

I moaned again. He repeated the motion and my whole body arched again. He was rubbing me inside just the right way, his thickness filling me just shy of too much, and with such a fucking delicious heat. My dick ached, but braced the way I was I couldn't stroke myself.

"Jesus," I said.

"Yeah?" he asked.

I nodded. "Yeah."

He moved faster, pushing in and out of me while I struggled to stay still. I wanted to throw myself down onto his dick with every thrust, but his left hand tightened when my arms shook.

"Stay," he said again. His lips curled in a grin, and I met his gaze.

"Fucking sadist," I said.

He laughed and pushed into me again. And again. And again. When I finally saw his control slipping and felt his left hand shaking, I dropped myself onto his dick, leaned forward, and pressed both hands to either side of his head. I ground him into me, and his head rolled back, his eyes shutting for the first time.

"Fuck!" he yelled, and I felt him come—the pulse of three surges in the condom that make me desperate to come myself. I reached down, keeping his dick inside me, and jerked myself off onto his hairy, sweat-soaked stomach.

I collapsed off him as carefully as I could, feeling him come free with a not unpleasurable pain, and lay on my stomach beside him, panting. My right arm lay across his chest, and I felt his right hand take mine and squeeze.

I turned my head to look at him.

His hand stroked along my arm.

"You have a great body," he said. "So smooth."

I smiled. "Thank you. You're pretty fucking fantastic yourself."

"I know," he said, smug.

I shoved his chest.

"Where did you get that?" he asked, his finger trailing the scar along my shoulder.

"One of the times I had the crap kicked out of me," I said. "Quite a while ago now."

"Oh," he said. Then he rolled onto his side and kissed it.

My whole body shivered at the touch of his rough stubble against my skin.

"Jesus," I said.

"Yeah," he agreed. Then, a moment later, he asked, "Now breakfast?"

❖

We wiped ourselves down, and I made bagels. We sat in our boxers, eating, and I tried not to stare too much at him. He wolfed them down. It made me want to pounce on him.

"You've done that before," I said, once we were done and he was standing beside me at the sink while I rinsed the plates.

He smiled at me. "A few times, yeah." He leaned forward and kissed me. My whole body relaxed into the kiss. He leaned back. "I'd like to do it a few more times, as well."

I shook my head. "I'm sorry. I'm confused—I thought…I mean, the Pop-Tarts?"

Mikhail shrugged. "It's an image thing."

I blinked. "So you're in the closet."

He raised his eyebrows. "I play in the NHL."

"Is that the same thing?"

He laughed. "Worse. Just ask the Thunder." He tapped his bad shoulder.

I didn't let that particular nugget distract me. "So this is…what?"

Mikhail smiled. "Sex."

"Right," I said. He leaned in again. I pulled away.

"What's wrong?" he asked.

"You know that kid?" I said. "The one from the canal?"

He frowned. "The little one?"

I nodded. "Yeah. That's what's wrong."

He shook his head. "I don't understand."

"You could make it better," I said. "I don't know if he's like me or not, not really, but you know what I didn't have at his age? Anyone like you to look up to." I felt my eyes well up, and blinked furiously, annoyed at myself. "Think of what you could do."

Mikhail crossed his arms. "I can't come out. Not if I want to play."

I sighed. "That sucks."

"You can keep a secret. We can still be…friends." He grinned at me. And his dark eyes were very tempting.

"No," I said. "No, we can't."

❖

Bart took it as well as I could have hoped.

"What did he say to you, exactly?"

I shook my head. "It's okay. I don't want to get into it. I just don't want to work with him anymore." I sighed. "I'm sorry. I know I let you down."

Bart shook his head. "No. He was difficult with Becky, too. And you said he's been making progress. I'll just tell Scott not to get all starstruck with him."

"Actually," I said. "I spoke with Becky. And she said wouldn't mind another shot at him."

Bart paled.

"Figuratively speaking," I said.

❖

I tried to put Mikhail Popov out of my mind. I arranged my schedule with other clients to be opposite when I knew Becky had time with him, and after a while, it wasn't so bad. She told me he seemed like a different guy to the one she'd helped four years ago—he was polite, paid attention, and did what he was told.

"Whatever you did to him," Becky said, "you should market it."

I hadn't had the heart to laugh.

As the days went by and became weeks, I tried not to ask questions, but she shared anyway. She had the same sinking sensation I'd had, that Mikhail wasn't going to fully regain his range of motion, and that between the shoulder subluxation and the rotator cuff injury, he might be off the ice for more than a season.

"How's he taking it?" I finally asked while we shared lunch one afternoon.

"He's announcing it on Friday," he said. She looked at me. "You should watch."

"I should watch hockey news?" I said, amused.

"He really respects you," she said.

That surprised me. "He does?"

She nodded. "I'm just saying. You made an impression."

I shrugged. "Just doing my job."

"Do me a favour," Becky said. "Watch it."

"Sure," I said.

❖

The little red indicator light lit on the PVR, but I didn't turn on the television. I sat with my book and glanced up every now and then, until the little red light turned off. Maybe I'd watch it later. I put my book down and went into my bedroom, opening the closet and pulling out the red, black, and gold jersey. I pulled it over my head, then looked in the mirror.

"You're an idiot," I said. "You need to find a nice guy who isn't a self-absorbed macho bastard."

My reflection regarded me with frank disbelief. It didn't seem likely to him, either.

"Right," I said and lay down on my bed. I stayed that way for about an hour, drifting on the edge of sleep, until there was a knock at my door.

I got up, and went to the door. I opened it.

Mikhail Popov took one look at my jersey and smiled. He'd shaved. He looked good without all the stubble. He reached in and grabbed me and kissed me before I could properly understand he was standing there. I forgot to protest at first, and took a step back when he let go.

"What…?" I said.

"I came as soon as I could get away from all the questions," he said, stepping past me into my apartment. He turned around. "I like your jersey."

I was lost. "Mikhail…"

He looked at me. "You didn't watch the announcement."

I felt my face blushing. "I recorded it." It sounded lame, even to me. I closed my door, avoiding his gaze.

He shook his head. "Becky said you were going to watch it."

"I was. I mean, I am." I shook my head. "What happened?"

"My shoulder is done," Mikhail said. "So that means I'm done. Retired."

"I'm so sorry," I said, and I meant it.

"And I came out."

"You—" I blinked. My mouth dropped. "Oh my God."

"That was the general response," Mikhail said, with a rueful smile. "I said it was too bad I didn't have the courage to come out while I played, but now that I was retired, I was going to try to make the sports world a place where people like me felt comfortable to be. Only it sounded better than that. I even apologized to the guy I'd been seeing."

I opened my mouth. Closed it.

"That would be you," Mikhail said.

"Oh," I said. We were seeing each other? I suppose we had seen each other pretty much every day for over a month. "You apologized?" I couldn't help but grin. "Like, in public?"

He scowled at my television. "I can't believe you didn't watch it. I had a really nice speech. Becky helped me write it."

"Becky knew?" I blinked.

"I told her. She told me about how badly you were beaten. I didn't know." He stopped, and I saw something new in his dark eyes: uncertainty. He'd just burned some major bridges.

I smiled at him. "Are you okay?"

He nodded. "I'm okay."

We stood there a moment.

"So if you didn't see the news," Mikhail said, a trace of his old self in his smile, "why are you wearing my jersey?"

"Because it's warm?" I tried.

"You think I'm hot," he said. "It was killing you not to be with me."

I went to shove him in the chest, but he grabbed me and tugged me tight against him. He even used both arms. I looked up into his eyes. He winked.

"You're such a self-absorbed macho bastard," I said.

"Oh good," Mikhail said. "For a second, I was worried you didn't like me anymore." Then he kissed me again, and this time I didn't even think of protesting. It was quite a while before we came up for air.

"Does this make me a Pop-Tart?" I asked.

He nodded. "My favorite flavor."

"Jerk. Are you really okay?"

"I'm terrified. But relieved. And horny."

I laughed and shoved him again. He didn't let go.

"Can we have sex now?" he asked. "I don't mind if you keep the jersey on, but the pants will have to go."

"Oh, shut up," I said, but I was grinning, and already tugging the jersey over my head.

He grinned and started stripping. Even with his bad shoulder, he beat me to it.

CHANGING LANES
MAX REYNOLDS

*They were like a pod of dolphins—sleek and smooth, their
backs arching up and then down and then up again. He could
see their legs flying out behind them, muscular and strong, cutting the
water and churning it up with beautiful, stark, animal precision. They
hit the wall, mere tenths of seconds between them. Not enough time to
blink, or he would miss the part he loved most—the sensuous flip as
they hit the wall and turned to go back for the next lap. One by one
they touched the tile and then arched up and out of the water, bending
artfully, gracefully, powerfully, and then dove down again, deep. The
movement was always literally breathtaking for him: he could feel the
quick intake of breath in the pit of his diaphragm as he felt how much
he loved watching men's bodies moving, pushing, and straining every
muscle, exuding their seemingly effortless power.*

*He could always see the outline of at least one cock against the
skin-tight Speedos during the turn, but that wasn't what excited him. It
was each of them and all of them—wet and sleek and smooth, muscles
rippling, shoulder blades flexing, arms up and out and down and in,
asses so tight and hard that he could almost feel them under his hands,
could almost see himself holding on to the tapered hips as he fucked
and fucked and fucked that hard, tight, hot, muscled ass, its delicate
rosebud hidden between those perfectly honed cheeks, ready to open
just for him when they were both ready.*

*He was ready now. He'd been ready for weeks. He was so ready
that after every meet he'd end up outside the showers, sitting on the
bench, leaning forward, towel in his lap to hide his cock, which was
never harder than it was when he was watching Ramirez swim, Ramirez
getting out of the pool, wet and dripping, and he knew, smelling of*

sweat and chlorine, Ramirez peeling off his Speedo, Ramirez slapping Cochran on the back, Ramirez throwing an arm around Miller, Ramirez snapping a towel at Thompson, Ramirez soaping up in the shower, Ramirez toweling off, Ramirez walking back to the lockers, muscled and still a little wet, like he would be after a workout or after sex, his hair jet black and falling just a little into his face, but his body smooth and waxed like they all were, to make them faster in the water. Sleek. Animal.

Then he'd watch Ramirez getting dressed—watch him pulling on his briefs—Ramirez liked the constricting kind with the legs and no flap—arranging his dick and balls quick and businesslike, not lingering the way he imagined he would when he finally got the chance to touch that dick himself.

This was the point where he always wanted to just whip off his towel and stand in front of Ramirez and jack it off right there, show Ramirez how hard he was, how hot Ramirez got him, how ready he was to give it to him however he wanted it—ass, mouth, hand, thighs. He'd do any of it. He wanted to do all of it. He wanted Ramirez, and every time he saw him swim, he wanted him more.

Jake McMahon had transferred into prestigious Halstead College as a junior. Never a good year to enter any college, especially a small one. It always looked like you'd failed at what you were doing before, or worse, that you'd been at some community college and now were ready for the real deal, the grown-up thing, the place where people could actually read and write in sentences that didn't use text speak. Or, at a place like Halstead, that Daddy's money had bought you a space.

But that wasn't what had happened. What had happened was Jake had been a point guard and a good one—he wasn't freakishly tall, just six feet two, but he was fast and an ace shooter. Ace. He'd had a future that was supernova bright and he was looking forward to every second of it, from the free shoes to the hot sex to the big house to the even bigger money. And the fame. He'd actually wanted the shove-it-in-your-face fame most of all.

He'd gotten a taste of it—the press, the offers to leave school and track into the NBA. But then in his sophomore season he'd blown his knee—blown it permanently. Gone. And not even on the court, but off on a dumbass ski trip in the mountains with a bunch of guys where he just had to do that extreme snowboarding and lost it completely, smashing his leg, blowing his knee, and lucky he could even walk, let alone play.

There had been press about it—about how the white kid from working-class Kensington in Philly who'd made it to a super school and had all the promise of being the first Irish guy since Larry Byrd to take it to the top had lost his scholarship and any hope of seeing the NBA as anything but another beer-guzzler with a big gut screaming in the stands with no clue.

Jake's NBA dream was done. He had to make other plans.

Halstead was his other plan.

Jake had always had a backup because he'd always known life demanded one. His mother hadn't had one—his father was a total loser, caricature of an Irish drunk who was out of work as much as in. He wasn't going to have a loser life like her or his father. The nuns had beat it into him that he was smart, too smart for sports, and that basketball was for "the ethnics" with no options and that he should be sure he had options.

So Jake could write well, loved literature, and was pretty good at math. And he had a second sport—swimming—but it was a sport he couldn't really afford, because all you needed for basketball was someone with a ball and some decent shoes, but to swim you needed a pool. All through high school he'd done regular favors for the parish priest, Father Gallagher—not that kind, but real favors, because the guy was old and the parish was poor and the diocese was busy paying out for those other priests, the bad ones—and so Jake had been able to guest at the diocesan pool for three years running. Which made him strong and fast—as good in the pool as he was on the court. But on the court he wasn't back up. In the pool he was.

Until now.

When he'd wrecked his leg and knee, pools were therapy. When he ramped up his speed again, could make that turn at the tile in splits of seconds, he started looking for small colleges with teams that might take him, blown knee and all.

Halstead was the place. The college needed another guy to replace their second lead guy, Evans. He'd been lost to rehab and a performance drug scandal. He'd taken down a lot of the support the team had gotten. But even with his blown knee, Jake still had star power, and so Jake was the fill-in, the replacement, the second-string would-be first-string hope to bring Halstead's team back from scandal and bad press.

Jake was it. His snowboarding accident had been seen as the whimsically tragic end to a spectacular career, a star athlete testing his athletic capabilities, not the dumbass move he'd known it was. Halstead was his second chance.

But he hadn't counted on Ramirez.

It wasn't that Javier Ramirez had taken his spot. Ramirez was already there, had been there since freshman year. He was the swim team leader after the Evans guy had gone through the whole drug drama that had forced everyone to be tested and checked and checked again. Ramirez was, everyone had thought until the scandal rocked the team, Olympic-bound. He was going to be another Michael Phelps or Peter Vanderkaay or Gary Hall—he was going to medal and big and take Halstead with him. But the scandal had tainted everyone with the drugs, including Ramirez. The money backing the team and the endorsement possibilities and all of it blew up, big.

Jake was clean. Totally. No taint. That was his bonus point. That was his entry pass. That was his second chance. But still, there was Ramirez.

Ramirez was a fish. They called him Ceviche and he loved it— he'd laugh and say, "Yeah, you want that spicy fish, and raw, don't you, *m'ijo*? Say it!" and then he'd slap his thigh or his ass and laugh again or whip a towel at somebody.

And when Jake first heard that, heard Ramirez's voice low and throaty and with just that hint of accent and the big laugh that followed, he knew a small school had been a huge mistake. Because he could hide gay back in California, just like he had hidden it in Philly. But there was no hiding it here. Here it would be as obvious as that dick poking through the towel as he sat waiting to jerk off in the shower to flashes of Ramirez after everyone else had left, when his desire for Ramirez was so great he'd just stand there, arm pressed against the wall, rubbing his balls and pulling on his cock under the warm, wet blast of the shower until he'd finally come, images of Ramirez pulling off his Speedo or pulling on his briefs so vivid and hot in his head that he could see himself with his hand in the Speedo or slipping inside the briefs while he had Ramirez's back against the shower wall, kissing him hard, thrusting his tongue into his mouth with all the sensual heat he intended to use with his dick when he got the chance and Ramirez kissing him back just as hard and urgent and...

It was always when he imagined his hand in Ramirez's briefs and his mouth hard against his that he would come, spurting into the shower with such force he'd feel his bad knee buckle sometimes.

Jake wasn't sure when he crossed the line from attraction to sexual obsession with Ramirez, but it was early on. He'd always been hot for guys with swimmer's bodies. He loved the broad shoulders and cut arms. He loved the ripped torsos and muscled legs. He loved the tight asses. He'd had more than a few tight asses out on the West Coast and there was nothing he liked more than a hot, hard fuck. He'd had to sneak around all through high school, but once he was out in California it was different—there were so many options for fucking, he never worried. He could drive up to San Francisco or just tool over to West Hollywood. It was all too big for him to care if someone took his picture with their cell phone. He knew he had a look that a lot of guys had—tall, lean, and muscled, with dark hair and fair skin and the kind of blue eyes his mother said would send good girls to hell. But he'd seen his own looks a lot in California—he wasn't the only Black Irish boy who'd gone west to get the kind of sex he couldn't get at home and he was more interested in doing the kind of fucking he wanted than he was in caring if some cell phone shot would end up somewhere later, when he was famous. His freshman year he'd spent studying, shooting, swimming when he could, and fucking every chance he got.

He'd read about how San Francisco and L.A. were a gay mecca in the 1970s when gay sex was out for the first time, and it had felt the same way to him when he got out there forty years later. He'd never seen so many available men, hot men, young guys and old dudes and guys with money and straight guys checking out the scene. Before he'd hit L.A. he'd been in Philly, down at K&A in his old 'hood looking for guys to trick with on the weekends or slipping into bars with fake ID or heading over to Jersey to this club or that party. But it always had that could-get-caught-any-time-and-screw-everything quality to it, and whether that was still a reality or not in L.A., Jake never felt it there. What he felt was years of not enough sex finally ended for good.

The weekend Jake had blown his knee, he blown a lot more. It was a sex party weekend and there was no way he wasn't going. Screw practice, screw everything. When he'd been there on the West Coast, all the guys on the team had said regular sex was important to playing good ball and he'd started to believe it to the point where if he didn't get it, he felt deprived and down on his game.

"Get yourself some regular pussy, man, or you won't shoot for shit. You feel me?" He'd heard it from Jackson and Williams and Tomlinson over and over again, and he knew they were hunting down girls night after night and there were girls ready and willing because every guy on the team was hot and going somewhere.

Except pussy wasn't what Jake had ever been interested in, so he'd feigned a regular girl out in Calabasas, which gave him upscale cachet and a good excuse to get out of town and fuck away a weekend.

He would have liked love, and before Ramirez, he'd tried for it a few times, but for all the fucking, he wasn't out, which meant love was almost as inaccessible as sex had been back in Philly.

Jake wasn't sure when he'd decided that heat and sweat and sex and desire were all one package for him, but he remembered the connection first when he'd been playing basketball in eighth grade and Tony Bylinski had been all up in his game and he could see the sweat dripping off his blond hair and running down his neck and he could smell the guy smell of him and he had felt that surge in his dick and it had scared him.

Later he'd gone home and jerked off into his own sweaty shorts and remembered the sexy look on Tony's face—concentration and a little bit of anger and whatever else happened to guys when they wanted to win—and he had come really hard and rolled over on his pillow and thought about his lips pressed to Tony's hot, sweaty neck and thought about Tony's mouth slightly open and wondered what Tony's dick would feel like in his hand, what those strong thighs would feel like underneath him and he had lain on his stomach and pumped himself again, this time thinking just about Tony, just about his strong thighs and soft, hot neck and those slightly full Polish lips that were a little like a girl's lips, but not really…

❖

In L.A. Jake had had the same locker room fetish—he knew it was a fetish now, he'd done it enough times to realize that the smell of other men and the total absence of anything female or feminine was part of what turned him on. This was a men-only world and that was what he loved about it, that was what fed his desire. In L.A. there had been someone else on his team he had wanted—Rashid Henderson, another shooter, but not quite as good as Jake was. Henderson was tall and built—he liked to lift weights and he was also into some weird stuff like shot put and javelin throw and things that made his arms incredibly strong. He was super light-skinned—his mother was Irish and his dad was half black, half Native American—and he had the kind of green eyes that reminded Jake of marbles he'd had as a kid.

He'd gone out to clubs with Rashid and they'd gotten high together and one night they were pretty lit down in Fairfax and Rashid had said what the hell were they doing there, and they needed to get some action and the way he had said action had made Jake laugh. And Rashid had faked seriousness and said in an exaggerated tone and fake dialect, "You laughin' at me, white boy? I'm gonna whup yo' ass so's you can't shoot no more. Don't know what they was thinkin' lettin' yo' on the team anyways, right—just felt sorry for yo' didn't they?" And then he had play-shoved Jake and they had wrestled a little and then Rashid had him pinned against the wall of the club and they were laughing and shoving and suddenly Rashid's mouth was so close to his and they had kissed.

It was the kind of kiss that Jake had remembered from high school—rough, "I'm not really doing this with another guy" kind of kisses that almost never led anywhere, except this one did. This one got harder and Rashid had his body slammed up against Jake's and Jake could feel Rashid's dick through his jeans and it was rock-hard and he wasn't sure if he wanted to touch it, suck it, or have Rashid fuck him. He'd never been fucked, but he was sure in that moment that if Rashid had wanted it, he'd have done it right there—bent over the hood of a car, with his tight white Irish ass out in the moonlight and let himself get fucked and hard.

Being there with Rashid was all the things Jake had remembered all through school—the way he commingled the smell and feel and sound of men as they ran across a locker room floor or a basketball court or around the acoustic tile of a pool. It was the ricochet of sound and the heady scent and the bodies—the muscles and the skin, the way a jock strap accentuated everyone's dick and ass and…all of it.

They'd moved back to the edge of the lot behind the club, Rashid sort of dancing him down the wall just like they were on the court, his mouth still hard against Jake's and his tongue hot and thrusting and tasting of vodka and something slightly sweet and there was a plot of bougainvillea and the scent of it rose up around them. Rashid had wanted to jerk him off, had wanted their dicks up against each other, had wanted to see Jake's dick against his own, and feel it—the two hot hard dicks touching each other. Rashid had unzipped Jake's jeans and pulled out his cock and his hands had been surprisingly smooth as he slid one into Jake's pants and massaged his balls and ran a finger back toward his ass.

Jake had been so hot then, with that move and the hard kissing, that he'd felt his cock wet and thought he was already coming, but it was just like it would be when he'd be jerking off at home and he'd stop and start again, edging a little and then waiting. But he didn't want to wait with Rashid and he'd wished they'd been someplace else, but there was that little danger thrill that he'd felt before back at K&A when he'd get in a car and drive around and jerk the guy off or let him suck him off and it would be barely dark out and there would be people everywhere and it would make the coming really intense, that little bit of danger.

Jake had asked Rashid if he wanted him to suck his dick and he'd said it low and whispery near his ear and he could feel the pulse in Rashid's thick cock when he said it and he knew Rashid wanted it, but didn't want to move from where they were and somehow if they stopped kissing it would be something else and tomorrow would be a very difficult day for them both.

So they stood there, rubbing each other's tight balls and stroking each other's dicks and pressing their dicks together and against each other's thighs and then fucking a little between each other's thighs, kissing like they were sucking dick, until they were both ready to shoot. Suddenly, Jake grabbed Rashid's hand and rubbed it hard against his cock—he didn't want to wait anymore, he was ready, he'd been thinking about this for weeks, maybe months, and he'd fucked eight or nine guys in between, but this was the guy he really wanted and he wanted to feel the intensity, he wanted to see Rashid's hand on his cock and he wanted to feel Rashid's dick against his thighs and he wanted to feel him come, he wanted that pulsing that he'd felt when he'd asked about sucking his dick and so he said it again, "You want me to do it right now—suck it? You want my mouth on your dick? You want it? Because I want it, if you want it. Do you? Do you?" And he was talking right into Rashid's mouth, their lips still against each other, and he'd let his tongue lick the edge of Rashid's upper lip and then Rashid made that sound, that sound that was the hottest sound Jake could imagine and he felt the hot cum on his hand as Rashid pressed his mouth hard into his as he was coming.

They stood against the wall for a few minutes, just standing, leaning a little, tilted back, legs wide apart. Jake wondered if one of those night-vision things would show the heat emanating from them both. Then Rashid said, "I need a drink—you need a drink?" and Jake had nodded and they had slid back upright and walked back to the club.

There had been one other night after that one, a night after a game, and it had surprised Jake because they had never talked about that night outside the club again and Jake had known that was the deal—he wasn't sure if Rashid knew that he wanted more, was maybe even close to falling for Rashid, but he knew Rashid was straight, or thought he was, and there was no talking about it.

It had been a bad game. Everything was wrong right from the start and they were all better than they'd played, and two of their guys had gotten injured and one had gotten fouled and the momentum was all in the wrong direction and this was one of those nights.

No one wanted to talk in the locker room. There was just a lot of lockers slamming and shoes being flung down and towels snapping, but not in any fun, weren't-we-great kind of way but in that depressed and angry how-could-we-fuck-up-so-badly kind of way. It was shower and get out. Jake had just sat down on a bench and put his head down for a bit and then swiveled to lie down, his towel stuck under his head. He'd gotten an elbow to the side of his head in the second quarter and it had screwed his equilibrium for the better part of the third and his right ear was still ringing. Williams had walked past and said, "You okay, man?" and Jake had said, yeah, he just needed to take five.

He'd still been on the bench, kind of dozing, when he felt the hand on his thigh. "Get up man, get in the shower. You practically got knocked out. You need to go home."

It was Rashid, and when Jake opened his eyes, Rashid's clear green eyes were staring down at him.

Jake wasn't sure what happened next—what made him think he could do what he did, but he sat up and ran his hand under the towel Rashid was wearing and then pulled it off.

Rashid's dick was hard and his balls were tight. Sitting there, slightly dazed from his injury in the semi-dark of the locker room where all the lights but one were off, Jake decided he didn't care what happened next. Rashid hadn't moved when Jake had touched his cock. Hadn't moved when he'd pulled off the towel. Now Jake slid down the bench just a little, his legs straddling it. And then he took Rashid's cock in his hand, ran his fingers up the shaft, and took it in his mouth.

There wasn't any sound Jake liked more than the sound of another man's desire. He'd figured that out years ago, the very first time he got in a car and heard what it sounded like when another guy was coming and he was making it happen. The power, the excitement, the heat—it made his own cock throb every time, made him want to come himself. That sound was the sound that made him love men. He'd never thought about what it would sound like with a woman—he'd never thought about it once. This was it for him, this was what he wanted. And now he realized with a kind of animal certainty that he really did want more from Rashid, but this was good for now, that sound and his making it happen. That was good for now.

Jake ran his tongue over the head of Rashid's dick, down the shaft, over his balls, down his thighs. He kept his hand tight on Rashid's cock as he tasted the sweat still on his stomach and thighs. Then he grabbed Rashid's ass and pulled him down onto the bench.

"No one's around—it's not like before," Jake said softly, his heart starting to pound, not sure if he should mention "before," but knowing that they both wanted something else this time other than a quick, if totally hot and so dangerous, hand job.

Rashid had his hands on the inside of Jake's thighs, rubbing hard. Jake's cock was tight inside his shorts. He wanted Rashid to pull it out. Now. He wanted to feel those long fingers on the head of his cock, wanted to feel him stroke it slow, then fast, then faster.

"Let's get in the shower," Rashid said then, his voice low with that sex sound. He stood up, lifting his leg over the bench and walking toward the far stall, Jake staring after his hot, tight ass. Jake pulled off his jersey and his shorts and went to meet him.

Rashid was soaping his dick and balls when Jake entered the

shower. The water felt amazing—not too hot, but like a liquid hand on his back and shoulders. Rashid handed him the soap and he lathered his own dick and balls and then rinsed off. He stood there under the water, not sure if he should make the first move, or if this was Rashid's play, just like last time. Jake knew he either wanted Rashid to fuck him or he wanted to fuck Rashid, but he wasn't going to ask. He was going to wait and see how it played out.

Rashid came over to him and pushed him back against the wall of the shower. He reached up and turned the spray so it continued to run over them, and then he kissed Jake—that same "I don't want to be doing this, I really don't" kind of rough, grinding, overheated kiss that had practically made Jake come in his jeans the last time. This time he knew what to do and grabbed Rashid's hand and put it on his cock and started to move it hard and fast.

"Get me off, make me come, do it," he breathed against Rashid's neck as he grabbed his ass and pulled him tight against him so that Rashid could barely move his hand.

"Turn around." Rashid's mouth was against Jake's ear and then his tongue was along his neck. He reached up and twisted each of Jake's nipples. That was new. He liked it. It went straight to his dick.

Jake turned around and braced himself against the wall. He had no clue what would happen next. Rashid was tight up against him—Jake could feel his dick against his ass, but there was no move to fuck him. Not yet.

Rashid slid his hand between Jake's legs, reaching up to touch his balls and finger the base of his cock. It was almost too much—he was aching to come, his cock was pulsing. He reached for his own dick, but Rashid pushed his hand away and told him not yet, which just made the ache more intense, along with the excitement.

Now Rashid had his hips up against him and had his ass in his hands and was grabbing at his cheeks and slapping them with his cock. He slid his finger into Jake's ass and the pressure was surprisingly intense—so intense that he was sure he was going to come right then, but didn't. But now he needed something—a hand on his dick, even if it was his own, Rashid's cock in his ass. He'd never felt such intense desire and he wasn't sure how long he could stand it. He didn't want to just come—he wanted to explode with the kind of intense heat he'd felt the last time.

"I want to fuck you." Rashid's voice was husky with heat and Jake had a momentary flush of fear—Rashid's dick was big, really big. And yet he wanted to feel it, wanted to feel Rashid pumping him and grabbing his ass and stroking his cock.

Jake said, "I want you to fuck me, but I've never been fucked before, so…easy."

Rashid rubbed his cock back and forth over Jake's ass. Water poured down Jake's back and into the crevice of his ass. He'd never felt such heat before as Rashid began to push his cock into Jake's ass, past the muscle, deeper, so that Jake gasped and pushed hard against the wall, but it was a mix of pleasure and pain with the pleasure suddenly washing over everything.

Rashid's hands were holding his hips and he was moving in a slow, steady rhythm, his balls slapping against Jake's ass. He kept one hand on Jake's hip and reached around to pinch his nipples, then began to stroke his dick. Jake felt his muscles closing over Rashid's dick, felt his own shaft so tight, so hard, in Rashid's hand. When Rashid stroked him, the pumping got faster and Jake heard sounds coming out of him and Rashid that weren't like anything else he'd ever heard with any guy he'd been with, never heard from himself, and this time when he came, as Rashid pumped hard into him, his muscles closing over Rashid's dick, Jake thought he might actually pass out. Was he breathing? Could he breathe? His legs were on fire with the tension, the muscles stretched beyond anything he could remember. It was searingly hot, hot through the core of him, and Jake felt overwhelmed with more than just the sex. He felt more than just desire for Rashid. But for now, desire was all he could have for sure, and he knew he had it. He knew it from the sound of Rashid fucking him. He knew it. And it made him hot and dizzy.

They had shared a shower afterward—a kind of soapy afterglow thing that felt a little like lying in a bed holding each other, but wasn't quite. Rashid had turned him around afterward and had just pulled him close, kissed him again, and then reached for the soap and had started washing him off. It was sweet—almost too sweet. Jake had felt some emotions that he supposed had to do with the fucking and tears had pricked behind his eyes a little and he had turned his face up to the water, just in case, and closed his eyes and Rashid had continued to hold on to him, and soap him down, and it had been way more feelings than he had expected or maybe even wanted and he had crossed some line in his head that he was pretty sure wasn't safe to cross. A line that was much bigger than the one where he decided to be the one being fucked, not the one fucking.

They hadn't said anything afterward. They'd left the shower and gotten dressed and walked to the door of the locker room without a word. Then Rashid had put his hand up against the door when Jake had reached for the handle and had said, "Next time, there's gotta be a bed, man. This standing up thing is a little rough." Then he had sort of body-slammed Jake against the door and kissed him, but this time it wasn't the rough not-really-gay kiss, but the kiss that went with whatever it was that Jake had felt when he almost started to cry in the shower. It was a long kiss and a deep kiss, but it wasn't a sex kiss, it wasn't meant to start anything new. It was meant to seal the contract between them. They had a secret now, and they were going to keep it. Both of them.

He and Rashid had gone on for a while. In secret. Hot sex as often as they could get it—secret sex. Jake had stopped looking for other people to fuck and had been trying not to think about Rashid the way he already thought about him—as way more than a regular and fabulous fuck. As the boyfriend he had never had before. Because Jake had never fucked anyone as regularly and as deeply and with as much feeling as he had Rashid.

Jake had been trying not to think about the kind of kissing he and Rashid always did after they fucked, in that brief window when Rashid was feeling what Jake was feeling and the emotional heat matched the sexual heat of minutes before. That deep, hands on his face, hands in his hair kind of kissing was something that Jake hadn't even known he'd wanted until that first time in the locker room when Rashid had kissed him like that and he realized no one had ever kissed him that way—like they didn't just want to fuck him, but like they loved him.

What hadn't changed was Jake and Rashid never talked about what they were doing. And the secret was starting to wear on Jake. The weekend before he'd gone up to Big Bear and ruined his life, he'd done something he'd never done before with Rashid. And that had pretty much ended things between them—or so it had seemed at the time.

Rashid had a small apartment off campus, benefit of being a junior, unlike Jake. It was a tiny place, but it was clean and tidy and kind of sweet in a straight-college-guy kind of way and Rashid was surprisingly neat. He used to joke that he was always afraid his grandmother might stop by and he didn't want to be embarrassed by having her sitting next to his dirty underwear on the sofa.

Jake liked it, that little apartment. He liked the window that looked out onto a small garden kept by the woman who owned the building, with the teacup-sized roses in soft yellows and dark pinks, the big fluff of magenta bougainvillea that cascaded over the fence, the little parade of succulents that lined the walkway and the one huge aloe that stood off to the side with its sharp, sword-like leaves. Rashid had told Jake he had found the place by accident, when he was taking a long run and had seen the little sign out front. The house had once been a family home for two generations, but then the daughter had gotten hooked on drugs and her kids had gone to live with their father up in Sacramento and now it was just the grandmother, who Rashid said reminded him of his own grandmother, the African American one. Except this woman, Mrs. Torres, was Mexican.

When Jake came over to Rashid's place, it always made things feel real to him. This wasn't someone's car or a parking lot or even the locker room—and he'd been satisfied with all those places before. But now, now things were different and this felt real in ways Jake ached to tell Rashid, but still didn't dare. Sometimes he wondered how it was he felt perfectly safe letting this guy put his big dick in his ass night after night but didn't feel safe telling him he wanted more. Now that he knew he wanted more. It wasn't that he wanted less of the sex—he couldn't get enough of it. If too many days had gone by and Jake hadn't been with Rashid, he'd find himself jerking off in the shower, or in his own bed when he woke up with a piss hard-on, always to thoughts of Rashid's perfect body, Rashid's big hands holding his ass, Rashid's full lips on the tip of his cock, because they did everything now, everything, Rashid's beautiful green cat's eyes as they looked at Jake with the same desire he felt himself.

No, it wasn't that the sex had become tiresome. It was that he wanted more, he just wasn't even sure what more meant. Did he want to go to gay clubs and dance with Rashid? Did he want to walk down the streets of West Hollywood holding hands? Or did he just want Rashid to tell him it was more, that those kisses after they fucked had words attached to them, words that he had never thought he needed to hear before now.

The night of the fight, the sex had been awesomely good. Jake could definitely say it was the best sex he'd ever had. And there had been a lot of it. Rashid had discovered new things he liked, things he liked Jake to do. After that night Jake had let Rashid fuck him in the shower, he knew Jake was open to whatever Rashid wanted.

He liked Jake talking to him, liked the hot sex talk Jake would whisper that made him fuck harder and come faster. And he decided he liked Jake on his back, legs up and ass wide.

"I want to see you when I fuck you," he'd said one night, and Jake had thought this meant Rashid was starting to feel what he was feeling. More than just the heat between them, which had overwhelmed both of them.

Rashid holding his legs up and fucking him, Rashid taking his dick down his throat, Rashid licking his balls, rimming his ass, sucking his nipples—Jake felt like he was in a sex stupor. They'd fuck and doze and fuck and doze and it would go on as long as they could get it up one more time. Once again, Jake felt like he was making up for all the time he had lost in Philly, missing out on anything more than those hot, fast nights in anonymous cars.

That last night, the night of the fight, Rashid had made dinner. When Jake got to the little apartment, he could smell the fabulous smells as he was coming up the stairs. The room was redolent of spices and Jake had no idea what was cooking, but he knew it would be delicious. Rashid had come over to him at the door and slung his arm around him in the "just guys hanging out" way he always had, but Jake had decided to let it go. Rashid was cooking for him. This was huge.

Or was it?

Jake never really knew. They'd eaten the meal—something complicated and Mexican that Mrs. Torres had taught him—and they'd been talking. School, their families—Rashid was from Phoenix, Jake from Philadelphia. It had felt a little like a date to Jake and he had been swept up in it. He'd cleared the table for Rashid and felt himself being watched. Rashid had come over to him at the sink and put his hands on Jake's shoulders and then held on tighter. Jake wasn't sure if this was a cocooning moment or a prelude to sex or both, but he leaned back into Rashid and then he turned around and they kissed—the good kissing that Jake liked so much. He could taste the hot spiciness of the meal between them and Jake had whispered, "I bet those chilies would warm up your dick," and then their clothes were off and they were on the bed. Jake had pushed Rashid back and was running his tongue down that smooth chest and stomach. He loved the color of Rashid's skin—truly the color of the lattes he got with extra milk. And then he was sucking Rashid's cock and Rashid was playing with his dick and balls and then Rashid had turned him over on his side and lubed up his dick and slipped it into Jake and held him tight as he fucked him harder, harder, harder, and Jake had come all over Rashid's hand as he jerked him off. It had been the most intense yet.

They were both sweaty and spent, sprawled on the bed that was just a little too short for both of them, and Rashid's arm was lying across Jake's chest and he had taken Rashid's hand and kissed the palm and then laid the arm back where it had been. And then, for reasons he couldn't explain, he had felt tears running down the sides of his face, into his ears and hair. Rashid had turned on his side then, and asked him what was up. He'd had no answer, afraid that if he spoke, the silent tears would turn to actual sobs and that was more than he would be able to handle.

They lay there for a while like that. Rashid's arm was still over him, but not holding him, exactly. Jake's eyes were closed and he was willing the tears to stop. He knew Rashid was watching him, but he couldn't open his eyes and look at him. Not then.

Jake lay there and thought about what he wanted to say, that the sex was more than sex to him, that he'd never been this close to any other man, that he was falling in love with—was already in love with—Rashid. That the dinner and the kind of sex they'd just had was different somehow, was more like being a couple and more like being lovers than the friends with benefits crap they'd been feeding each other, with the offhand chatter after sex—once those special kisses had been delivered. He'd wanted to tell Rashid that he was gay, not just playing around, not just trying it on, not just in between girls but full-on queer since the day in eighth grade when he'd gone home from that layup game and fucked his pillow to images of pretty blond-haired Tony Bylinski's face with his soft, girly, Polish cocksucking lips. He wanted to ask Rashid if things could change, if they could say what this was instead of pretending it was something else.

And so he did. He lay there, the tears still coming, his voice barely under control, and said all of it. Said that he'd been sucking and jerking off with guys in cars since he was fifteen and he wanted more now. That the weeks when he and Rashid had been here at the little apartment that always held a hint of the roses and bougainvillea that wafted up from the garden had been the best thing he'd felt in possibly his whole life. That he was really done with the one-week fuck fests with guys he then dropped or the unrequited romances he had in his head with classmates while he jerked off nightly to thoughts of them sucking his cock.

Rashid had been quiet. He'd lain there silent. Jake could hear his breathing, could hear his own heart pounding. And then Rashid had gotten up off the bed and pulled on his shorts and walked into the bathroom and washed his face and come back.

"I can't do that," was all he'd said as he sat down on the end of the bed.

"Can't do what?" Jake had asked, trying to keep fear out of his voice.

"Can't do what you want. Can't just be gay, man. I'm not really gay. I thought you knew that. I thought—" He stopped and then said, "I didn't really know you were gay, Jake. I mean you don't—"

"Don't look gay? Were you really just going to say that?" Jake was sitting up now, standing up, looking for his clothes. He wanted to leave. This had been a mistake, he'd known it was a mistake. He could hear his mother's voice in his own and it was not the voice he wanted to hear—the semi-pleading, tinged-with-anger voice he'd heard her use with his father his whole life. No, that was not who he was and he was not going to be that guy, the guy who begged for another chance, a real chance, for love or attention or whatever. Fuck that, he was done, it was his own fault for thinking some straight guy with issues over his racial identity was going to be any clearer about his sexual identity. This was nuts, he had to get out of this place with its cozy, rose-scented lie.

He was dressed, he was sitting on the edge of the bed, tying his shoelaces, and Rashid came over and sat down next to him, still wearing only his shorts.

"Don't go. Seriously, Jake, don't go. There's no reason why anything has to change. We can just forget this part happened. People do that all the time, right?"

Jake turned and looked at him. Looked at the pale green cat's eye marble eyes that were so unlike anyone else's. Looked at the short corked dreads. Looked at the face that showed the whole mix of Irish and black and Native American and was so handsome, so sexy. He leaned into the kiss Rashid was about to give him, leaned into it like he was going to give in, pretend he didn't feel what he felt, pretend they were going to go back to bed, back to the sex that was so mind-blowingly hot, back to the secret.

But he couldn't. Jake knew who he was, even if Rashid didn't. He knew what he wanted, now that he'd had all the bits and pieces of it, and Rashid had filled in a lot of those bits and pieces. Jake knew that he would likely go back to fucking one guy after another until he found another something like this, and that was okay, because he knew that there was another something like this and he was going to find it, just like he found this. Only next time, he was going to find it with a guy who wasn't straight, or thinking he was straight, or whatever it was when a guy was fucking other guys but thought he wasn't really gay.

So Jake had leaned into that kiss from Rashid. He had leaned into another round of sex, this time with Rashid lavishing his cock with his hot lips and tongue and throat, sucking his balls—all of it, until he was moaning and grabbing at Rashid's hair and fucking his mouth until he came. Jake had even fallen asleep with Rashid's arm over his chest, and he had wanted all of it, no matter what he'd said before. But then a couple of hours after they had fallen asleep, Jake had woken up and the reality of it all had washed over him in a cold, harsh wave and he had gotten dressed quietly and left, hoping that the next time they saw each other on the court, it would be okay and that they could both do exactly what Rashid had asked of him: pretend none of this had happened.

But they didn't ever see each other on the court again. Three days after the fight at Rashid's place was the weekend when Jake had wrecked his leg and his budding NBA career. He'd been invited up to Big Bear and he had decided to go after all. Screw Rashid, screw all of it. He was up for some mindless fun and he knew that's what it would be and he needed it. He really needed it.

And it was definitely fun. There had been six of them—Jake had been with three of them before—no one in a couple, all of them wanting to unwind and just have a lot of sex, do a lot of drinking, and just a little bit of drugs. Jake had had his cock sucked over and over and it had felt raw and hot and uncomplicated and he thought he could reenter this part of his life just as easily as he had exited when he'd been with

Rashid. That kissing thing wasn't as necessary as he thought, maybe. But getting his dick sucked, and often, was.

The sex and alcohol—Jake never did drugs—helped Jake stop thinking about Rashid and the sex and those kisses and the dinner. He'd done a lot of tearing it up in the snow. And then it happened—the accident where he been flying like something out of *Crouching Tiger, Hidden Dragon*, and it had felt so unbelievably amazing as he flew through the cold, white air, sailed on the snowboard so far, so high, right up until he had dropped to earth like freaking Icarus, slamming himself into a twisted mess and nearly killing himself. Ending his basketball career instead.

Rashid had come to the hospital to see him, had acted like they were best friends from the team and that it was his job to go see Jake and make sure he was okay and then report back to the rest of them—Tomlinson, Stewart, Sullivan, Jackson, Williams, and the other guys. Jake had been on intense drugs and that had helped. But Rashid had kept looking at him with those eyes of his and even through the drug haze and the pain and the creeping knowledge that his life the way he'd planned it was over, Jake had felt all those things he didn't want to feel anymore.

Before he left, Rashid had looked toward the door of the room and then bent over and kissed him. Quick, but one of those kisses, one of the real ones. Then he'd said, "Really sorry, man, about your knee," and left.

Now Jake was here, at Halstead, with a new hot straight guy he was obsessed with fucking and he could see himself spiraling down the same rabbit hole, only this time he would be blowing everything, not just his knee.

Since he'd landed at Halstead, Jake had been sitting in his dorm room every night—nice little cottages with single rooms the upperclassmen got—and jerking off to Internet porn until he fell asleep, his laptop on the bed next to him with twink after twink sucking dick or getting fucked or jerking it off themselves.

It wasn't enough. He wanted more. He wanted Ramirez.

He couldn't help it. He wasn't sure if it was that Ramirez reminded him of Rashid—they both were beautifully built. But Ramirez had eyes that were deep and dark, not those pale green cat's eyes that Rashid had. Ramirez had wavy black hair that fell into his face when it was wet. And he wasn't as tall as Rashid, who was NBA tall, nearly six-eight. Ramirez was about six feet—not as tall as Jake.

Rashid had no tattoos, but Ramirez had an elaborate tattoo on his left arm. Jake had asked him about it in passing one day when he'd been sitting there, towel in lap, wondering just how close he could get to Ramirez without having the towel drop or exposing—literally—himself to everyone in the locker room.

It was Our Lady of Guadalupe, Ramirez had told him. He'd gotten it in honor of his mother, Lupe, who had died two years earlier from cancer.

Jake had nodded, said he was sorry about Ramirez's mother, had said his own grandmother had died the same way when he was still in high school. Had said he understood how bad it could be. Their eyes had locked briefly then, and Jake had seen how deep and dark Ramirez's were. How they threatened to lure him in, make him drop the towel, make him blow yet another sport, yet another team, yet another school. Threatened to take him back to Philly where he'd end up like his asshole father, drunk and useless and nothing. Probably paying guys for sex down at K&A.

Ramirez had said, "Hey, man, we should get together. Go have some beers or take a run or something. I hardly know you, since you got here." And he had snapped his towel at Jake's arm, done the thing Jake knew he did with members of the team he liked. Jake had felt his cock throb, had wondered what would be more likely to lead to sex with Ramirez—the beers or the run.

Jake had tried to pull himself together after that one exchange with Ramirez, tried to tell himself that Ramirez hadn't been looking at him the same way Rashid had looked at him that night in Fairfax when they'd ended up jerking each other off in the parking lot of the club beneath the bougainvillea. Instead, now where he'd once seen Rashid's eyes in his head, he saw Ramirez's.

For three nights in a row he'd been surfing the Internet for porn with guys who looked like Ramirez—toned Latino guys with swimmer's builds who would somehow be Ramirez for him as he jerked himself off. He'd found one guy in a YouTube sex video who looked a lot like Ramirez. He was kneeling on a bed in gym shorts and he was cut and buff and had almost the right build. His hair was a little long in front like Ramirez's, but he didn't have the elaborate tattoo. He did, however, have eyes you could fall into and he was talking in the video, not just performing with his hand in his shorts to some dumbass music.

Jake had moved his laptop to the side of his bed and stretched out. The video was meant for men, but the guy was talking as if he were straight. The first time Jake had watched it, he'd gotten hard almost immediately, but the irony of the I'm-not-really-gay thing hadn't been lost on him.

The kind of talk reminded him of Ramirez—the guy in the video was saying how hot he was and how hot it would be to fuck him or to be fucked by him. And there was a slightly rough, edgy tone to the talk and at first he had bent forward in the bed, like he might—might—just offer up his smoking-hot ass. That kind of tone Jake had always heard with the guys he'd been with. Then the guy, the faux Ramirez, had started to play with his own dick, first running his hands down his ripped abs and then playing with the waistband of the gym shorts, teasing himself and the viewer, moving his fingers down to the head of his cock and just barely touching it, pulling at the tip, which showed now, just a little, out of the waistband of the shorts, glistening. Then he was saying something dirty in Spanglish that was, Jake knew, about the wet tip of his cock and did someone want to suck it.

Jake felt like he could come just from watching that part over and over. It was like how he felt when he watched the lap turns at the pool. It was hot, but hidden, and Jake had begun to realize that there was something about the hidden and the dangerous that he liked, that he couldn't actually get enough of. Like all those nights in the cars at K&A. Or with Rashid in the parking lot, or the locker room shower. He wanted more, yes. But that element of the forbidden—and the dangers that went with it—really did excite him.

He'd thought about turning the video off then. Just lying on the bed in the dark and jerking himself off into the pillow the way he had back when he was a kid and he'd first realized that was what he wanted—to come in his bed with another guy, over and over and over.

He'd pulled the pillow over, but the guy in the video had changed position now and Jake was drawn back into it. His ache for Ramirez was throbbing in his dick and he wanted more than just the wank into the pillow—he needed the kind of intensity he used to feel when he'd masturbate after he'd been with Rashid. Back then he was jerking off to the scenes in his head of Rashid's cock or Rashid's mouth or Rashid's ass or Rashid fucking him or Rashid sucking his dick or Rashid rubbing his balls.

Now it was Ramirez. Or this fake Ramirez on the screen who was getting ready to jerk himself off for Jake. The guy was pulling his hard dick out, the shorts pushed down as he began to jerk off in Jake's direction. He was talking about how hot he was, and how hot it was in the room. He was using a lot of the same words Ramirez would use to joke around about sex in the locker room, and that just intensified the connection for Jake. He could see that there was a film of sweat on the video guy's chest and thighs, and the gym shorts made it seem like he had just gotten back from working out and had to blow off the rest of the steam by getting off with as much heat as he could.

Jake was stroking his own cock now, stroking it and stroking it, watching the guy he wanted to be Ramirez as he rubbed his balls and ran his hand down his thighs and pumped his dick harder and faster. Something about the tone in the voice of the guy in the video was getting him hotter and hotter—the way talking into Rashid's ear had always made them both come.

The guy on the video was getting close to coming now. He was groaning a little and his voice wasn't as smooth as it had been and he kept looking down at his cock as he pumped it. He wasn't a porn actor, just an amateur with a hot body and a hotter dick and a little story for the viewers, of which there had been thousands, and Jake knew why. The guy was really rubbing himself now—he twisted his nipples and ran his hand over his chest and those ripped abs and never took his other hand off his dick. You could tell he knew he should slow it down, hold it back, but he was too close and he wanted to come. It wasn't just for the camera. He'd worked his cock and he was ready to let it go, to just shoot right into the camera, right in Jake's direction, just the way Jake wanted to with Ramirez.

It wasn't just how good the guy in the video looked that was hot. It was the talk. The rough, you-know-you-want-me-and-you've-never-had-anything-this-good-*m'ijo* talk with the faint accent that finally made Jake come just as the guy in the video was making himself come with his hot talk and fast hand and rubbing his balls through the gym shorts that Jake knew had that smell of the locker room and the just-got-in-from-playing-hard sweat that Jake had loved since that first time after he got stiff from watching Tony Bylinski all sweaty and flushed like he'd been fucking instead of playing basketball.

It was good when Jake came—it was intense and hard and he'd morphed Ramirez's face into the video guy's by the time he was getting off. He closed the computer and lay there, near sleep, thinking about what it would be like to take Ramirez in the shower after everyone had left.

Ramirez was sleek and wet, like some kind of merman, when he pushed himself up and out of the pool with his strong arms. He shook himself off, water flying from his black hair, which hung over his forehead. The tattoo of Our Lady of Guadalupe was glistening, almost shining, on his arm as he raised it to run his hand through his hair.

He walked toward Jake, who was standing in the doorway of the locker room, and Jake could see Ramirez's cock starting to get hard in his Speedo as he got closer. As Jake watched him, he stopped and rubbed his hand over the outline of his dick and smiled at Jake, nodding his head toward the showers.

Jake backed away and walked toward the showers. He had his towel around his waist, but he was naked underneath. Ramirez slammed through the door and flipped off the lights as he walked toward Jake. The only light was the small one over the showers that was golden and glowing—more like candlelight than anything else.

Jake stood by the open shower stall and waited while Ramirez bent over and pulled off the Speedo, turned, and tossed it onto a bench behind him. Jake looked at him as he turned back around and his cock was big and hard and the only hair on Ramirez's merman's body was the black tuft around his balls. Jake let out a small gasp.

"You want this, *m'ijo*?" Ramirez asked him as he pulled on his cock and ran his hand over his balls. "You like it spicy? You like it raw? Which you want—this?" and Ramirez had pulled his dick some more, "Or this?" and he had turned slightly and slapped his ass, hard.

Then he had come up to Jake, who was just standing there, watching, suddenly unsure what he did want, and pushed him against the shower wall.

"I know you been watching me since you got here, *m'ijo*, and I know you want it. *Toca mi verga. Toca.* Do it. Touch my dick—you know you want it."

Ramirez was standing in front of Jake, the arm with the tattoo raised, his hand flat against the wall of the shower. His other hand pulled the towel off Jake, exposing his hard dick. The dick he had wanted Ramirez to touch and suck and fuck was now in Ramirez's hand. Jake could feel his heart pounding out of his chest, his bad knee a little weak as he tried to brace himself against the slick tiled wall of the shower. He was so ready for this—for whatever Ramirez wanted.

"Take mine, *m'ijo*. Take it, take it." Ramirez's voice was low and sexy and Jake was looking down at his hand on the beautiful big dick and Ramirez was pumping him, not hard, just enough to keep him hot and ready for whatever he decided he wanted.

"Tell me what you want, *m'ijo*, tell me."

"I want to fuck you—can I fuck you? I've been thinking about fucking you for weeks. Last night I was jerking off in my room thinking about you doing the turn in the pool, thinking about this—" Jake looked down at Ramirez's dick in his hand. He felt almost reverent toward it, it was so magnificent, and he'd wanted it for so long. He wanted to lick it and suck it. He wanted Ramirez to bend over and show him his ass and open it for him. He was so ready for this.

"Suck my dick first. I want to be close when you start to fuck me." And then Ramirez leaned in and put his mouth on Jake's. A kiss to start. A kiss to get the taste of them on each other. Ramirez tasted like chlorine and something sweet and flowery.

Jake slid down the wall and held Ramirez's cock to his lips. He ran his tongue over his balls, sucking them into his mouth. Then he ran his tongue up the shaft and took the head in his mouth. Ramirez tasted the same all over—chlorine and something flowery and sweet. He really was like a merman, a creature of the sea—a hot, sexy, creature of the sea.

Ramirez pumped his dick into Jake's mouth, his hands were in Jake's hair, on his shoulders.

"Ay, sí, más rapido, más suave, ay, sí, sí..." The words flowed over Jake, Ramirez's voice was thick and low and full of heat and Jake could feel that power he liked so much. He stopped sucking Ramirez's dick and stood up, his hand still on the thick cock. He put his arms around Ramirez and pulled him tight, their cocks pressed against each other. He ran his tongue across the edge of Ramirez's ear as he said,

"I want to fuck you, turn around, let me fuck you, I want to fuck you hard—"

Jake wanted to feel his balls slapping against Ramirez's ass, wanted to pump him hard, harder, until he came, wanted to…

"Do it," was all Ramirez said, then stopped. "Wait." He stepped back out of the shower and disappeared around the bank of lockers. Jake stood there, rubbing his balls and stroking his cock, once, twice. Stopping, because he was so hot, he didn't want to come, not yet.

Ramirez returned with something in his hand. Jake couldn't see clearly in the dim light.

"Use this, *m'ijo*—I like it with this."

Jake took the lube and the condom, somehow even hotter now as he tore the wrapper and handed the condom back to Ramirez.

"Put it on me," he said, and Ramirez rolled it over his dick, rubbing it as he did. Jake lubed himself, then Ramirez. He rubbed the head of his cock against Ramirez's ass over and over before he finally slid into it. Hot, tight, ready. Just as he had imagined. He could feel Ramirez squeeze him and release him as he started to fuck him.

It was blissful. Everything he had been waiting for, jerking off to fantasies of every night in his dorm room. Now Jake had him—the sexy, hot, Latino merman, the real one, not the video porn guy, but Ramirez. He had Ramirez's ass in his hands, he was reaching around for Ramirez's cock, he was stroking him, faster and faster, pumping him harder and harder, feeling his balls slapping against his ass, hearing him moaning and telling him over and over, *"Más rápido, más suave, más fuerte. Ay, sí, sí, sí…"* until there was nothing but heat between them and he could feel the hot spurts from Ramirez on his hand as he started to come in Ramirez's tight, hot hole, and he thought he might actually pass out, it was so intense. Jake leaned into Ramirez as he gently slid his dick out. He had his arms around Ramirez as he reached up and turned on the shower. He held him as they moved together under the hot water. Jake was used to seeing Ramirez wet. He really thought of him as a creature of the sea, just as *he* had once been a creature of the shiny, squeaky surface of the basketball court.

The water felt good. Ramirez felt good. The sex had been just as magnificent as Jake had thought it would be. He looked into Ramirez's deep, dark eyes, eyes that had almost lured him into another disaster, just as Rashid's had. He leaned in to kiss Ramirez. His lips were full and hot and wet from the water coursing down on them both and Ramirez whispered, "You know you wanted it, *m'ijo*. You know you wanted it."

The pillow was wet with cum when Jake woke up. His computer was on the edge of the bed and Jake grabbed at it before it hit the floor. He checked his watch—almost six thirty. If he hurried, he could get to practice on time.

As he ran across the chill quad toward the gym in the brisk semi-dawn, Jake had flashes of the night before—jerking off to the YouTube guy, the dream about Ramirez. He was starting to feel out of control of his own obsession with the swim team leader, starting to feel like he might lose control of everything he had rebuilt here, if he didn't try to get this obsession out of his system. He'd already screwed up his life in reaction to the breakup—or whatever it was—with Rashid. Was he going to let another guy with gorgeous eyes and a beautiful body take him down permanently?

Jake had spent the last three weekends hitting the gay clubs in town, away from the college, away from Ramirez or thoughts of Ramirez. He'd sucked some dick, had his dick sucked, and gotten a really excellent hand job in the car of a guy he had danced with for about an hour. It wasn't like he hadn't been laid since he'd left California. And it seemed as if he spent as much time jerking off as he spent swimming and studying combined.

He stopped running as he neared the building that held his future and walked briskly the last leg of the path to the gym. Glassy-eyed students staggered past him, all looking just as tired and dissipated as he felt.

He slammed through the double doors and checked his watch. He had more than ten minutes. He wanted coffee, but knew from experience it didn't mix with the early morning laps. Not for the first time he wished he hadn't screwed up his knee. Swimming hours were brutal. And he had a full day of classes after this practice.

Ramirez was sitting on a bench just inside the locker room doors when Jake careened through them.

"Hey, McMahon—you look a little rough this morning. Hard night?" and Ramirez pointed to his own dick. Jake tried not to look stunned, knew it was just the kind of thing guys in locker rooms said to each other and he'd heard it before. But the timing was bad for him and he had to keep from blurting something stupid or over-the-top in response.

"Yeah. You know how that goes," was all he said and opened his locker and started to strip down.

Ramirez came over to him as he was almost naked. "You want to go out tonight and get some beers and talk about it, man? Seriously—I didn't mean anything, but you do look like it's not going so good."

Jake looked up, his jeans in his hand over what he knew was going to be yet another hard-on in about two seconds. He needed Ramirez to back off, at least until he was in his Speedo and in the cold safe water of the pool.

"Yeah, man, that sounds great. It's been a little tough, you know—settling in, that kind of thing. This wasn't my first choice, you know. I mean the accident—changed my direction. I know you get that. I know I'm lucky and all that—it just wasn't where I thought I would be."

Ramirez reached out and put a hand on his shoulder. His touch was surprising—soft and warm and suddenly deeply reassuring. "I get it, man. Really. You know Evans blew my life up, here, with the drug thing. Stayed clean my whole freaking life just to have someone else screw it up for me with their mess. So yeah, I totally get it."

Jake looked up at Ramirez. It wasn't that his desire was gone, it was just where it should be—elsewhere for now. He'd averted one disaster by maybe creating another. Had he blown it with Ramirez with sheer callous stupidity?

"I never—you must think I'm a real asshole. Sorry, man. Here I am just coming in here, taking Evans's spot. Not thinking about what you've been through. It's just been a really rough time for me. The accident, the scholarship, some other stuff." He thought fleetingly of Rashid, how he'd sent his whole life into a spiral with that. He wasn't about to do it again. He was going to control this, no matter what.

"It's okay, McMahon. I get it. We come from the same place. I know about you." Jake stood up, stuffed his jeans in his locker. What did Ramirez mean?

"Yeah? How's that?" Now he was on his guard. What had Ramirez heard?

"You're from Philly, right? I'm from the South Bronx via

Dominica. Not a lot of pools there, you know? So yeah, we're from the same place. I know about you. You know about me, too."

Ramirez put his hand back on Jake's shoulder. "Rich dudes like Evans, they don't get it. If that'd been me, I'd be doing time now, or on probation—something. No cushy rehab in Boston for me, that's for sure." There was a bitterness in Ramirez's voice that surprised Jake. They really were from the same place. Well, that part, at least.

A whistle blew out by the pool.

"Get that thing on, man. We're gonna get our asses kicked by Nelson." The coach gave points for lateness. Jake couldn't afford points.

Ramirez headed out to the pool while Jake got into the Speedo, grabbed his goggles, and slammed his locker shut.

As he went through the doors to the pool, Coach Nelson blew his whistle again and shouted, "Ramirez!"

He walked to the side of the pool as Ramirez dove into it and butterfly-ed with lightning speed through the lap. Nelson was clocking him. Jake watched as Ramirez touched the tile and did the beautiful, sensual flip, his powerful body sleek and animal as it cut through the water. Jake felt the sudden intake of air that always came with the turn.

"McMahon, you're late. No points this time, next time, twenty extra laps. Believe me, you'll wish you'd gotten up ten minutes earlier." His voice was gravelly, but he eyed Jake with the kind of fake gruffness Jake remembered from Father Gallagher when he'd helped him at the parish.

The whistle blew again and the team lined up. It was going to be a long practice, Jake could feel it. But he didn't care. "No crossing lanes," Nelson yelled as they all dove in at once.

❖

Later, as Jake sat in the bar near the square where they'd agreed to meet, waiting for Ramirez to show, he thought about the past few weeks—how long it had seemed as he had tried to acclimate not just to the chill New England climate, but the tectonic shift his life had taken in the past year. His obsession with Ramirez had been some kind of buffer between him and the reality of his feelings for Rashid, the terrible losses from his accident, the disasters that he'd brought on himself. It wasn't that Jake had lost his desire for Ramirez since that morning at practice—if anything he felt more now than he had before. He'd remembered that dream so vividly. Jerking off or just coming in his sleep, he wasn't sure which, it was so hot. And yet.

And yet now it was even more complicated. Now Ramirez wasn't just the sleek and sensual merman he wanted to fuck. Now he was another probably straight guy like Rashid who he saw naked almost every day and wanted to fuck who also was getting under his skin, making him feel things. Just like Rashid had done.

Jake got up from the stool where he'd been sitting at the bar and turned around to look at the crowd, keep his eye on the door. He was thinking maybe he should just leave. Not even meet Ramirez. That it might all go really wrong if he did. The place was starting to fill up and it was getting much louder. A mix of students from Halstead and people who wanted to fuck students from Halstead leaned against walls, the bar, piled into the booths that lined the far wall, hunkered over the pool tables and the jukebox.

Ramirez was wearing a leather jacket, jeans, and a black T-shirt when he came through the door of the bar, three laughing co-eds right behind him. He looked around for Jake before Jake made a move to signal him. He looked just as hot out of the water as he did in it. Jake was getting hard again as Ramirez walked toward him. Flashes of last night's dream went through his head, only adding to his mounting desire. What had he been thinking, meeting Ramirez when he had such totally uncontrolled lust for the guy? He really did want to blow up his life and end up like his loser father, didn't he?

Ramirez slapped him on the back as he signaled the bartender. He ordered a Becks and leaned into Jake to be heard above the din.

"One beer and we're out of here, man. Too crowded to talk. I forgot how it gets on Fridays."

Out to where, Jake wondered. Ramirez practically chugged his beer, making aimless chitchat about the place while Jake finished his lager. Then they left.

The air was crisp and almost cold as they walked out of the bar and onto the square. Neither said anything and Jake followed Ramirez's lead as he turned and walked toward what Jake had already discovered was the gayborhood. He wasn't sure what was happening, but he decided to go with it.

"So why haven't we talked before this morning, McMahon?" Ramirez asked him, a tone Jake couldn't discern in his voice.

"Not sure, really. I've been feeling my way. I've talked with Wilson and Cochran on the team. Some guys at the cottage. A girl in my chem class and a few people in Irish Lit—I'm working a kind of weird literature major that I carried over from…where I was." Jake sounded lame even to himself. They walked another block in silence.

Then Ramirez stopped, turned, and stepped back toward a shop window. Jake walked toward him. They were a block from the bar where Jake had met the guy who had given him the magnificent hand job last weekend. He wasn't sure he wanted to go further in this direction. They were standing under an awning, near a little alleyway. Jake wanted to turn and run down it. The street was almost deserted. All the foot traffic seemed to have ended a block earlier, but he could see people milling around down by the bars at the other end of the block. He wished he were there, or back at the dorm cottage. Anywhere but here, now, so close to Ramirez and suddenly having no idea what to say or do.

Ramirez was leaning against the wall of the shop, facing Jake. He had one foot up against the wall and a hand in his pocket. He looked like he'd been hanging out there forever, comfortable, relaxed. All the things Jake wasn't.

"You know I've seen it, right? You sitting with your dick all hard, looking at me in the shower after practice, thinking that stupid towel thing could hide it."

Jake felt his stomach churn. He'd been so careful, he thought. It never occurred to him Ramirez had ever noticed him, let alone known what was going on.

"Look man, I'm not sure what you're talking about here—" Jake's voice trailed off. He was looking everywhere but into Ramirez's dark, deep eyes.

Ramirez put his hand out, touching Jake's shoulder, just like he had in the locker room that morning. He moved closer. Closer. He glanced toward the gay bar less than a block away, then leaned in, put his hand on Jake's neck, and pulled him in for a kiss.

It took less than a minute for them to move into the alley, hands all over each other—grabbing ass, pinching nipples, rubbing dicks hard against their jeans. Ramirez tasted crisp, like the October air and the flinty Becks. Jake could barely catch his breath. This wasn't a dream he was going to wake up from, this was what he'd been fantasizing about for weeks, since he'd first seen Ramirez push himself out of the pool, wet and glistening like a merman from some Irish myth.

Ramirez was unbuckling Jake's belt and unzipping Jake's pants now, his fingers nimble and swift as he pulled Jake's dick out, his mouth hot and soft as he took Jake's cock in. Jake was up against the wall of the alley, his hands twisted in Ramirez's wavy black hair, and he whispered that if Ramirez didn't stop, he was going to come. But Ramirez didn't stop—wouldn't stop. He sucked his dick hard, his fingers running over his balls and back toward his ass. Jake felt himself thrusting again and again as he came harder than he had even in last night's dream. Ramirez was amazing.

Ramirez stood up, leaning into Jake, put Jake's hand on his own cock and whispered, "Jerk me off, *m'ijo*. *Toca mi verga*. Touch it, touch it…"

Jake pulled Ramirez close and stroked his dick, rubbing it hard and fast. He could tell it was only going to be seconds now before Ramirez was coming in his hand and he wanted to hear the sound of Ramirez's desire, wanted to hear him moan and talk to him in Spanglish as he was coming. Jake whispered, "Is this what you want, or do you want my mouth on your cock? I want to make you come so hard, I've wanted to make you come for weeks."

"Faster, *fuerte*, hard, please, oh—" Ramirez was grabbing his ass, pulling him close as Jake jerked him off. He felt waves of desire crash over him as Ramirez's hot cum hit his hand and the small sighs of *"Sí, sí, sí,"* made his own cock twitch to life again.

They stood, arms around each other's waists for several minutes before Ramirez handed Jake a handkerchief to wipe his hand and zipped up his jeans.

"You didn't have to sit all this time with the towel, *m'ijo*," Ramirez told him. "I was ready the first time I saw you get out of the water. I wanted you then, I've been thinking about it for weeks."

Jake laughed then—a laugh of sheer spontaneous relief. This

could work, this second chance, this merman, this hot night in a cold alley. He pulled Ramirez close. He smelled sweet and slightly flowery, a hint of chlorine in his hair, just like in his dream.

"Let's go get a drink," he said, and slung his arm around Ramirez's shoulder. "Let's do this."

"A drink and some dancing," Ramirez responded.

They walked out of the alley, the air brisk, the wind picking up. Fallen leaves swirled at their feet as they walked toward the lights and the muted music of the gay bar down the block, walked toward everything they'd been ready for through all these long, tense weeks, ready to begin their night—and days and nights—all over again.

CONTRIBUTORS

JOSEPH BANETH ALLEN grew up in Camp Lejeune, North Carolina. An avid reader and writer, his short stories have appeared in *Blood Sacraments*, *Wings*, and *Riding The Rails*. His nonfiction has been published in *OMNI*, *Popular Science*, *Final Frontier*, *Astronomy*, *Florida Living*, *Dog Fancy*, *Pet Life*, *eBay* magazine, and many others. He now lives with his family amongst an ever-growing collection of Big Little Books, Gold Key Comics, and G.I. Joes in Jacksonville, Florida, where he continues to write fiction and nonfiction.

JONATHAN ASCHE's work has appeared in numerous anthologies, including *Exotica Erotica*, *Nice Butt*, and *Cruising*. He is also the author of the erotic novels *Mindjacker* and *Moneyshots*, and the short story collection *Kept Men and Other Erotic Stories*. He lives in Atlanta with his husband Tomé.

'NATHAN BURGOINE (http://redroom.com/member/nathan-burgoine) lives in Ottawa with his husband Daniel. His previous erotic fiction appears in *Tented*, *Blood Sacraments*, *Wings*, *Erotica Exotica*, *Afternoon Pleasures*, *Riding the Rails*, and *Melt in Your Mouth*. His non-erotica short fiction appears in *Fool for Love*, *I Do Two*, *Saints & Sinners 2011: New Fiction from the Festival*, *Men of the Mean Streets*, *You Can't Shoot the Cancer Squad* (the second *Machine of Death* anthology) and *Boys of Summer*. His non-fiction appears in *I Like It Like That* and *5x5 Literary Magazine*. 'Nathan can't skate, but does enjoy Winterlude.

JAY DICKINGSON says: I am a dreamer, a lover, a teller of tales. I am the dream spinner. I can be anything I want, and anything you want me to be. Presently living in a little house on the prairie in Southeastern Alberta, Canada, dreaming of stampedes and bull riders. Previous work published: "Adidas Feet" in *Quickies 2 Anthology*, "Banff Rim Off" in *Buttmen 1 Anthology*, "In Blackhaven Forest" in *Buttmen 3 Anthology*, "Still Life with Brie and a Spent Condom" in Volume 17 of the Ezine *suspect thoughts: A Journal of Subversive Writing*, and assorted stories in the now defunct gay sci fi pay site *Chaos Law*.

TODD GREGORY is the author of the bestselling erotic novel *Every Frat Boy Wants It* and its sequel, *Games Frat Boys Play*. He has edited numerous erotic anthologies, including *His Underwear*, *Wings*, *Rough Trade* (Lambda Literary Award finalist), *Blood Sacraments* (ForeWord Award finalist), and the forthcoming *Raising Hell*. He has published numerous short stories, and his next novel, *need*, will be released by Kensington in December 2012.

JEFF MANN's poetry, essays, and fiction have appeared in many literary journals and anthologies. He's published three poetry chapbooks, *Bliss*, *Mountain Fireflies*, and *Flint Shards from Sussex*; three full-length books of poetry, *Bones Washed with Wine*, *On the Tongue*, and *Ash: Poems from Norse Mythology*; two collections of personal essays, *Edge: Travels of an Appalachian Leather Bear* and *Binding the God: Ursine Essays from the Mountain South*; a volume of poetry and memoir, *Loving Mountains, Loving Men*; two novels, *Fog: A Novel of Desire and Reprisal* and *Purgatory: A Novel of the Civil War*; and a book of short fiction, *A History of Barbed Wire*, which won a Lambda Literary Award.

MAX REYNOLDS is the pseudonym of a well-known East Coast writer and academic. Reynolds's short stories, erotica, and essays have appeared in numerous anthologies, including *Fratsex*, *Men of Mystery*, *Inverte*, *Rough Trade*, *His Underwear*, *Blood Sacraments*, *Wings*, and *Men of the Mean Streets*. Reynolds is currently at work on a novel set in London.

JEFFREY RICKER (http://jeffreyricker.wordpress.com) is a writer, editor, and graphic designer. His first novel, *Detours*, is available from Bold Strokes Books. His writing has appeared in the literary magazine

Collective Fallout and the anthologies *Paws and Reflect, Fool for Love: New Gay Fiction, Blood Sacraments, Men of the Mean Streets, Speaking Out, Wings, Riding the Rails*, and others. A magna cum laude graduate of the University of Missouri School of Journalism, he lives with his partner, Michael, and two dogs, and is working on his second novel.

NATHAN SIMS grew up knowing he wanted to be a storyteller. Somewhere along the way his storytelling turned from the written word to the stage and he spent many years acting, directing, and teaching before returning to his first love: writing. He currently lives outside Washington, D.C. with his partner. His fiction can be found in various anthologies and magazines. He is currently at work on his first novel.

TROY SORIANO is the author of *The Beginning: An Allegory, Coffee Is Everywhere and You're Not: A Poem*, and most recently *The Push Back: What To Do With Apocalypse Fatigue, Toxic-Nostalgia and Malignant Worry*, as well as other erotic stories including "America's Passion Kings," "The Thrill-Seekers Luncheon," and "Matthew's Total Fitness." His next book will be called *How to Be Relentlessly Happy.* He lovingly dedicates "The Ravishing of Sol Stein" to Rose Sanchez.

From Vancouver, Canada, JAY STARRE has written for numerous gay men's anthologies. His imaginative and stimulating stories can be found in anthologies such as *His Underwear, Full Body Contact, Kink, View to A Thrill, Wired Hard 3*, and *Wings*. His short story "The Four Doors" was nominated for a 2003 Spectrum Award. Two of his erotic gay novels, *The Erotic Tales of the Knight Templars* and *The Lusty Adventures of the Knossos Prince*, have been published recently. Contact Jay Starre on Facebook.

CAGE THUNDER worked as a professional wrestler for BGEast.com for a number of years before starting to write wrestling erotica. He has published numerous short stories, which are being put together as the forthcoming collection *Learning the Ropes*, and is currently writing an erotic wrestling romance called *Going Down for the Count.*

AARON TRAVIS's (www.stevensaylor.com/AaronTravis/) first erotic story appeared in 1979 in *Drummer* magazine. Over the next fifteen years he wrote dozens of short stories, the serialized novel *Slaves of the Empire*, and hundreds of book and video reviews. In 2003, his story "The Hit" was voted their all-time favorite by readers of Susie Bright's *Best American Erotica* anthology series.

Over sixty of **MARK WILDYR**'s short stories and novellas exploring developing sexual awareness and intercultural relationships have been acquired by such publishers as *Freshmen* and *Men's* Magazines, Alyson, Arsenal, Bold Strokes, Cleis, Companion, Green Candy, Haworth, and STARbooks Press. *Cut Hand*, a historical novel, was published in June 2010. His second book, *The Victor and the Vanquished*, a contemporary story, came out in October 2011. His third novel, *River Otter*, a sequel to *Cut Hand* is scheduled for release in fall 2012. Wildyr presently lives in New Mexico, the setting of many of his stories. A list of Wildyr's publications is contained on his website: www.markwildyr.com. He enjoys and appreciates contact by readers.

LOGAN ZACHARY is a mystery author living in Minneapolis, Minnesota, where he works as an occupational therapist and is an avid reader and book collector. He enjoys movies, concerts, plays, and all the other cultural events that the Twin Cities have to offer. *Calendar Boys* is his new collection of short stories out with Bold Strokes Books. His other short stories can be found in *Hard Hats*, *Taken By Force*, *Boys Caught in the Act*, *Ride Me Cowboy*, *Best Gay Erotica 2009*, *Ultimate Gay Erotica 2009*, *Surfer Boys*, *SexTime*, *Queer Dimensions*, *Obsessed*, *College Boys*, *Teammates*, *Skater Boys*, *Boys Getting Ahead*, *College Boys*, *Men at Noon*, *Monster at Midnight*, *Homo Thugs*, *Black Fire*, and *Rough Trade*. He can be reached at LoganZachary2002@yahoo.com.

Books Available From Bold Strokes Books

The Marrying Kind by Ken O'Neill. Just when successful wedding planner Adam More decides to protest inequality by quitting the business and boycotting marriage entirely, his only sibling announces her engagement. (978-1-60282-670-0)

Sweat: Gay Jock Erotica by Todd Gregory. Sizzling tales of smoking-hot sex with the athletic studs everyone fantasizes about. (978-1-60282-669-4)

Missing by P.J. Trebelhorn. FBI agent Olivia Andrews knows exactly what she wants out of life, but then she's forced to rethink everything when she meets fellow agent Sophie Kane while investigating a child abduction. (978-1-60282-668-7)

Touch Me Gently by D. Jackson Leigh. Secrets have always meant heartbreak and banishment to Salem Lacey—until she meets the beautiful and mysterious Knox Bolander and learns some secrets are necessary. (978-1-60282-667-0)

Slingshot by Carsen Taite. Bounty hunter Luca Bennett takes on a seemingly simple job for defense attorney Ronnie Moreno, but the job quickly turns complicated and dangerous, as does her attraction to the elusive Ronnie Moreno. (978-1-60282-666-3)

Dark Wings Descending by Lesley Davis. What if the demons you face in life are real? Chicago detective Rafe Douglas is about to find out. (978-1-60282-660-1)

sunfall by Nell Stark and Trinity Tam. The final installment of the everafter series. Valentine Darrow and Alexa Newland work to rebuild their relationship even as they find themselves at the heart of the struggle that will determine a new world order for vampires and wereshifters. (978-1-60282-661-8)

Mission of Desire by Terri Richards. Nicole Kennedy finds herself in Africa at the center of an international conspiracy and is rescued by the beautiful but arrogant government agent Kira Anthony—but can Nicole trust Kira, or is she blinded by desire? (978-1-60282-662-5)

Boys of Summer, edited by Steve Berman. Stories of young love and adventure, when the sky's ceiling is a bright blue marvel, when another boy's laughter at the beach can distract from dull summer jobs. (978-1-60282-663-2)

The Locket and the Flintlock by Rebecca S. Buck. When Regency gentlewoman Lucia Foxe is robbed on the highway, will the masked outlaw who stole Lucia's precious locket also claim her heart? (978-1-60282-664-9)

Calendar Boys by Zachary Logan. A man a month will keep you excited year-round. (978-1-60282-665-6)

Burgundy Betrayal by Sheri Lewis Wohl. Park Ranger Kara Lynch has no idea she's a witch until dead bodies begin to pile up in her park, forcing her to turn to beautiful and sexy shape-shifter Camille Black Wolf for help in stopping a rogue werewolf. (978-1-60282-654-0)

LoveLife by Rachel Spangler. When Joey Lang unintentionally becomes a client of life coach Elaine Raitt, the relationship becomes complicated as they develop feelings that make them question their purpose in love and life. (978-1-60282-655-7)

The Fling by Rebekah Weatherspoon. When the ultimate fantasy of a one-night stand with her trainer, Oksana Gorinkov, suddenly turns into more, reality show producer Annie Collins opens her life to a new type of love she's never imagined. (978-1-60282-656-4)

Ill Will by J.M. Redmann. New Orleans PI Micky Knight must untangle a twisted web of healthcare fraud that leads to murder—and puts those closest to her most at risk. (978-1-60282-657-1)

Buccaneer Island by J.P. Beausejour. In the rough world of Caribbean piracy, a man is what he makes of himself—or what a stronger man makes of him. (978-1-60282-658-8)

Twelve O'Clock Tales by Felice Picano. The fourth collection of short fiction by legendary novelist and memoirist Felice Picano. Thirteen dark tales that will thrill and disturb, discomfort and titillate, enthrall and leave you wondering. (978-1-60282-659-5)

Words to Die By by William Holden. Sixteen answers to the question: What causes a mind to curdle? (978-1-60282-653-3)

Tyger, Tyger, Burning Bright by Justine Saracen. Love does not conquer all, but when all of Europe is on fire, it's better than going to hell alone. (978-1-60282-652-6)

Night Hunt by L.L. Raand. When dormant powers ignite, the wolf Were pack is thrown into violent upheaval, and Sylvan's pregnant mate is at the center of the turmoil. A Midnight Hunters novel. (978-1-60282-647-2)

Demons are Forever by Kim Baldwin and Xenia Alexiou. Elite Operative Landis "Chase" Coolidge enlists the help of high-class call girl Heather Snyder to track down a kidnapped colleague embroiled in a global black market organ-harvesting ring. (978-1-60282-648-9)

Runaway by Anne Laughlin. When Jan Roberts is hired to find a teenager who has run away to live with a group of antigovernment survivalists, she's forced to return to the life she escaped when she was a teenager herself. (978-1-60282-649-6)

Street Dreams by Tama Wise. Tyson Rua has more than his fair share of problems growing up in New Zealand—he's gay, he's falling in love, and he's run afoul of the local hip-hop crew leader just as he's trying to make it as a graffiti artist. (978-1-60282-650-2)

Women of the Dark Streets: Lesbian Paranormal by Radclyffe and Stacia Seaman, eds. Erotic tales of the supernatural—a world of vampires, werewolves, witches, ghosts, and demons—by the authors of Bold Strokes Books. (978-1-60282-651-9)

Derrick Steele: Private Dick—The Case of the Hollywood Hustlers by Zavo. Derrick Steele, a hard-drinking, lusty private detective, is being framed for the murder of a hustler in downtown Los Angeles. When his brother's friend Daniel McAllister joins the investigation, their growing attraction might prove to be more explosive than the case. (978-1-60282-596-3)

Nice Butt: Gay Anal Eroticism edited by Shane Allison. From toys to teasing, spanking to sporting, some of the best gay erotic scribes celebrate the hottest and most creative in new erotica. (978-1-60282-635-9)

Murder in the Irish Channel by Greg Herren. Chanse MacLeod investigates the disappearance of a female activist fighting the Archdiocese of New Orleans and a powerful real estate syndicate. (978-1-60282-584-0)

Initiation by Desire by MJ Williamz. Jaded Sue and innocent Tulley find forbidden love and passion within the inhibiting confines of a sorority house filled with nosy sisters. (978-1-60282-590-1)

Toughskins by William Masswa. John and Bret are two twenty-something athletes who find that love can begin in the most unlikely of places, including a "mom-and-pop shop" wrestling league. (978-1-60282-591-8)

me@you.com by KE Payne. Is it possible to fall in love with someone you've never met? Imogen Summers thinks so because it's happened to her. (978-1-60282-592-5)

Bloody Claws by Winter Pennington. In the midst of aiding the police, Preternatural Private Investigator Kassandra Lyall finally finds herself at serious odds with Sheila Morris, the local werewolf pack's Alpha female, when Sheila abuses someone Kassandra has sworn to protect. (978-1-60282-588-8)

Awake Unto Me by Kathleen Knowles. In turn of the century San Francisco, two young women fight for love in a world where women are often invisible and passion is the privilege of the powerful. (978-1-60282-589-5) http://www.boldstrokesbooks.com

Bold Strokes
B O O K S

victory
EDITIONS

Drama

LIBERTY
EDITION

AEROS
BOOKS

Mystery

C
CRIME

Sci-fi

Sf
SPEC FIC

e-Books

HE
erotica

Erotica

BSB
SOLILOQUY

Young
Adult

BS
BOLD
STROKES
BOOKS

MATINEE BOOKS

Romance

WEBSTORE
PRINT AND EBOOKS